'This debut from a former M of the most exciting I have read in a page rings with authenticity, the tension is s and the central character is all too believable: a man wary of the power to kill'   *Daily Mail*

'A non-stop, fast-paced thriller set in contemporary Britain and reeking of authenticity'   *Independent*

'It's awesome'   Mark Billingham MBE,
                                                        SAS: Who Dares Wins

'Tom mixes tense drama with fascinating insight into the lives of security service operators, to deliver a blistering read'
                                                        Jonny Lee Miller

'You can't create authenticity without having lived it. *Capture or Kill* is spy fiction which is brutally immersive. The most protected author in history – we had to disguise his identity to appear on Sky News – writing one of the best books I've ever read. You won't be disappointed'   Kay Burley

'*Capture or Kill* is certainly one of the most gripping books I've ever read. A thrilling, tough, vivid and rewarding experience from start to finish. Tom's writing is so honest, it opens the book to a whole new audience who may not think a "spy book" is   series'

                                                        r Phelps

... their thing, I can't wait for the next in the series.
Olive, Here

DEFEND OR DIE

Tom Marcus, former MI5, grew up on the streets in the north of England. He joined the Army at sixteen and went on to become the youngest member of the Armed Forces to pass the six-month selection process for Special Operations in Northern Ireland.

He was hand-picked from the Army into MI5 as a Surveillance Officer. He left the Security Service after a decade on the frontline protecting his country due to being diagnosed with PTSD.

An extraordinary battle and recovery took place which led Tom to write his first book, *Soldier Spy*, which has been vetted and cleared for publication by MI5. It's the first true ground-level account ever to be told and the first time in the Security Services' history a Surveillance Officer has told the real story of the fight on our streets. His debut book went straight to number one on the *Sunday Times* bestseller list.

Tom now consults on projects within TV and film including the TV dramatization of his book *Soldier Spy*. *Defend or Die* is his second novel, following on from *Capture or Kill*.

Due to the ongoing specific threat to Tom Marcus, MI5 insist he keep his identity hidden and he continues to work with the Security Service and other agencies to ensure he stays safe.

www.tommarcus.com

BY TOM MARCUS

Fiction
CAPTURE OR KILL
DEFEND OR DIE

Non-Fiction
SOLDIER SPY
I SPY

DEFEND
OR
DIE
TOM MARCUS

PAN BOOKS

First published 2020 by Macmillan

This paperback edition first published 2021 by Pan Books
an imprint of Pan Macmillan
The Smithson, 6 Briset Street, London EC1M 5NR
EU representative: Macmillan Publishers Ireland Ltd,
Mallard Lodge, Lansdowne Village, Dublin 4
Associated companies throughout the world
www.panmacmillan.com

ISBN 978-1-5098-6364-8

Copyright © Tom Marcus 2020

The right of Tom Marcus to be identified as the
author of this work has been asserted by him in accordance
with the Copyright, Designs and Patents Act 1988.

1 3 5 7 9 8 6 4 2

A CIP catalogue record for this book is available from the British Library.

Typeset by Palimpsest Book Production Ltd, Falkirk, Stirlingshire
Printed and bound by CPI Group (UK) Ltd, Croydon, CR0 4YY

Visit **www.panmacmillan.com** to read more about all our books
and to buy them. You will also find features, author interviews and
news of any author events, and you can sign up for e-newsletters
so that you're always first to hear about our new releases.

This book is dedicated to my wife. My one true constant.
Always inspiring me to go bigger!

DEFEND
Or
DIE

PROLOGUE

The woman eased her foot off the accelerator just a little as she turned into the bend, and made a conscious effort to breathe. In the erratic sweep of her headlights, the landscape remained an amorphous blur of dips and ridges; the only thing she could see clearly were the white lines on the narrow ribbon of road unspooling ahead of her.

Driving fast on open roads was the only way she knew to combat the tension that had gripped her. Not that tension was really the word.

More like fear.

She thought back to her little girl, Poppy, tucked up snugly in her cot back in the cottage, and the dread gripped her even tighter. What was she thinking, leaving her there, alone and unprotected?

No, that was just paranoia. She needed to think clearly, remain rational. She gritted her teeth and focused on steering into the next curve. That was why she had grabbed her car keys and sped off into the night in the first place: to calm down. To sort her thoughts out so she could decide what was real and what was imagined.

So she could decide what the hell she was going to do.

For the next five minutes she just concentrated on keeping the car on the road, savouring the feeling of being right on the edge of control as she sped through the winding moorland road, the hum of acceleration and the whining of the gears like a soothing lullaby.

When had she realized they were on to her?

There hadn't been a particular incident, a single trigger. More like a growing sense of things not being quite right: the instinctive reaction of a trained watcher when they themselves were being watched. And then once she really started paying attention, things that had remained unnoticed in her peripheral vision suddenly came into focus.

The same dark-green saloon in her rear-view mirror twice within an hour.

The man in the dark raincoat pushing a trolley round the supermarket without buying anything.

The wrong number at seven in the morning.

It all added up.

The question was: what did it all add up to?

Or, rather, *who*?

Back in the day, she would have just called it in, carried on as normal and let the counter-surveillance lot deal with it. But that wasn't an option any more. She wasn't family. As far as they were concerned she'd burned her bridges. If she called, they'd probably just fob her off.

No one here of that name, I'm afraid. Are you sure you have the right number?

Someone would log it, of course: a curiosity to be looked into at a later date. When they had the time.

She rounded another curve and there was the moon, three-quarters full and impossibly bright, revealed briefly between scudding clouds. It was like a giant searchlight, and she felt dangerously exposed in its silvery glare. Flicking her eyes back to the road, she caught a sudden movement and dabbed her brakes just in time as a hare or a weasel flashed into the gorse.

She smiled to herself. *Don't go off the road, you silly bitch. You're supposed to be calming yourself down, not driving into a ditch.* But she didn't slow. In fact, she gripped the wheel harder and put her foot firmly back on the accelerator. The adrenaline was doing her good, the need to focus on keeping control of the car freeing up the rest of her mind to sift through the data.

So, who could it be on her tail? Nobody connected to the last op, surely. There was simply no way anyone could have connected the dots and drawn a line back to her. Further back? Even less likely.

Unless . . .

She looked in her rear-view and saw headlights, a mile or so behind her, playing now-you-see-me as they vanished into a dip before reappearing at the crest of the rise. Should she slow, in case it was a patrol car? Unlikely: surely they had better things to do than roam the moors at one in the morning. But she eased her foot off the gas, just in case. She had nothing to hide if she was pulled over, but she could do without the aggravation.

As the headlights got nearer, she rehearsed what she would say. 'Sorry, officer, was I going a little fast? I find going for a drive late at night clears the head, sometimes, don't you? Have I been drinking? Absolutely not! But you can breathalyse me, if you like.'

That was when she saw the other pair of headlights, coming in the opposite direction towards her. 'It's getting like bloody Piccadilly Circus around here,' she muttered wryly to herself. So much for the solitude of the moors at night.

The car behind must have been going a lot faster than she thought because it was suddenly right on her tail. She frowned and put her foot down to put a bit of distance between them again as the road straightened, but the other driver instantly matched her, his lights now filling her rear-view.

What's he fucking playing at? she thought.

But she wasn't worried. She couldn't see what kind of car it was, but she knew she had enough under the bonnet, together with a local's knowledge of every twist and turn in the road ahead, to outrun it if she had to.

It was only when she saw the other pair of headlights coming straight for her down the middle of the road that she felt the first beginnings of panic. She nudged the wheel, hugging the edge of the road as close as she could and inviting him to move over, but instead he moved further over to her side, making a collision inevitable. She only had seconds, but she waited until the very last moment to wrench the steering wheel to the right, her heart in her mouth as she put her foot down even further to try and keep her wheels on the road, but instead of letting her past, the other driver swung back into his lane, meaning she had no choice but to continue the turn. She heard the tyres screaming as they left the tarmac, suspended in mid-air for a moment before settling with a crunch onto the turf, then the whole car started bouncing crazily over ruts and ditches as it careened down an incline, the headlights tracing a crazy stroboscopic lightshow against the blackness.

She braced herself, the sickening feeling of the car being tossed around by forces out of her control making her gasp. She saw the boulder a split second before she hit it, a solid shape suddenly looming at her out of the darkness, then felt rather than heard the crash, an irresistible force lifting her out of her seat and smashing her head and shoulders against the roof of the car as it continued spinning though the air.

Time stopped.

She felt herself revolving in slow motion, and then nothing.

The car she'd been trying to avoid had come to a stop a hundred yards or so beyond the point where she'd left the road. Slowly it reversed back until it was alongside the second car. Two men got out. They were dressed in dark clothing and both wore black driving gloves. One was short and thick-set, with close-cropped grey hair and a fleshy face. The other was taller, his jacket hanging off his bony frame. With a mop of dark hair and sculpted cheekbones, he would have been handsome if it wasn't for the long scar that bisected his cheek and tugged at the corner of his mouth, giving him a permanent sneer.

'Nice job,' said the short man.

The tall man shrugged. 'She had some balls, I'll give her that. I thought she was going to run *me* off the fucking road.'

The short man chuckled, pulling a small torch out of his pocket. 'Better go and make sure, though.'

Together they followed the helter-skelter route she'd taken down the slope. The car was lying on its roof, one headlight still casting a mournful beam into the night. As they approached, they could hear the ticking of the engine as it cooled in the night air. The passenger door was open and hanging off its hinges. The short man leaned in carefully and played the torch around the interior.

'She dead?' the tall man asked.

'Looks like it,' the short man said after a few moments. The tall man took a step closer and peered in. She was hanging upside down like a puppet whose strings had been cut, her face dripping blood onto the roof.

'"Looks like" ain't good enough, though, is it?' the tall man said.

'Christ almighty, give me a fucking chance, will you?' the short man replied.

The tall man stood back to give him room so he could shine the torch into what was left of the woman's face. Bloody bubbles formed between her lips, and a sound emerged halfway between a moan and a whisper. The short man strained to hear.

Papa? Puppy?

Not quite dead, then. It would probably only be a matter

of minutes, but in his experience it was best to be certain. Belt and braces, that was his motto.

Slowly, he reached forward until he was able to cup her jaw in one hand. He put one knee down to brace himself, then reached his other hand behind her head as far as he could and took a firm grasp of her hair.

'Right then,' he said.

With a quick movement he rotated her skull, as if he were trying to open a giant jar of pickles. Both men heard the crack.

'There you go.'

He eased himself backwards out of the car, trying not to brush his clothing against the seat.

'OK, all done.'

They walked back to the cars, careful not to step in the muddy ruts the wheels had carved out of the turf. The short man quickly shone his torch over the road. One set of skid marks.

Good.

He turned to say one last word to the tall man, but he was already in his car. As he got into his own car and started the engine, the tall man was pulling away. The short man did a three-point turn and drove off in the opposite direction.

Only after he had been driving for a mile or two and could no longer see the tall man's tail lights in his rear-view did he allow himself a smile of satisfaction at a job well done.

1

The pub was out of the way, but not *too* out of the way. A habit from being surveillance operatives, I suppose. Stay out of the limelight, but don't go so far off the beaten track that you stand out. It was on a quiet street, but still close enough to the centre of town for a few tourists to have wandered in by accident. Otherwise it was locals, and being a Friday night at nine thirty, most of them seemed to be here.

The place wasn't much to look at: a couple of TVs above the bar if you didn't feel like talking and your phone didn't have any charge, and some sort of noisy slot machine in the corner by the door to the toilets that could just about be heard flashing and beeping over the noise of conversation, as if vainly trying to get the patrons' attention. A handful of framed photographs were stuck wonkily on the walls, some of them signed, suggesting local minor celebs – TV soap actors, maybe. I didn't recognize any of them except, bizarrely, one: a photo of Michael Jordan, hanging improbably in the air over the basket. I was willing to bet he'd never stopped in for a pint here. All in all, it suggested an old man's pub that someone had half-heartedly tried to liven up a bit before giving up.

It suited my mood. *Good choice, Alex*, I thought.

We hadn't seen or spoken to each other for two months. In fact, the whole team had deliberately gone to ground since the op. Not that we suspected anyone was aware of our involvement. You'd never seen a D-Notice clamped so tight. But in these digital days you could never be a hundred per cent sure. There's always some smart alec with a phone, always the chance that you got snapped somewhere you shouldn't be, or talking to someone you shouldn't be, and once those images were on the net, then anyone who was actually looking would eventually find them.

For the first few days after it all went down, the team hung around the hospital where I was recovering – a particularly brutal carjacking was the official line – just making sure there was always someone keeping an eye on who came and went. After all, it wasn't as if they could put an armed policeman outside my door. But after I was discharged, they melted away. As if Blindeye had never existed.

As if we hadn't just rescued the Foreign Secretary from being beheaded on live TV.

My injuries had pretty much healed by now. The muscle damage from the round I took in the chest seemed like a small price to pay. A nasty slash to my left forearm had been deep but managed to miss any vital tendons. A gashed cheek from somewhere. The details of the fight with the two jihadis on the houseboat were fuzzy now. And while my knee still gave me a bit of pain from time to time, the rest of the bumps and bruises had faded away.

To look at me, you wouldn't think I'd gone toe to toe with two knife-wielding fanatics in the service of Queen and country.

Not that the Queen had known anything about it. Likewise the PM, and everyone else in the top echelons of the government and intelligence services. That was the whole point of Blindeye: because no one knew we existed, we didn't have to play by the rules. If there was a threat, if a bad guy needed to be taken out, we just did it, no questions asked. And the operation against the two brothers had shown it worked. MI5 – my old employers – had dropped the ball. We'd been keeping tabs on the brothers, knowing they were planning something big, but at the crucial moment word came down that we had to let them go. Rules are rules. And so we did.

It made me mad. It made me wonder what the fuck I was doing, putting my life on the line to try and stop terrorists from killing innocent civilians on our own streets, when the powers that be made sure you had one hand tied behind your back. When the Director General told me he felt the same way, and that he was trying to put together a clandestine team who weren't afraid of crossing the line if it meant taking bad actors off the board, who would do whatever needed to be done to keep our streets safe, due process be damned, it was just what I wanted to hear.

Alex felt the same way, too. We'd both had experience of the plug being pulled on surveillance ops, leaving dangerous terrorists in the wind. It was only a matter of time before a bloodbath was the result. There were only so many times you could drop the ball without scoring an own goal.

I hadn't known the others – except for Alan Woodburn, of course, our tech guy – before we became a team, and I have to admit I was suspicious at first. First rule of intelligence: don't trust anybody in a suit who hasn't done the business at the sharp end. Second rule: don't trust anybody else, either – not unless they've had your back and you've had theirs.

Well, there wasn't time for that. With Blindeye it was straight in the deep end. But by the end of it we were a team. I liked them. Trusted them. And, I had to admit, two months on, I missed them.

Well, it wasn't as if there was anyone else in my life, was there? Soon after the DG had made his pitch, I'd lost my wife Sarah and my little boy Joseph to a knife-wielding madman. He ripped my heart out at the same time.

I picked up my bottle of lager and took a swig, trying to put those dark thoughts out of my mind. Right on cue, Alex appeared, making her way through the crowd to the little corner table where I was sitting. As usual, she had changed since I'd last seen her. The shoulder-length mousy hair was gone, replaced by a Day-Glo blonde buzz cut, set off with a handful of ear piercings. She was wearing jeans, workman's boots and a white tank top. All a bit dykey. I liked it.

There was a brief awkward moment. Did I get up and give her a big hug or stay seated and keep it low-key? I wasn't sure what parts we were playing, and believe me, when you're a surveillance operative, you're always playing a part, even when you're not on an op. You don't have a job – or even a life – you can be upfront about, so wherever you go, you have to ask yourself, 'Who am I today?' Not a great recipe for mental health, perhaps, but it could sometimes keep you alive.

While I was still dithering, Alex practically hauled me out of my chair and put her arms around me, enfolding me in a fierce bear hug. Without thinking I hugged her back, and we stayed like that for a long time, the memories of everything we'd been through together flooding through me.

Eventually we pulled apart and sat down. No need to say anything now. That part was over. She picked up the second bottle of lager and took a long swig, then looked at me.

'So how have you been? You're looking good.'

'Not bad, not bad. Ready to get back in the game, that's for sure.'

'What've you been doing?' She said it casually, but I could sense an undertone. She was worried I'd gone back on the booze, or worse, I'd let my demons back in. I could see it had been hard for her, being under strict orders not to reach out, not to make contact, until now, until we knew the coast was clear and there would be no comeback.

I smiled, trying to look like a man without any demons, or, rather, a man who knew his demons well enough to be able to knock them back down when they threatened to get the upper hand. 'You know, just getting fit again. Getting my strength back. Lots of running, hitting the bag in the gym. It's amazing what a few days lying on your back in a hospital bed doing fuck all will do to you. I must have lost a stone.'

'Didn't they feed you?'

I made a face. 'There's a reason they call it hospital food, you know.'

'Funny. But now? You're eating properly? Not just take-away curries every night?'

She was right about the curries, as it happened, but I needed to put a stop to this or she'd be asking me about my laundry next, and whether I was wearing clean boxers.

'Just the low-fat veggie ones. All right, Mum?'

She winced, realizing she'd gone too far. 'Sorry. I'll shut up. It's just . . .'

'I know. I've been worried about you, too.'

'About me? Why?'

I shrugged. 'I don't know, I thought maybe you'd get bored and try to set a speed record on that bike of yours.'

She shook her head. 'Nah. Just long walks in the country. A bit of birdwatching.'

'Back to nature.'

'What's left of it.'

That was the thing I could never figure out about Alex. As part of A4, MI5's undercover surveillance unit, she'd ridden a motorbike – a big, powerful one. Her job was to stay on a target when other vehicles were too unwieldy, dodging though traffic at high speed to make sure we didn't lose them, making manoeuvres and taking risks no car driver, however well trained, could even think about. And she was damned good at it too – a natural. But when the helmet and the leathers came off, she didn't really behave like a biker.

Instead of doing wheelies and a ton-up on the motorway like any self-respecting petrol head, her idea of letting off steam was to put on her hiking boots, grab her bins and a bird book, and head off for the boonies in search of something small, brown and endangered.

I remembered taking the piss out of her about it once, probably after a couple of beers too many, and she hadn't cooled off for days. When she did finally start speaking to me again, she pointed out that twitching and undercover surveillance weren't really so different when you thought about it, which I admitted was a fair point. She offered to take me along on her next jaunt, to see if I had what it takes, but I politely declined.

What I didn't say was that it was the adrenaline rush that I was addicted to: the knowledge that if the mask slipped and you got made, it didn't just mean the op had gone tits-up; it might also mean a violent and potentially armed individual now had you in his sights. A lesser-spotted hedge-warbler might be harder to keep track of, but if you spooked it, it was unlikely to come after you with a butcher's knife.

'So have you heard from any of the others?'

'I got a text from Ryan yesterday. Hoping I'd had a nice holiday. You?'

'Just Alan. Something about having a check-up at the optician's.'

She looked puzzled for a moment, before the penny dropped. 'Oh, Jesus.'

I shook my head sadly. 'Yeah, there's a reason they keep

him in the back office. Tradecraft's not really his thing. I'm surprised he didn't send it in code.'

'Thank God he knows what he's doing when it comes to comms.'

'Well, he certainly came through last time when the chips were down.'

'True enough.' She held up her now-empty bottle. 'Same again?'

'Sure.'

As she made her way to the bar, I noticed one or two heads turn. That's the thing about surveillance: habits become ingrained and then you can't switch off. As soon as you enter an unfamiliar location you find your spot, start living your cover, and then check everyone out. The pub was already busy when I'd arrived, with people constantly entering and exiting the premises and generally forming a very fluid and dynamic group. It was hard to identify and keep track of individuals without drawing attention to the fact that you were observing them. But, still, there were one or two who'd got my attention.

Top of the order was the bald bloke leaning back against the bar, with a mate on either side. As the pub filled up, room at the bar was at a premium, and already a couple of people trying to buy a round had politely asked if they could squeeze past, and both times he'd given them a look. The kind of look that made them decide to try their luck further down the bar.

Now Alex was approaching him and my antennae instantly started twitching, sensing trouble ahead.

I sat up a little straighter in my chair, hands loose on the table in front of me. Alex's back was to me, and the background noise was too loud to hear her, but I assume she'd asked him if he'd move because he was grinning at her, then nudging one of his mates. Then he made a big show of standing to the side, waving her past like a traffic cop. Obviously whatever Alex had said had done the trick.

While she stood waiting to be served, he moved a little closer again and said something into her ear, then stood back, grinning. Alex didn't turn her head or show any other reaction, which was not a good sign. If it had just been regular banter, she'd have smiled and given it back.

After a minute, she turned, holding two fresh bottles by the neck in one hand and her purse in the other, and started walking back to our table. I could see the bald bloke's hand reaching behind her and she suddenly froze, before taking a deep breath and continuing on her way. At that moment the bald bloke looked straight at me. Our eyes locked and he gave me a wink.

I was half out of my chair when Alex put the bottles down on the table with a shake of her head. 'Don't, Logan. Let it go. He's just an arsehole.'

'I know what he is,' I said.

She put her hand on my arm. 'I've had my bum pinched by bigger bastards than that. I'll survive. The last thing we want to do is get in any aggro. If we find ourselves talking to the local plods, things might get a bit tricky. Just let it go.'

I sat back, to let her know I was calm and in control. 'What did he say?'

'Does it matter? He asked if my boyfriend – that's you, I think – knew I was a lesbian, and when I got married to my girlfriend, could him and his mates come to the wedding. That's the clean version, anyway. I may have left some of the choicer language out.'

I shook my head. 'What fucking year is this? 1973?'

She shrugged. 'They've got cans of Skol behind the bar. Maybe it is.'

'I think I'd better go over and have a word.'

She sighed. 'Do you have to?'

'I think so, yes. Look, he's looking for trouble. If I don't rise to the bait, he'll just come over here and piss us around some more until I do. Might as well nip it in the bud.'

'Well don't nip his bud too hard, OK?'

I gave her a nod and went over to the bar. Baldy and his mates weren't grinning now. They were standing to attention, getting ready for action, waiting for the first punch to be thrown. I walked up to them with a big smile on my face, then rolled up my sleeves.

It only took a couple of minutes, and then I was back at the table. Baldy and his mates were no longer looking in our direction.

Alex looked impressed. 'What the fuck did you say to him?'

I rolled my sleeves back up. 'I just told him how I got these scars, and one or two others. I told him how many men I'd killed and explained how I did it. I asked him how many he'd killed.'

'You show me yours and I'll show you mine.'

I shrugged. 'He didn't have much to show.'

We clinked bottles and tried to remember what we'd been talking about before we'd been interrupted. 'So what do you think's going to happen now?' Alex asked.

'With Blindeye? Hard to say. That first op was ad hoc. I mean, we had to hit the ground running, no time to set things up properly. It's been a couple of months, plenty of time to organize something a bit more permanent, you know, so we're not just ghosts, drifting around.'

She looked at me. 'Is that how you feel?'

Yes, actually, that was exactly how I felt. Unreal. Insubstantial. Not quite alive. Except in moments like the confrontation with Baldy and his mates, when my heart briefly seemed to start beating properly again. But I didn't want to tell her that.

'Nah. Figure of speech. I just mean we need a base, you know.'

'Well, maybe we'll find out tomorrow.'

'What?'

Alex grinned. 'Didn't I tell you? I got a message.'

'No you fucking didn't. Saying what?'

'Just a date and a time. And an address.'

'Where?'

'Office building, somewhere in Pimlico. Buy me another drink and I'll give you the details.' She looked at her watch. 'Then I've got to shoot.'

I raised my eyebrows. 'Meeting your girlfriend?'

'Fuck off.'

I put my hands up. 'Didn't mean to pry.'

The fact was, I didn't know very much about Alex's private life. I knew she had been with one guy for a long time, but that had ended: the pressure of the job, the reason why so many intelligence operatives' relationships hit the rocks.

She knew all about mine, of course, poor cow.

'It's OK. Just a friend. Someone I was at school with but haven't seen for years. It's sort of like I want to see what my life could've been like if I hadn't gone down this path, you know?'

'Sure.' Well, sort of. I couldn't really do that with the people I grew up with. Not unless I wanted to spend a lot of time visiting prison or hanging out in graveyards. For all that my life was a complete fucking disaster, I'd probably still have ended up top of the class. Not that we ever went to class, of course. School of hard knocks. And some of those knocks were hard enough to be fatal. 'Right, come on.'

We drained our bottles and made our way to the door. There was no sign of Baldy and his mates. I looked both ways quickly as we stepped onto the street, just in case he'd been waiting outside, holding a bottle by the neck, but the coast was clear.

I turned to Alex. 'Which way you going? You on your bike?'

'Nah, left it at home. Look. I'm just going to pop to the loo. Wait for me, yeah?'

'Sure.' I zipped my jacket up against the early September chill. The street seemed to have emptied, as if everyone had settled down for whatever evening they'd planned, either staying in the pub till closing time or dozing at home in front of the TV. A fox had stopped at the kerb opposite and was looking at me, utterly unconcerned, as if he knew he belonged out here on the street just as much as me. I suppose he did.

I was just turning back to the pub to see where Alex had got to when something hit me like a sack of concrete on the back of my head. The next thing I knew I was face-down in the road, my head exploding with pain from where I'd just cracked it on the tarmac. I tried to lift myself up, my hands scrabbling for purchase on the road while I tried to get my legs to work. I turned my head, my vision blurry, and was suddenly blinded by headlights. I heard the grinding of gears as someone put their foot down hard. *Shit*, I thought.

The next thing I knew, I was being hauled upright, strong arms around my chest jerking me back towards the kerb. I felt the rush of air as the car screamed past, then watched it barrel down the road, brakes screeching as it turned the corner.

'Jesus, Logan. Are you OK?'

I staggered onto the pavement. 'Yeah. Bloody hell. That was close.'

Alex stood back to take a look at me. 'What happened?'

I put a hand to the back of my head. 'Somebody blindsided me. Then before I could . . . Fuck, that hurts.'

'Just sit down a minute. Come on.'

I plonked myself down on the kerb and took a couple of deep breaths. 'It's OK. I'm fine.'

Alex did a quick three-sixty, scanning both sides of the street for further threats. 'Baldy?'

'Dunno. I didn't think he had it in him, to be honest.'

'I guess you never know.'

I stood up. 'OK, let's make a move.' People spilling out of the pub were looking our way, trying to decide if we needed help or were just a couple of drunks.

We walked as briskly as we could up the road towards the station. My knee didn't like it, but I focused on making my gait seem normal. I put my arm round Alex's waist for a bit of extra security, just in case the joint decided not to play ball. We looked like an ordinary couple on the way to getting their train home. People drifted away or went back inside the pub.

I looked across the road, and the fox was still there, still not bothered, as if he saw people almost mown down by speeding cars every night of the week. I gave him a thumbs up.

'All right, Foxy?'

He looked straight back at me, and for a moment I thought he was trying to tell me something. I held his gaze, trying to work out what it was, but before I could he gave the air a quick sniff and trotted away into the darkness.

2

It was still muddy at the bottom of the rise, and my trainers were soaked through as I geared myself up for the final push. Five miles of hard running through boggy fields and farm tracks, driving myself until my muscles screamed and my lungs ached, with the grand finale of Hangman's Hill waiting for me at the end. One good thing about the pain in my thighs and calves was at least it took my mind off the thumping headache I'd had ever since the incident outside the pub. There were several routes to the top of the hill, but it didn't really matter which one you took: all of them were brutal. Strangely, though, the harder I pushed myself, the less my knee hurt. In fact, over the last mile or so, I'd forgotten I still had a problem and had stopped instinctively favouring the good one. I managed a wry chuckle in between heaving for breath: all that fucking physio, all that pushing and pulling and stretching and kneading, and all it needed was a brutal spanking like this to sort it out. Bloody sight cheaper too.

As I passed the rock that marked the halfway stage on the ascent, I thought back to those lung-bursting runs during basic training, often in full kit. If you had anything on your mind, any problems weighing you down, that was the way to clear your head. Everything felt better when all you could feel, all you could think about, was the pain wracking every inch of your body. Yep, no doubt about it: pain was good. It was the only philosophy I had and it had proved its uses over the years. Unless you took it too far, of course, but that was true of everything, wasn't it?

Three more strides that made me feel as if I was pushing the weight of the world up the hill and I was at the top. I jogged over to the flat boulder that marked the summit and sat down. Amazingly, my whole body now felt as if it was glowing, pulsing with an energy that seemed to come straight out of the earth beneath my feet. I held my hands out in front of me and spread my fingers, almost expecting to see sparks fizzing from the tips.

'Budge up.'

I turned my head and Sarah was settling herself on the stone beside me.

'Good run?'

I nodded, looking at her. Her eyes were screwed up against the sun, her shining blonde hair tossing in the wind. 'Never better.'

'Look at the little rascal. What does he think he's doing?'

I turned and looked where she was pointing. Joseph had a stick that was almost as big as he was and was swinging it round and round as if it was a sword.

'I told him there was a monster up here – a big, shaggy thing with horrible teeth.'

I smiled. 'Well, if there is, I don't fancy its chances.'

'Joseph! Your dad's here!' Sarah had to shout against the wind to make herself heard.

The little boy paused in mid-swing, the big stick held above his head in two hands, and looked over. When he saw me he smiled.

'I'm going to kill the monster! I'm going to smash him!'

I felt my heart swelling in my chest. 'Go get him, Joseph!'

Sarah smiled. 'He's growing up so fast.'

I was puzzled for a moment, a bubble of anxiety forming in my chest. Then it passed.

'And what about you, Logan?' Sarah said, looking at me.

'Me? Too late for me to grow up, I reckon.'

She laughed, that lovely soft sound I'd missed so much. 'Don't worry, we like you just the way you are.' She touched the bruise on my forehead gently with a finger. 'How did you get that?'

Her touch was like a magic wand, filling me with warmth and light. I reached up to put my hand over hers, but it was no longer there. I sighed. 'I'm not really sure. An accident, I think.'

She frowned. 'Well, try to be careful. We wouldn't want anything to happen to you.'

'Look—' I started to say, but she cut me off with a finger to my lips.

'No, Logan. Don't start that again. It's not your time. Not yet. You've got a job to do. An important job. Joseph and I are very proud of you.'

I bowed my head, knowing it was no use arguing. We'd had this conversation before.

She changed the subject. 'So the house is all packed up?'

'Just about,' I said with a sigh. 'It doesn't feel right, though.'

'It's only bricks and mortar, Logan. Nothing important.'

'I know, I know. But it's where Joseph was born. Our own little home. It's where we were happy. Mostly happy, anyway. When we weren't, that was my fault.'

'Always happy,' she said, giving my arm a squeeze.

We looked down at the valley below, spreading out towards the city in the distance, and we could see the little house at the edge of the estate. I knew you couldn't really see it from up there, but today we could.

'Let someone else have it. Someone else can be happy there.'

She was right. That was the way to think about it. I looked up to see where Joseph had got to, but he was gone. 'Sarah . . .' I started to say, reaching out, but she was gone too. My hand closed on empty air.

I closed my eyes and took a deep breath, filling my lungs with cold air. It was not the first time Sarah and Joseph had appeared to me, but it still left me wondering what it meant. I didn't believe in ghosts, in visitations from the spirit world. I never had. When I was little and my dad had died, my mum had some sort of spiritualist medium come to the house. I remembered her, a big woman in a bright floral dress and large hoop earrings (for the gypsy look, I suppose), collapsed in an armchair with her eyelids fluttering, beads of sweat forming on her brow, pretending to be tuning in to the right spiritual frequency.

Lo and behold, after a couple of minutes of moaning and wriggling about, while she let the dramatic tension mount, she made contact with the old bastard, and began to deliver a series of messages that even to a ten-year-old's ears were stunning in their banality.

'He's missing you! He wants you to wear that special dress for him – you know the one – because up in heaven he can see you! Tell little Matthew I'll be watching him playing football next Saturday!'

What a load of bollocks – especially since I'd been kicked out of the football team the week before for fighting – but my mum lapped it all up and even asked for a second helping (for another twenty quid, naturally) of vague drivel which any idiot could have made up without knowing my dad from Adam. Leaving aside the football (to be fair, Dad was usually so pissed he might have forgotten about me being banned), just the fact that he was supposed to be in heaven should have sent up a bloody great big red flag.

That bastard in heaven? Not unless they had a special section for wife beaters. Come to think of it, seeing Mum crying her eyes out listening to these post-mortem endearments from a man who'd beaten her black and blue every Saturday night had probably been the last straw. I left home for good soon after, preferring to live on the streets, where the people who beat you up and stole your stuff at least had the excuse that they weren't family.

So, no ghosts, then. But if I wasn't seeing ghosts, what was I seeing? Hallucinations? That was a normal part of the grieving process sometimes, I knew that much, so it didn't necessarily mean I was crazy. But at the time it was all so real. I could touch her. Well, she could touch me. It was impossible to accept it was all just a trick of my mind.

Fuck it. I got up and started jogging back down the hill, my muscles already beginning to tighten up, resisting the temptation to look over my shoulder to check one more time if Sarah and Joseph were still there. In the end it didn't matter whether they were real or not. All that mattered was that I didn't want their visits to stop.

I got back to the house just in time, before my hamstrings started to seize up good and proper. I stood under a scalding shower until my skin was raw, then put on a fresh T-shirt and jeans. I stuffed my filthy trainers and running gear into a black bin liner, put them in the holdall with the rest of my clothes, toiletries and a few books, then did one more look through each room to make sure I hadn't missed anything.

Nope: all packed away and gone, either to the charity shop or the tip. Nothing left to show that Sarah and Joseph and me had ever lived there. Like she said, just bricks and mortar. Time for a new family to move in with all their stuff, all their life.

I caught sight of a mark on the wall where Joseph had somehow managed to flick a spoonful of raspberry dessert right across the room. Not quite every last trace gone, then. I felt a lump tightening in my throat and knew it was time to leave. I took my jacket from the back of the chair, picked up the holdall and walked out, closing the door firmly behind me. I opened the boot of the car with a beep, slung in the holdall, then got in. Before starting the engine I took my phone out of my back pocket and quickly tapped out a message.

Hi Alex. I'm on my way.

3

I walked briskly past the entrance, head down against the drizzle, trying to look like an office worker running late, a takeaway coffee cup clutched in my hand. It was the second time I'd walked past it in the last hour. I'd also sat in the coffee shop on the corner with an unrestricted view of the building for half an hour, keeping an eye on the comings and goings, seeing if anyone was parked up – especially if two or more men were in a vehicle and showed no sign of going anywhere – or if the same person or persons walked past the building more than once.

Was I just being paranoid? Maybe. The message Alex had shown me had been encrypted; the timing seemed right. Everything made sense.

But then it would, wouldn't it? Blindeye, I was fairly certain, had pulled off the rescue of the Foreign Secretary without anyone outside of the team being aware of it. I wasn't expecting Special Branch or SCO19 – the Met's firearms unit – to be waiting to pounce. But there was always the possibility that the DG had had a change of heart, realized the whole thing was too risky even though it was his baby

– actually *because* it was his baby – and decided to clean house. Kick over the traces. Get rid of the awkward bastard who had actually done his dirty work for him.

I had no reason to think he would, no reason to suspect he didn't have our backs. But there was always the first rule of intelligence: never trust a man in a suit.

I got to the end of the road and entered the newsagent on the corner, buying a packet of gum. I exited and began walking back the way I'd come, towards the nondescript office building that was my destination. I was as certain as I could be that there was no surveillance: no parked cars with no reason to be there, no pedestrians doing repeated walk-bys, no clear observation points in the buildings opposite. It was time to press the buzzer and see what happened.

If there was a squeal of brakes and four men in jeans, trainers and bomber jackets hauled me into the back of a van, I'd know I'd been wrong.

There were four brass plates with company names, one for each buzzer. The top one said Clearwater Security International. It was shinier than the others, as if it had only been screwed on that morning.

'Yes?' a voice came through the intercom. A woman, not young, sounding as if visitors were an unusual and unwelcome occurrence.

'Logan,' I said simply.

The door clicked open and I went in.

As I walked up the four flights, I paused briefly at each floor, but I could detect no activity from behind the doors of the other businesses occupying the building. I felt another little surge of adrenaline. The place had been cleared of civilians. Maybe a street snatch was too obvious. Maybe the offices of Clearwater Security, beyond the gaze (and the smartphones) of random passers-by, was where the action would be. *Oh well, too late to abort now.*

At the top, another door, another brass plate. I turned the handle and walked in.

Instead of hard-faced men with buzz cuts pointing Heckler & Koch sub-machine guns at me, I found myself looking at an elderly, grey-haired lady sitting behind a desk in a matching charcoal jacket and skirt, with a string of pearls around her neck, apparently absorbed with the *Times* crossword. She looked at me over a pair of horn-rimmed glasses.

'You can go through, Mr Logan,' she said, indicating a door to the right.

I walked in and the gang was all there. Or, at least, three of them. Alex had dressed up a little for the occasion, now looking more like a sales rep who had come down to London for a job interview in a neat dark-blue suit. Alan was, well, Alan: black jeans, black T-shirt just about keeping his belly under wraps, thick glasses and greasy hair over his eyes. And then there was Ryan, wearing a loud and distinctly unseasonal Hawaiian shirt, his long black hair in a neat ponytail.

If you'd known these were the people standing between you and a major terrorist attack, you might have felt a little uneasy. The truth was, they were the best of the best.

They were sitting at a round table in the middle of what

looked like an open-plan office, a scattering of PC terminals and random office supplies giving it a *Mary Celeste* look, as if the staff had had to evacuate in a hurry because of a fire alarm or had just been raptured.

I smiled. 'Hi, guys.' I shook hands with Alan and Ryan and sat down. Yeah, I'd missed them.

There was one member of the team I hadn't missed, though. In fact, thinking about seeing him again had been making my guts churn uncomfortably for the last twenty-four hours.

Jeremy Leyton-Hughes. The DG's number two and the man who had directed Blindeye's operations. My bad feelings towards him weren't just on account of the fact that he was Eton and the Guards from his spit-shined shoes to his regimental tie, although that would be more than enough in my book; it was more the fact that he'd been playing a double game, taking us off the board just when we had the brothers in our sights, so the SAS could terminate them live on TV, thereby making the PM look good. The trouble was, the house where the brothers were supposedly holed up was a clever fake, a booby-trapped death-house, while the brothers were actually on a houseboat near Millwall Dock, preparing to do the business with the Foreign Secretary. In the end it was a fucking miracle there hadn't been a bloodbath.

When he briefly visited me in hospital, the DG had hinted that despite almost fucking the whole thing up, Leyton-Hughes was too useful to get rid of. I had to disagree, and if I hadn't been hooked up to a drip at the time, I would have volunteered to do the job myself. Now I was dreading seeing the bastard back in charge.

Before I could ask the others why he wasn't here, the door opened and the receptionist walked in. I instantly clammed up, uncertain what the set-up was, and how much she knew about Blindeye.

She closed the door behind her, a thick pile of files held to her chest.

'Well, not exactly a full house, but perhaps we'd better begin.'

I threw Alex a questioning look. She gave me a shrug in return.

'My name is Margery Allenby,' she began. 'There's no reason you should know this, I suppose, but I had the privilege of working for the Director General for the last twenty-six years as his personal assistant. A month ago, I retired.' She made a sour face. 'Or, rather, I *was* retired. It seems that in the Service, once you reach three score years and ten, it's assumed by the powers that be that you've gone gaga.'

She caught the look of bewilderment on our faces.

'I can see by your expressions that perhaps some of you share that prejudice. Well, let me cut to the chase, as they say. I'm pleased to say the Director General has agreed that I still have something to offer my country, that some things even improve with age, like a fine wine. He also told me he had a vacancy he would like me to fill.'

I really was getting bewildered now, though I managed to keep it from showing on my face this time. Was the DG's seventy-year-old PA the latest recruit to Blindeye? Apart from top-notch typing skills and being able to help out when one of us was stymied by a tricky crossword clue, what exactly did she have to offer? We weren't trying to infiltrate the WI, as far as I knew.

'Mr Leyton-Hughes,' she continued, 'has been assigned a new, non-operational role in our Rio consulate. In his absence, I will be taking over the day-to-day operations of Blindeye.'

She looked at each of us in turn, gauging our reaction.

I thought for a moment. Actually, it made perfect sense. If she'd been the DG's PA for twenty-six years, she'd know how to keep a secret. She'd know where all the bodies were buried and even whose fingerprints were on the shovel. She was probably the only person in MI5 the DG really trusted. And on top of that, now that she was retired, she didn't have to explain her absence from Thames House.

Which made me think of the brass plate on the door.

'If Blindeye is to continue to operate in secret, it will need a legitimate front,' she continued. 'If half a dozen intelligence officers just disappear off the radar, eventually someone, somewhere will join the dots. Or one of you will be arrested –' for some reason her eyes came to rest on me at this point – 'and your cover story might not stand up to scrutiny. So, from today, all of you work for Clearwater Security International, an ultra-discreet consulting firm offering intelligence-based solutions for companies operating in high-risk environments. Our client list is highly confidential, so no one will be able to see that it has no actual names on it. Secrecy being our watchword, we don't have a website, we don't tout for business, and if clients try to approach us directly, we simply tell them that all of our resources are currently employed – and will be for the foreseeable future. Everything else about the company, however, is entirely legitimate. You are all salaried employees, paying your taxes and even contributing to a pension fund, though whether you will ever be able to draw on it is another matter. The main thing is that you will be able to come and go, getting on with your real job, without attracting undue attention. Please don't ask me how all this was organized or where the money comes from. But you can rest assured that it's not the first time I have had to concoct such a fiction.'

I nodded to myself. Definitely more than just a secretary, then.

'Any questions?'

Ryan put up a hand. 'Just one. Where are the others? Craig, Claire and Riaz?'

'I'm afraid Mr Ahmed has decided to quit Blindeye for personal reasons. Mr McKinley, I am sad to report, recently suffered a fatal heart attack while on holiday in the Grampians. And Miss Maxwell . . .' She frowned, looking at her watch. 'Miss Maxwell should have been here some time ago.'

We all took a moment to digest the news. Craig was ex-Army like me; he'd seemed tough and fit. It was hard to believe he'd gone, just like that. He was a solid guy, and Blindeye's capability would be diminished as a result.

Riaz deciding to turn his back on Blindeye was a shock,

too. Like the rest of us, he'd seemed utterly dedicated to the cause. You didn't join an outfit like Blindeye unless you were asked, but you didn't say yes unless you believed wholeheartedly in its mission: to take the fight to the terrorists on a level playing field. I wondered if seeing me kill a man with my bare hands because we couldn't risk him exposing the operation had been eating away at him. Maybe he'd finally come to believe the ends didn't always justify the means.

'Well, I don't think we can wait any longer, I'm afraid.' Mrs Allenby started handing out the folders.

'What's this?' I asked, trying to dispel my dark thoughts with a quip. 'My pension details?'

'No, Mr Logan,' she said, tossing a folder into my lap. 'This is some background information on Blindeye's next target.'

'Our target? You mean Blindeye has another op already?'

'Yes, Mr Logan,' she said, giving me a serious look, 'we most certainly do.'

I'd never been the fastest reader. Books weren't my thing when I was growing up. When you were sleeping in shop doorways and under bridges, a bedtime story before lights out wasn't usually an option. Even on the streets, though, you'd find some people whose most precious possession was a battered paperback they'd clearly read six times before, and you could see that immersing themselves in a familiar fictional world, whether it was learning spells at Hogwarts or slotting bad guys with the SAS, was the only thing that kept them going. Until some cunt came and grabbed their book off them and tossed it on the fire, of course.

When it came to processing information, however, I was lightning quick, and I'd absorbed the salient points of the file before the rest of them were halfway through.

The target: Viktor Shlovsky. Russian oligarch. Born in the small town of Lensk, Siberia, 1963. Houses in Monaco, Geneva and Montenegro plus a luxury yacht currently moored off Cannes, but his permanent home is a big pile on The Bishops Avenue, north London, bought for £47 million. Estimated net worth £4 billion, mostly from mining: minerals, precious metals, etc. Acquired the mines for a song during the great post-Soviet sell-off of state assets. Considered a loyal supporter of the current president. Wife: Ekaterina, a former model ten years his junior. Unconfirmed rumours of a previous spouse, fate unknown. Children: a son, Mikhail, aged twenty-two, and daughter Anastasia, nineteen. Playboy and man about town, often frequents high-end clubs and casinos in the West End, but otherwise tries to stay out of the limelight.

I flipped the file closed. 'This guy's our target? A Russian oligarch? Sorry, I don't get it.'

The only thing I could think of that would make him a person of interest would be money-laundering. As a rule, no Russian ends up with that much money in the bank without having got their hands dirty somewhere along the way (there had to be some reason Shlovsky ended up with those mines and not someone else, right?), and the UK was a good place to invest some of that money in legitimate businesses. The trouble was, everybody knew that was going on. In fact, the UK government practically put up a bloody big sign saying: NEED TO GET RID OF YOUR DODGY ROUBLES? THEN COME TO LONDON! EVERYTHING FOR SALE! NO QUESTIONS ASKED! Unless Shlovsky had done something the government couldn't overlook, like pushing a business rival off the top of the Shard, it was hard to see why they'd be interested. And MI5? They had other, bigger fish to fry.

'You're quite right, Mr Logan. There's nothing in this file to indicate why Blindeye might want to get involved with Mr Shlovsky.'

I shrugged. 'Then . . .?'

Ryan, Alex and Alan had all now finished reading, and looked up to see what Mrs Allenby had to say.

'You recall the Novichok attack on Sergei and Yulia Skripal in Salisbury? You might also recall that the two GRU officers responsible left a remarkably conspicuous trail. Perhaps the Kremlin wanted the world to be in no doubt who had done this – or rather they wanted other former Russian intelligence officers around the world to know what would be coming their way if they decided to start chatting indiscreetly with their new hosts.'

'Well, at least after being caught red-handed, they won't try the same thing again,' Ryan said.

'That's no reason for complacency,' Mrs Allenby replied. 'It would be foolish to rest on our laurels. And the Russians are certainly not resting on theirs. In fact, we have every reason to think that they are scaling up their plans to destabilize Western democracies in general and our own in particular – and I don't just mean troll farms and fake Facebook accounts. I'm talking about bombs and guns and bodies on the streets.'

'But if they're not going to risk infiltrating their own intelligence people, then how?' Alex asked.

Mrs Allenby smiled, like a schoolteacher who had nudged her pupils into finally asking the right question. 'That's where our Mr Shlovsky comes in. If the Russians can't bring in their own assets, then they have to use what's on the ground.'

Ryan frowned as the penny dropped. 'You mean they're going to get Russian billionaires to start planting bombs?'

'Nothing quite as simple as that, Mr Oldfield. But if you think about it, these people have considerable assets. Not just money, but security personnel, often highly trained, some of them ex-Spetsnaz or even GRU and FSB. The expertise is definitely there.'

'But what's the motivation?' I asked. 'You're living high on the hog, strippers and coke every night, taking full advantage of Her Majesty's generous hospitality – why piss on all of that? They'd have to be mad.'

'Or someone would have to be twisting their arm,' Mrs Allenby said. 'Someone back in Moscow, for instance. We have information that all of Viktor Shlovsky's assets in Russia have been frozen: bank accounts, real estate holdings, you name it. And a prosecutor has been appointed to investigate tax fraud relating to his businesses. All in all, it sounds as if someone at the very top is holding a loaded gun to Mr Shlovsky's head.'

'So what do we do?' I asked.

'We do what we're best at. We watch. We try and find out if Shlovsky is planning an attack. And if he is, then we stop it.'

'But why us? Why Blindeye?' I persisted. 'If HMG knows all this, why don't they just stick A4 on him?'

For the first time, Mrs Allenby looked ill at ease. 'The PM won't allow it,' she said tightly.

We all took a moment with that: so MI5 thinks Russia is planning terrorist attacks through billionaire proxies resident in the UK; Viktor Shlovsky looks like he's been prepped for the first try-out; and the PM doesn't want him put under observation. In what universe did that make any sense?

I was beginning to get a nasty feeling that things at Clearwater Security International were not really clear at all.

'Which is why the DG tasked Blindeye with the job,' Mrs Allenby concluded, with a tight-lipped smile. 'Now, if there are no more questions, I suggest you all start putting together a plan of operation.'

4

Mrs Allenby closed the door behind her. I wondered if she would now be sitting outside at her desk, playing receptionist again. Something stopped me from opening the door and taking a peek.

Ryan was the first to break the silence. 'I can't believe Craig . . . I mean, how old was he?'

Alex shrugged. 'Forty? Bit younger, maybe.'

'Did he have any sort of history of heart problems? Something in the family, maybe?'

'Not that I know of,' Alex said.

But then, the truth was, most of the team hadn't known anything about each other before we started working together, and we hadn't found out much more on the job. None of us really talked much about our lives before Blindeye, partly for operational reasons – the less you know, the less you can give away – and partly, perhaps, because throwing ourselves into Blindeye was a way of escaping something. Something you didn't want to talk about.

At least, it was for me.

Ryan shook his head. 'Bloody hell.'

There didn't seem to be anything to add to that. 'Anyone fancy a brew, before we get down to it?'

Alan pointed to a kitchen area in the corner. 'Over there, mate. I might have a decaf soy latte, if you can manage it.'

'No you fucking won't,' I said. 'You'll have a tea with four sugars as fucking usual.'

'Same for me, minus the sugars,' Alex said.

I looked at Ryan. 'Just a coffee. Black. And out of a jar is fine, before you go off on one.'

I walked over to the kitchen and put the kettle on. It all looked like a real office, even down to the jokey mugs. Somebody had clearly put a bit of effort into creating our cover. I should have been impressed. Instead, I wondered what it was I wasn't seeing, what else our new boss was covering up. I was thrilled to bits that that cunt Leyton-Hughes had been given a sideways promotion that left him halfway across the world, of course, but at least he'd been easy to read. One reason he'd never have made a halfway decent surveillance operative, of course.

But what about Mrs Allenby?

I brought a tray of mugs over and put it on the big table. 'Right, then. Where do we start?'

Ryan flipped through the file on Viktor Shlovsky. 'Well, we know who he is. Now we need to find out what he does. We need to see the underlying pattern: where he goes, who he talks to – every day, right from taking his first crap to taking his teeth out before bed. Then when we have the whole picture, when we can see it all in three dimensions, we'll be able to see where something doesn't fit.'

'Let's hope he doesn't do too much jetting around, then,' I said.

'I dunno,' Alex said with a grin, 'I wouldn't mind checking out the Riviera this time of year. I hear Monaco's quite nice, too.'

'We'll just have to hope that Putin's got him by the balls, and he's going to stay close to home,' Ryan said. 'But from what I can see, he likes to spend most of his time in London, anyway. Plenty of billionaire buddies from the motherland to hang out with, of course. Keep your friends close and your enemies closer and all that. And this is where the money is, don't forget. Plus all the glitz and glamour of the world's most exciting city.'

Alex pulled a face. 'He needs to spend more time in Lewisham.'

'OK, so first thing, we need to find out what goes on inside that big pile on The Bishops Avenue.' I turned to Alan, who was sipping his tea suspiciously, clearly not convinced I'd put in the requisite number of sugars. 'What kind of audio can we get from outside?'

He put his mug down. 'Well, that depends. I don't suppose we'll be able to set up with a van full of gear parked outside his front door.'

'A bit too conspicuous,' I agreed. 'What kind of kit have we got?' I was aware that however long Mrs Allenby's reach might be, we no longer had access to any of the specially designed gear that A4 used.

'Anything commercially available, just like any regular security firm. Money's not a problem, apparently, so I should be able to get my hands on some decent stuff. Depends what you need.'

I nodded. 'I'll be able to tell you that after we've taken a look at the lie of the land.'

The truth was, I was itching to get out there. Gathering and analysing as much information as you could while sitting at a desk with a laptop made sense, but there was no substitute for eyeballs on the ground. All the megabytes of data that were freely available floating around the internet if you knew where to look could only tell you so much. I wanted to see Viktor Shlovsky for myself. I wanted to hear his voice, see how he moved, how he walked, how he carried himself – the subtle human behaviours that can only be analysed by the human brain, that evolutionary super-computer designed specifically to work out whether another human being is friend or foe. At least, that was the way I saw it.

'First thing we need then is a decent plan of the property, inside and out. You all right sorting that, Ryan?' Alan was no slouch when it came to IT, but hacking into other people's databases was something Ryan did for fun.

'Sure. Should be able to get the estate agent's specs, plus any surveys – architect's plans, maybe, depending on how long ago it was built. If they had a security firm come in and look the place over, they might have something useful, too.'

I nodded. 'That was my next question. We'll need to see what kind of systems they've got in place. They're bound to have the usual off-the-shelf stuff, but I'm guessing they might have something a little bit more bespoke as well. Plus plenty of size-twelve boots on the ground, of course. Let's start with the commercial stuff, find out which company installed it and do some digging around in their files, and we'll take the mantraps and tiger pits as they come.'

'I'll see what I can find in terms of directional mikes,' Alan said. 'And there's lots of fun stuff you can do with drones these days, of course.'

'Don't bother with the drones,' I told him, 'unless you just want to piss off the dog walkers on Hampstead Heath on a Saturday afternoon. We don't know how sophisticated his set-up is yet, but we can't risk him getting spooked before we've even started. If he finds himself sitting on the toilet one morning and there's a fucking drone hovering outside the window, he probably will fuck off to Cannes.'

Alan looked down despondently.

'Look, if it ends up that there's someone with a backpack full of plastic explosive climbing up a drainpipe in Buckingham Palace, you have my blessing to blast the fucker to kingdom come with one of those little drone missiles, OK?'

Alex frowned. 'Remember who pays for the bleedin' repairs on that place, Logan. It all comes out of your and my taxes, you know.'

I grinned, taking a gulp of tea. I looked at Ryan and Alan. 'How about if me and Alex leave you two here to dig up some more info and see what our tech options are, and we'll get over there and have a discreet little look-see?'

Ryan nodded. 'Sounds good. Alan?'

'Yeah, sure.' He was looking a bit happier now, no doubt looking forward to browsing some glossy high-tech catalogues with a few quid in his back pocket.

Alex was just grabbing her bag when the door opened. We all turned, expecting to see Claire. Instead, Mrs Allenby stood in the doorway with a sombre expression.

'I'm afraid I've just received some bad news. It appears that Miss Maxwell has been in an accident.'

I saw Alex pale. 'What sort of an accident?'

'It appears her car came off the road at high speed on a stretch of the Yorkshire Moors in the early hours of the morning. I'm afraid she's dead.'

5

In the car, Alex stared out of the driver's side window into the drizzle, chewing meditatively on one of her nails. I left her to her thoughts. No doubt she was doing the same as me – trying to make the pieces fit together.

As we started the long climb up Fitzjohn's Avenue towards Hampstead, she finally broke the silence.

'Are you thinking what I'm thinking?'

'If you're thinking that losing one member of Blindeye is bad luck but losing two is either very bad luck or something a fuck of a lot worse, then yes.'

'And what about Riaz?'

'As far as we know he's OK, at least according to Mrs Allenby.'

She wasn't convinced. 'We need to make contact. Get a message to him, at least.'

'Saying what?'

'I don't know – watch your back?'

'You think he isn't?'

'Was Claire? Was Craig?'

I focused on my driving for a minute. 'Mrs Allenby said

no one else was involved in Claire's accident. She was driving at high speed on a lonely road in the middle of nowhere at one in the morning.'

'So?'

'So, that's the sort of thing you do when there's something on your mind.'

'And that's why she went off the road?'

'I don't know. *Maybe*. Maybe she lost concentration for a second.'

'And Craig?'

I tapped the steering wheel with my fingers. 'I guess a heart attack's a heart attack. Maybe that *was* just bad luck.'

She gave a dismissive shake of her head. 'Isn't there something else you're forgetting?'

There was, of course. Not that I'd really forgotten it. It was the big, fat elephant in the room.

'Baldy?'

'You really think he tried to run you over because you made him look like a twat in front of his mates?'

'He might have wanted to give me a scare – maybe just run over my legs or something. Whoever it was behind the wheel wasn't necessarily trying to kill me.'

'Jesus, Logan, remind me to leave you pissing your pants in the middle of the road next time some arsehole tries to use you as a human speed bump.'

'You know what I mean.'

We drove on another fifty yards. The traffic was slowing as cars fed in from the adjoining roads, all headed up the hill.

'OK,' I said finally. 'Let's assume they're all hits, all connected. Who'd want the three of us dead and why? The only thing connecting us is Blindeye. But who knows Blindeye even exists? Can't be the brothers, because they're dead. And they never knew we were on to them until it was too late. They had no way of identifying us, anyway. Their counter-surveillance drills were pretty slick, they were savvy with the comms and all that, but at the end of the day they were just two blokes. That's how it works.'

'I don't believe that,' Alex said. 'The whole thing was too sophisticated, with the fake live feed from the killing house and everything. Someone very smart thought all that up. And that someone is still out there.'

I hit the revs and scooted in front of a big SUV that was trying to nudge out in front of me. Driving in London, you run out of peace, love and understanding pretty quickly.

'Yeah, sure, but how does that person know anything about us? The only other people in the magic circle are the DG and Leyton-Hughes. I can't exactly see our Old Etonian friend masterminding a purge of his former comrades from his deckchair on Copacabana Beach. So unless the DG has decided he wants to smash up his new toy, who could it be?'

'Maybe the DG wasn't as clever as he thought he was,' Alex suggested. 'Maybe someone in the Service found out what he was doing, rang the alarm, and the PM saw her damehood in the balance and let the dogs of war loose on us.'

'In that case we're well and truly fucked,' I said.

We finally made it to the top of the hill, then along Heath

Street, past the tube station and up another hill towards Jack Straw's Castle.

'Look, all we can do is crack on, watch our drills. In the meantime, let's get Ryan to see what he can find out about Craig and Claire: police reports, post-mortems, toxicology – all of that. Just in case we're jumping at shadows.'

'And Mrs Allenby? The DG?'

I thought for a moment. 'Let's keep them out of it for the moment. She might look like Miss Marple, but we don't even know if she really was his PA yet, do we?'

'Fair enough,' Alex said.

We turned right past White Stone Pond with a view of Hampstead Heath sloping down to our right and onto Spaniard's Road, the long, straight road that would lead us to Viktor Shlovsky's mansion. Conversation stopped as we both tried to clear our heads and get into operational mode.

There was no more time to worry about someone hunting us down.

It was time for us to become the hunters.

6

Millionaire's Row, they used to call it. Billionaire's Row now, of course. A million might buy you a garden shed on this street, but not much else. Snaking its way gently north from the edge of Hampstead Heath, The Bishops Avenue was still the only street in London where you could buy a property big enough to house an extended family, plus all the servants and bodyguards, along with the pool and the tennis court, the gym and the cinema, without having to dig down halfway to Australia. Every mansion sat on its own two or three acre plot, giving the impression of a country estate slap bang in the heart of London. Definitely no need to worry about noisy neighbours.

No need to worry about neighbours, period. As we drove slowly down the road, most of the properties looked uninhabited, locked up tight behind steel gates and bolted window shutters. Some of them looked as if they'd been empty so long they were actually falling down.

'Fucking hell, Logan, does anybody actually live here? It's like something out of a zombie movie.'

We passed a vast, odd-shaped mansion that looked as if it

had been constructed out of giant sandstone blocks. You could imagine gangs of slaves dragging them along the A1, being mercilessly whipped by men in loincloths and hard hats.

'Maybe they're like the pyramids,' I suggested. 'You know, they lock you in with all your servants, your concubines, your Lamborghini and your favourite Rottweiler, and you never see the light of day again.'

'Jesus, I can believe it.'

'A lot of them were bought as bolt-holes by Saudi royals when it looked like Saddam was going to seriously fuck up the region. But in the end they never had to use them. So they just left them to rot.'

'And increase in value, I suppose.'

'Oh, yeah. Most of them were just bought as investments or tax dodges, anyway. The owners were never planning to live there.'

Alex nodded to herself. 'You can see why.'

'What do you mean?'

'Have you seen a corner shop anywhere? Where are you supposed to go for a pint of milk or a bottle of Chardonnay at ten o'clock on a Saturday night?'

'You want to see inside, Alex. Some of these places have wine cellars bigger than your average offie. You may have a point about the milk, though.' I nodded to our left. 'There we are: Wyvern Lodge.'

Architecture wasn't my thing. Anything with central heating and indoor plumbing was a palace as far as I was concerned. And if the roof didn't leak and the windows weren't broken, that was a bonus. I guess for me the bar had been set pretty low early on in life.

But when I looked at Viktor Shlovsky's mansion, even I wondered if you couldn't get something a bit classier-looking for forty-seven million. Sure, it was big: a sweeping driveway leading up to a pillared entrance with all sorts of fairy-tale castle bits on top; but something told me a genuine toff would have turned his nose up at it. It certainly didn't look anything like a stately home that had been in the family for generations: more like a cookie-cutter McPalace for people with more money than style.

We carried on down to the junction. I turned left onto the A1 and then first left onto Winnington Road, Billionaire Row's slightly poorer cousin. I parked halfway up, near the entrance to Hampstead Golf Course, and we both got out.

'Right, see you back here in twenty.'

The idea was for each of us to do a walk-by, coming at the target from different directions. It wasn't ideal: pedestrians on The Bishops Avenue were few and far between, so somebody somewhere might be taking note of who came and went, but we could risk doing it one time, just to get a proper feel of the geography.

I walked south and Alex, in baseball cap and trainers, started jogging north. I turned left again at the end and was soon back at the top of the Avenue. Now I knew where Shlovsky's mansion was situated, I had a better idea of what I was looking for.

I walked on the left-hand side, too close to see much more

than a sliver of driveway and the two pillars flanking the entrance when I went past Wyvern Lodge. But it didn't matter.

I was much more interested in the crumbling pile on the other side of the road.

Without a security gate and a ten-foot wall all the way round, it was easier to see what you were dealing with: three stories of faded stucco with a green tiled roof, a little more modest than Shlovsky's mansion, and more importantly, no cars out front and all the shutters on the windows looking as if they hadn't been opened in a while. I took out my phone and pretended to answer a call, while taking in every detail of the house.

This place was definitely unoccupied, and had been for some time. But what I really liked about it was the view.

From the third floor, I reckoned you'd be able to see more or less the whole frontage of Wyvern Lodge.

I put my phone back in my pocket and carried on past without a backward glance. Alex passed me on the other side of the road, looking like a jogger who'd run out of steam. In my peripheral vision I saw her stop, leaning forward, breathing hard, her hands on her knees, then straighten with a hand on her hip, as if she had a twinge in her back.

For Christ's sake, don't overdo it, I thought, quickening my pace.

Ten minutes later, back in the car, we compared notes.

Alex was keen to impress me with how much she'd managed to glean from her performance as a stricken jogger, but I cut her short.

'The house opposite. That's the OP,' I said.

7

I dropped Alex back at her flat, then drove to the place that was going to be my new home for the foreseeable future – in other words, the next three weeks. Alex had offered to let me doss down at hers until I found somewhere permanent; she didn't have a spare room, but the couch was comfy, apparently, and she said she needed someone to do the washing-up.

I didn't know how serious the offer was, but I thanked her and said I didn't want to cramp her style. I also didn't want her to find me sitting at the kitchen table talking to someone who wasn't there at three in the morning.

A couple of Sarah's musician friends who'd moved down south were touring in Europe for a month and needed someone to house-sit. I'd never met them and they didn't really know anything about me except that I was ex-Army, but they obviously liked the idea of someone who could handle the odd burglar looking after their place, and I liked the fact that nobody else would know I was living there.

I found a parking spot fifty yards up the road, grabbed all my worldly possessions from the boot and made my way to the front door. The key was under a flowerpot on the third step, just like they said. I shook my head. For people who were worried about burglars, they didn't seem to have thought much about security. Maybe that was musicians for you.

I dumped my bag in the hall and did a quick recce. A front room with lots of books, ethnic knick-knacks, stacks of old-fashioned vinyl and a beanbag instead of a sofa – the sort of place you'd have to be stoned to feel really comfortable in. A small kitchen out back, looking onto a postage-stamp back garden crammed with flowerpots full of half-dead plants. Upstairs a bedroom that continued the ethnic theme, with a big, fuzzy painting of a woman in a sari, a couple of guitars on stands and something hiding in the corner that looked like a lute made out of some kind of exotic vegetable. A small office space with more books and magazines scattered on the floor and a knackered-looking PC completed the picture.

I went back down to the kitchen, found milk and teabags and made myself a brew. 'Make yourself at home,' they'd said, but that didn't really feel like an option. I'd probably sleep on the floor in the hall, I decided, touching as little as possible. I wouldn't even disturb the dust. I'd be a ghost.

I finished my tea, rinsed my mug and put it on the drainer. Finsbury Park was round the corner: I'd go for a run, have a shower, find somewhere that did a decent chicken jalfrezi, then try and get a bit of kip before it was time to go back to The Bishops Avenue.

* * *

I'd set the alarm on my phone for 1.30 a.m. but my eyes snapped open promptly at 1.25, as I knew they would. Despite the odd creaky floorboard, I'd slept like a kitten and woke up with a clear head, raring to go, already dressed in black jeans and black T-shirt. It felt good, having a plan, like being back in the job. A nice little adrenaline buzz was quietly building as I laced up my army boots, then I put on a black tracksuit top and stuffed a black balaclava into my pocket before grabbing a black daysack. I'd already checked the contents before going to sleep.

I took it easy on the drive, despite feeling that old familiar itch to press play and start the action; if I didn't look like someone planning a bit of breaking and entering, I don't know who did, and I didn't want to give some over-eager plod a chance to improve his stats for the night. By the time I got to Hampstead Lane, the traffic was getting sparse, but there were plenty of cars parked on the road, so I could blend in without too much trouble. I drove past the top of the Avenue and took the third left, the street that bordered the other side of the golf course. The houses weren't quite so palatial on this side, but one owner seemed determined to change that, having bulldozed whatever inadequate fifteen-bedroom hovel had been on the site. The resulting wasteland was now hidden behind a ten-foot security fence, but the little panel set in the black metal sheeting had been left unsecured, presumably as there was nothing on site to nick yet. That was going to be my way in.

At least, that was the plan.

When I'd been a surveillance operative, working for MI5's

A4 unit, improvisation was the name of the game. It didn't matter how much planning you'd done, how many briefings you'd half dozed through, how many different scenarios you'd prepared for; the target almost always did something you weren't expecting, meaning you were either suddenly at risk of being compromised, or they were going to slip out from under your control. Sometimes you had to create a diversion; sometimes you had to switch instantly from the part you were playing to a quite different one. Whatever you had to do, it wasn't something you'd prepared for.

And with Blindeye the chances of that kind of situation happening were multiplied tenfold. Maybe more, now that there were just the four of us (I wasn't quite ready to call Mrs Allenby one of 'us' yet).

I parked up as far from the nearest street light as I could manage while still being in sprinting distance of the entrance point. If things went tits-up, I needed to be ready for a quick getaway. I sat there for a few minutes, trying to get a sense of whether my arrival had disturbed the slumber of this leafy backwater, but there were no twitching curtains or front doors opening curiously as far as I could tell. Maybe no one actually lived here, either.

I slipped out of the car and made my way down towards the building site, staying light on my feet and keeping close to the shadows, before ducking through the panel and across the empty expanse of rubble-strewn mud until I reached a low wooden fence bordering the golf course. I hopped over the fence and into the trees.

That was when I realized a bit more planning would have been good.

I'd looked at the layout of the course, and calculated where the nearest point to the back of the house would be. But now that I was there, the online map didn't seem to correspond to reality. I was aiming to keep to the trees until I reached the two big bunkers alongside the sixth fairway, then sharp left past the green and straight down the fifteenth fairway and I'd be more or less there.

I stood in the shadows, looking out at the gently rolling landscape faintly lit by a quarter moon, and realized I had no idea where the hell the fifteenth fairway was. I knew they moved pin positions around on the greens, but did bunkers come and go as well? I leaned back against an old oak tree and tried to get my bearings. There was nothing else for it; I'd have to get out onto the course until I stumbled across a feature I recognized.

Feeling uncomfortably exposed, I left the safety of the shadows and started walking in a vaguely westerly direction, with the mansions of The Bishops Avenue somewhere through the dark smear of trees ahead.

Where was my one, though?

I'd always thought golf was a game for cunts; now I was sure of it.

I skirted a little bunker then stood still, letting my boots sink into the turf and my heart rate steady. Some infrared goggles would have been handy, I thought.

It was no good. The map and the territory refused to

slot together in my mind. I might as well have been on the moon.

I saw a movement to my left and made myself stay loose. Sat on the lip of a bunker, his outline grey in the moonlight, was a fox. He must have caught my scent, because he was now stood stock-still, too, his nose pointed straight at me. I was sure I caught a glint of moonlight in his eyes, a quick flash of silver.

I stared back, trying to make contact, trying to bridge the unbridgeable gap between us. I took a step towards him and he turned lazily away, not spooked, not even wary, as if we were just two pals out for a moonlight stroll together.

'All right, Foxy, show me where to go.'

He ambled on, checking behind him once, but I couldn't help thinking not because he was worried I was gaining on him: more to check that I was keeping up. Finally he reached the edge of the trees, threw me one last look and disappeared.

I walked into the undergrowth at the point I'd lost sight of him and let my eyes adjust to the gloom. Ahead, through the trees, I could just make out a shape, a faint area where the dark felt a tinge more grey than black. I took a few steps closer, brushing the brambles out of my path, and the shape began to solidify. Soon I could see the outline of a roof. Then three black-shuttered windows in a neat triangle. I didn't need to see any more.

It was my house.

I picked my way carefully through the bushes, taking it slowly. It was impossible to know what was underfoot and

I didn't want to turn an ankle at this point in the game. But I still almost walked into the fence before I saw it. I thought of going over, but reckoned I could make out razor wire at the top and didn't fancy having to deal with that every night. I needed a proper back door.

I took off my daysack and rummaged around until I had the wire-cutters, then got to work. When the hole was big enough, I pushed through, then fitted the chain-link back in place. The garden was almost as much of a jungle as the woods surrounding the golf course: a pain to get through, but otherwise good news. I wasn't going to be interrupted by the under gardener trimming the wisteria.

The back door was inside a pillared portico (they did like their pillars round here) and secured behind a metal sheet bolted to the frame. No way in there, then. I edged round to my right and found a pair of French windows. A gap in the curtains revealed a solid-looking metal grille. I took a step back onto what had once been the lawn and looked up. The first-floor windows were covered over with metal plates, just like the door. There was a drainpipe to my left. I hefted my daysack again and found a torch, then played the beam quickly along the length of the drainpipe. It was leaning slightly to one side, as if someone had pushed all their weight against it. The wall jutted out a couple of feet, just to the right. Maybe someone had used the drainpipe as leverage as they hauled themselves up the wall. I decided to see if the trick would still work.

Putting my left foot on the drainpipe's first join, I planted my right against the wall and pushed. I was half expecting the drainpipe to give way, but it held firm and I was able to take another step, pushing off my left, then my right, with one hand on the pipe and the other wedged into the angle of the wall to steady myself, inching my way up crab-wise.

Two more pushes and I was level with the first window. Still holding on to the drainpipe with my left hand, I took the torch out of my back pocket and leaned round so I could take a look at the bolts. Each sat in an aureole of rust, marked with deep gouges, but the bolts themselves looked relatively new.

My hunch had been right. Someone else had taken this route before. They'd unscrewed the bolts (which were probably rusting somewhere in the undergrowth below me) and got in through the window. But they'd obviously been discovered, and the metal plate had been reattached with shiny new bolts. I reached round and fumbled in the daysack for my toolkit.

Twenty minutes later, with my knee shaking and my back threatening to go into spasm, I was in. I'd loosened the bolt in the top-right corner but left it in place, so I could swing the plate round on its axis, push open the sash window, scramble inside and then carefully manoeuvre the plate back to its original position.

I jumped down, my boots landing with a soft thud, and turned on the torch. I was in a bedroom. The door opened on to a corridor, leading to a grand staircase sweeping down to the front entrance. I moved the beam of the torch in a slow three-sixty. As it caught the teardrops of a massive chandelier, there was a brief sparkle of faded glamour, but it quickly died as the torch beam lit up a tableau of rotting floorboards, crumbling plaster and peeling wallpaper. The stairs had begun to collapse, pulling the gilded bannisters along with them. There was rat shit everywhere.

Weird. A house on one of London's most exclusive streets, where only the super-rich could afford to buy, and inside it was a fucking tip. Someone had paid a fortune for this house once, and then literally let it fall to bits.

I found some more stairs and made my way up to the next floor, testing my weight on each step first so I didn't find myself crashing down to the floor below. Another corridor: more bedrooms, it looked like. I opened the door to the second one, guessing it would be the one with the view I was looking for. There was a crunching sound as I stepped in. I shone the torch over the floor to see a syringe, along with a scattering of broken wine bottles. So this is where the intruder had ended up. I hoped they'd enjoyed the party. Back in the day, it was the sort of party I might have had an invite to.

I picked my way through the broken glass to the window. The shutters were locked but not bolted. A couple of minutes' work and I was able to open them an inch or two, just enough to make sure I hadn't fucked up. Across the way, Viktor Shlovsky's double-fronted Disneyland castle was lit up like a Christmas tree.

I hadn't bothered lugging a sackful of gear on the

off-chance I'd find a way in, but now that I was here, I thought about what else I'd need if this was where I was going to be hunkering down for a while. I had a couple of ideas. Maybe tomorrow Alan could go and do some shopping.

I'd seen what I needed to see. No point in hanging around. I closed the shutters and turned back towards the door, shining my torch in a wide arc across the floor, just to check how much more crap there was I'd have to clear up.

The torch beam stopped when it reached the corner.

'Jesus.'

She was crouched in the angle of the walls, her knees drawn up, looking as if she was trying to make herself as small as possible. I assumed it was a she, from the long blonde hair that still half covered her face on its way almost to the floor. Otherwise there was no real way of telling. Most of the flesh had gone; the rats had seen to that. Before they'd started on her clothes. A few scraps of blackened, leathery skin, some wisps of fabric and a pair of much-chewed ankle boots were all that was left.

I stepped closer, holding the torch out in front of me as if to ward off something evil. Her blonde hair shone incongruously in its beam.

How old had she been when she'd put the fatal dose in her arm? I wondered if someone was thinking about her, even now, wondering where she was, what had happened to her. Well, there was nothing I could do about that. If there was a loved one out there waiting for closure, they were going to have to wait a while longer.

Something caught my eye. A rust-coloured stain on the wall by her head. A smear of something that had once been red. And on her temple, I could see, the bone had cratered, as if it was collapsing inward.

Or as if someone had smashed her hard with something. Like an iron bar, or a baseball bat.

I let out a breath I hadn't realized I'd been holding.

So they'd found her here. They'd seen the window at the back where she'd managed to get in, followed her footprints in the dust, up the stairs to the third floor. And then? I could imagine how it had happened. She'd been young, pretty and off her head. Easy meat. Then afterwards, they knew they couldn't let her leave, couldn't sling her out on the streets again in case she went crying to the cops. That would be the end of their cushy little security job, for starters. So they hit her with the bat, until she had no more stories to tell, and then they fixed the steel plate back over the window and left her to the rats.

My nostrils flared at the smell of something rotten.

I turned the torch off and let the darkness swallow her again.

8

It was hard to find anywhere without any cameras these days. There are more cameras per head in London than anywhere else in the world, so they say. But is it really true? What about a real police state – what about North Korea? Why would a decent country like Britain need to keep more of a watch over its citizens than a brutal dictatorship like that? It didn't make sense.

It was also a pain in the arse.

It meant fixing a meet was like trying to find a pub where the bar staff were older than his daughter, spoke proper English and knew how to pull a pint without spilling it all over the bar. Bloody difficult, in other words. Sometimes he felt like the only way to be a hundred per cent certain you weren't being watched was to meet in the middle of Epping Forest, but he wasn't about to suggest that. Apart from anything else, he always liked to stay in the car.

Just to be on the safe side.

He pulled into the car park and looked for the silver Lexus. That could be it, in the far corner, under the billboard advertising a payday loans company, just like they'd said. He wasn't sure if that was meant as a joke. But otherwise they were true to their word: no cameras. He was surprised the place was so empty, even as late as this, and not full of people selling drugs, racing stolen motors and having gang fights, seeing as none of it would be recorded for posterity.

Some people just didn't have the gumption to grab life's opportunities. Another thing that was wrong with this country.

Still, he wasn't complaining.

He drove in a wide arc, approaching the Lexus head to head, then eased in beside it so the driver's windows were next to each other. He powered down the window and the other driver did the same.

She hadn't changed from the last time he'd seen her: the same navy-blue suit and white blouse. She looked like an accountant.

And was that what she was? An accountant? Someone who did the books, looked after the money and occasionally handed over envelopes full of cash in out-of-the-way car parks?

You could never tell with people. That was another of his mottoes. And a bloody good thing, too. It meant people looked at him – the sharp suit, the monogrammed cufflinks, the expensive haircut – and saw a modestly successful entrepreneur with their own consultancy business in sales or marketing.

Not a man who killed people for a living.

'Is he happy with things then?' he asked.

'Is who happy with things?'

'Your boss.'

'What makes you so sure my boss isn't a woman?' she asked.

Jesus, this isn't twenty questions, he thought. *If I wanted to know who your boss was, male or bloody female, I'd stick the barrel of a gun up your arse and count to ten.* But of course he was intrigued. You couldn't help being curious about why one person would pay a lot of money to have another person killed. There had to be an interesting story there. Just think of all the dramas he'd played a part in without ever knowing the plot, or even who the main characters were.

But he was never going to ask who and why. That was information it was better not to have. Better for people to *think* you didn't have it, anyway. Unless, of course, you fucked up or were just unlucky, and you ended up in an interview room with the cameras rolling. That was when you needed a bit of leverage: when you were looking at fifteen to life, and that was if the judge had had his jollies the night before and woke up in a good mood.

'Anyway, to answer your question, the person I represent is quite satisfied.'

He nodded. 'No comeback, then?'

'Not so far.'

'What the fuck does that mean?'

The woman in the Lexus shrugged. 'You never know.'

She opened a steel briefcase on the passenger seat and

took out a fat manila envelope. She held it out of the window and he reached out and took it.

He raised an eyebrow. It weighed a little heavy.

'Think of it as an advance. On your next job.'

9

I didn't mention the girl. I don't know why, really. It's not as if it would have made any difference to anything. But I suppose they might have wondered what sort of person would happily spend time in an empty, shut-up, decaying mansion with a corpse.

'Happily' wasn't exactly the word, but it was true I didn't really mind the idea as much as perhaps I ought to. And what did that say about me?

I liked to think it said I took people as I found them, dead or alive, but they probably wouldn't have understood.

Mrs Allenby wouldn't have approved; I was sure about that. She was sitting at one of the desks with a notepad on her lap and a fountain pen in her hand, peering over her specs at us like a conductor waiting to begin a concert. The notepad made me nervous, but I suppose she wasn't going to change the habit of a lifetime just because she was now running Blindeye.

I explained the set-up at the mansion and what I thought we needed for the surveillance.

Mrs Allenby scribbled away on her pad for a bit, nodding to herself, then turned to Alan. 'So, what have you got for us?'

He pushed an SLR with a telephoto lens across the table. I picked it up and had a squint through the view-finder. 'I hope it comes with a tripod. This thing weighs a ton.'

Alan looked as if his professional pride had been hurt. 'Of course.'

Mrs Allenby made a note. 'Fine. Once we get a sense of Mr Shlovsky's routine, who comes and goes, etcetera, then we can take the next step.'

'Meaning?' Alex asked. I could tell she was itching to get into the action.

'We need a way in,' Mrs Allenby said. 'A chink in his armour. He'll assume he's being watched, so it won't be easy.'

'But there'll be something,' I said. 'There always is.'

Mrs Allenby turned to Ryan. 'What do we know about the security arrangements?'

'Not much. Shlovsky's a bit of a man about town, so there are one or two snaps coming out of nightclubs and casinos, always with a bodyguard in tow, and another guy hovering around who could be his security chief. Always the same driver too, so we'll assume he's on the firm.'

'And we don't know who they are?'

'Not a private firm, that's for sure, or we'd have been able to identify them. I'm assuming they've been flown in from the motherland. The usual motley crew.'

'What else?'

'Well, there's the staff. Cooks, maids, butlers . . .'

'Very *Downton Abbey*,' Alex said.

'Maybe we could send you in as the new scullery maid,' I suggested.

'Fuck off.'

'You never did like hard work,' I smirked.

'If we could get back to the subject in hand,' Mrs Allenby said, giving us both a look. 'That's the downstairs, as it were; what about upstairs?'

'Just the wife, Ekaterina,' Ryan said. 'The son, Mikhail, is doing a masters in business at NYU.'

'So he can look squeaky clean when he takes over Daddy's dirty business, presumably,' Alex said.

'Not sure he's got the brains, actually, judging by his school reports,' Ryan said.

'What about the daughter?' Mrs Allenby asked.

'She seems to be the one with all the smarts. Currently at the Sorbonne doing a degree in something fancy with the word "literature" in it.'

'So Mr and Mrs Shlovsky have the place all to themselves.'

Ryan nodded. 'Apart from the hundred and fifty staff, yes.'

'Anything else?'

'I tried to find out something about the previous marriage. Ancient history, I know, but it was niggling at me.'

Alex nudged him. 'Plus you like showing off.'

'It's bad enough with the unknown unknowns,' Mrs Allenby said. 'We don't want to leave any known unknowns unexplored, if we can help it.'

It took me a moment to work out what she was talking about. A fancy way of saying loose ends, I suppose.

Ryan continued. 'Anyway, the first wife seems to have been a childhood sweetheart from his home town. All I can tell you is that she died in childbirth.'

'So Shlovsky didn't just get rid of her when he wanted to trade her in for a newer model?' I said.

'Doesn't look like it.'

'What a gent,' Alex said, rolling her eyes.

'What about audio?' Mrs Allenby asked, looking at Alan again.

He started riffling through what looked like a technical manual. 'I think we can rustle up something you can use in the OP. I don't think a parabolic mike is going to be much use to you. Too conspicuous apart from anything else.'

'Quite,' Mrs Allenby said. 'In which case?'

'Worth giving a laser set-up a go, I think. They can be bulky, but it sounds like Logan might be able to handle it.'

I nodded. Aiming a laser beam at a window meant you could pick up the minute vibrations in the glass caused by the sound of people speaking in the room, bounce it back and turn it back into sound. It was amazing what you could get, and from a serious distance too.

Alan turned to me. 'I should be able to source that some-time tomorrow. I'll just need to tinker around with it a bit first. And we'll just have to hope he doesn't have triple glazing.'

'Or bulletproof glass,' I added.

Alan grinned. 'Yeah, that can be a bitch.'

Mrs Allenby closed her notebook and stood up. 'Well, it sounds as if we're ready for the next phase. I'll leave you to it.'

She put her notebook in her handbag, along with her fountain pen, took her jacket from the back of the chair and gave us a brisk nod before walking out. I wondered who those notes were for. The DG? Leyton-Hughes had kept him out of the loop, to put it mildly, so maybe this time he wanted to make sure he knew what we were doing every step of the way. Or was there someone else she was reporting to?

The door closed behind her. We listened for a few seconds and heard the sound of another door closing, then the clack of her heels on the stairs going down to the street.

I imagined her returning to a little flat in a nice Victorian block in Pimlico, taking off her shoes, then putting on Radio Three before feeding the cat and watering the plants. Twenty minutes later she'd be deep in the *Times* crossword, or Skyping the grandchildren in Australia.

Or was she actually on her way back to Thames House? Or somewhere else? I felt like asking Alex to get on her bike and follow. We'd quickly see if Mrs Allenby had the sort of skill set that went beyond shorthand and efficient diary management. But we had enough on our plates.

Now that she was gone, Ryan was looking at me expectantly.

'Go ahead. What have you got?'

'Not much,' he admitted. 'As far as Claire's concerned, it's a bit early to say, but as of now it's definitely being treated as an accident. Autopsy won't be for a while yet. The initial report doesn't mention any other vehicles. Unless there's a surprise with the toxicology or a witness pops up out of nowhere, it's hard to see the story changing.'

Was that what I wanted to hear? You couldn't call a tragic accident good news, especially when there was a kid left without a mother, but I suppose it was better than the alternative.

'What about Craig?'

'That was a bit longer ago, so in theory there should be more information, but the cupboard is a bit bare.'

'Curiously bare?' Alex asked.

Ryan adjusted his ponytail. 'Hard to say. Definitely a heart attack. No previous in the medical records, no mention of any family history.'

'And he was on his own when it happened?'

'Looks like it. At least, he was when they found him.'

'And let's say it wasn't natural causes. How could it have been done?'

'Still working on that.'

'OK.' I put my hands behind my head and rocked back in my chair, thinking. 'Either it's all just what it looks like, including my bit of bother outside the pub, or there's a bloody sophisticated operation going on: someone putting a lot of effort into covering their tracks.' I looked at Ryan. 'If you start to see signs of an online clean-up, information disappearing, that'll be the tell.'

'Meaning what?' Alex asked.

I looked at all of them. 'That we're up against the big boys.'

10

I thought I'd better give her a name, seeing as how we were going to be spending a bit of time together. I saw her as a bit of a hippy, a flowerchild, for some reason. Then, of course, there was the hair. And half hidden by a stray wisp, something I hadn't noticed first time round: a tiny brooch pinned to what was left of her top. A yellow flower with white petals.

'Daisy,' I said. 'Sorry if it's not your real name.'

Daisy didn't say anything.

'Daisy it is, then.'

It had been a bit of a slog, lugging all my stuff into the house. Finding my way had been no problem – no need for Mr Fox this time. But I wanted to be extra careful about leaving any traces, so made sure I didn't disturb the foliage too much when I left the fairway and stepped into the woods. I didn't want anyone else following in my footsteps.

I took my time climbing up to the window, too. The wonky drainpipe had stood out to me, so it might to someone else. I pushed it back to the vertical as best I could. And I brought a slab of builder's putty with me so I could fix the metal sheet over the window more securely behind me.

Inside the house, too, it wasn't just that I didn't want anyone to know I was here; I didn't want anyone to know I had been.

Everything I brought in, I was planning to take out. And that meant everything: along with the energy bars and the water, I'd packed a couple of empty two-litre plastic bottles and a handful of polythene bags. Daisy would just have to avert her eyes.

I turned on the torch and set it on the floor, then brushed the broken glass away from a section of the floorboards under the window and put my daysack down. That was going to be my bed, not that I was planning on doing much sleeping.

I took out the collapsible tripod and the SLR and set them up in front of the window. With a piece of cloth, I wiped a layer of dust and grime from the window pane, then crouched down and looked through the viewfinder.

All set. I looked at my watch. Another couple of hours until dawn.

'Such a lovely girl.'

I turned. Sarah was crouched on the floor next to Daisy, stroking her hair. I could see that Daisy had her eyes closed. Her skin was very pale in the torchlight. I thought I could see blood seeping down one side of her face, but she looked peaceful: asleep, not dead.

'You know what happened to her?' I asked.

'Of course.'

I waited for her to say more but she just smiled and carried on stroking her hair.

'She should have stayed at home,' I said.

'Home's not always the safest place, Logan. You know that.'

True, I thought: some people spend their lives running away from home; others spend their lives trying to find it. I suppose I was somewhere in between.

'Where's Joseph?'

'Oh, he's around. But I didn't want him to see Daisy like this.'

I nodded. 'You're right. This isn't a good place. Not for a child.'

'Not for Daisy, either,' she said sadly.

I noticed a little vase, with a spray of yellow flowers, on the floor.

'I thought she'd like them,' Sarah said. 'Brighten the place up a little.'

'That was thoughtful,' I said.

'And she's got you. Some company. At least for a little while.'

'Company for me too.'

I stepped closer. Daisy was very thin. Her wrists were like sticks. But you could see how pretty she'd been before she'd got sick.

'Will she stay like this? After you've gone?' I asked.

'I'm afraid not, Logan. You'll just have to remember her

the way she was. A beautiful young girl with her whole life ahead of her.'

'I'll try.'

Sarah got to her feet and brushed herself off. 'I'd better go now. See what mischief Joseph's getting into.'

'Give him my love.'

'Of course.'

I closed my eyes, knowing that when I opened them again she'd be gone.

I woke up just after dawn. I wasn't hungry, but I had an energy bar anyway. From now on it was going to be all about staying focused.

Daisy was back to being a heap of bones and gristle. I said good morning to her anyway.

I gently eased the shutter open an inch or two then put my eye to the viewfinder. 'Right, Mr Shlovsky. Let's see what's going on in your world.'

Three hours later I was beginning to seriously wonder if he wasn't on his yacht after all. To call The Bishops Avenue a quiet street was an understatement. No one came, no one went. It seemed as pointless as watching Buckingham Palace hoping to catch a glimpse of the Queen letting herself in at the front door with her trusty Yale.

But maybe that was the point. When the tennis court and the gym and the swimming pool and the cinema were all on site, not to mention the restaurant-grade kitchen and wine cellar, why bother going anywhere? Especially when you'd forked out forty-seven million for the privilege – plus another couple of mil making sure the carpets all matched the wallpaper just the way the missus liked.

Daisy thought I was being a bit sexist there.

'Sorry, Daisy.'

At 10.07 I was just thinking of doing a few stretches to keep my back loose when finally there was a bit of action. A black SUV pulled up to the gates, a young guy in a dark suit spoke into the intercom, and the gates slowly swung open. He drove in, but instead of pulling up in front of the pillars, stopped halfway down the drive, the engine idling. Suddenly there were three more men in dark suits: one at the front door, one at the gate and one leaning into the driver's window of the SUV. Maybe I was losing my touch, but they seemed to have appeared out of nowhere.

The one at the gate stepped into the road and scanned the avenue in both directions for a good thirty seconds. Then, satisfied that all was well, he stepped back into the property and the gates swung closed behind him. By this time the SUV was moving again, waved on by the second guy. It crept round to the left and I could just see it disappearing under a roller door built into the brick facade.

An underground car park. Natch.

I waited to see what the guy by the door would do but he stayed where he was. So did the guy by the gate. Then a minute later the SUV reappeared. I was expecting to see passengers now, but no: just the driver. The second guy trotted behind, then put his hand on the roof and said something to the driver. He added a quick hand gesture I couldn't interpret. The driver kept looking straight ahead, pretending not to be interested. Then the second guy walked away, nodding in the direction of the guy by the gate as he went.

The gates opened and the SUV drove out. I looked back at the house and the three guys had disappeared. All very slick. I almost felt like applauding.

That was all the excitement Daisy and I had until lunchtime. Then, promptly at half past twelve, the roller door went up again and a white Range Rover appeared. A second later the front door opened and there was Mrs Shlovsky.

At least I assumed it was. I'd seen pictures, and very glam they were, too, but although the woman I was looking at certainly carried herself like the lady of the manor, straight back, head held high, just like a ballerina, her face was hidden behind a scarf and big Jackie O sunglasses, almost as if she knew there was a bloke pointing a camera with a great big telephoto at her from across the street.

Snap, snap.

She skipped down the steps and the driver nipped out smartly to open the door for her. I was looking forward to seeing how elegantly she managed to fold herself into the car when she stopped, a hand on her hip, and looked back with a frown.

There at the top of the steps was hubby. No mistaking him: short, iron-grey hair, dark eyes, a little bit jowly and with a slight paunch, but still a powerful-looking man, square-shouldered and solid. Not exactly a gym body, more something forged in the fields or a factory.

And right now he was looking pissed. He put his meaty hands in the pockets of his tan slacks, less to affect a casual look than to keep them out of harm's way, I suspected, and let loose with a volley of angry Russian.

She gave it about three seconds, then responded with a volley of her own, while the driver, hand still holding the door, froze in place as if someone had just hit pause. My Russian wasn't up to much, but I knew sarcasm when I heard it, and she was giving him a barrel load.

Shlovsky turned to his left, where another black-suited guy had magically appeared, and started talking quickly, his speech punctuated with little shakes of his head, as if women simply couldn't be reasoned with.

Seeing that hubby wasn't listening to her, Mrs Shlovsky brought the driver back to life with a flick of her hand and got into the car. The driver shut the door then looked questioningly at Shlovsky. Shlovsky gave him a curt nod, then turned on his heel and went back into the house. The Range Rover went through the gates and disappeared up the road, towards Hampstead.

'Well, Daisy,' I said. 'What do you think of all that to-do? I think you're right: that's definitely not the first time they've had *that* conversation. I'm also pretty sure I know what's going to happen next.'

Sure enough, less than a minute later, another Range

Rover, black this time, emerged from the underground garage and the guy in the suit jumped in.

'Not too close, Boris,' I murmured as he sped up the road, 'or she'll suss you.'

After that little drama, things got quiet again.

At 13.57 a short-haired brunette in what looked like some sort of maid's uniform went out in a Mini and came back forty-five minutes later with a couple of shopping bags.

A UPS truck tried to gain admittance at 14.34 but the men in black were having none of it and sent it on its way.

At 15.15 two men came out and had an animated discussion, with lots of pointing up towards the first-floor windows. Something to do with the security system? They looked too serious to be discussing the double-glazing.

I was less interested in what they were talking about, though, than who they might be. One guy was heavyset, looking relaxed in jeans and loafers with a navy jumper that did nothing to hide his belly. The other guy was a little bit more dapper: flannel trousers, blazer and tie. Everything about him said ex-Army, and I didn't mean the Russian Army. He seemed to defer to the big guy, so was the big guy the capo? I kept snapping as they talked, hoping Ryan would be able to get a match.

Mrs S came back at 16.07, walking up the steps with slightly less balletic grace than she'd gone down them – or was that my imagination? She was clutching a couple of bags, the boxy kind you get in fancy clothing stores, but I didn't recognize the names.

Daisy said she didn't either.

The black Range Rover returned twenty minutes later.

And that was it for the day. I imagined a little shut-eye for Mrs S, then perhaps a swim, a massage, try on her new frocks, until it was time for a glass of wine.

I had to admit a beer would go down well at this end, too. But I still had work to do. Another energy bar, a slurp of water and a quick piss in the bottle while Daisy wasn't looking, and I was back at my post.

I had a feeling that if Shlovsky was going to make another appearance it wouldn't be until late. He had the look of a night owl. And if he did go out on the town, would he be accompanied by Mrs S? I reckoned not. A frosty dinner with him wolfing down a steak and her picking at a salad while sipping another large Chablis, then early to bed with a headache was my bet.

At 22.27 it looked as if I was right. Shlovsky appeared, suited and booted, and with the big guy at the wheel and our ex-Army chap and another security guy in the back, they headed off.

I wanted to follow. They looked like they were planning on a proper night out. But I contented myself with taking a few more snaps. At least I had all the plates now. We'd see if that turned up anything interesting.

I wasn't expecting anything else to happen before they returned, and that wouldn't be for a while. I thought I could risk a bit of kip and Daisy agreed. I watched the foxes for a while, trotting up and down the Avenue as if on patrol. One of them stopped outside the gates, and I swear he turned and looked at me.

I put a finger to my lips and gave him a wink.

11

'You look like shit, Logan.'

A long, hot shower, a change of clothes and a pint of orange juice chugged down straight from the fridge obviously hadn't done the trick: I still looked like someone who'd just spent the last seventy-two hours crouched over a camera tripod in a room full of broken glass and rat shit, not to mention the corpse of a young girl with her head bashed in. Still, considering that I'd passed on the full English my stomach was craving so I could debrief the team ASAP, Alex's reaction seemed a bit harsh.

'Thanks, Alex. Nice to see you, too.'

I handed over the camera and Alan plugged it into his laptop. Soon he was scrolling through the hundreds of pictures I'd taken. I gave a running commentary as Alex, Ryan and Mrs Allenby huddled round the screen.

Ryan was particularly interested in the security team, especially the big Russian guy and his British sidekick. 'Can you get me some decent headshots, Alan? Enhance them a bit?'

Alan started photoshopping. 'Shouldn't be a problem.'

'Great, I'll run them through the system. See what the

facial recognition gizmo turns up. Let's have a gander at those number plates as well.'

'You're not thinking maybe he hasn't been paying his parking tickets?' Alex said.

Ryan shrugged. 'You never know.'

'I hope you've got more for us than that, Mr Logan,' Mrs Allenby said, giving me a sour look.

The truth was, I wasn't sure if I did.

I was still sorting through it all in my mind, knowing from experience that you didn't always know what you had seen until you reviewed it all again from beginning to end, like when you emptied out someone's bin and laid all the rubbish out on the floor. Things that had seemed significant could turn out to be nothing and things you weren't even aware of at the time suddenly jumped out at you.

But nothing was jumping out at me yet, and I had a nasty feeling it wasn't going to.

I let them work their way through all the pics, pausing every now and then so I could explain what it was they were seeing. Maybe another member of the team was about to say bingo.

No one did.

Mrs Allenby pushed her chair back as Alan scrolled through the last few images. I noticed she was drinking tea out of a fancy cup. She looked at me over her glasses. 'Would you like to sum up for us, Mr Logan?'

I took a breath to clear my head. The last of the adrenaline was long gone and I was beginning to feel properly knackered.

'The first thing is there's no point looking for unusual visitors, because Shlovsky doesn't have any. I mean, *no one* comes to the house. There was the guy in the Range Rover on day one, but he was in and out; I don't think he put a foot inside. Apart from him, anyone breezing up at the gates gets told to fuck off pretty bloody quickly, unless it's one of the maids coming back from a caviar run. So if Shlovsky is meeting anyone he shouldn't, he's not doing it at the house.'

'Not very helpful,' Mrs Allenby said.

'No,' I agreed. 'But it does tell us something useful: he's nervous.'

'Perhaps,' she conceded.

'He's definitely a bit edgy where the wife's concerned,' Alex said. 'What's going on there?'

'Well, the way it looks to me, she likes going into town with just the chauffeur, and Shlovsky wants her to take the heavy mob along. Hence the screaming match.'

'I think it's nice. It shows he cares,' Alex said.

'Cares about his bank account, you mean,' Ryan said. 'If she gets kidnapped, he could get taken for a couple of billion.'

'No wonder he was a trifle annoyed,' Mrs Allenby said.

'Of course, it could be that she's having it off with the driver,' I suggested.

'Doubtful,' Mrs Allenby said.

I shrugged. 'They say love is blind.'

'But not mentally impaired. I think our Mr Shlovsky would be feeding that young man to the pigs as soon as he got the slightest whiff.'

'Of course, it could be she's just fed up of being followed round by a bunch of goons wherever she goes,' Alex said.

'Either way, perhaps that provides us with an in of some sort,' Mrs Allenby mused. 'Clearly Shlovsky himself doesn't step foot outside of the gates without a full complement of minders.'

'Yeah, he doesn't take a shit without the big guy being right by his side,' I said.

'Personal bodyguard?'

'Maybe once upon a time, but now I think he's running the show. More Tom Hagen than Luca Brasi.'

'Konstantin Titov.'

We all looked at Ryan.

'Sorry?' I said.

'The big guy. Konstantin Titov. Formerly Major Titov of the FSB.'

'Christ, that was quick.'

'Well done, Mr Oldfield,' Mrs Allenby said.

'Wonders of modern technology,' Ryan said. He shrugged. 'Or maybe he's just got one of those faces. Anyway, that's our guy. Another boy from the wilds of Siberia who made good.'

I looked over his shoulder at the image of a younger and slimmer man in a spiffy uniform. 'So maybe they go way back.'

'If they did, he would have been a useful person to know.'

'Or to have in your back pocket. Unless it was the other way round, of course.'

'In Russia, everyone with money is in someone's back pocket,' Mrs Allenby said. 'But where does that get us?'

'If Titov's ex-FSB, then maybe he's still getting his orders direct from Moscow. He could be the conduit. Maybe he's the one we need to be putting under surveillance,' Ryan suggested.

'The security chief,' I said, leaning back. 'You don't ask for bloody much, do you?'

'I think for now we should be focusing on Mr Shlovsky,' Mrs Allenby said, pursing her lips. 'Mr Woodburn? I believe you have something for us?'

Alan got up from the table and ambled over to one of the desks. I hadn't noticed until now that it was covered in cables and electronic equipment. I followed along behind.

'Comes in two parts, basically.' He picked up a smallish black box with an antenna-like projection. 'You aim this at the window. That's the laser beam. And then –' he picked up another, similar-looking box – 'this is the receiver. You obviously need to get the angle right so it bounces back to you and not into next door's bathroom. I can show you how to do it.'

I clapped him on the back. 'Looks like the business. Thanks, mate.'

Wait till I show Daisy, I thought. Despite my fatigue, and the lure of a good night's kip, part of me was already eager to get back.

'Similarly,' Mrs Allenby said, getting up from the table, 'there is little point in going to the trouble of setting up this device if we're aiming it at a broom cupboard. Mr Woodburn?'

Ryan turned his laptop round so we could all see it.

'OK, here's the layout, all twenty-four thousand square feet of it. There's actually a ballroom, if you can believe it.'

'Handy for someone who never has visitors,' I said.

'Maybe him and Mrs S take a little turn every Saturday night under the chandelier,' Alex said.

'You are an incurable fucking romantic, you know that?' I said.

Mrs Allenby made a tutting sound.

'So,' Alan continued. 'Nine reception rooms, twelve bedrooms, grand dining room, slightly less grand dining room, blah, blah, blah – OK, here we go, at the front, first floor, we've got two bedrooms, a dressing room and what's described as an office suite, whatever that is.'

'If that's where he makes important phone calls, that could be what we're looking for,' I suggested.

'Worth a crack,' Ryan agreed.

I turned to Alan. 'I think I know the answer to this, but there's no chance of getting the other end of the phone call, is there?'

Alan wiped a lock of hair out of his eyes. He looked genuinely pained. 'Sorry, mate. We don't have the resources to jump on the landline – not that he probably uses it for anything confidential, anyway; he'd assume it's got a tap on it. And mobiles . . . in theory, if I had the number, I might be able to do something, switch the audio on and listen in to that, but it's going to take time.'

'No point,' Ryan said.

Mrs Allenby looked at him quizzically. 'Because?'

'I've pulled up his mobile account. He stopped making calls a week ago.'

'Maybe he just switched to another provider?' Alex suggested.

'No, I think he ditched the regular phones altogether. I'll bet you anything you like they're using burners.'

'Fuck me, they've gone to the mattresses,' I said.

Mrs Allenby looked at me pointedly. 'Then I think you'd better get back there as soon as you can.'

12

Ryan sat on the tube and thought about patterns. He'd left Logan and Alan messing about with the laser microphone set-up. Mrs Allenby was sitting at one of the work stations doing admin; whether for Blindeye or Clearwater Security it was hard to tell, which was presumably the point. Alex was doing some research of her own, based on the visuals from Wyvern Lodge.

Ryan felt he had been staring at a screen all day, soaking up information; now it was time to let everything settle in his mind while he focused on something else. It was like those pictures that looked, at first sight, like one thing, but if you managed to flip a switch in your mind, a totally different image appeared. But you had to step back and look away first; otherwise you'd always be stuck seeing only what was on the surface.

If Ryan had a skill, he supposed that was it: the ability to see the face when all everyone else could see was the tree. The picture he was looking at right now, however, was nothing to do with Viktor Shlovsky.

Claire. Craig. Logan. Put them together and what did the picture show?

Two deaths, one near miss. Was that two murders and one failed attempt? Or one accident, one natural causes and a random altercation in a pub that got out of hand? Or, of course, a different combination; Craig's heart attack could be genuine but that didn't mean the other two weren't hits.

There were two ways to approach it: look at each individual incident on its own terms, drilling down into the detail as far as you possibly could; or try to see the connection first, the thing all three had in common, and then work back, seeing the separate incidents in a new light.

Part or whole. Thread or pattern.

He had begun the first process, hacking into police and coroners' reports, anything that was online and accessible, which, though he said it himself, meant pretty much everything. Now it was time to have a go at the second.

He put that thought on hold as the train pulled into the station. Time for some counter-surveillance drills. Nothing very fancy; it was a while since he'd been in the field, and his skill set was probably a bit rusty, but it was better than nothing. He'd certainly look like a fool if someone jabbed him with a poisoned umbrella just at the moment he figured out who was trying to kill him.

He found an unoccupied bench and sat down, waiting for the next train. When he'd got on the train at Victoria he'd clocked the other passengers in the carriage. Logan had been impressed by the way Major Titov had been identified by a computer algorithm, but our own natural ability to recognize faces was actually more astonishing, as far as Ryan was concerned. Every day, just walking down the street, we were processing this vast mass of visual information, scanning every face we saw without even knowing we were doing it, then storing the data away, ready to access it at a nanosecond's notice when we came across the same features again. The evolution of this ability quite possibly explained the impressive size of the human brain.

And that's what Ryan had been doing on the train. The idea was that if you were being followed by one person, or even a basic team of two, then when you got out at a stop, they would too. And when you got on another train, so would they.

Do that enough times, make your journey complicated enough, and when you got to your final destination (carefully selected so there was a convenient observation point, a bottleneck through which every exiting passenger would have to pass), all you had to do was wait for a visual data match.

In layman's terms, a face that rang a bell.

It was basically rinse and repeat, until the carriage was clean. Or not, of course. What you were supposed to do if that was the case, when there was no backup team to call on, he wasn't entirely sure.

He got up and followed the signs to the southbound Northern Line platform. At least there were no stairs involved this time. Forget to plan in advance and you could find yourself doing the equivalent of walking halfway up the Shard before you'd reached home. Not that that would be a bad thing, necessarily. He was aware he spent too much time sitting in front of a screen and that was not what the human body had evolved for. He wasn't really a gym person (running or cycling in place, in a recreation of the office environment where you'd just spent eight hours, defeated the whole point of exercise as far as he was concerned), so clocking up a few miles getting on and off tube trains was probably as good a way of improving his fitness as any.

Particularly if you factored in the increased heart rate due to the awareness that somebody might well be trying to kill you.

He looked up at the train indicator. Three minutes. Leaning back against the wall, half watching the passengers pass along the platform, he felt the wave of new faces wash over him, letting two million years of evolution quietly do its work.

The train arrived and he found a seat at the end of the carriage. He went back to thinking about randomness, and coincidences, and pictures that could tell two different stories. The first thing to do was to make a list of all the things that connected the three of them. Blindeye was the obvious one, but it didn't seem feasible that someone connected to the terror threat they'd eliminated, or to the intelligence organization they used to work for, had either the capability or the motivation for targeting them.

Of course, he knew his Sherlock Holmes: *When you have eliminated the impossible, whatever remains, however improbable, must be the truth.* So he'd park the twin possibility of terrorists or their own former employers being the bad guys for the moment without definitively dismissing it.

The train rattled on down the Northern Line as he thought. Claire, Craig and Logan: what possible connection could there be between three strangers who'd never met before they were recruited to Blindeye? And what if he enlarged the data set to include himself, Alex and Alan? Maybe even Mrs Allenby too, for good measure?

From a purely analytical point of view, of course, another death would certainly help to clarify things.

The train pulled in. Time to get off again. Clock up a few more metres on the Fitbit. He waited for the exiting passengers to disappear. Soon he was alone on the platform with his thoughts. He looked at his watch. How did it get so late?

A man wearing a tan raincoat and holding a briefcase entered the platform, quickly looked both ways, then made his way towards Ryan. As he approached, Ryan looked up. The raincoat and the briefcase didn't raise any flags, but something about the face made the hairs instantly prickle on the back of his neck.

13

I stood back and took a look at my handiwork. 'What do you reckon, Daisy?'

Considering the effort of getting the bloody thing here, not to mention fitting it all together, I was hoping for a more positive response. I'd brought her fresh flowers – nothing fancy, just some little yellow things I found at the edge of the golf course – but she seemed to be in a bit of a sulk.

That was the trouble with dead people: sometimes you just couldn't tell what was going on in their heads.

Or maybe it was just teenage girls.

I shrugged and went back to tinkering with the equipment. The problem was, you had to have a reasonable space between the unit that fired off the infrared beam and the receiver, which was then connected to an equalizer and an audio unit. We were a bit cramped for space, so the margins were tight. More worryingly, I'd had to open the window; otherwise all the microphone would pick up would be mine and Daisy's conversation, and that was hardly going to make riveting listening. There was an overhanging tree, which helped, but across the way, anyone really paying attention in daylight would be able to see the window was open. Which meant my own window of opportunity was pretty narrow.

Maybe Daisy was right, and it was all a waste of time.

I couldn't really set the camera up at the same time, so I watched the house and made notes of the timings. Not that there was much to see. All the signs were that this was going to be a quiet night. Mrs S had been out on a major shopping trip and experience told me that she wouldn't have the energy for another out of doors expedition for a while. I'd always found any kind of clothes shopping a pain in the arse, so I knew how she felt.

I hadn't seen any sign of Shlovsky himself. I was just hoping he hadn't slipped out while I'd been away. If I'd seen Titov or the English guy, I'd have been reassured; I couldn't imagine Shlovsky going very far without those two. But I hadn't seen them either.

Fuck. This was not looking good.

I paced up and down a bit, wanting to kick something, then told myself to fucking calm down. I could tell by the coolness in the room that Daisy wasn't impressed.

At 10.27 p.m. a car stopped abruptly opposite the house and a couple started having a row. One of the guys in suits came out to have a peek through the gates, making sure it was all kosher, took the opportunity to have a quick fag, then went back in.

At 11.05 the light in one of the bedrooms went on. Five minutes later the light went on in the office.

Showtime.

I switched everything on, the infrared beam arrowing invisibly towards the window opposite, then picked up the headphones and sat down with my back against the wall.

For the first couple of minutes, nothing. I got up, tugged on all the connections and checked the indicator lights. Everything seemed to be in order. I sat back down again and waited.

The first sound didn't really sound like anything. Maybe the equalizer wasn't properly equalizing or something. Alan told me it would all be crystal, but I was beginning to have my doubts.

Then my ears got used to it or something and it started to make sense. It was liquid being poured into a glass. Someone was making themselves a drink.

I felt better. Shlovsky was having a stiff one before he started making calls.

I still didn't hear any voices. Maybe he was having a bit of a think. Figuring out what he was going to say. Or maybe he just wasn't looking forward to talking to whoever it was.

That's fine, Viktor. Take your time. Just make sure you speak loudly and clearly. And in English, if you wouldn't mind.

A sound like a cupboard opening or a door sliding or something. Then a sort of metal scraping sound.

Then singing. I couldn't pick out the words, but it was a woman's voice. Little snatches of song, followed by humming, more of the scraping noise, then a soft thump.

What the fuck was going on? Maybe it was the maid doing

some dusting, and helping herself to a glass of the boss's premium vodka while she was at it?

No, that didn't seem right.

I looked over at Daisy and I could swear she was grinning. Then I twigged.

I listened some more: *la la la, scrape, thump; la la la, scrape, thump*. The sounds assembled themselves in my mind and became attached to a memory. I was listening to a woman picking dresses out of a wardrobe and tossing them on the bed *(This one? Hmm. This one? No. This one? Maybe.)*, singing along to herself while she took sips from a glass of wine.

This definitely wasn't Viktor Shlovsky's office. This was his wife's dressing room. Even on the off-chance of Shlovsky making an appearance, the best we were likely to get was, 'Yes, the red one. No, of course you look good in the blue. If you want to wear the blue, wear the blue.' That sort of bollocks. And I doubted we'd even get that. For hubby the dressing room was probably off limits.

I pulled the earphones off and tossed them on the floor.

'You knew, Daisy, didn't you? You knew all along.'

I waited until I'd calmed down a bit, then closed the window and started disassembling the laser mic. There wasn't much point in hanging around. We'd got all we were going to get from this OP. But I didn't want to leave right away, not while there was still a bit of tension between me and Daisy.

I tidied up, or rather, did the opposite, sweeping all the crap back over my little patch of floorboards, so at least it wasn't so obvious I'd been here. I looked across the road.

The dressing room was in darkness. Mrs S must have called it a night. I pulled the shutter closed.

I swept the torch around the room to make sure I hadn't left anything. My little bunch of flowers was already starting to look a bit sad.

'Look, I'd better be going now. I've probably been lucky so far. Stay much longer and they'd be bound to spot me.' I knelt down. 'Sorry if I've been a bit on edge. I really thought we were going to get lucky tonight. You know, get Shlovsky on tape.'

It felt like the temperature instantly dropped a couple of degrees.

I decided to change the subject.

'Sorry the flowers are a bit crap. I couldn't really see what I was doing. Actually, I've always been crap at getting flowers. Sarah will tell you that.'

I reached out a hand towards the flowers. I really should have taken them. But I didn't.

I wanted to tell her to take care of herself, but the words died in my throat.

I picked up the torch, hoisted my bag and left.

14

Mrs Allenby looked as if she was about to spit. She was leaning on the table while me, Alex and Alan sat sullenly on the other side.

'I had tea with the Director General yesterday afternoon. He told me the chatter from Moscow is that things are being ramped up. The timetable is accelerating.'

'What's the hurry?' Alex asked.

'It could be any number of things, but my guess is that they want to strike before the election, to cause maximum political damage.'

'Putin wants the PM out?'

'Not necessarily. Simply creating chaos in the democratic process would probably serve his ends just as well. We don't know what they have planned –' she paused to give us a withering look – 'so we can't yet judge the aim, but whatever it is, if it's devastating enough, it might even mean postponing the election.'

'We need to hear what's going on in there,' Alex said, looking at Alan.

Alan held his hands out, palms up. 'I can give you a dozen

different kinds of transmitter. Small, medium, large – just tell me what you want.'

'But we've still got to get it through the front door somehow,' I said. 'Any bright ideas?'

Alex shrugged.

'Where the hell's Ryan?' Mrs Allenby snapped. Alex and I exchanged a look. We'd never heard her swear before. The DG must have really put the screws on over the cucumber sandwiches at Fortnum's. Alan looked as if he desperately wanted to go and tinker with some equipment.

I tried to think through our options. There weren't too bloody many, and none of them sounded good.

Alex was chewing on a pen thoughtfully. 'When she goes shopping, she always has lunch after, right?'

It took me a moment to work out what she was talking about. 'I don't know. She's usually a bit wobbly on her pins, like she's had a couple of Martinis.'

'Let's look at those photos again.' Alex fired up her laptop and started scrolling through, then started making notes on a pad.

Mrs Allenby looked intrigued. 'Miss Short? Do you have a suggestion?'

Alex scribbled down a couple more notes. 'Yeah, maybe.' She closed her laptop. 'OK, so Mrs S likes her retail therapy, and as you'd expect, her idea of fun isn't standing in line for the one-pound tank tops in Primark. She doesn't go for the big department stores, either. She likes the little boutiques, the exclusive ones where you don't have to rub shoulders with any of the hoi polloi. This one seems to be her favourite – Dulcima Drew, off South Molton Street.'

Mrs Allenby frowned. 'This is all very interesting, but how exactly does it help us?'

Alex tapped her pen against her teeth and gave us all a big grin. 'I think I've figured out a way of getting our bug into the house.'

An hour later I was standing in the men's department in Selfridges wearing a fashionably uncomfortable midnight-blue suit and feeling like a twat.

'Give us a twirl. Let me see the back,' Alex said, making a circular motion with her hand.

I turned round slowly.

'You're a funny shape, Logan. Has anyone ever told you that?'

'Nobody who kept their front teeth after, no.'

Alex grinned. She was enjoying this about as much as I wasn't.

'I'm just trying to make you look the part.' She tilted her head to one side. 'All right, this'll have to do. We haven't got time to go to Jermyn Street and get you something made to measure. We'll just have to do something about your walk. Now, what about a shirt to go with it? I'm beginning to think lavender is your colour.'

I gave her a look.

'That's it, Logan. The mean look, like you want to give me a slap. Perfect.'

We bought the shirt, along with some fancy-looking loafers. Alex wanted me to wear a tie as well, but in the end she agreed that the open-necked look would be more in character. All I needed to complete the effect was a nice heavy Rolex and she trusted me enough not to fuck that up while she went to sort out her own gear.

Forty minutes later we walked out onto Oxford Street and I gave her the once-over. Even I could see the loose-fitting pale-green trouser suit was classy. With the chunky gold necklace and the shades, she looked a million dollars, which was more or less the idea.

'Nice,' I said simply.

'Thank you. Now, we just need hair and make-up and we're all set. And I mean you, too, Logan. The stubble's fine, but the hair's a disaster. You need to look as if you at least give a tiny fuck about your appearance.'

By 11.45 we were sat in the car on a double yellow, breathing in the heady mix of Chanel No. 5 and some nasty aftershave I'd been doused with, while keeping an eye out for parking attendants.

'Now we cross our fingers and wait,' Alex said.

'Let's just hope she didn't wake up this morning and decide the fashion industry's killing the planet,' I said.

Alex wagged a finger. 'Don't be negative, Logan.'

We got the call from a car parked up on the Avenue at 12.03. Mrs S was on her way. We reckoned it would take her thirty-five minutes, tops. That's if she was actually planning on throwing away a few grand at Dulcima Drew's this afternoon and not going somewhere else.

By 12.30 we were strolling down South Molton Street in the sunshine, trying to blend in with the other mega-rich couples out looking for an opportunity to burn through some cash. We'd done one side of the street and were walking back the other way when we spotted her. The chauffeur had obviously dropped her off on Brook Street, at the south end of Great Molton Street, so she could do a bit of window shopping before the main event.

'Bloody hell,' I murmured. 'You can see it from Viktor's point of view. She's a sitting fucking duck. I'm surprised she hasn't been lifted before now.'

'Well, let's just hope no one's planning to do it today,' Alex said. 'That would properly fuck things up.'

Ekaterina Shlovsky was walking towards us as we loitered in front of a jeweller's shop. Alex nudged me. 'Buy us a fucking diamond, Logan. Go on – one of those big ones.'

I turned my head as Mrs Shlovsky passed. She was wearing a camel-hair coat and humming to herself with a dreamy expression behind her shades. I thought I recognized the tune. Even through a telephoto lens, the camera hadn't been able to do justice to her sculpted cheekbones, her wide, thin mouth and slightly turned-up nose.

'Give it a couple of minutes,' Alex said. 'Pretend you're really thinking about buying me that diamond.'

'If this works, I'll seriously consider it,' I said.

Alex nudged me and we turned, arm in arm, and followed Mrs Shlovsky down a little side street.

Dulcima Drew was the sort of place where you had to ring a bell and get buzzed in once they'd looked you up and down and decided you might be rich enough to actually buy some of their overpriced wares. Same as whenever your cover's first tested, I felt my heart rate go up a notch. If they didn't let us in, apart from anything else it was a couple of grand down the drain, because I wasn't planning to wear the suit twice.

The door buzzed and I held it open as Alex stepped inside. A model-thin assistant in a black trouser suit sashayed over with a hundred-watt smile, as if we were just the people she'd been waiting for.

'Can I offer you a glass of champagne?'

I scowled, trying to get in character.

Alex returned her smile with interest. 'That would be lovely.'

I looked around. For a clothes shop, there didn't seem to be many actual clothes. No racks of dresses or piles of T-shirts, just the odd shapeless scrap of fabric hanging from a fancy stand. It felt more like a museum or an art gallery than a shop and for a moment I wondered if we'd come to the wrong place.

Alex, however, was like a pig in shit, instantly swigging champagne and yukking it up with the assistant as if she'd been born to it.

I scowled again in her direction and looked at my watch.

Mrs Shlovsky was down the other end, nodding at another young woman in black, who held a curtain open for her. Presumably the changing rooms: where the real action was.

I paced up and down for a bit, not having to work too hard at being pissed off. After a few minutes I could hear Alex's voice.

'Oh my goodness, I hope you don't mind me saying, but you look so lovely in that. I'm so jealous! I couldn't wear it – with my hips it would look like a paper bag on me, but oh my goodness on you . . . really, soooo lovely.'

I couldn't make out what Mrs Shlovsky said in reply, but she laughed, which was good, and soon they seemed to be chatting away like long-lost mates.

So far, so good.

I left them to it, making sure to bang the door shut after me. I walked back up towards Oxford Street and found myself a coffee shop. Alex would send me a text when she was ready.

Forty minutes later and I was just starting to get twitchy when my phone pinged.

Time for phase two.

I marched back to the shop, and there were Alex and Mrs Shlovsky, laughing like schoolgirls, while the two assistants gleefully boxed and bagged their purchases. From the growing pile on the desk, it looked like the shop must have had some clothes hidden away somewhere after all.

Alex spotted me and waved me over. 'I think there may be a teeny problem with my card, darling. Could I use one of yours?'

'I just paid the fucking thing off. How can you have maxed it out again?'

Alex shrugged with a sheepish smile. 'Oh, I don't know. This thing never has as much money on it as I think it does.'

Mrs Shlovsky turned away, pretending to look at her phone, while keeping a discreet eye on me.

I crossed my arms. 'Well if you can't count, that's not my fucking problem.'

Alex whirled on me, eyes blazing fury. 'Just give me the card!'

'Sorry, darling.' I shook my head.

Alex stomped over, breathing hard, her hand out. I gave her a nasty smile. She made a grab for my wallet and I put a hand on her arm.

'Get off me!'

I gripped her by the shoulders and she tried to shrug me off. Both assistants had gone white, their mouths open. Out of the corner of my eye, I could see Mrs Shlovsky furiously texting. I needed to get a move on.

Alex gave me a tiny nod and I counted to three then flung her away as hard as I could. She careened against the wall and fell to the floor, taking down a couple of clothes stands with her. I turned on my heel and was out the door before the chauffeur could pitch up.

I jogged back to the car and waited for phase three.

15

Fifteen minutes later Alex texted me the name of what I was hoping was a restaurant: Sollozzo's.

I grinned to myself. *You fucking star. Give that girl an Oscar.*

It seemed like a while since anything had gone to plan, but so far this one was working a treat. And that was all down to Alex, though I had to say I was quite proud of my tightwad boyfriend act, too. If Mrs Shlovsky had been a cold-hearted bitch, or just a bit savvier about her own personal security, it wouldn't have worked. But Alex had had a feeling that this was a woman who would instantly bond with someone being given a hard time by her domineering partner – especially if he manhandled her a bit in the process. And what would be more natural than to invite poor old hard-done-by Alex to lunch, so they could both drown their sorrows with a nice bottle of chilled Sauvignon Blanc?

It was only a few streets away, so I took my time, driving slowly past the restaurant. The chauffeur had parked up the Range Rover more or less opposite on a double yellow. Either he was going to move off when a meter maid turned up or he had some other arrangement – like not giving a fuck about the fines, for instance. I cruised by on the lookout for a parking spot, and found one two streets away, managing to beat a spanking-new Porsche to the punch as someone pulled out. I guess it always helps if you give less of a fuck about your paint job than the other guy.

I settled down to wait, hoping Alex could keep up the performance until she got the opportunity she needed.

From the look on her face when she tapped on the window an hour or so later, it seemed like she had.

'Bloody hell, Logan, I'm pissed,' she said, slumping into the passenger seat.

'Don't expect any sympathy from me. A nice bit of shopping, a slap-up lunch with a bottle of bubbly . . . What are you bloody complaining about?'

'OK, you can stop being an arsehole, now, Logan. You were very convincing in the role, but the play's over.'

I grinned. 'Come on, let's get out of here before we get spotted. We don't want to fuck it up now.'

I pulled out and we headed back to the office.

'So what's she like?'

'A sweetheart, actually. I think she must have been a nurse or a physio or something before she married Shlovsky. She gave my ankle a real going-over. And she was all for paying for the stuff I'd bought. I almost let her, too. Well, I did let her pay for one thing.'

She caught my look.

'No! I couldn't stop her. Look, isn't it lovely?'

113

She held up a scarf. It was a bit bright for my taste, but it looked expensive.

'Very nice. And she paid for lunch, too, I suppose.'

'Well I haven't got any money, have I? Because meanypants over here won't give me any,' she pouted.

She gave me a dig in the ribs.

'Oi, I'm driving. So apart from her warm heart and her medical skills, what else did you find out?'

'Not a huge amount. She was pretty tight-lipped about Viktor, just said she was married to a businessman, couple of grown-up kids, blah blah blah. She mostly asked about me, which kept me on my toes. Especially after a couple of cocktails. I told her about you, obviously.'

'Only nice things, I hope.'

'Oh, you know, what a bully you are, how controlling, always trying to see what's on my phone. Then you go off for two nights running and don't tell me where you've been. She said I should dump you. She said forget about the money; it would only make me unhappy in the end. Actually, she said, "Find a man whose wallet is empty but whose heart is full of love."'

'Very poetic. She really fucked up when she married Viktor, then, didn't she?'

Alex shrugged. 'He wasn't always a billionaire.'

'So she didn't invite you home for a cup of tea then?'

'Yeah, that would have been good, but no. She was nice, but she kept her distance too, you know? Like a part of her was still wary.'

'Not too wary, I hope.'

She grinned. 'Nah.'

'So how'd you do it?'

'Cloakroom. We went to get our coats and she went to the loo. I'd already swapped our coat check tokens when they handed them out, so they handed me her coat and I managed to pull the seam in the pocket and slip it in before she came back.'

'Sweet.'

'Best I could do. I couldn't get near her bag.'

'We'll have to hope she doesn't give the coat to Oxfam as soon as she realizes it's got a couple of stitches loose.'

'Let's just hope the bloody thing works as well as Alan says it does,' Alex said.

Back at Clearwater Security, Mrs Allenby was making tea. She'd obviously got fed up with the instant coffee and teabags that gave the place its authentic workplace feel, and we were now being treated to the best Darjeeling, poured from a silver teapot that looked as if it had been in the Allenby family for at least a couple of generations.

Alex looked as if what she really needed was a couple of paracetamol and a lie down, but she sipped her Darjeeling with a smile on her face and her pinky finger stuck out like the rest of us.

Ryan was the only one who didn't have a cup in front of him. I imagined he was more a green tea sort of guy.

'Where the fuck were you this morning?'

'Had a bit of trouble on the tube.' He gave me a meaningful look.

I glanced at Alex. 'Right.'

'Shall we have another look at those architect's plans?' Mrs Allenby suggested.

'Sure.' Ryan clicked on the file and turned his laptop round so we could see. 'OK, so this space was originally designated as an office.' He tapped the screen. 'And this was supposed to be the dressing room. But it looks like they swapped.'

'Maybe he didn't like the idea of someone aiming a listening device at his window,' Alex suggested pointedly.

'Anyway,' Ryan continued, 'if we can get the transmitter into the dressing room, ideally in a wardrobe against the adjoining wall, we have a chance of picking up something from the room on the other side. That right, Alan?'

'It's not a hundred per cent. Depends how thick the wall is, obviously. But yeah, technically it's possible. It's a powerful little thing. I'm looking forward to seeing how it performs, actually.'

'As are we all, Mr Woodburn,' said Mrs Allenby, taking a sip of her tea. 'We'll just have to hope she's the sort of person who hangs her things up properly and doesn't just fling them on the floor, won't we?'

'I'm sure the maid will take care of it,' I said.

It reminded me. I needed to get out of the suit and back into civvies. 'I'm going to change out of this,' I said, heading for the loos.

'Don't just chuck it on the floor, Logan,' Alex called. 'You never know when you might need it again.'

'Quite,' Mrs Allenby added. 'The pair of you have used up a good deal of our budget today. Let's hope it proves to have been worth it.'

Amen to that, I thought to myself. *Otherwise we're screwed.*

After I'd changed, I went out and grabbed a sandwich from the place on the corner and ate it walking round the block. While Alex had been scoffing her lobster salad at Sollozzo's, my stomach had been rumbling. I thought about going back to the flat for a few hours, maybe getting in a run and a couple of hours' kip before the evening shift, but I was hoping if I hung around, Mrs Allenby might disappear off somewhere, and we could have a proper chat with Ryan about what happened last night. Also, if things kicked off earlier than expected, I didn't want to risk missing the party.

I closed my eyes and tried to work the cricks out of my neck.

'She'll be all right, you know.'

I opened my eyes. Sarah was sitting at the other end of the bench, throwing crumbs from a paper bag at the pigeons.

'I told her you'd be back. When this is all over. You will do that, won't you, Logan?'

'I'll try. It was nice having someone to talk to. She got a bit, I don't know, she got in a mood or something the last time.'

'Not a mood. She was just upset. And frightened.'

I thought about that. What could frighten a dead girl? Only memories, surely. And Daisy must have had some pretty bad ones. But you'd think she'd be beyond all that by now. I wanted to ask Sarah, but I knew she wouldn't tell.

I was trying to remember what I'd said that could have triggered Daisy's reaction when my phone pinged. I fished it out of my pocket and looked at the message.

'You need to go,' Sarah said.

16

'So what happened?'

We were all grouped around Ryan's work station. Mrs Allenby had left for the day, leaving instructions to message her if there was any activity at the house.

'I can't be sure. I was on the tube, trying to pick out any followers. I ended up alone on the platform, and then this guy appears. I got the feeling he hesitated, like he was expecting a crowd and didn't know what to do when there wasn't one. Then he made a decision and started walking towards me.'

'Not what you'd normally do,' I said. 'Just two people on a platform.'

'Unless he was a creature of habit, always stands in the same place,' Alex said.

'Could be. Description?'

Ryan thought for a moment. 'Short, I guess. Five foot six? Fawn raincoat, black briefcase, looked like a salesman who'd been stuck late in the office and was on his way home. I didn't get a chance for a better look because he came and stood behind me and a little to the side. I could just see him in my peripheral vision.'

Alex pulled over a chair. 'What did you do?'

Ryan started twisting his ponytail. 'Tell you the truth, I was bricking it. I could just feel him there, you know?'

'If he'd been planning to push you in front of a train, he'd have wanted a crowd. Just the two of you and he would have had to practically pick you up and throw you,' I said.

'Yeah, well, I didn't fancy taking the chance. There was a bench on my right, so I went and sat down. I tried not to let him see my knees were shaking. Started reading my book. A few more people came onto the platform, but I kept thinking he was going to stick a needle into me or something.'

'And when the train pulled in?'

'I stayed where I was, and so did he. It was a Bank train, and the next one was Charing Cross, so I thought he's got to get on that one.'

'Did he?'

'Yeah. I stayed put, like I was so engrossed in my book I wasn't paying attention.'

'And you got on the next one?' Alex asked.

Ryan shook his head. 'I left the station. Thought I'd get out on the street. I needed some air. And I thought he's not going to be able to pick me up again if I leave the area quickly.'

'And you think he clocked you were on to him?'

Ryan shrugged. 'We never made eye contact. I didn't just leg it as soon as I spotted him, which is what I bloody well wanted to do.'

'You did all right,' Alex said. 'Would you recognize him if you saw him again?'

'Maybe.'

'That'll be how we know this is for real,' I said.

'And in the meantime?' Ryan asked.

'We try not to get into a routine. Stay in pairs when we can. Keep working on the "why?"'

Ryan chewed a pen thoughtfully. 'You think it's got anything to do with Shlovsky?'

I looked at him. 'A bit of a leap, isn't it?'

'I don't know – the PM doesn't want him watched. I'd like to know why.'

I didn't have an answer for that.

On the other side of the room, Alan had a pair of headphones on and was tapping away on his laptop. 'I'm getting some audio,' he said, waving us over.

He took his headphones off and turned up the volume.

'There was some unidentifiable stuff earlier, which at least means it's working, and could be consistent with the coat being hung up in the walk-in wardrobe. But I'm picking something else up now.'

We listened. A few pings and whistles. Some deeper rumblings. It sounded to me like a bunch of humpback whales having a singalong.

Alan frowned, trying to adjust the balance. 'OK, this should be better.'

Nothing for a few seconds. Then some buzzes and clicks. Finally a voice emerged out of the background, faint but identifiably human.

And Russian.

'. . . should meet. What . . . you mean? I . . . not Stasi . . .'

I put a hand on Alan's shoulder. 'Can you turn it up a bit?'

Alan shook his head. 'You'll get too much distortion.'

I closed my eyes, trying not to force it, just letting the words take shape of their own accord.

'Yes . . . yes. What? . . . don't care. The merry . . . OK. No, I don't think . . . kill? Yes, or there will be . . . eleven, tomorrow, yes. OK . . .'

Silence. I thought for a moment the receiver had stopped working. Then something very loud – shouting, in Russian, and what sounded like glass shattering. Then a bang that could have been a door slamming.

I looked at Ryan, our resident linguist. 'Fuck was that?'

'He called someone a rabid dog, I think. Then maybe threw a glass against the wall?'

Alex had made a transcription. I looked over her shoulder. It seemed to be mostly gaps and question marks.

'That was Shlovsky?'

'Stands to reason,' Ryan said.

'OK, so he's setting up a meet with Rabid Dog. At eleven tomorrow. A.m. or p.m? And where? It's not a lot to bloody go on. And what was that about the Stasi?'

Alex tapped her teeth with her pencil. 'Maybe Stasi means spies in general. Or just non-Russian ones. Maybe Five?'

'Could be. Which means he's worried about being under surveillance.'

She folded her arms. 'So why "not Stasi" then?'

'You can't enhance any of it?' I asked Alan.

'Good as it gets, mate. Actually, considering it's through a bloody wall, it's a miracle it's as clear as it is.'

'So where would he go if he wanted a meeting away from prying eyes? He's not going to pick a bench on Hampstead Heath. And he's definitely not going to risk whoever it is coming anywhere near the house.'

'Somewhere private. Secure. A controlled environment. But where there's people. So he has cover.'

'Like a private club?' suggested Alex.

I nodded. 'Yeah, could be. But it would have to be a very exclusive one.'

'Can't be that exclusive if he's meeting someone he calls Rabid Dog there,' Ryan said.

I read through it all again, checking that Alex's transcription chimed with what I thought I'd heard.

'The "merry" something. Is that the location? But the "merry" what?'

'The "Merry Widow"?' Alex suggested.

'Sounds like a pub,' I said.

'There's a hotel, the Merridale, off Piccadilly,' she added.

I rubbed my chin. 'I suppose. Book a suite, maybe? It's still a bit public, though.'

Ryan was tapping away at his laptop. 'You said a private members' club? There's a *very* private one called the Merrick in Mayfair.'

'Never heard of it,' Alex said.

Ryan smiled. 'Exactly.'

'And is Shlovsky a member?'

'Let's find out.' He tapped away for another couple of minutes, then frowned. 'This is going to be harder than I thought. Hold on, here we go. *Ta da*.'

We all took a look as Shlovsky's face appeared on the screen. 'That's our boy.' I looked at the membership details. 'Joined in 2009. What about Rabid Dog?'

Ryan looked at me. 'You're joking.'

I shrugged. 'Maybe someone with the initials RD?'

Alex rolled her eyes. 'He was speaking Russian, remember. Different spelling.'

'Different alphabet,' Ryan added.

'All right, all right. So I didn't go to bloody Oxbridge like you posh cunts.'

Alex grinned. 'You didn't go to school, Logan. Anyway, Rabid Dog doesn't necessarily have to be a member. He could be Shlovsky's guest.'

'So how are we going to identify him, then? No point setting up an OP to see who goes into the club unless they waltz in together. We have to have eyes on the meet.'

The door opened. It was Mrs Allenby, carrying a Harrods shopping bag. I wondered if she was about to hand out cakes. 'Sorry to have missed all the fun. I understand we managed to intercept a phone conversation. What do we know?'

'Shlovsky's meeting someone at his private club tomorrow night, the Merrick. At least that's what we think. Someone he doesn't like, too,' I added.

She put the bag on the floor, looking thoughtful. 'So not a friend. And not a business associate he could meet with openly.' She nodded to herself. 'I suppose it could be the person we're looking for.'

'My gut tells me it is,' I said. 'Shlovsky was prickly. He wasn't happy about having to meet this guy.'

Mrs Allenby looked at me over her glasses. 'Then we need to get you in there.'

'How?' Alex asked. 'No offence, Logan, but even you wouldn't be able to blag your way into a place like that. And I'm guessing you need a couple of million in your bank account before they'll let you become a member.'

'I imagine application is by referral only,' Mrs Allenby said. She took her glasses off and started polishing them with a piece of cloth. 'Mr Woodburn?'

Alan had drifted back to his work station and was fiddling with some wires. He scuttled over.

'We need a membership card. Do you think you might be able to produce one for us?'

Alan looked dubious. 'Mind if I . . .?' He pulled Ryan's laptop towards him. 'Let's have a look. Membership card . . . OK, here's one. Hmm.' He clattered away at the keyboard for a couple of minutes, then sat back, staring hard at the screen. 'I don't know . . .'

Mrs Allenby raise an eyebrow. 'You don't think you can do it?'

'If we could get hold of one, I could clone it, I reckon.'

'I don't think that's a feasible plan,' Mrs Allenby said dryly. 'Any other thoughts?'

Alan chewed the end of a pen. 'I could try taking the

member information off the website and inputting it on a dummy card, but there'd be a unique signature. It wouldn't work.'

'Plus it would mean Logan trying to pass himself off as someone else. What if the real guy turns up?' Alex pointed out.

'So what you're saying is you could make a card that looked authentic, but that's all,' Mrs Allenby said.

Alan nodded.

Mrs Allenby gave him a disappointed look, like a schoolteacher who'd just been let down by her star pupil.

'We can make it work,' I said. 'As long as it looks like the real thing, I can bluff my way in.'

Mrs Allenby looked at me sceptically. 'If you cause a scene, that might put paid to the whole operation. Shlovsky could realize he's being targeted and simply go to ground.'

I looked around. 'Anybody got any better ideas?'

'All right. You go in. But with Miss Short. You'll be less conspicuous if you're accompanied by your wife.'

'I don't think it's the sort of place where members bring their wives, to be honest.' I grinned at Alex. 'But I'm sure a high-end call girl wouldn't look out of place.'

17

I knew the Merrick Club was going to be tricky to get into, but I wasn't worrying about that right now. First we had to find the bloody place.

Located somewhere along a narrow lane off Curzon Street in Mayfair, it wasn't exactly advertising its existence. I wasn't expecting a big neon sign, but a discreet brass plaque would have helped.

In fact, there weren't even numbers on the row of black basement doors lining the street. Everything looked dark, shut up, uninhabited. Ryan had dropped us off on Curzon Street – pulling up in anything less than a top of the range SUV or luxury saloon would have put up a red flag right away, assuming the club had a camera or two on the street. But wandering around like a couple of lost souls looking for number 58 wasn't an option either.

'Should have started counting at the top of the road,' Alex muttered, trying to keep steady on her six-inch heels.

'Yeah? Which end do the numbers start, then?' I asked, shaking my head.

We both knew if we passed the door and then had to double back, we'd be sunk. We slowed to a snail's pace.

'We could always have another row,' Alex suggested.

'They might be a bit leery of letting you in if we have a screaming match in the street,' I said. 'Just take out your phone and look like you've had a call from your sister and she's about to top herself or something.'

Alex frowned but slipped her phone out of her bag and pretended to answer it. We both knew this wasn't going to buy us much time. We just had to hope Ryan had realized we had a problem and would send us a text when he'd figured it out.

Just then a big black Mercedes off-roader turned the corner and started nosing its way slowly down the street.

'Here's fucking hoping,' I said under my breath.

The Merc pulled up twenty yards ahead of us. The driver got out and hopped round to the rear passenger door but a man was already getting out. Dinner jacket, bow tie, slicked-back grey hair to his collar, he spoke briefly to the driver while a second, younger, wide-shouldered man in a plain dark suit got out on the other side.

The talent and the hired muscle. I suddenly wondered if bringing Alex along was such a good idea after all. If the place was full of old men in DJs accompanied by their security, a bleached blonde in a tight red dress tottering around in her stilettos was definitely going to look out of place.

Cross that bridge when we come to it, I thought. We hadn't even got into the place yet.

The grey-haired geezer and his minder went down some

area steps. At least we knew where the front door was now. While Alex continued to hand out sisterly advice, I kept half an eye on our friends. The old guy knocked on the door, light and noise briefly flooded the area as the door opened, and they stepped inside. It closed noiselessly and the street returned to darkness and silence.

Alex dropped her phone back in her bag.

I raised my eyebrows, continuing to play the part, even if no one was watching. 'Everything all right?'

Alex rolled her eyes. 'Cry for help. I told her to pull herself together and stop being such a drama queen.'

'You're all heart,' I said.

She shrugged. 'Us high-class tarts are a tough lot.'

'I'll remember not to stiff you on your fee, then.'

'Just fucking try it,' she said with a wink. She took my arm. 'Come on then, I reckon it's show time.'

We walked down the steps and I knocked on the door. I couldn't see any cameras but they had to be somewhere. I just hoped there wasn't a secret code and I'd just demonstrated that I wasn't in the know.

I waited ten seconds, thinking the door wasn't going to open, that they'd taken one look at us and decided we were fakes. I was beginning to feel the sweat under my collar when it swung open with a hiss and a short, barrel-chested guy with a buzz cut and a dickie bow ushered us in.

Regiment or just Paras? I wondered.

Down at the end of a short corridor with shiny black and white tiles was a large desk. A brunette in a cocktail dress sat behind it with a slim laptop open, while another ex-Special Forces type lurked at the bottom of the stairs. Through a door to the right of the desk I could hear the muffled buzz of conversation.

I got out my wallet and pulled out the black card Alan had knocked up for me an hour ago. 'Thank you,' the brunette smiled as I handed it over. She swiped it through some sort of card reader and looked at her laptop screen. She was pro: her expression didn't change, but I could tell from her eyes she didn't like what she was seeing.

'I hope there isn't a problem,' I said with a tight smile, trying to sound like the sort of man who had waiters killed for bad service.

'I'm afraid the system doesn't seem to be bringing up your details,' she said, swiping the card through a second time. 'If you wouldn't mind waiting for just a moment, let me just talk to Mr Riccardi.'

I leaned over and put a hand on her arm as she reached for the phone. The last thing I wanted her to do was talk to Mr Riccardi, whoever he was. Alex had casually sauntered over to stand between the brunette and the heavy so he couldn't see what I was doing.

'I've got a meeting with Viktor Shlovsky,' I said, keeping the smile in place but putting as much menace into my voice as I could. 'If I was to be late for my meeting because you're having some IT problems, that would be very inconvenient.'

I took my hand away, but maintained eye contact. I could see the wheels going round in her head as she tried to figure out which was worse: getting fired because she let a non-member into the club, or getting fired because she pissed a genuine member off. I was hoping the threat of physical violence behind my nasty expression was going to tip the balance.

After what seemed like an eternity, she switched her professional smile on and handed me back my card. 'That'll be fine, Mr Schmidt.' She pushed a ledger across the desk. 'If you'd just care to sign the lady in?'

'Thank you,' I said, hoping she'd got the message that she'd made the right decision and there might be an opening as a hostess on one of my yachts if she kept up the good work.

The brunette nodded to the heavy and he opened the door. I put a hand on the small of Alex's back and we stepped through.

We were in.

We just had to hope the brunette didn't get straight on the blower to Mr Riccardi and we would find out that getting out again was going to be the real problem.

We walked towards the long, zinc-topped bar at the end of the room, trying to look as if we belonged. Booths lined the walls, with a scattering of tables surrounded by deep leather armchairs. The lighting was low and the carpet underfoot was deep-piled. This was clearly the opposite of any normal club: a place to not be seen and not be heard. I could see why Shlovsky had chosen it.

Now it was just a question of finding him and his mystery guest.

The barman made his way over. 'Good evening, sir. Good evening, madam. What can I get you?'

'Brandy and coke, please,' Alex said. She'd already decided that this was the sort of thing high-class tarts drank, and I wasn't going to contradict her. The barman didn't bat an eyelid, either, so maybe she was on the money.

'Wyborowa on ice,' I said. 'A large one.'

'Of course.' He turned back to the array of bottles above the bar and went to work.

With our drinks in our hands, we turned to make a discreet survey of the room. The tables were mostly occupied by men, a lot of them in evening dress, deep in serious conversations. Thank fuck there were a handful of bored-looking women too. I didn't spot any professionals, but they all looked considerably younger than their male companions, so Alex didn't look too out of place. I assumed a lot of these guys were getting some business done before heading out to the gaming tables, where a beautiful girl at your side might bring you luck, or if she didn't, could at least help you forget how much cash you'd just lost.

Alex took a sip of her drink and touched my arm. 'Three o'clock. Don't look now but I think I've spotted Major Titov and the British guy.'

I waited for thirty seconds, then stood up, patting my pockets as if I was looking for something. Over Alex's shoulder I could see the big Russian sitting at a table opposite one of the booths. On the other side of the table was another man with his back to us, but from the ramrod-straight posture I was pretty sure it was our Army friend. Both had what looked like glasses of sparkling water in front of them but they weren't drinking. They weren't chatting either. Instead, they were slowly quartering the room with their eyes, first right, then left, taking in the full three-sixty between them, without even bothering to hide what they were doing.

Alex swivelled slowly on her stool until she had an unobstructed view. 'So where's Shlovsky?'

'In the booth,' I said. I looked at my watch. It was 22.55. The meeting must have started early.

To the right of the booth was a long, padded bench. A young, unshaven guy was lounging with his back against the wall, arms crossed, looking bored. Was that the mystery man's minder? If so, he wasn't doing a very professional job. Nothing ex-Army about him. But he looked like a killer all the same.

'Can you see them?' Alex asked.

'Nah, but they've got to be in there. Titov and his mate aren't doing drills for nothing. And there's another guy over by the wall I reckon is watching out for someone.'

'We need to get closer,' Alex said.

She was right. Hearing any of their conversation would be a million to one shot, but if we could get a decent pic of the guy Shlovsky was meeting, at least we had a chance of identifying him.

Two men were sat at a table between Titov's and the bar. One of them got up and the other followed.

Perfect.

I took Alex's arm. 'Here we go.'

We made our way over to the table, trying not to look too eager. As I sat down, I made sure my jacket was open and the miniature camera masquerading as a shirt button was in line with the booth. Because of the angle, I could only see one occupant. It wasn't Shlovsky but that was about all I could say; the lighting in the booths was even worse than in the main bar. He looked animated, though, with some energetic head-tossing and a couple of forceful finger jabs. Obviously not a happy bunny, but was he telling Shlovsky to piss off, or were they just haggling over the price?

My eyes began to adjust to the low light and his features started to come into focus. Dark hair, a hawk-like nose, a neatly trimmed beard. Did he look Middle Eastern, or was that just my own confirmation bias? We'd speculated about where Shlovsky would most likely try to outsource his dirty work, and it was hard to see who else had the people on the ground: the human weapons just waiting to be primed, aimed and fired.

I looked away, aware that Titov might register my interest if I made it too obvious.

'Having a nice time?' I asked.

'Terrific,' Alex said. 'Can't believe you've never brought me here before. Tell you what, though, the women in here: I bloody well hope they're getting paid at the end of the night. They've bloody earned it.'

'Well, I'm afraid all you're getting is another tart's drink,' I said. 'Do you want it with a little umbrella this time?'

'I'm fine, thanks,' she said. 'These heels are bad enough when you're sober. You wouldn't want me going arse over tit and causing a scene, would you?'

'I might actually, now that you mention it,' I said. A neat little man in a grey suit was making his way slowly through the room, stopping to shake hands and exchange pleasantries with the members.

A monkey says that's Mr Riccardi, I thought.

'Look, Alex, I've got a feeling the manager's going to introduce himself in a minute. We may not have much time. Can you just swing by the booth on the way to the ladies' and confirm Shlovsky's actually in there? If I'm not here when you get back, I've been made and you're going to have to find another way out.'

'No problem,' she said.

The fact was, we didn't have an exit strategy. If Mr Riccardi and a couple of his goons decided to brace me, I wasn't quite sure what I was going to do. Carry on acting like a mega-rich arsehole and hope for the best, I guessed.

Alex got up and headed towards the booth just as Mr Riccardi reached our table.

'May I?' He bowed his head deferentially, but his beady eyes were like lasers.

I waved a hand towards a chair and he sat down.

'Forgive me for interrupting, Mr Schmidt, but I like to think I know all our members. I don't believe we've met, have we?'

I sat back and tried to give him some laser beams of my own. 'I've only just joined. That might explain it.'

'And can you remind me who your sponsor was?'

I was ready for that one. We'd looked through the members list and picked the oldest, a reptilian South African precious minerals baron in his eighties, hoping he'd be tucked up in bed with a cup of cocoa at this time of night, and so wouldn't be on hand to tell Riccardi he didn't know me from Adam.

'Mr De Vries. You know him, of course.'

Riccardi's smile got a bit more brittle. 'Unfortunately we haven't had the pleasure of Mr De Vries's company for some time.' The lasers continued to bore into me.

Shit. Was De Vries not just old but dead? Why didn't Ryan fucking think to check if the old bastard was still breathing?

'And what happened was such a shock.'

I didn't answer. I knew a fucking trick question when I heard one. I looked up, trying to see if any of the ex-Special Forces guys were waiting in the wings. Sure enough, the big one was stationed by the door.

I waited for a scream and the sound of someone being slapped, hoping Alex had seen the spot I was in and had decided to create a diversion, but as the silence lengthened, I realized it was a vain hope. I could see the guy from the door in my peripheral vision, sidling slowly towards us. Riccardi had me boxed in good and proper.

I tossed a coin in my head. If I caused a scene, Shlovsky would know something was up and that might put the kibosh on the whole operation. On the other hand, if I followed Riccardi meekly back to his office, there'd likely be a couple of plods waiting for me – and then things could get complicated.

Heads you win, tails I lose. Not much of a choice, really. I was leaning towards option number one, just because I felt like punching someone, when I heard a shout. We both looked over at Shlovsky's booth. He was stood up, pointing a finger at the other guy, who was still sitting down. The room went quiet as the other tables clocked what was happening, and for a moment all you could hear was Shlovsky's voice, hard and angry as he jabbed the air. In an instant Titov was on his feet, managing to intercept the guy sitting on the bench, who looked as if he was about to tackle Shlovsky. Now the young guy was shouting, trying to wrestle out of Titov's grip, as his boss barged past Shlovsky and out of the booth, then turned on him, the two men now standing chest to chest, only inches apart, looking like they wanted to kill each other.

Part of me wanted to see what happened next, but I knew a window of opportunity when I saw one. Riccardi was on his feet, obviously weighing up whether intervening would make things better or worse. His two heavies were cautiously approaching the booth, no doubt wondering the same thing.

I walked smartly between the tables and out through the door. Alex would have to fend for herself. Hopefully no one would bother too much with a call girl who could plausibly claim she'd never met me before tonight and had no idea who I was. I marched past the brunette without making eye contact and yanked the street door open, then I was up the steps and quickly jogging down the street.

It was only when I got to Berkeley Square and sat down on a bench that I realized how fast my heart was racing. *Too fucking close*, I thought.

I waited ten minutes. I reckoned I'd give her twenty and then call it a night. If Alex hadn't made it out of there by then, the plods had got hold of her and were giving her a grilling.

Three minutes later Alex appeared, holding her stilettos in one hand and a wine glass in the other. She plonked herself down and started rubbing her feet with her free hand.

'Fucking things.'

'You made it out all right, then?'

'There's a reason they don't wear high heels in the hundred metres, you know.' She rubbed some more. 'Yeah, no problem. I tagged along when a party of four got up and left. No one gave me a second look.' She took a swig of her drink.

'Good girl.'

'You reckon you got some decent pics, then?'

I shrugged. 'I fucking hope so. If you want some more you can go back and get them yourself.'

She tossed back the last of her drink and threw the glass into the bushes. 'Right then, let's go back to the office and see who it is that's got Viktor so riled up.'

18

It turns out wearing a concealed camera is a little bit like firing a rifle from the hip. Instinctively you aim along your sight line, as if you're looking down the barrel, without compensating for the fact that the camera is actually at a different angle to the target. I'd used a similar device before, but both times the target had been up close, and I couldn't really miss. Looking at the images on Alan's laptop, I realized I'd been trying too hard to see the guy Shlovsky was meeting for myself, and not thinking about where the camera was pointing. It looked like CCTV footage from a shopping centre, pictures of a fuzzy blob that could have been anyone.

Jesus, what a fucking amateur.

Thank fuck their shouting match eventually spilled out of the booth. It was almost as if he was posing for the camera. He even glanced towards Titov as he lumbered out of his chair.

Alan pressed a key to freeze the footage. 'Got him.'

Alex squeezed my shoulder. 'Good job, Logan.'

'More by fucking luck than judgement,' I said, shaking my head. 'If they'd stayed nice and cosy in their booth, we would have got fuck all.'

'So that's Rabid Dog,' Ryan said.

Mrs Allenby leaned closer. 'Well, he's certainly very well groomed.'

I had to admit I was impressed with the old bird. It was gone two in the morning, and she was bright as a button, making a pot of strong coffee for us all and bustling around with a lot more energy and enthusiasm than I felt, if I was honest. Maybe I'd been wrong to doubt her.

'Anyone recognize him?' she added.

Head shakes all round.

'Let me double-check the membership list again, just in case,' Ryan said, going back to his work station and firing up his laptop.

The rest of us carried on looking at the face on the screen, as if staring at him for long enough was going to tell us who he was.

'I think if I was going to give him a nickname, it would be some sort of bird of prey, not a dog,' Mrs Allenby mused. 'That nose, those black eyes, the rather cruel mouth. He has the look of a predator.'

'Does he look like a terrorist, though?' I asked.

Mrs Allenby frowned. 'Well, that's hard to tell, of course. As we know to our cost.'

'Definitely not a member,' Ryan called over. 'Let me run him through the usual databases and see if we can get a hit.'

That was definitely our best bet. But it depended on Rabid Dog already being on somebody's watch list. What if he'd been under the radar until now? A minor Middle Eastern royal happily playing the part of a mega-rich playboy, just biding his time until the opportunity came to strike?

But if that was the case, how did Shlovsky zero in on him?

I rubbed my hand over my face. The truth was, it was all bollocks until we had a name.

Mrs Allenby turned to Ryan. 'How long do you think it might take?'

Ryan pulled at his ponytail. 'No way of knowing. Depends on how deep he's buried. There are some databases I'm still trying to access, but it's tricky.'

Mrs Allenby gave him a thin smile. 'It's supposed to be tricky, Mr Oldfield. It's what we call national security. We don't want any Tom, Dick or Harry hacking into them. In fact, I think I will have rather mixed feelings if you do manage it.'

Alex put an arm round Ryan's broad shoulders as he worked. 'It's a good thing Ryan's on our side, then, isn't it?'

I got up and put my hands behind my head, stretching out my neck muscles. There was no point just hanging around while Ryan went through the laborious process of putting Rabid Dog's face through every terror suspect list he could get access to. And there was no way I was going to sleep; I was too wired for that, and Mrs Allenby's killer coffee hadn't helped. But I was too tired to make any sort of positive contribution to things. I needed to clear my head before I could get back in the game and help the team. What I really fancied was a good, hard run, preferably up a bastard of a mountain. But I'd settle for a long walk along the river.

'I'm just going to get some air. Ping me if we get a name.'

Mrs Allenby nodded.

'Take care,' Alex said, with a meaningful look.

'Always.'

Out on the street, I realized I still had my tie on. I pulled it off and put it in my pocket. I took a deep breath. The air was crisp and cool. I headed south, not really knowing where I was going. It was almost three in the morning and nobody was about, unless you counted the homeless people sleeping in doorways. I rummaged in my pockets for change and put a handful under the ratty-looking sleeping bag of one guy who was spark out in front of a shop full of wedding dresses. I hoped he'd find it before anyone else did.

As I walked on, increasing my pace, I felt the last traces of adrenaline from our emergency exit from the club leaving my system. With a bit of luck, Mr Riccardi would have had his hands full smoothing things over with Shlovsky and Rabid Dog, and the mysterious Mr Schmidt would be forgotten. We'd got away with it. And we now had a better than even chance of identifying the man Shlovsky was so anxious about meeting.

We were getting somewhere at last.

I turned the corner at the end of the street and smelled the river. At this time of night you could imagine it like it must have been before Londoners started dumping all their crap into it, from used condoms to dead bodies. I leaned out over the embankment wall and looked down at the water. Over to my right, I could see the street lamps on Battersea Bridge. It seemed like as good a place to go as any.

As I strolled along the Chelsea Embankment, I suppose I should have been more worried about being followed. But with the streets so empty, it would have been hard to tail me effectively, even for real pros, so I reckoned I could afford to take my eye off the ball a bit. There was also a part of me, to be honest, that was hoping they would have another crack. I was tired of trying to figure out what was going on. I wanted to see the bastards face to face.

I stopped and looked at the water for a bit, then turned and surveyed the street. Plenty of cabs and Toyota Priuses on the prowl, but the traffic kept on flowing and nothing else caught my attention. I went on and stepped onto the bridge. The breeze was stronger here and I started to shiver.

On the other side a couple were walking unsteadily arm in arm, laughing and hanging on to each other to stay upright. I watched them to the end of the bridge, where they stopped to flag down a cab, then I turned back and kept walking.

As I got to the middle of the bridge, I saw a figure looking out over the river. It was a woman: tall and pale with long black hair. But there was something odd about her. She wasn't leaning against the wall; she was just standing a foot away, stock-still, arms by her sides, like a soldier on parade. I wondered what the hell she was doing, how long she'd been standing like that.

As I got nearer I could see the breeze whipping her hair around her face. But she didn't try to brush it away. It was like she was made of stone.

I was six feet away now, and she must have clocked me in

her peripheral vision, but she didn't turn to look at me. She was focused very intently on something in front of her, something that only she could see.

I held my breath. Something in the way she held herself struck a chord. Suddenly I knew exactly what she was about to do.

Before I could move she'd reached forward and hoisted herself onto the top of the wall. She stood there for a moment, looking down into the water, then I sensed everything in her body going loose, letting everything go.

I hurled myself forward and just managed to wrap my arms around her knees before she tipped forward. She cried out as we both tumbled back onto the walkway. I felt a lightning bolt of pain shoot up my arm as I took most of our weight on my elbow.

Fuck.

She picked herself up and I thought for a second she was going to have another go. If she did, I wasn't sure I'd be able to stop her. I felt her wavering. Then she saw me cradling my elbow.

'Are you all right?' Her voice was deeper than I'd expected.

I couldn't help grinning. 'Am *I* all right? You're the one that's just tried to top herself.'

'I'm sorry,' she said, looking down at her feet.

'Don't be,' I said. 'I'm glad I was in the right place at the right time for once.'

I looked at her. She seemed lost. I reckoned I knew how she must be feeling. All those hours and hours screwing up your courage to do it, then you finally close your eyes and pull the trigger and . . . you open your eyes and here you are again, back where you started.

'Look, my name's Logan.'

She nodded. 'Lucy.'

'Hello, Lucy.'

We stood looking at each other. What now?

I started talking to fill the awkward silence, not really knowing what was about to come out of my mouth.

'I had a go at it once. You know, trying to kill myself.'

'Really? How did it go?'

There was a pause, then we both started laughing.

She put a hand to her mouth. 'I'm sorry.'

I smiled. 'It's fine. I totally cocked it up. As you can see.'

She tried to smile, but I could see the moment had passed. The adrenaline was draining out of her body, the crazy rush of finally letting go was gone, and all the sadness and pain that had made her want to do it in the first place was seeping back.

'What I meant was, I've been there. I know what it's like.'

'OK,' she said uncertainly.

'So if you want to talk about it . . .'

'You could help?'

'I could try.'

She smiled sadly. 'You've saved my life. I can't expect you to mend a broken heart, too.'

I smiled back. 'You're right. That might be too much. In one evening, anyway.'

She looked at me, searching for something in my eyes. 'You don't have to worry, you know.'

'About what?'

'That I'll do it again. Try to do it again, I mean.'

'Are you sure?'

'Yes, it took all I had to do it once. I think I'm just . . . I don't know . . . too tired now.'

I nodded. I knew how that felt, too. But eventually she'd find the strength again. I could see that in her eyes. And this time there might not be anyone on hand to stop her.

'Look, can I give you my number? In case you want to talk.'

She patted the pockets of her long cardigan and smiled. 'I left my phone at home. Didn't want it getting wet. How stupid is that?'

I found a ballpoint in my jacket pocket. In my wallet was an old train ticket. I scribbled down my number and held it out.

'Please.'

As she took it our fingers touched. Hers were icy cold.

Just then my phone pinged. She saw my expression as I looked at the message.

'You need to go,' she said.

19

I was looking at the face of the man Shlovsky called Rabid Dog, but my mind kept drifting back to the woman on the bridge.

Lucy.

I realized that was all I knew about her: her name. What had led her to that dark place where there's no hope left? She'd said she had a broken heart, but I didn't think she was the type to end it all over some bloke who'd ditched her. No, her heart was properly broken into bits, like mine had been, leaving nothing but a big hole where all the pain rushes in.

I'd stopped her from killing herself, but I couldn't help wondering if all I'd done was delay the inevitable. Maybe she was on her way home now, figuring out Plan B. Pills, maybe: something where some interfering bastard can't put a spanner in the works.

'Are you all right, Logan?' Alex was giving me the once-over. 'You look like you've been in a fight.'

I looked down. I'd torn a hole in one knee of my trousers and my jacket was scuffed where I'd fallen on my elbow.

'Walked into a lamp post. Just knackered, that's all.'

'Right . . .' She gave me a look which meant, *We'll talk about this later.*

I turned to Ryan. 'So, who's our boy?'

'Danilo Melnyk.'

'Not a Saudi princeling, then,' Mrs Allenby said.

'Nope,' Ryan said. 'He's Ukrainian. From Kiev.'

'This looks like a booking photo,' I said.

Ryan nodded. 'Top marks. Melnyk was arrested in Paris in 2007. Currency irregularities. Money-laundering to you and me. He's a banker, basically. But it looked like some of the businesses he chose to invest in were not exactly kosher. Like drug smuggling, for instance.'

'Did he do time?'

'No, it looks like they didn't have enough to charge him and the French cut him loose. He went back home for a couple of years, then pitched up in London in 2010.'

'And since then?'

'He's been investing in various businesses, but it's hard to see where his money's been coming from. There's chatter he's still involved in drugs, and the NCA have an ongoing interest, but he's managed to keep his nose clean up to now.'

I rubbed my eyes. My arm was beginning to freeze up but I didn't want to draw attention to it. I got up and walked over to the kitchen area, trying to think it all through. I filled the kettle and switched it on. I needed more coffee.

I leaned on the counter and glanced over at the team. 'He's basically the bag man for a drug gang, then.'

'Looks like it,' Ryan agreed.

'So how's he going to organize a terror attack?'

Ryan frowned. 'Hard to figure that one.'

'But they had a meeting about something. An urgent meeting, and they argued. What else could it have been about?' Mrs Allenby asked. 'Unless Shlovsky's suddenly decided to get involved in the drugs trade.'

Alex had been very quiet. She was looking at something she'd written on a notepad, rocking back and forth in her chair.

'*Shit.*'

Mrs Allenby looked at her over her glasses. 'Miss Short?'

'I think I might have an idea,' Alex said. 'Alan, can you play the tape?'

Alan switched on his laptop. 'Sure. Give me a minute?'

'What tape?' I asked.

'Alan picked up another conversation.'

'From Shlovsky's office?'

'No, from Ekaterina's dressing room.'

I frowned. 'How does that help us? You're not telling us she's the one trying to set up the terror attack, are you?'

Alex ignored me. 'Just have a listen.'

We crowded round Alan's laptop. 'Sorry, that's just her moving around. OK, now she's hitting the speed dial. Here we go.'

I folded my arms and listened. She had quite a nice voice, sort of musical. And she put a lot of emotion into it, in a Russian sort of way.

But that was the point. She was speaking Russian. For all I could tell she was ordering a takeaway.

I looked at Alex and shrugged my shoulders. She held a finger up. 'Just wait.'

Another minute of sing-song Russian and there it was.

'Stasi.'

I listened more closely.

'OK, this next bit,' Alex said.

'Stasi, Stasi, Stasi . . .'

'She says it thirteen times in three minutes.'

'OK,' I said, still not getting it. 'Do we know who she's talking to?'

'I think so,' Alex said. 'I've managed to translate some of it. Nothing very earth-shattering, I'm afraid. It's mostly just girly chit-chat. I think she's talking to her daughter. Anastasia.'

Mrs Allenby smiled and put a hand on Alex's shoulder. 'Or Stasi for short.'

'Exactly.'

'OK . . .' I said slowly. 'That makes sense. But where does it get us?'

Mrs Allenby looked at me as if I was the class dunce. 'Shlovsky used the word "Stasi" when he was setting up the meeting with Melnyk. He was quite irate, as I recall. Why do you think that might be?'

I was too tired to play games. 'Beats me.'

She turned to Ryan. 'Could you take a look at the list of students at the Sorbonne for me?'

He nodded, a knowing smile on his face. Had everybody

figured it out except me? We waited while he tapped his way into the database.

'Bingo.' He turned his laptop round and we all looked into the face of a young man, late teens, early twenties, with dark hair to his shoulders and a wide smile. He was slightly pudgy, like there was a bit of puppy fat still to burn off, but he was a handsome kid, no doubt about it. And that smile said he knew it.

At last the penny dropped. 'Melnyk junior,' I said.

'Krystiyan, to be precise,' Ryan said. 'Studying engineering.'

'I wonder if Anastasia has a Facebook page?' Mrs Allenby said.

Ryan grinned. 'Just give me a second.' He turned his laptop round again and his fingers danced over the keys for a couple of minutes. 'Here we are. And look who we have.'

Yep, there they were: the happy couple. Krystiyan looking like the cat that got the cream in a velvet tux, his arm round the shoulders of a dazzling blonde in a strapless cocktail dress. You didn't need a DNA test to see she was Ekaterina Shlovsky's daughter.

'Another word that came up a few times was *pomolvlen*,' Alex said. 'Engaged.'

I nodded. 'And I'll bet Daddy's thrilled about that. His little princess marrying the son of a Ukrainian drug dealer. No wonder he's pissed off.'

Mrs Allenby sat down and tapped her lips with the end of a gold pencil. 'So we've managed to solve one mystery. We know what Shlovsky and Melnyk were arguing about.

But unfortunately that takes us back to square one as far as the terror attack is concerned. Which means we have even less time to stop it. Quite possibly not enough time. Does anybody have any ideas?'

I had one idea: that we were being played for suckers by somebody. I tried to think through the sequence of events: first Six picks up chatter about the Kremlin using Russians living in the UK to instigate terror attacks. Then Shlovsky looks like he's having his arm twisted back home. SIS wants to put him under surveillance but the PM won't have it. The DG decides to do it anyway, and Blindeye is tasked with the job, directed by his old PA, Mrs Allenby. We put him under the microscope and come up with fuck all. Meanwhile two members of the Blindeye team are dead, a third has a near miss and a fourth thinks he might have had one, too.

Put that all together and what did you get? Which one of those pieces didn't fit? I was too tired to bloody think.

'I think perhaps we should call it a night,' Mrs Allenby said. 'Let's resume in the morning when our minds are fresh, review what we have and look at our options. As I've said, the meter is running. I have a meeting with the Director General tomorrow afternoon and I would like to have something to report.'

Ryan closed his laptop and reached for his jacket. Alex got up, yawning. Mrs Allenby started putting her things in her bag.

I stood frozen in the middle of the room, not wanting to quit but not knowing what the hell to do next.

I looked over at Alan. He was licking his lips and fiddling with his glasses. I'd known him long enough to recognize the signs. He had something on his mind but wasn't sure if he should speak out.

'Alan, mate, what's up?'

The others stopped what they were doing. Alan smiled nervously. 'Er, probably nothing. Don't worry about it.'

Mrs Allenby put her bag down on the table. 'If you have something to share with the team, Mr Woodburn, even if you think it's of no consequence, I'd like to hear it.'

'Well . . . I was looking at the footage from the club. The first thing we see is Shlovsky and Melnyk in the booth – well, we assume it's them, we can't really see – and sitting at a table is Titov and his number two – we think it's his number two, anyway, the Brit. Now, when Shlovsky loses his rag and comes out of the booth with Melnyk, Melnyk's minder jumps up and tries to get in between them, but Titov's too quick for him and gets him in a bear hug. Then Riccardi tries to calm things down and we don't really know what happened after that. Does that seem like a fair summary of events?'

'Pretty much,' I said.

'Sure.' Alex nodded.

Alan hesitated, licking his lips again. He looked over at me. 'So where was the British guy?'

Fuck. Where *was* he? You don't go for a piss or a fag while your boss is out in the open, I knew that much about being a bodyguard. But one minute he was there and the next he'd vanished. And he didn't come back, even when things kicked off, leaving it to Titov to run interference for Shlovsky all on his own.

Alan looked up sheepishly. 'It might be nothing, I mean there's all sorts of . . . I don't want to be . . .'

'No, Mr Woodburn,' Mrs Allenby said firmly. 'It's a loose end. And I don't like loose ends. I think we should take a closer look at our ex-Army friend and see where it leads.' She turned to me. 'Go home, Mr Logan, and get some rest. Tomorrow you have work to do.'

20

Alex started on me the moment Mrs Allenby closed the door behind her.

'So what really happened? And don't give me any more of that "walking into a lamp post" shit.'

I was so fucking knackered, and there were so many strange thoughts churning around in my mind, I felt like just telling her to fuck off and mind her own business. But I just about had enough sense left to know that she was only badgering me because she cared. And come to think of it, she was the only person I had in my life who did. The only one living, anyway. It might be annoying, but her heart was in the right place.

I gave her a sheepish grin. 'Yeah, sorry, I was crossing Battersea Bridge and these arseholes were hassling this couple who were, you know, trying to have a romantic moment. I told them to clear off and, well, they needed a bit of persuading. Sorry, I've messed up the suit.'

Alex shook her head. 'Fuck the suit. It's you I'm worried about. Anything could have happened. You could have ended up at the nick, trying to explain who you are.'

I shrugged. 'It was only kids.'

I didn't even know why I was lying. But there was something about the whole thing with Lucy I just wanted to keep to myself for the moment. Until I'd – I don't know, sorted it out in my mind. I decided to change the subject.

'Ryan, how's the homework going?'

Ryan had his head buried in his laptop, as usual. Was he planning on being here all night?

'Sorry?'

'Claire and Craig. Connections.'

He frowned. 'I'm not really getting anywhere, to be honest. Apart from the obvious link, that they were both part of Blindeye, I just don't have enough to go on. There aren't enough data points to do a proper analysis. It's just guesswork.'

'What if you add us both to the mix?'

'That doesn't actually help. Again, apart from the one thing, there are even fewer commonalities. There's nothing else that links all four of us – at least nothing I can see.'

'Maybe there's nothing *to* see, then,' I said.

Ryan sighed. 'That's the point. Because they worked for Five, their personnel files are classified. Whatever's there, I can't see it. I can't even get access to mine.'

Alex brought a mug of coffee over and sat down. 'We need those files, then. Anyone fancy trying to break into Thames House?'

'There is another way,' Ryan said. 'We could ask Mrs Allenby. She's about the only person I can think of who could get them.'

I folded my arms. 'I don't know. What if that just tips our hand?'

'You still don't trust her?' Alex asked.

I shrugged. I wasn't sure what I thought any more.

Alex and Ryan exchanged glances. 'Do we have any choice?' she asked.

I looked at them both. At least it would end things one way or another.

'I guess not.'

I turned to Alan, who'd gone back to his work station where he was fiddling with some wires. I couldn't work out whether he was trying to set up some equipment or it was just therapy, his way of dealing with all the stress. Not for the first time, I wondered if he had the right stuff for Blindeye. I mean, tech-wise he was a wizard. I used to take the piss by calling him Q, but he'd saved my bacon on more than one occasion when I'd been on a covert surveillance operation and the comms had failed. He always seemed to have a backup plan, could always cobble together something that *worked* when some fancy new piece of equipment didn't do what it said it would on the box.

But he was a backroom guy to his fingertips. Being in the field was never part of the plan, and although he hadn't said anything, I think the idea that someone might be targeting the lot of us was scaring him shitless.

'Alan, mate, are you listening?'

He put down what he was working on. 'Uh, yeah, sure.'

'It needs all of us on board if we're going to do this. Are you OK with it?'

He blinked a couple of times behind his thick glasses and licked his lips. 'If it's the only way, yeah. I mean, we need to know, don't we?'

'OK, agreed. We'll talk to her tomorrow.'

As soon as I said it, I felt a little shiver, as if we'd just signed our death warrants. But Alex was right: what choice did we have?

'In the meantime, we don't take any chances. Before anyone leaves here, we do a sweep of the area, then go in pairs, one on follow to pick up any surveillance. Make sense?'

They all nodded.

'OK, then tomorrow we reassess our options. I'm pretty sure no one's tailed me home, but we may need to look at moving to different locations. In the meantime, this is the nearest thing we have to a safe house. If things get really hairy, we may need to hole up here for a bit. At least until we can get hold of those files and find out what the fuck is going on.'

I looked at Alan. 'Right, get your coat on, mate. We're out of here.'

It was 4 a.m. before I got back to the flat, with Alan safely installed in the ground-floor flat in a Peabody building in Victoria he shared with his elderly mum. I did one more circuit to make sure I was clean and let myself in. I stood in the hallway with the lights off, just listening and breathing in the air, trying to pick up any telltale traces of aftershave or body odour. Even cigarette smoke, although something told me the people we were dealing with weren't stupid enough for that. But there was nothing except the faint aroma of incense.

I turned on the light in the hall and went into the kitchen. It felt like a week since I'd eaten anything but I was too tired to do anything about it. I could maybe manage a cup of tea, but then all I wanted to do was sleep. I threw a teabag into a mug and filled the kettle, then took my shoes off and padded quietly upstairs, checking each room, then all the doors and windows, to make sure everything was the way I'd left it. I came back downstairs, put my shoes back on, took off my jacket to use as a pillow and lay down on the floor. I was asleep as soon as I closed my eyes.

The church was packed. I was sitting with Joseph and Sarah, feeling self-conscious in my new suit. As long as I was sitting down, no one could see the ragged holes at the knees or the tear in my sleeve, but I knew Sarah was going to give me hell when we got home. There was blood on my shirt, too, a bright splatter all down the front. It looked fresh; in fact, new spots were seeping through the crisp white cotton as I looked, which meant it must be mine. Which was odd, because I couldn't feel any pain.

I looked at Joseph. He was fidgeting in his seat, looking round at all the strange people, the men in morning suits and top hats and the women in bright dresses and big, flowery hats. I tousled his hair and he stuck his tongue out. Now that I looked, there were flowers everywhere, huge sprays of yellow in niches along the walls and two big urns by the font.

I caught sight of Mrs Allenby in the front row, wearing a green dress and a little black hat with a veil. She was sitting next to Viktor Shlovsky, whispering something in his ear. She was smiling as she spoke, but his expression was grim. On his other side, Ekaterina, in a black cocktail dress and pearl necklace, had a firm hand on his arm, as if she was afraid he was going to jump up and attack someone.

His eyes flicked to his left and I followed his gaze. On the other side of the aisle was the bridegroom's family. Melnyk was dressed in a gaudy sharkskin suit, his arm around Krystiyan's shoulders. He was wearing dark glasses so I couldn't see his eyes, but you could tell from his grin he was enjoying the proceedings. Krystiyan was dressed in a white silk suit. Not the best choice, I thought. Attention grabbing, yes, but try getting bloodstains out of it.

He didn't seem to be able to sit still, casting nervous glances towards the back of the church. I couldn't help smiling, remembering how that felt. I turned to Sarah, wanting to share the moment together, but she was busy wiping jam from Joseph's mouth. I looked towards the font. The priest was standing there, his thin lips pursed, looking at his watch. With his nose like a hawk's beak and cold grey eyes, I recognized the Director General. *Where's his security?* I wondered, a trace of panic growing in my guts. Unless that was me? I patted the inside of my jacket. I didn't have a weapon. I looked at my hand and it was sticky with blood. Sarah frowned, shaking her head. *Sorry*, I mouthed. *Sorry sorry sorry.*

I looked around for something to wipe the blood on, but then the music started. I noticed Viktor wasn't in his place any more. Mrs Allenby was now chatting with Ekaterina, who was pointing admiringly at Mrs Allenby's hat, saying, 'Beautiful, beautiful.' *Somebody's missing*, I thought. *There's somebody who should be here.* But I couldn't think who. I turned to Sarah to ask her who it was, but she and Joseph had gone. In her place was Lucy, the woman from the bridge. She was wearing the same dark skirt and cardigan as before, but they were soaking wet. I noticed her hair was wet, too. There were puddles forming around her feet on the cold flagstones and I could smell the river. She put a hand to her cheek.

'Weddings,' she said, sniffing. 'They always make me cry.'

There was a rustling as the bride made her way down the aisle. I turned round as she passed. She was arm in arm with Shlovsky, and held a little bunch of yellow flowers in her hands. I caught a whiff of something coppery, then realized it must be me. I looked down at the front of my shirt but I couldn't see any blood.

I looked at the bride. She was wearing an ivory silk dress that emphasized her tiny waist before ballooning into a big, puffy skirt. Her long blonde hair was loose, almost covering her face. Her veil was made of cobwebs.

I tried to catch her eye. 'You look beautiful, Daisy. Really beautiful.'

Shlovsky peeled off as she approached the priest, and returned to his seat. The DG took her hand and looked towards the opposite pews. Krystiyan Melnyk got up with a sheepish grin, getting one last pat on the back from his father as he squeezed past. He walked forward and the DG took his hand. The happy couple had their backs to me as the DG spoke the words of the ritual. I strained to hear but he spoke so quietly it was just a mumble, until he looked up and said loudly, *'Till death do us part.'*

The bride and groom turned towards each other. I could see the sweat dripping off Krystiyan's face. The music had changed. Deep and moody: not so cheerful any more. I thought I recognized it from that movie about Mozart. Daisy started lifting her veil, the cobwebs sticking to her tiny fingers.

This isn't right, I thought. I'd been feeling happy for her, but now a sick feeling was creeping up my spine.

I heard a ringtone.

'Sorry!' Lucy whispered, rummaging in her bag for her phone, but the ringing just got louder.

'Can't you stop that?' I snapped.

She made a face. 'Sorry! Sorry! Sorry!'

I turned with a frown.

Krystiyan was looking at his bride with horror as she offered up her bone-white skull to be kissed.

Jesus.

* * *

I jerked awake, banging the back of my head against the floorboards. My shirt was soaked, my heart hammering. I felt along the floor until I found my phone.

'Yeah.'

Silence.

'Hello? Who is this?'

'Is that Logan?' Her voice was soft, uncertain.

I took a deep breath, trying to get my mind back into gear. 'Hold on. Give me a second.'

'I've woken you up. I'm sorry. Look, I shouldn't have called . . .'

'No, it's fine. It's fine.' I looked at my watch. Six o'clock. I took another deep breath. 'I'm glad you did.'

'Are you OK?'

'Yeah. Yeah. I was just having a funny dream.'

I could feel her smiling on the other end of the phone. 'Tell me. I could do with cheering up.'

'Not that kind of funny. Not that kind of funny at all.' I shivered as the last pieces of it melted away, leaving nothing but a feeling of vague dread. 'Look, do you want to meet, get a coffee or something? I could do with one right now.'

'Are you sure that's OK? You don't mind? I'm sure you were hoping the crazy suicidal lady wasn't going to take you up on your offer.'

'No, that would be good.'

'All right. It'll be your own fault if I bore you to death.'

We let the word sit between us for a moment, neither of us knowing what to do with it. Eventually she said, 'There's a place near the bridge, where we . . . met. Patsy's. Do you know it?'

'Yeah, sure. I can be there in twenty minutes.'

'Thank you. I'll be waiting for you. Then I can tell you all about my sorry, fucked-up life.'

21

I had a shower, brushed my teeth, threw on jeans and trainers and made it in twenty-five. I wasn't sure she'd still be there. I reckoned she'd bail after twenty, figuring I'd thought better of it.

'Strong and black, is that all right? You sounded like you needed it.'

'Perfect.'

She'd found a corner table by the window. The way the sun was streaming in, it felt like another lifetime when I'd pulled her off the bridge. Or a bad dream.

She smiled, that sad half-smile I was beginning to recognize, and took a sip of her cappuccino.

'Gosh, I certainly wasn't expecting to be sitting here this morning.'

'No? Where were you expecting to be?'

Fuck. Stupid question. My head wasn't working properly yet.

'Well, at the bottom of the river, I suppose. Or floating gently downstream, with my hair all around me, like Ophelia.' She sighed. 'Probably not very realistic. More likely I'd be on a slab in some morgue, I suppose, being sliced open so they can take all my organs out.' She made a face. 'Yuck. Why do they always weigh them? I've always wanted to know that. What bloody difference does it make? Lucy Jane Pargeter, dead as a doornail, but here's the good news: her kidneys are a perfect size seven.'

I smiled. 'So how does it feel – to be alive? Not on a slab having your organs weighed.'

She looked thoughtful. 'Better, in one way.' A shadow seemed to pass over her face. 'Worse in another.'

I nodded. That pretty much summed it up.

She looked at me. 'So how did you . . . do it? Try to do it, I mean.'

I frowned. 'I don't know if I . . .'

'Look, it's all right, I'm not asking for tips. But if you don't want to talk about it . . .'

'No, it's OK.' I took a gulp of coffee. 'I . . . tied a rope to a lamp post, put the other end round my neck and then drove straight at a wall.'

She put a hand to her mouth. 'Oh my God. That's . . .'

I shrugged. 'The end result's the same, however you do it.'

'I suppose. Why didn't you go through with it?'

'My wife stopped me.'

'Your wife?' She looked puzzled.

'She was dead at the time. That was why I wanted to end things, you know? But she persuaded me to carry on, told me there was a reason to go on living. At least, I could hear her voice in my head, like.'

She nodded. 'And do you hear her voice now? Does she still speak to you?'

'Yeah. Every now and then. When I'm least expecting it. I . . . see her as well. And my boy. He doesn't say much, though. He's only little.'

She put her hands to her face. Her eyes were suddenly brimming with tears. 'I'm so sorry.'

I handed her a napkin. 'It's OK. You know, I've never told anyone that.'

'Can I ask what she said to you? The reason for going on living, I mean.'

I took another gulp of coffee and wiped my mouth with a napkin, trying to buy myself some time. I didn't want to lie to her, but I couldn't exactly tell her the truth, either.

'To help people, I suppose.'

'Like you're helping me?'

'Something like that.'

'My God, how many people have you stopped from jumping off bridges?'

I smiled. 'You're the first, actually. I mostly try and help people in . . . other ways.'

Other ways that sometimes involve killing them, I thought. I needed to try and steer the conversation in another direction.

'Sorry, I haven't eaten for a while. I need to get some sugar in my system or I'm going to crash. I'm going to get a bun or something. Do you want anything?'

'No. Thank you. Caffeine's all I need.'

I went to the counter and grabbed a Danish pastry

oozing carbs. But I knew how she was feeling. Eating means living. When you want to die, it just seems wrong. You need the caffeine, though, so you don't go to sleep. Then you won't dream.

I brought my breakfast back and sat down. I took a bite and felt the glucose hitting my bloodstream. That was better. She waited patiently while I finished it off.

'So, I was going to tell you about me, wasn't I?'

I brushed crumbs off the front of my T-shirt. 'If you still want to.'

She closed her eyes and took a breath. I could see this wasn't going to be easy for her.

'I'm a teacher. *Was* a teacher. God, I don't know. It feels like my life's been cancelled out, even though I'm still here. Does that make sense?'

'Sure. It's like you've said goodbye to everything. But you haven't gone.'

She nodded. 'Including saying goodbye to yourself. In a way it feels as if I *did* die. Like I'm not the same person any more.' She smiled bitterly. 'One of the living dead. A zombie.' She glanced at her reflection in the window and brushed a strand of hair from her face. 'I'm sure that's what I look like, anyway.'

'I know what you mean – I mean about feeling like a zombie.'

'Not about looking like one?' There was a smile hovering at the corner of her lips.

I looked away, feeling awkward. 'No.'

She picked up a packet of sugar from the bowl on the table and started turning it over in her fingers. 'Would you like another coffee?'

'Sure. My shout. What are you having?'

She shook her head. 'I'm fine.'

I went to the counter. I didn't really want another coffee either. But I figured she needed a couple of minutes to herself, to work up the nerve for the next bit of the conversation. This was going to be the hard bit, when she told me what had ripped the heart out of her and made life seem not worth living. I took as long as I could, pretending to search in my pockets for the right change before giving up and paying with a card. The woman in front of me was waiting for a takeaway. She was wearing a blue dress with yellow flowers, and a fragment of the dream came back to me.

Organ music. A funeral – no, a wedding. Daisy's? I looked down at the front of my shirt, expecting to see blood.

When I got back to our table, Lucy was blowing her nose. I could tell she'd been crying.

'You OK?'

She nodded. That half-smile again. 'For a zombie.'

I waited. She closed her eyes and took a deep breath and then it all came out in a rush.

'They died in a car crash. I can't say their names. I'm sorry. We were going to Cornwall. His uncle had a cottage. We'd stayed before. It was lovely – perfect for the kids. I . . . stayed at home. I was going to take the train the morning after. I had all this admin to do for the school. I wanted to get it done, out of the way, so it wouldn't be on my mind and we could really enjoy the holiday. They were going to go crabbing. Janey said she was going to catch a big one for me.'

Her voice cracked and she covered her face with her hands. Her body heaved with great, wracking, silent sobs. I reached out a hand, then left it hanging in mid-air, feeling useless. Gradually her breathing returned to normal and the tears tailed off. She dabbed at her eyes and blew her nose again.

'Is everybody looking?' she asked.

I shrugged. 'Fuck them.'

She nodded. She kept her eyes closed, trying to still the whirlwind of emotions she'd just unleashed.

After a while she said, 'How did you go on? I mean, get up every day afterwards?'

'Like I say, Sarah told me I had a job to do.'

She sniffed. 'I suppose I do, too. I mean, teaching is helping people. Making a difference. But I just couldn't do it now, I mean teaching other people's kids. So what do you do?'

'You mean work?'

'Yes.'

I paused. 'Security.'

'What, like a security guard?'

'It's a bit more complicated.'

'It sounds very mysterious.'

'Not really. Sometimes I stop bad people from doing bad things. That's all. If I'm lucky.'

She put her hands on the table, so her fingers were almost touching mine. She had blood under a couple of her nails.

'Thank you.'

I felt there was something else I should say, something that would stop her getting sucked back into that black hole of despair. But I knew it would sound hollow. The best I could do was share my experiences, the story of a fellow member of the undead, and hope she found her own path, the way I had mine.

'You're welcome.'

'Look, I'm going to go now. But maybe we could meet up again?'

Despite myself, I felt a little jolt of electricity, as if I'd just touched a live wire. 'Sure. I mean, yes, that would be good.'

She stood up and swung her bag onto her shoulder. She turned to go, then looked back with a smile.

'Remember, I've got your number now.'

22

I took my place at the round conference table, hoping I didn't look as ragged as I felt. I kept replaying bits of my conversation with Lucy in my head, and then underneath was the dream, just odd fragments, nothing that I could really get a hold on: more a vague feeling of menace. It was like treading water, knowing there were sharks circling somewhere in the murky depths beneath you.

Luckily for me, if I looked bad, Ryan looked even worse. He was unshaven with dark circles under his eyes, and looked as if he was wearing the same baggy blue golf shirt as yesterday. There was a mug of steaming black coffee in front of him but he hadn't touched it.

Alan looked a tad better; at least he'd showered and changed, but his complexion was still sweaty and grey. Another troubled night, I reckoned. He was spooning sugar into his tea like there was no tomorrow.

Even Alex, who prided herself on always being ready for action, looked a little bit the worse for wear. But I knew it wasn't about being physically or mentally tired; it was the frustration of feeling like we'd hit a brick wall.

Mrs Allenby, on the other hand, looked fresh as a daisy, dressed in a crisp navy-blue suit with a cream silk blouse, her notepad and gold pencil placed neatly on the table in front of her. As usual, I wondered if she knew something we didn't.

As soon as I'd taken my seat, she called the meeting to order.

'Good morning, everybody. Before we proceed, I think it might be helpful to summarize the current situation regarding Viktor Shlovsky. So far, we have uncovered no evidence of covert communication with a third party capable of executing a terror incident or campaign. That does not, unfortunately, rule out the possibility that such communication is ongoing, merely that we have been unable to detect it. Blindeye's resources are, in that regard, limited.'

She glanced at me over the top of her glasses. Was I just being paranoid, or did she mean me? I clenched my fists, my instinctive distrust of office-bound pen-pushers starting to bubble up.

'We have no choice, however,' she continued, 'but to proceed on the basis that we have been looking in the wrong direction, and that the link we are seeking to establish is somewhere in our peripheral vision. In that regard, Mr Woodburn has suggested that the target of our surveillance should now be Shlovsky's deputy head of security. While I agree that this is the only logical way forward, I would also remind you all that this is something of a last throw of the dice.'

She looked round the table, making eye contact with each of us in turn.

'I would also remind you that the stakes could not be any higher. We do not know the scale of what is being planned, but we can assume it is intended to cause significant disruption, and that means significant numbers of dead or injured. We do not want the blood of those innocent people on our hands.'

She paused, letting that all sink in. I couldn't help wondering if it was more of a threat than a warning. If we failed now, that would be the end of Blindeye. And then what would happen to us? We'd be loose ends. And she'd already said she didn't like those. No doubt her former boss, the DG, didn't like them either.

Find the link or we're fucked, I thought. A last throw of the dice all right.

Mrs Allenby turned to Ryan. 'I believe we now know who our target is.'

So that's what he'd been doing all night.

'Yes,' Ryan said. 'A slightly laborious process, I'm afraid. If he'd been regular army – even Special Forces – it would have been a lot easier. But it turns out he's a former military intelligence officer, so there were a few more firewalls to negotiate. He'd been hidden away quite well, in fact.'

'That's unusual,' I said. 'Russian oligarchs tend to be like everyone else when it comes to security: they want ex-SAS or Spetsnaz if they can get them. Paras at a pinch. But military intelligence? Isn't that overdoing it a bit?'

'Maybe it's a status thing,' Alex said. 'So he looks impressive when he's hobnobbing with his oligarch mates.'

'Does he have a name?' Mrs Allenby asked.

'Assuming it's his real one,' Ryan said. 'Major Douglas Weston.'

'And how long has he been working for Shlovsky?' I asked.

'We don't know,' Ryan said. 'Honourable discharge five years ago. After that, he's been off the radar.'

'Why Shlovsky?' I persisted. 'What's the connection?'

'Maybe through Titov, somehow?' Alex suggested. 'Maybe he got passed over for promotion and his Russian oppo persuaded him to move over to the dark side.'

I nodded. 'The pay's got to be better. Or it could just be he holds a grudge. People have betrayed their country for less.'

'All of that is beside the point at this moment,' Mrs Allenby cut in. 'What we need to know is if he can lead us to the terrorists. And that means one more trip to our observation point, I'm afraid.'

I felt a fluttering in my guts. I was glad to have an excuse to go back to the house. After the dream, there were things I wanted to ask Daisy. But I was also nervous about what I'd find there. Maybe one of those sharks would decide to break the surface.

'Hopefully it will be a quick in and out job,' Mrs Allenby continued. 'Just long enough to install a remote video camera so we can see if Weston goes AWOL again.'

'And if he does?' Alex asked.

'Then you and Logan follow.'

* * *

It was gone 2 a.m. when I finally got to the boarded-up window. I knew we needed to get that camera in there ASAP: if Weston made his move before we were set up, that could be our one chance down the tubes. But still, I wasn't going to hurry. I wanted to make sure no one else had been in the house since my last visit. As I loosened the bolts on the metal plate, all seemed to be in order. I hoisted myself in and re-secured it, then swept my torch over the floor, looking for fresh footprints in the dust.

Nothing.

When I got to the room, the first thing I did was open the shutters and set up the camera, making sure it was focused on the driveway. I switched it on and waited for Alan's text, confirming the connection was live. Thirty seconds later the ping told me we were in business.

Only then did I turn and look for Daisy.

She was where I'd left her, still slumped in the corner, a bag of bones slowly turning into dust.

What the hell had I been expecting? That she'd shifted to a more comfortable position? That she'd done something new with her hair? Not for the first time, I wondered if I was entirely sane.

But then, if it meant no longer seeing Sarah and Joseph, sanity was overrated. I'd stick with being nuts.

Now that I'd set up the camera and checked it was working, I had no reason to stick around. Alex would already be waiting in the car a hundred metres or so down the road in a little turn-off. And if Weston appeared on Alan's screen now and

I wasn't there, she'd fucking kill me. But I decided to take that chance.

I sat down with my back against the wall just a few feet from Daisy. She must have been so used to having the place to herself, I didn't want to crowd her. But I wanted to be close enough to feel it, if there was anything she wanted to tell me.

'I had a dream last night, Daisy. And you were in it.'

I thought I'd try that for starters, see if it got a reaction. I paused, then went on.

'I can only remember bits now. But it was a wedding. You've never been married, have you, Daisy?'

I'd propped the torch up on my daysack so the beam wasn't aimed right at her. I didn't want her to think this was an interrogation. I shuffled a bit closer so I could see her properly. Did a shadow pass over her face?

'Anyway, Viktor Shlovsky was there. He was giving you away, in fact. And the bridegroom, you probably don't know him—'

I didn't get any further.

The room was suddenly filled with a piercing, high-pitched sound, except that it wasn't really a sound, even though it was making my head hurt; it was more like a terrible, silent scream that went on and on until I couldn't bear it any more.

I don't know how long I sat there with my hands clamped over my ears. After a while, the screaming in my head died down to a sort of buzzing, like white noise, and the pain just became a dull ache. I opened my eyes and saw something glinting on the floor.

I crawled forward on my hands and knees. How had I never noticed this before? It was wedged into a crack between the floorboards by Daisy's feet. I fished a coin out of my pocket and waggled it around until it popped out onto the floor, a dull gold in the torchlight. I picked it up. It was a cufflink. I turned it over in my fingers. On one side was some sort of engraving but it was too grimy to make out. I spat on it and gave it a rub on my shirt, then looked again.

A grinning skull, complete with crossbones, looked back.

23

Alex gave me a sideways look as I got in the car. 'You took your time.'

'Yeah, sorry. It took me a while to get the camera set up right. Alan always makes things sound a doddle, you know what he's like.'

The truth was, I'd needed a few minutes to myself after I'd exited the house and secured the window again, just standing in the undergrowth, listening to the night sounds, waiting until my heart rate calmed down a bit. My skin still felt clammy, like I had a fever, sweating and freezing at the same time. I wiped a drop of sweat out of my eyes, hoping Alex would think it was just the physical effort of getting in and out of the house.

'Well, it seems to be working all right now.'

I nodded. 'We could be in for a long night, then. You brought your knitting?' After what had happened in the house, I needed to try and lighten the mood.

'Duh.' Alex put her fist to her forehead. 'I knew there was something I'd forgotten.'

I shook my head. 'Call yourself a covert surveillance operative.'

She smiled and we didn't say anything for a minute or two. We'd done this enough times before to be comfortable just sitting in silence.

'D'you want to have a kip for a bit? It doesn't need both of us. You look like you could do with it, if I'm honest.'

I shook my head. 'Nah. I'm good.'

In fact, a nap was exactly what I needed. But I had a feeling there was a big, fat nightmare with my name on it, just waiting to jump on me if I nodded off. The last thing I wanted to do was start gibbering like a maniac with Alex in the car.

'Suit yourself. I might have forty winks, then.'

'Go for it.'

Alex put the front passenger seat back and got herself comfortable.

We were parked up in a little lane just off the avenue, about halfway down, well out of sight of Shlovsky's place, but close enough that if Weston headed south we could pick him up, and if he went past us going the other way, he wouldn't spot us. The challenge was going to be keeping him in sight without making ourselves conspicuous, given that there wasn't going to be a hell of a lot of other traffic around to give us cover.

That, of course, was if he showed his face at all. Most likely we'd be here all night with fuck all to show for it. And the next night after that. And the next.

And then?

We'd turn on the news one morning and find out the attack had already happened.

I didn't want to think about that.

I looked over at Alex. With her biker's jacket, scuffed jeans and boots, she looked like a tough cookie, but right now she was sleeping like a baby. I watched her hands, clasped together on her lap, gently rising and falling with her breath, and felt a stirring of envy. *All right for some*, I thought.

'You look tired, Logan.'

My eyes flicked to the rear-view mirror. Sarah was sitting in the back. Joseph was fidgeting in his seat next to her, trying to undo his seatbelt.

'Not you as well,' I said.

'Well it's true. What you need is a good night's sleep.'

'Chance would be a fine thing,' I said.

'Bad dreams?' she asked.

I suddenly remembered how the Daisy dream had begun, with the three of us sitting together in the church. And at the same time, the feeling came back: that I was dressed wrong or showing her up, somehow. I started feeling guilty.

'She seems nice,' Sarah said.

I frowned. 'Who?'

'Lucy, of course.'

'Oh, right, yeah – you know about her?'

She smiled. 'It was a good thing, what you did. She was lucky you turned up at the right moment.'

I shrugged. 'I don't know if she felt all that lucky.'

'Don't be silly. And it's nice you talked to her.'

'I . . . I'm not . . .' I suddenly felt tongue-tied. I didn't even know what I was trying to say, but whatever it was stuck in my throat.

'It's all right, you know.'

I coughed, trying to get my voice back. 'What is?'

'Liking her.'

'I don't. I mean—'

'It's *all right*!'

Joseph stopped fiddling with the seat belt and looked up at her. He wasn't used to her raising her voice.

I glanced over at Alex, but she hadn't stirred.

Sarah kissed the top of Joseph's head. When she spoke, her voice was quieter. 'Look, Logan, I know you love us. And you always will. And one day we'll all be together again.'

'Sarah—'

I tried to butt in but she ignored me.

'But even though it's hard sometimes, you're still here for a reason. To save people.'

'I did save her,' I insisted.

'You stopped her from ending her life. But that's only doing half the job. If you're really going to save her, you need to help her to live again.'

'How am I supposed to do that?' I said, but I already knew what she was going to say.

'And she can help you, too.'

I twisted round in my seat. 'Look, Sarah—'

My phone pinged. A second later, Alex's did, too. She snapped awake and reached into her jacket pocket.

'Target on the move,' she said.

I looked in the mirror. Sarah and Joseph were gone.

I breathed in, trying to focus. 'Which way?'

'South.'

I turned the engine on and nosed out onto the Avenue. Up ahead I could see a pair of red tail-lights.

'Black Bimmer. That's him,' Alex said.

The trick now was to tuck ourselves out of sight while maintaining visual contact. Easy enough as we crawled up the road after him, but there was a set of traffic lights at the top of the Avenue and what we definitely didn't want was to get stuck there together bumper to bumper. The lights were green as he reached the junction.

'Come on, come on,' I muttered under my breath as we started to close on him.

He made a right just as they turned red.

I pulled up at the lights. I wasn't bothered about waiting until they turned green again. I was just waiting for another vehicle to be the meat in the sandwich. The seconds ticked away. Much longer and we'd be in danger of losing him before we'd even got started. We'd have to tail him without any cover and hope for the best.

A silver-grey Mercedes went past. Perfect. I pulled out and we settled in thirty yards behind him. Just as well: once we'd squeezed past the Spaniards Inn, it was a long, dead-straight stretch ahead, with nowhere to hide.

'Is he alone?' I asked Alex.

'Alan said the picture quality wasn't great, but yeah.'

I reckoned that was a good sign. 'OK.'

The Mercedes was slowly gaining on Weston's BMW, keeping us nice and tight. With a bit of luck, we'd hit some more traffic as we headed into town and we could add some more ingredients to the sandwich.

Weston turned left at Whitestone Pond, with the Mercedes right on his tail, then carried on down the hill towards Hampstead. It felt good to have a target under my control, instead of running round in circles trying to figure out what the fuck was going on.

So long as he didn't make us, of course. I knew the longer we followed him the likelier he would. Even if he wasn't actively taking counter-surveillance measures, he'd be trained to a high level and it would just be instinct. Somewhere his brain would be logging everything he saw, and if our profile popped up more than a couple of times, he'd know it wasn't coincidence.

So the sooner he got where he was going, the better.

At the lights by the tube station, Weston carried straight on through, but the Merc turned left down the High Street, leaving us with another long, straight run down Fitzjohn's Avenue but this time without any cover. I knew there'd be plenty of traffic and therefore opportunities to merge into the background again once we got down to Swiss Cottage, but by then I was sure our presence would have already been filed away.

I'd just have to make sure we stayed invisible after that.

'You all right, Logan?' Alex asked.

'Never better,' I replied. The truth was, following a target, I was like a pig in shit. Yes, the stakes were about as high as they could be, and I knew from experience that when you thought you had everything under control, that was when some random piece of shit usually happened to fuck things up, but at least I knew what I was doing. No more dreams, no more ghosts; just follow the bad guy in the car and see where he goes.

We'd joined the traffic going past the station, a steady flow even at this hour, and managed to keep him in sight as we skirted Regent's Park and merged onto the Euston Road, heading east. Alex was looking at a map on her phone, trying to work out where he was headed, but I knew it was pointless. We'd know when we got there.

We carried on in the same direction, past Angel tube station and along City Road, like we were on a conveyor belt, sometimes with only one car between us, sometimes as many as three, but without any bumps along the road, until we turned south, towards Spitalfields.

He's too relaxed, I thought. He's not going anywhere. He's just an insomniac who gets in the car and drives around aimlessly when he can't sleep.

'What are you thinking?' Alex asked, seeing my knuckles tightening on the steering wheel.

'I don't know. It's too easy. He's too bloody casual. Either he's going nowhere or he clocked us miles back and he's just leading us on a wild goose chase.'

'Or maybe he has no reason to think anyone would be following him?' Alex suggested, but I could tell she didn't really believe it.

It turned out it was me who was getting too relaxed, though.

At that moment, with only one car between us, Weston made a sharp left and I had to brake quickly so I didn't overshoot. I hauled the wheel to the left and gave it some gas coming out of the turn, not wanting to lose sight of him before he got to the end of the street.

And then almost went into the back of him.

24

I just managed to swerve round and squeeze past him without clipping his wing mirror. Alex resisted the temptation to look back.

'Did you see the number of the house?'

I shook my head. 'That's not his destination. I think he's finally doing some counter-surveillance.'

'Fuck. What now?'

'Have a look at the map. Right or left at the end?'

Alex quickly scanned her phone. 'Left – no, right. If that really is what he's doing, he'll be waiting to see if we turn round and come back. Then, if he's still aiming to go in the same direction he was before we went on this little diversion, he'll go round the block and back onto the main road.'

'Got it.' Unless he was being very sneaky, he'd turn right at the end of the street like we did, and then right again, before finally turning left. If we took the second right instead, we could wait at the end of the street until he went past and pick him up again.

And if he didn't go past?

Fuck knows what we'd do then.

I drove on and took the second turn. I parked at the end, cut the engine and turned off the lights.

'How long do we give him?' Alex asked. It was a good question. How thorough was he going to be? Was he spooked or just going through the motions? Did he have plenty of time to get to his meet – if that's what it was – or did he need to get a move on?

'We'll give him ten minutes. Then we go looking.'

'And if we bump into him again?'

'We say we're tourists looking for Buckingham Palace and got a bit lost?'

'At three in the morning?'

'If you've got a better suggestion, I'm all ears.'

'I'd say we take a look at the house he stopped outside of. Maybe he wasn't playing games. What if he was picking someone up? In which case, maybe we should wait until they come back.'

I was sure it was a dead end, but I didn't have anything better. 'OK.'

'No, wait. There he goes.'

Damn. I'd missed it. 'Good girl.'

I turned on the engine and pulled out, then waited at the junction until another car went past before turning left. There he was. 'Got him. Now, with a bit of luck he'll think he's clean and go straight to his destination.'

After a quarter of a mile he slowed and turned right down another gloomy Edwardian terrace. There were no vehicles in between us now so I had to make a quick decision: follow and risk another contact, or keep going and risk losing him. I delayed making the turn as long as I could, then followed. We were just in time to see his tail-lights disappearing at the end of the street. I resisted the temptation to put my foot down, cautiously making the same left turn as he had. The street narrowed, hemmed in by a housing estate on one side and a row of dingy lock-ups on the other. A couple of the street lights weren't working. I scanned the road ahead, my eyes adjusting to the gloom.

There was no sign of him.

'Keep going,' Alex whispered, sensing my hesitation. I carried on past the housing estate. I slowed to a crawl as we passed a left turn, squinting down the narrow street, then drove on. Next right: same thing. Still no sign.

Suddenly a pair of red eyes appeared in the middle of the road, caught in my headlights. It was a fox, his snout deep in a black bin bag he must have dragged there. He raised his head and looked at us.

'Come on, which way now, Foxy?' I muttered under my breath.

Alex looked at me. 'What was that?'

'Nothing.'

She shook her head. 'It's not natural. He should be out in the country eating chickens, for God's sake.'

'Maybe he prefers them coated in the Colonel's secret recipe,' I said.

She sighed. 'Come on, get out of the road, you silly animal. *Shoo.*'

He showed no signs of moving. In fact, he'd gone back to rooting around in the bin bag. I skirted round him, my wheels almost scraping the kerb. He didn't even turn his head.

There was a little alley on our right. I peered down it as we passed.

'Where now?' Alex said. 'He can't have just disappeared. How the fuck did we miss him?'

I shook my head. 'He's better at this than we thought. He's taken us for mugs.'

We got to the end of the road. Right or left? I went right, knowing it was pointless. Once you'd made one wrong turn, the chances of picking up your target again were already receding fast. Two and it was a hopeless cause. Before you knew it, you were just going round in circles for the hell of it.

I saw a dark shape up ahead, then a rusting sign wonkily fixed to a lamp post: *St Saviour's Church*.

As we got closer I could see the church itself wasn't in much better shape than the sign. There was tarpaulin stretched across part of the roof and a row of windows along the side had been boarded up, like it had been stripped of all its lead and stained glass. But the big, arched front door was showing a sliver of light, so it looked like it was open for business. I'd only ever been in a church for weddings (well, one) and funerals, so I couldn't really imagine what anybody would be doing in one at three in the morning. A Black Mass, maybe? Some kind of Satanic orgy? Or was it just a bunch of lads scraping the last bits of copper off the wiring?

I slowed to get a proper look.

'Don't stop,' Alex hissed, nudging me with her elbow.

I gave her a look, but put my foot back on the gas anyway.

'He's parked up, opposite the church.'

I felt a little surge of adrenaline. 'Is he still in the car?'

'Nope. I couldn't see him, anyway.'

I carried on. The road curved round to the right, and then stopped at a fence with a spool of barbed wire at the top. On the other side I could see the wrecks of rusting cars and heaps of other junk. To the right was a low warehouse with most of its windows smashed. It looked like gentrification hadn't made it to this part of town yet.

I made a U-turn and parked up behind an abandoned van sitting on its wheel rims. Weston's car was out of sight, but we had a good view of the church.

'You're sure he's not in the car?' I asked.

'Yes.'

'You didn't see him get out?'

'Nope.'

'So we don't know where he went.'

Alex pointed at the front door of St Saviour's. 'Have a bit of faith, Logan.'

I grunted and settled myself in my seat. Nothing to do now but wait. I focused on the target and tried to get my mind into that halfway state where I was relaxed but alert. I'd decided he was a tricky fucker and I was determined I wasn't going to let him slip through our fingers again.

After twenty minutes I started to lose my grip on consciousness, like I was treading water and something was trying to pull me down into the depths. I powered down the window and took a big breath of the cold night air.

Then the door of the church opened wider and a figure slipped out. He was dressed in jeans and a dark windbreaker, but the military bearing was unmistakeable. He did a quick scan of the street and I instinctively hunkered lower in my seat, even though we were hidden by the van. Then he turned back to the church. The sliver of light had been extinguished and a second man was now pushing the heavy door shut. The two men exchanged a few words, then nodded to each other, before Weston turned his back and walked briskly towards his car. The other man stood for a few moments, looking after him, an unreadable expression on his face, allowing me to take a mental snapshot. Medium height, thinning blond hair, glasses. Difficult to see his build under the loose chinos and baggy grey pullover, but somehow I got the impression of physical frailty. There was an intensity, though: something I couldn't put my finger on. Like there was a flame burning inside him. Finally he turned and went in the opposite direction, down an alley running alongside the church.

I looked at Alex. 'Heads or tails?'

She nodded towards the alley. 'The contact. No point tailing Weston back to Shlovsky's.'

'What if he has another meet? What if this bloke was just the set-up man?'

She chewed her lip for a moment. 'I don't think so. This is our guy. I can feel it in me waters.'

'You don't want to split up? You take the car and follow Weston and I'll go with the contact?'

Alex blew out her cheeks. 'This is where we could do with some more bodies.' She shook her head. 'Sorry, wrong word. But you know what I mean. What if the contact has a car round the corner?'

'Let's take that chance.'

She nodded. 'OK.'

We heard Weston starting his car, then we caught a glimpse of his tail-lights as he did a sharp three-point turn and started back the way he'd come.

'If he acts twitchy, just let him go,' I said, opening the door and stepping out.

Alex rolled her eyes. 'Any more helpful advice, Grandad?'

I grinned and shut the door.

I entered the alley and stood still for a moment, just getting my bearings. I didn't want to get sandbagged a second time in one night. No sign of the target. Just the usual stale-piss smell and a scattering of used laughing gas canisters. One flickering street light. *Good place for a mugging*, I thought. I jogged down to the end where it opened out into a scruffy-looking housing estate. *Is this where he lives?* I looked for a window with a light on, but everywhere was dark.

Then I spotted him, walking between two of the low-rises. I looked for another way through the estate. Maybe I could head him off. I jogged left, past a patch of worn grass with a pair of rusty swings, past a couple of blocks, over a low wall, and then I was on the street again.

I stopped, hearing voices, and looked to my right. A queue had formed in front of a white van. A panel opened in the side, and someone was handing out styrofoam cups. A mobile soup kitchen. I pulled my hood down lower over my face and put my hands in my pockets. My clothes were too clean to really blend in, but if no one looked too closely, I could do a passable impression of a down and out just from the way I moved. I shambled over and joined the queue, behind a middle-aged woman with long grey dreadlocks, all the time keeping an eye out for the contact. Apart from the van and our little band of derelicts, the street was empty.

Maybe I'd guessed wrong and he hadn't come through the estate at all. *Fuck*. If I'd let him go, I'd need more than a cup of bloody soup to give me a warm feeling inside.

I shuffled forward, thinking fast. Could he have got through the estate and out onto the street before I did? Or was he still there?

Before I could decide what to do, I found myself standing in front of the hatch. Someone was holding out a cup of soup. I reached out and took it, mumbling my thanks. As I turned away I glanced back over my shoulder and for a second our eyes met.

He had a lanyard round his neck now, with some sort of ID on it. But the blond hair and the glasses hadn't changed, even though the intense expression had been replaced with a gentle smile. What really struck me, though, was the dog collar.

Weston's contact was the parish priest of bloody St Saviour's.

As soon as I was out of sight of the van I chucked the soup into the gutter and crushed the cup in my hand.

There was no avoiding the obvious conclusion. Whatever Weston was doing, it wasn't planning a terror attack. He must have woken up in the middle of the night, having a nightmare he was going to hell or something, and couldn't wait until morning to go to confession, so the man in black could tell him Jesus still loved him and he could go back to sleep.

My phone pinged. A message from Mrs Allenby. Please update.

I texted back. One word: Bust.

She took a minute to digest that, then: Reconvene 0900.

I shoved my phone back in my pocket. There was one last shred of hope. Maybe the St Saviour's jaunt was just a diversion, and the real meeting was somewhere else. But I didn't put much faith in the idea. And even if it was true, it meant Weston had already outwitted us once. No disrespect to Alex, but the chances were he'd do it again.

I didn't much fancy 'reconvening' in a few hours' time. Not unless Alex had managed to pull a rabbit out of the hat. That's if there was a rabbit in the hat in the first place, which I was beginning to seriously doubt.

Any minute I was expecting a message saying Weston was back home safely tucked up and saying his prayers.

I'd been wandering aimlessly without thinking where I

was going. I needed to get my bearings and start heading in the vague direction of the flat, otherwise I'd be halfway to Southend before I knew it.

That was when I saw the bloke with the dog. I was walking in the middle of the road, and so was he. I stepped onto the pavement so we wouldn't walk into each other.

So did he. So we would.

This was all I bloody needed. Some twat looking for easy pickings on the night shift. Maybe I'd still been unconsciously walking with the homeless shuffle, giving off a vulnerable vibe. I pulled myself up straighter, making myself look like a tougher proposition. With a bit of luck, he'd think better of it and just carry on his way.

The dog seemed to have other ideas, unfortunately. It was a nasty-looking pit bull, all neck, jaws and teeth, and I could tell from the way he was struggling to keep it on the leash that it was locked on to me like a guided missile.

We stopped at ten yards. He was wearing jeans and a white T-shirt, both half a size too small, so there was no missing he worked out. I could have stepped back into the road to let him pass, but by this point that was only going to make me seem weak. A victim.

Best to look like I couldn't give a fuck and wait it out. You never know, maybe he just wanted a light.

'What are you looking at, you cunt?' he said.

Maybe not.

I grinned, shifting my weight onto the balls of my feet. 'Just admiring your poodle. What's his name?'

He grinned back. 'You can pet him if you like.' He squatted, unclipping the lead from the dog's collar.

I didn't wait, just turned and started sprinting back the way I'd come, trying to think where I could find a weapon. Behind me I heard the rattle of chains as the dog was set free, then the scrape of its nails on the tarmac as it came after me.

How long before it caught me up and sank those jaws into my leg? Over distance I was pretty sure I could outlast it. Pit bulls were bred for power, not stamina, and I was still in decent nick. But that was if I made it past the first twenty metres.

There was an alley off to my left, black bin bags spilling out. Was there an actual old-fashioned dustbin? A dustbin lid would be handy right now.

A shape materialized from between the bags. A fox. He took one look at the pit bull hurtling towards him and dived back into the alley, scattering refuse in his wake.

I had a split second to make up my mind. Forgetting about the dustbin lid, I veered right.

Behind me I heard a furious tearing and scraping as the dog plunged through the bin bags after the fox.

I stopped to get some air into my lungs. With a bit of luck, Foxy would know a way out of the alley and take the bastard pit bull with him. I looked round. His owner was marching towards me, the chain wrapped round his fist.

'That dog cost me two grand,' he snarled. 'If he gets fucked up, you fucking owe me.'

'Fair enough,' I said. I pulled my wallet out of my back pocket and held it out to him. 'Should be a few hundred in there, mate.'

He narrowed his eyes. He looked at me, then at the wallet. The next thing he felt was my fist crashing into his cheekbone. He went down like a puppet with its strings cut, hitting the back of his head on the tarmac.

I stood over him. His eyes were closed. I couldn't tell if he was breathing.

I was tired. It had been a long night with nothing to show for it except bruised knuckles. I had dead people running around in my head.

I didn't particularly care if he joined them.

I gave him a kick in the ribs. He grunted. Not dead, then. His lucky night.

I put my wallet back in my pocket and headed home.

25

It was nine in the morning and I felt like I was at a funeral. It didn't help that Mrs Allenby was dressed in black to match the mood.

'Mr Logan, if you would like to brief us on last night's activities.'

I gave them the shortened version: Weston had his meeting at a church in a run-down part of the East End. His 'contact' turned out to be the priest.

'Not what we were expecting,' Mrs Allenby said.

'He couldn't have met anyone else? The priest wasn't just the go-between?' Ryan asked.

I shook my head. 'Nope.'

'St Saviour's, you said?'

I shrugged. 'Does it matter?'

'Let's have a look, anyway,' Ryan said.

I went and made myself a coffee, trying to think what our next move was going to be.

'Paul Martindale. Made parish priest of St Saviour's two years ago. Does a lot of outreach for the homeless, drug addicts, people with mental health problems, etcetera. Bits and pieces in the local paper, building an inclusive community, blah blah blah.'

I came back and sat down. 'Just your average happy-clappy do-gooder, then.'

Mrs Allenby tapped her pencil on the table. 'He can't be.'

I made a face. 'Why not?'

'Because Weston went to see him, alone, in his church, at three in the morning. There's something about that that's just not right.'

Mrs Allenby turned to Ryan. 'This "outreach". Do you have any more details?'

'Let me see. He runs a soup kitchen three nights a week. Then he has what he calls "surgeries", when homeless people are invited to come to the church to develop a "spiritual action plan".'

'When are those?'

'Ah . . . Mondays and Fridays.'

Mrs Allenby wrote something down on her notepad. 'Today is Wednesday. On Friday, Mr Logan, I would like you to attend one of these surgeries.'

I looked at her. 'You're kidding.'

'Not at all. I want us to take a closer look at the parish priest of St Saviour's, and the best way to do that is to see him at work. Mr Logan, you have less than forty-eight hours to work up your legend and make yourself presentable. I'm told this is one of your specialities.'

It was true. Having grown up on the streets, passing myself off as an authentic down and out was basically a piece of piss. Which was why as an A4 covert surveillance officer, I'd usually been the one who volunteered. I used to say you never really appreciated clean clothes, a warm bed and a full stomach until you hadn't had any of them for a few days. But usually it was a question of just sitting in your sleeping bag collecting pennies while you kept an eye on targeted premises, watching who went in and who came out. Apart from the odd conversation with a kindly soul who wanted to buy you a sandwich instead of giving you money you could waste on drink or drugs, or a beat copper who wanted to move you on, you didn't have to talk much. In fact, the less you talked, the better.

This was going to be different, however. Mrs Allenby wanted me to try and worm my way into St Saviour's outreach programme, and that would mean really living the part.

And what then? What was she expecting me to find?

'Sure. Not a problem.'

'And while you're doing your homework, I want Mr Oldfield to keep digging to see what else we can find out about Paul Martindale.'

'Do you want me to wear a wire, or anything?'

She thought for a moment. 'Not at this stage. Mr Woodburn, if you could have one or two options prepared, in case we need video or audio later on, that would be appreciated.'

She turned to Alex. 'In the meantime, we will continue to monitor the feed from the house. If Weston moves again, I want you to be ready to follow. Just in case we're going down a blind alley.'

Yeah, just in case, I thought.

That seemed to be it. We all had our tasks. Mrs Allenby picked up her notepad. I caught Alex's eye and she gave me a subtle nod.

'There is one more thing,' I said.

Mrs Allenby put her notepad down again. 'Yes?'

'We've been thinking,' I continued. 'The four of us. About Craig and Claire. Whether their deaths were entirely accidental.'

She pursed her lips. 'Is there any evidence they weren't?'

'Not exactly. It's more a question of probability. What are the chances? And a couple of us may have been targeted, too.'

'*May have been?*'

'Yes.' Now that I'd actually said it, it sounded lame, even to me.

'By whom?'

'That's the point. We don't know. And the only way we can find out is to pin down a connection, something that ties Claire and Craig together, apart from the fact that they were both part of Blindeye.'

'Which we must assume nobody knows. I take it you've already started looking for this connection.'

I glanced at Ryan.

'Yeah,' he said. 'So far we've come up with nothing. But that's because most of what we need to see is classified. *Very* classified.'

I watched the penny dropping for Mrs Allenby.

'Out of the question,' she said. 'You're forgetting I'm retired. I don't have security access any more, whatever you may think. I would have to ask the Director General, and if you think he's going to remove classified files from Thames House and hand them over to you, on the basis of . . . "probability", you've got another think coming.'

She got up to go.

'I suggest we all get on with the job in hand, and stop wasting our time with far-fetched conspiracy theories.'

Great. Now we had the worst of both worlds: we'd let the cat out of the bag but had nothing to show for it.

I caught her eye, and saw a glint of steel.

I'd like to see your file an' all, I thought to myself.

26

When it came to the game of life, Stevie Nichols was definitely one of the losers. Dumped in an orphanage at birth, he was picked on by the other kids as soon as he could walk and talk and they had something to take the mickey out of. Maybe his mother being a teenage alcoholic had affected his brain, but he was always a little bit on the slow side compared to the rest of them, not that any of them were exactly booking their places on *University Challenge*. He was handy with his fists, though, and quickly learned that smacking people in the mouth before they'd had a chance to open it was a good way of making sure they didn't say anything nasty. Unfortunately, it also meant he was soon in trouble with the law, and since the only lesson he'd ever really taken to heart was that if you were in trouble the best thing to do was to lash out, the trouble only got worse.

When there was casual work on building sites to be had, Stevie could make enough to have money in his pocket, even if most of it went to the landlords of various pubs in Kentish Town before it ever reached home. When he couldn't get work on the building sites, Stevie's income took a nosedive.

The truth was, he wasn't really cut out for the service economy. Telling people to have a nice day, rather than to go and fuck themselves, didn't exactly come naturally. McDonald's failed to see the funny side, and soon every coffee shop and fast-food restaurant in north-west London knew that taking on Stevie Nichols was the quickest way to get sued by an angry customer with a fat lip.

The streets took him in with open arms, as if they'd always known this was where he belonged, and even though it was no fun being cold and tired and hungry most of the time, deep inside, a part of him was relieved. At least he didn't have to try and fit in any more. Shops would still take your money, even if they wouldn't give you the time of day, and when he crouched in a doorway out of the rain with a half-full bottle in his hand, he had a feeling that this was as good as life was going to get.

Still, there were some advantages to being Stevie Nichols. When I was Stevie, for instance, I didn't have to worry about the fact that my wife was encouraging me to have some sort of relationship with another woman.

And I didn't have to worry about whether, deep down, I wanted to.

I also didn't have to worry that somebody might be trying to kill me.

Yep, being Stevie Nichols might be no picnic, but for me it was beginning to feel like a holiday. Rainy Southend rather than Ibiza, maybe, but a holiday nonetheless. And if he woke up with a sore head from time to time, at least it didn't feel like it was going to explode with all the crazy shit going on inside it.

It was one in the morning and I'd walked the last mile or so. I didn't want any of the other dossers who turned up at St Saviour's seeing Alex dropping me off. It also gave me time to fully become Stevie: to walk and talk and think like he did. By the time I turned the corner, dressed in out-of-fashion grey trackies with a matching top, and saw the church looming up ahead, I was in the zone: lonely, confused and generally pissed off with everything, but with a sort of numbness over it all like a grey cloud.

The church door was open all the way this time, spilling warm yellow light onto the steps, where a man in a stained raincoat and pinstriped trousers, wearing mismatched trainers, one blue, one red, was rolling a cigarette. I sat down beside him and he looked up warily. He had grey hair tied in a ponytail, and a patchy beard. He could have been anything between forty and sixty.

'Me last one,' he said.

I shrugged. 'I don't smoke.'

'Bollocks,' he said, following it up with a rasping cough that might possibly have been a laugh. 'I bet you don't drink neither.' He looked at me more closely. 'You one of them vegans, then?'

'What?'

'Vegans. They're all cunts. I fucking hate them. You better not be a vegan.'

'Yeah, I'm the king of the fucking vegans,' I muttered.

He cough-laughed again, his hand shaking so much he started spilling tobacco on the steps. 'Fuck,' he said, trying to scrape it up again.

'Here.' I handed him a couple of shreds. Or it might have just been dirt.

'What you doing out of your palace, then?' he said with a grin.

'I heard this bloke was all right.'

He nodded to himself. 'He don't give you no money, though.'

'What does he do, then?'

'Talks, mostly.'

'What, Jesus, and all that?' I spat onto the steps. 'I had enough of that shit from the nuns.'

'It's a fucking church, you cunt. He's a cunting priest. What do you expect?'

At this point, I could feel Stevie getting annoyed. My fists were already clenched, my throat tight. There was a faint buzzing in my head, like a wasp had got trapped between my ears. I wanted to hit someone, this bloke for preference. I looked away until the feeling passed.

He finished rolling his fag. 'You got a light?'

'I told you. I don't smoke.'

He threw the roll-up into the bushes and got to his feet. 'Bollocks. You comin' in, then?'

'All right.'

'I'll introduce you. What's your name?'

'Stevie.'

He held out a hand with yellow-stained fingers. It was shaking slightly. 'Augustine,' he said. 'Stupid fucking name, I know.'

'Then change it,' I said. 'It's easy.'

Outside, the church looked in need of repair. Inside, it was almost derelict. Half the pews were missing and it looked as if someone had taken a sledgehammer to the font. There was a ladder against the wall, and bits and pieces of timber on the floor. The light was coming from a hurricane lamp on a table.

As my eyes adjusted to the semi-dark, I looked for Martindale. At first it seemed like the church was empty. Then I spotted him in a corner, under a boarded-up window. He was sitting on a packing case, reading. He put the book down and looked over.

'Welcome to St Saviour's,' he said. His voice was surprisingly strong. He gestured to his ramshackle surroundings. 'The house of God.'

Augustine nudged me forward. 'This is Stevie. He's a vegan.'

Martindale smiled. He was wearing camouflage combat trousers and a grey hoodie. There was no sign of the dog collar.

'He's taking the piss,' I said. Then all those beatings from the nuns kicked in. 'Sorry.'

Martindale waved a hand dismissively. 'You think Christ never swore? Not even when he was overturning the money-lenders' tables? He felt anger, just like we all do. And what about when he was carrying the cross, being abused by the soldiers? And then on the cross. Remember, he was a man as well as the Son of God.'

'What did he say then? "Jesus fucking Christ"?' Augustine slapped his knee as he went into a fit of coughing.

Martindale smiled gently. 'I've missed your humour, Gus. Remember, that comes from God, too.' He waited until Augustine's coughing fit had passed. 'How are things with you? Did the hostel work out? I did talk to Mr Sykes.'

Augustine nodded. 'Yeah, he said.' He licked his lips. 'You haven't got a fag, have you?'

Martindale felt in the pocket of his combats and came up with a roll-up and a box of matches. I thought of aid workers handing out sweets to starving children.

Augustine took them, nodding. 'Bless you.'

'Outside, if you wouldn't mind,' Martindale said.

When Augustine had gone, he gestured to another packing case. 'Please, sit. So, Stevie, what brought you to St Saviour's?'

I clenched and unclenched my fists. 'I dunno. People talking, you know. Said you were all right.'

He smiled. '"For a priest", no doubt. And what did they say I could do for you?'

I looked at my feet. 'Dunno, really.'

'If you need food, there's a van serving soup, later. But I can't give you a bed for the night. The diocese, I'm afraid – not to mention the council . . .'

'Right,' I said, as if I had the faintest idea what the diocese and the council were doing. Just being cunts, I supposed, if experience was anything to go by.

'I thought you could give me some help, like.'

'With finding somewhere to stay?'

'No, I'm all right. It gets a bit shit in the winter, like, but it's all right now.'

'What about health issues? Are you drinking? Taking drugs?'

'Nah, not really. I hate fucking junkies, anyway, you know. Slit your fucking throat for tuppence. I try and keep to myself, like.'

'What about family?'

I winced, feeling old memories, long dead, being stirred up.

'Never had any.'

I glanced up. He was looking at me steadily, like he was X-raying me. But I was confident all he would see was Stevie Nichols all the way through, like a stick of rock.

He took his glasses off and started polishing them with a tissue. 'Something must have brought you here.'

'Yeah, I suppose.'

'You felt you needed something. And you thought you might find it here.'

I kneaded my hands together nervously. 'Look, maybe I should be on my way, like.'

'Why? Something brought you here, so we ought to try and find out what it was, don't you think?'

There was something in his eyes that definitely gave you the shivers. For a split second I wondered if he knew I was a fake. I considered picking up a lump of wood and chucking it through a window. At least that would have been in character.

'Do you believe in God?' he asked eventually.

'Used to. When I was little. Didn't have much choice, like. Get a caning, otherwise.'

'And now?'

'Don't see the point. I believe in hell, like. Reckon I've seen it. But heaven? Clouds and angels and all that? I mean, who thought that up? Walt Disney?'

I wondered if I'd gone too far, but he seemed pleased. 'Oh, I agree with you. If heaven exists, it certainly won't be like that. And perhaps the reason people see it wrong, is because they've been looking for it in the wrong place. Have you ever thought of that?'

I squinted at him. 'What do you mean?'

He spread his hands. 'Maybe it's here.'

I looked around, an uncertain expression on my face.

'I mean, perhaps it *could* be here. It's up to us to create it. The world's a long way from being perfect at the moment. You know that as well as anyone. But maybe that's only because we've let the forces of darkness get the upper hand.'

'Yeah,' I said eventually, genuinely confused. What was he on about?

He stood up and put his hand on my shoulder. I thought maybe he was going to bless me, but he just gave it a squeeze then turned towards the door, putting his hands in his pockets.

'I think you've been searching, Stevie. You don't know what for, but that's OK. That's normal. In fact, it's part of the process. And your search has led you here. But let's see if this is your real destination. Go away and think about what I've said. Then, if you want to, come back. Does that make sense?'

'Yeah, sure.' I sucked in a breath as I got to my feet. My joints were sore from all those nights in freezing doorways.

'Be safe. God be with you. And perhaps we'll meet again soon,' he said.

Outside, I looked for Augustine, but he was gone. Maybe the roll-up was all he'd come for. Fair enough: when you were on the scrounge, putting up with a bit of Jesus Loves You bullshit was the price you had to pay, and tonight he'd got a freebie.

But what had led Douglas Weston to St Saviour's? Not the prospect of a cigarette and a mug of soup, I was fairly certain. So did he just see a star one night and decide to follow it down the City Road? Or was there a lot more to Paul Martindale than met the eye?

I started walking. After a couple of minutes, my arthritic knees started to loosen up. I lengthened my stride and started to feel the strength coming back into my limbs. I was becoming more and more myself with every step. Stevie Nichols got smaller and smaller, then gradually faded away, as if he didn't exist.

27

I got to the Clearwater office early, hoping I could catch Alan before Mrs Allenby got there. As usual, he was tinkering with some electronic equipment as if he hadn't moved since the last time I'd seen him, the only difference being he now had a fresh mug of black coffee steaming in front of him. He pressed a couple of buttons on a small black box then bashed away at his laptop for a few moments, before looking up.

'So how'd things go at St Saviour's?'

I sat down. 'Hard to say. Martindale's an interesting character. Is it OK if we wait for the debrief? I wanted to ask you something before the boss gets here.'

He looked intrigued. 'Sure. What is it?'

'Are you still monitoring the calls from the house?'

'Not really. We can only pick up Mrs Shlovsky's calls and I think we've established she doesn't know anything. Mostly she's calling her girlfriends when she gets a bit tipsy, that sort of thing. Then she calls up Anastasia every couple of days for a mother–daughter catch-up. That's about it.'

I nodded. 'Can you do me a favour? When she calls Anastasia, can you listen in on those calls for me?'

He scratched his chin. 'I guess. It's pretty boring stuff. Like listening to the Kardashians, you know? It's actually more interesting in Russian, before I can translate it.'

I grinned. 'Don't worry, I just want you to pick up one or two keywords. Well, one, actually.'

'Which is?' He grabbed a notepad and picked up a pen.

I put a hand on his arm. 'Don't write anything down, OK? This is just between you and me, off the books. No need for anyone else to know.'

'Bloody hell, Logan. What are you up to?'

'Just trust me, Alan.' I gave him my most winning smile. 'When have I ever let you down before?'

He shook his head. 'Now you've really got me worried.' He pushed the notepad away. 'OK, what is it.'

I paused, feeling like I was standing on the edge of a precipice.

'Daisy.'

He looked bemused. 'Like the flower?'

'Yep.'

The click of the door closing made me look round. Mrs Allenby was hanging up her coat. I turned back to Alan, a finger to my lips. He nodded dubiously.

Alex and Ryan arrived a few minutes later, and we all busied ourselves with getting a brew before sitting down at the conference table. Mrs Allenby got out her notepad and gold pencil.

'Before Mr Logan tells us about his meeting last night, I would like an update on what we know about our subject, Paul Martindale. Mr Oldfield?'

Ryan already had his laptop open. 'He's not one for social media, I'm afraid. Doesn't seem to be his style.'

'Perhaps also not the best way to communicate with people living on the streets who may not have the latest smartphone?' Mrs Allenby added with a thin smile.

'Yes, quite. Anyway, we do know he studied theology at Trinity College, Oxford, but left without taking his degree. He disappeared off the radar for a year or two before turning up at a Franciscan monastery near Carlisle. But that doesn't last long, for some reason. Next thing he's made parish priest of St Jude's in a little village in Wiltshire, but gets into a bit of bother with the locals about letting heroin addicts use the church, so he leaves there, and then a few months later he gets the job at St Saviour's, which had been vacant for a while.'

'Not exactly a plum job, then,' Mrs Allenby said. 'It sounds like our Mr Martindale has had a somewhat fractious relationship with the church authorities.'

'A bit of a rebel, I'd say,' Ryan agreed. 'The Franciscans are big on poverty, so you can see why they might appeal to him.'

'But maybe not the monastic life,' Mrs Allenby said, 'since he didn't stay with them long. Too cut off from the real world. He likes to get his hands dirty, I think.'

'He must be like a pig in shit at St Saviour's, then,' I said.

Mrs Allenby gave me a look, then turned back to Ryan. 'Do we know anything more about his time at Oxford?'

'Not really. He didn't make a splash in any of the university societies, if that's what you mean.'

'What about his studies?'

'Like I say, he didn't stay the course, but not because he was a lousy student. He got top marks in his first-year exams.'

'Interesting.' Mrs Allenby tapped her gold pencil on the desk. 'Did he have any special areas of interest?'

Ryan scrolled though whatever documents he was looking at. 'He was writing a dissertation on the theology of the crusades, apparently, when he left.'

Mrs Allenby nodded to herself, making a note.

Alex had her arms crossed and was shaking her head. 'This is all very fascinating, but what could it possibly have to do with the Russians? Martindale might be a bit of a rebel, as priests go, but apart from letting junkies shoot up in the vestry, what's he ever done? Do you honestly think he's taking orders from the Kremlin to blow up the Houses of Parliament? Why would he? It doesn't make any sense.'

Mrs Allenby looked up at her mildly. 'Patience, my dear. Let's gather all the pieces, and then see if we can fit them together.' She turned to me. 'So, Mr Logan, what was Mr Martindale like in the flesh? I take it you did meet with him?'

'Yeah. We talked for a few minutes, that's all.'

'Just you and him?'

'There was another homeless bloke but he buggered off.'

'And what did you talk about?'

'The usual stuff. Did I believe in God? What had brought me to St Saviour's? He wanted to know if I had any family. He seemed to have a thing about creating heaven on earth.

Then he sent me on my way, said come back when I'd thought about things.'

Mrs Allenby scribbled on her notepad. 'Interesting.'

'You reckon? I mean, he definitely had something about him, a charisma, you know. But apart from that . . .'

She looked at me. 'So how did you feel? When he dismissed you.'

I thought about it for a moment, trying to remember what it felt like being Stevie. That sense of being on the outside of everything. Frustration. Anger, simmering away constantly like a saucepan on a low heat. My fists clenched instinctively under the table.

'Pissed off, I suppose. Like I was expecting him to do something for me, to help me, and he wouldn't.'

She nodded. 'You were expecting a quid pro quo. Sit through a sermon and you get a cup of tea and a bun, that sort of thing.'

'Yeah, he said to think about what had brought me to St Saviour's before coming back. Like it was some sort of test.'

Mrs Allenby smiled. 'It was. And now we have to make sure you pass it.'

Alex looked confused. 'What do you mean? I don't get it.'

'Classic recruiting technique, my dear,' Mrs Allenby said. 'He's sorting the wheat from the chaff, finding out how you react to being rejected. Do you shrug your shoulders and slink away? Or does it make you determined to do whatever he wants to be accepted?'

I thought about it. How did Stevie feel? Like he wanted

to set fire to the church and watch it burn down from a cosy doorway with a bottle of vodka, probably. Actually . . . no. I waited, letting the feeling of being Stevie grow stronger. When Martindale talked about something having led him to the church, Stevie felt something he'd very rarely felt before. Belonging. It didn't matter what he was supposed to belong to; just the feeling of being accepted, of being where you were supposed to be, was enough. Deep down in the dark of his lonely, pissed-off soul, he felt a tiny flame bursting into life. He desperately wanted Martindale to say, 'Yes, Stevie, no doubt about it, you were led here, to me.' Maybe Mrs Allenby was on to something after all.

'So if Martindale's recruiting down and outs, what's he recruiting them for?' Ryan asked.

'And what's the deal with Weston? He's not a down and out; he's living on Billionaire's Row, for God's sake,' Alex added.

Mrs Allenby looked at us impatiently, as if we were a particularly stupid remedial maths class.

'To answer the first question, Mr Logan needs to make sure he passes Martindale's test. Then, hopefully, we will find out. And the answer to the first question should also provide the answer to the second.'

'So what do I need to do?' I asked, feeling a little tremor of excitement from Stevie bubbling up.

Mrs Allenby looked at her notes. 'If I'm right, Martindale is looking for empty vessels.'

Alex looked at me and grinned. 'You're just what he's looking for, then, Logan.'

I didn't smile back. The Stevie part of me didn't like people taking the piss.

Mrs Allenby continued, taking no notice. 'He needs to see you're being compelled by forces beyond your control. At least, that's what you feel is happening. You want to give up your selfhood, your individuality. You want to be absorbed by something bigger than you, so you don't have to think for yourself any more.'

I thought back to my talk with Martindale. When his eyes were boring into me, was that what he was looking for? A void he could fill? He wasn't just trying to reach out a helping hand to one of life's unfortunates? It was true, he had freaked me out a little, but was that just because Stevie was weak-minded and vulnerable?

Alan spoke for the first time. 'To be honest, you make him sound a lot like an Islamic State recruiter.'

Mrs Allenby put her hands down flat on the table. 'Yes, I do rather, don't I?'

28

I decided to walk home. I needed time to figure out how I was going to play my next meeting with Martindale – or, rather, Stevie's next meeting. But I had a feeling all I really needed to do was let Stevie get on with it and just say whatever came into his head. If Martindale was looking for restless, tormented souls, desperate to be absorbed by something bigger and more powerful than themselves, then he couldn't do any better than Stevie Nichols. I already suspected that my real problem was actually going to be keeping my own head above water once Stevie had taken the plunge.

I pushed thoughts of Stevie to one side and focused on my surroundings. I needed to stay sharp and make sure I didn't miss any followers. I turned into the park. If anyone came with me, they'd be easy to spot in the open, and if they decided to wait for me at the exit on the other side, I could lose them by going through a hole in the fence and sneaking out down the back of a row of shops.

I pulled out my phone and pretended to take a call, turning 180 degrees back towards the entrance.

There was someone following me.

It was Alex. I put the phone away and waited for her to catch up.

'You were out of there a bit sharpish,' she said.

I shrugged. 'The nine to five doesn't really suit me.'

'You going back to the flat?'

'Nowhere else to go. What about you?'

'Thought I'd take the bike out, get some miles under my belt. You know me; I need to be doing something. Be good to get out of London. And I can practise my counter-surveillance drills while I'm at it.'

'Sounds good. What held you up?'

She rolled her eyes. 'Mrs Allenby wanted a word.'

'About you speaking up about Martindale? I'm surprised you didn't get a detention.'

'No, not that. It was about you.'

I gave her a quizzical look. 'Me?'

'She wanted to know whether I thought you were unstable. "Coming apart at the seams" was the phrase she used.'

'And?'

'I told her the truth.'

'Jesus, I fucking hope not.'

'I said you'd been through a tough time, and you still had some dark moments, but when it came to the crunch you still had what it takes.'

I swallowed. 'I hope that's true.'

'You don't think so?'

'Yeah, I mean . . .'

I suddenly realized there was so much I wanted to tell

her. About Sarah. About Daisy. About Lucy. Alex was my only real friend – the only living one, anyway – and I desperately wanted to empty out all the crazy thoughts filling my head in front of her and let her sort them out.

But I knew I couldn't risk doing that. Not if I wanted to keep her as a friend. Plus, what if she then told Mrs Allenby what sort of nutjob her partner really was? Alex was as loyal as they come, but if she thought I was going to compromise the operation and possibly risk the lives of the rest of the team, that would put her in a tough situation.

'Yeah, I'm good,' I said finally. 'You don't have to worry about me.'

She gave me a long look, then took my arm and we started walking along a path that skirted round the edge of the park. 'OK, good. I'll cross that off my list. It's not like we haven't got anything else to worry about.'

'Like Mrs Allenby stonewalling over the files?'

'Exactly. But if she's not on our side, whose side is she on?'

I shook my head. 'I can't figure it out. Maybe she really does think we're just being paranoid.'

'And . . .'

'Maybe we are.'

She frowned. 'So what's the plan? Wait until someone else gets killed, and go, "Aha! See!"'

I shrugged. 'Maybe that's the only way we're going to get those files.'

'And then we can use them as a bloody tombstone. Brilliant.'

'If you've got a better idea . . .'

'I'm going to get on the bike. Put myself out there. See if I pick up a tail.'

'And if you do?'

'I'll see if I can draw them out of their comfort zone, funnel them somewhere where we can box them in. I'll text you.'

I didn't like the sound of that. Alex knew as well as I did we didn't have the manpower to pull off that kind of stunt. It was just frustration making her think like that. And when you got frustrated, that's when you started making bad decisions. But I was hardly the one to tell her that, was I?

'Watch yourself, yeah?'

She grinned. 'Always.' Then she gave me a peck on the cheek and walked away.

I watched her strolling casually towards the entrance across the grass, wondering if I was doing the right thing, keeping everything bottled up. The trouble was, once you'd pulled the cork, there was no getting it back in, was there?

I pulled my phone out and checked for missed calls. Nothing. I hadn't realized it until that moment, but I'd been waiting for Lucy to call again. Was it a good sign that she hadn't? Did that mean everything was OK? She didn't need my help any more? Or did it mean she was looking at a big glass of wine and a bottle of pills at this precise moment? I'd tried to pull her out of the abyss but maybe only halfway, and now she was being dragged back under . . .

I looked at the list of recent calls. I had her number now. All I had to do was call. My thumb hovered over the button.

Then I realized. The reason I'd wanted her to call wasn't really because I was worried about her – or, at least, that wasn't all of it. If I was being honest with myself, I wanted her to call because I wanted to hear her voice. I remembered the brush of her fingers against mine and felt a flutter of something deep, deep inside, like a voice calling faintly from the bottom of a well.

Bloody hell, Logan, what have you got yourself into?

I looked over my shoulder, expecting to see Sarah, but the park was empty.

I sat down on a bench and took a deep breath, staring at my phone as if it were an unexploded bomb.

Fuck's sake, you pathetic twat. Just make the call. If she's feeling OK, and doesn't want to see you, then fine, you've done your bit. You can stop worrying, can't you?

I pressed 'call back' and held the phone to my ear. I remembered she'd left it at home when she'd tried to jump off the bridge. Maybe she was clutching it in her hand now as she lay on her bed, eyes closed, with a half-finished glass of wine and an empty bottle of pills on the bedside table, her fingers slowly tightening around it as rigor mortis took hold. When someone finally found her, they'd have to prise it out of her grip, and if they bothered to look, they'd see one final missed call. I felt an odd stab of hurt that she hadn't left me a message before she did it.

The image of her dead body vanished as her voice interrupted my thoughts.

'Hi, this is Lucy. I'm not here right now, or I've seen who's calling and don't want to speak to you – only kidding! Leave me a message and I'll call you back.'

I tried to speak, but my breath caught in my throat. For some reason this was the last thing I was expecting: a funny voicemail message from the time before, when she had a husband, a family, a life. When she wouldn't have looked twice at a deadbeat like me.

I felt . . . what? *Jealous?*

For fuck's sake, Logan, it's a fucking recording. Pull yourself together.

'Hi . . . Lucy . . . this is Logan. You know, the guy . . . I'm just calling to see if you're OK. Er . . . if you want to meet up or something, you know, just give me a call back. I'm gonna be—'

I was cut off by the beep, feeling like a dickhead. What would she think? I sounded like a fucking teenager.

I took a deep breath, still looking at the phone. Maybe she was listening to the message now and deciding whether to call back. I realized my heart was racing. I waited some more.

After a while I put the phone back in my pocket.

Nice one, Logan. I felt an urge to throw the phone as far as I could into the bushes or pound it into bits under my boots.

I smiled ruefully to myself, realizing that was Stevie, trying to get involved. I could feel him now, squirming irritably under the surface.

I hauled myself to my feet, grimacing as I felt a little twinge in my knee.

All right, Stevie mate, let's get going. You and me, we've got stuff to do.

29

The short man put another golf ball on the rubber tee, settled himself into his stance, waggled the club head a couple of times, then took the club back nice and easy until he could feel the tension coiled in his arms and back and hips, before letting go, the club head flashing through the ball with a satisfying *thwack*. Poised at the end of his swing, his torso twisted round to the left, his eyes facing the target, he watched the ball veering off to the right before landing just short of the 150-yard marker.

'Fuck,' he said, and not for the first time.

He'd hit a hundred balls, first with a seven iron, then with a three, and now with a big, clunky titanium three wood, but never mind the club, almost all of them had followed the same trajectory: a big, fat, arse-cunting slice.

It was a good thing he'd said no to a round with Shanks and Andy. They'd have fucking murdered him, and if there was one thing he didn't like, it was looking like a twat on the golf course. That's not what he paid the exorbitant membership fees for, never mind the lessons and the clubs and all the other fucking gear. No, golf was like anything else: he played to win, and if possible to make the other fella look like a cunt into the bargain.

But today his swing was definitely off and the only person looking like a cunt was himself. He gave the bloke in the next bay a nasty look, just in case he was thinking of offering him some tips, but he was doing a good job of pretending not to have seen anything.

Smart lad, he thought.

He slammed the three wood back into his bag then walked over to the ball dispenser and put another token in, holding his basket underneath as another hundred rattled in. The basket overflowed, and several rolled onto the concrete, but he didn't bother picking them up before placing the basket by the tee.

He looked at his bag and took out the seven iron again, then put it back. Maybe he should just start with the nine. Get some rhythm back, some confidence, then take it from there. Or maybe he should just call it quits and hit a few balls on the putting green instead.

He put his hand on his hips and sucked his teeth for a moment. He definitely had a problem. But the problem wasn't his wonky driving. Or, at least, his persistent slice was only the symptom of the problem, not the cause. The cause was somewhere in his mind, and if he wanted to cure it, that's where he needed to look. There was something nagging away at him, fucking up his rhythm; he just didn't know what it was.

Could it be the job? Sure, it was taking a little more time

than he would have liked, proving to be a bit trickier than anticipated. But that was par for the course. If one thing didn't work, you did something else. You had to be adaptable. If the army had taught him one thing, it was to always have a Plan B. And then a C and a D. After that, you'd probably be dead, so there wasn't much point worrying about an E.

So what was it?

His hand strayed over the club heads, searching for the right one. His fingers came to rest on the three iron. Definitely not the club to choose if you were having a bad day. So why had his hand stopped there?

Three.

Fuck. That's it.

It wasn't anything specifically about the third hit that was bothering him. It was the fact that it was number three. He'd done a double once, but that was essentially one hit. Now the same client was commissioning three separate hits, one after the other.

So why was that a problem? He peeled off his glove and searched in one of the pockets of his club bag until he found a cigar and a lighter. Standing, looking out towards the 300-yard flag, he sparked up, puffing on the cigar until the end glowed. He didn't bother looking over at his neighbour. If he didn't like it, he could have a three iron up his arse, slice or no slice.

Perhaps he'd been blinded by greed. The money was good, top of the range, and a third job had seemed like the cherry on the top. It was always good to let cash cool off a little before putting it into circulation, but to be honest, he'd already started spending this one in his head. A new Range Rover, or something a bit flashier this time? Dory was always going on about electric, but fuck that. Or he could buy her one just to shut her up. Watch her on the phone to the garage stamping her six-inch heels when it ran out of juice in the middle of Oxford Street. That would be worth a couple of grand just for laughs. He could buy her some more jewellery; that would keep her sweet for a while. But what was the point? She couldn't tell a fake from the real thing; as long as it sparkled and made a noise when she shook her wrist, she was happy. Until she lost it down the plughole, that is.

He drew on the cigar and let the smoke out slowly, bringing his mind back into focus. OK, so he'd been distracted. He wasn't thinking properly. But even so, what was so wrong with three? They liked the way he did things – no fuss, no mess – so why go elsewhere?

Because one was . . . well, a one-off. Two was riskier, but still. Three in a row, though: that was different. That was a pattern. That was a giant fucking invitation to join the dots. And if you joined the dots, you might just see your client's face staring back at you. So why were they taking the risk? It was almost as if they didn't care if he figured out who they were.

Then it hit him. *That was it*. They didn't care. Because once he completed number three, they were going to take care of *him*. Maybe they'd get Hansen to do it. And then they'd take care of Hansen. That would be neat and tidy.

He felt a flutter of adrenaline in his chest. So what to do? Just walk away? No, that would be tipping his hand. They'd come after him anyway. He could give them back the money, tell them it was too tricky? No, same difference; once he knew who the target was, he was already compromised. He'd have to complete the job.

So, what then?

He pulled out the driver and swished it back and forth.

Then he'd just have to turn the tables, wouldn't he?

30

I'd decided to wait until a bit later this time before making my way to the church. I wanted to make sure Martindale was alone, and I didn't think there was any harm in keeping him waiting, anyway. I didn't want to seem *too* keen. But Stevie had other plans. As soon as I put on my filthy old jeans and a manky hoody, he was raring to go, his swollen feet doing a nervous tap dance on the kitchen floor as I sat with a final cup of tea, trying to relax and focus my thoughts.

'Easy, Stevie, mate. Plenty of time,' I muttered, taking another sip. But after a few minutes I'd had enough. It was like sitting on a bench trying to read the paper with a hyper-active pit bull pulling at his lead. 'Fine. Just let me take a piss, and we'll be off.'

Once we were on the street, Stevie calmed down a bit. I wasn't sure whether it was because we were on our way to St Saviour's or just because he was finally walking, concentrating on putting one aching foot in front of the other so the riot of angry thoughts in his head faded into a meaningless background buzzing. I sympathized, knowing how effortlessly I could eat up the miles when I was running if there was something in my head I was trying to run from. Stevie was no runner, but he shuffled along at a decent pace, given the state of his legs.

An hour later I turned a corner and there was St Saviour's. At first it just seemed dark and shut up, and I wondered if I'd left it too late. 'My bad, Stevie,' I muttered. But as I got closer, I could see a faint glow flickering jaggedly in one of the windows, as if someone had put a brick through it since the other night.

I tugged at the heavy door and it opened just enough for me to squeeze through. Not very inviting. So much for *me* playing hard to get. I was beginning to wonder if Martindale's homeless recruiting drive was a figment of Mrs Allenby's imagination. Maybe he wouldn't even remember me.

Inside, the only light was coming from a torch placed on the floor near a stack of planks covered in a dirty tarpaulin. The rest of the church was sunk in gloom. No sign of Martindale.

'Stevie.'

I turned in the direction of the voice and a figure materialized out of the darkness.

'I'd almost given up on you. I suppose I should have had more faith.'

Martindale was dressed in dark-grey combats and a black hoodie pulled low over his face. No wonder I hadn't seen him. It made him look like a monk – but one dressed for action. The torchlight glinted feebly off his wire-rimmed glasses and I guessed he was smiling.

'Yeah, yeah, right.'

He took me by the elbow and guided me towards the tarpaulin, then bent down and picked up the torch.

'Stay here for a moment.'

Darkness swallowed me up as he walked to the door. I heard the clank of heavy bolts as he pulled it closed.

'Good. Now no one can disturb us. Would you like a cup of tea, Stevie?'

I nodded. 'Be nice, yeah.'

'Come on, then.' He shone the torch in an arc to his right, picking out the polished brass of a doorknob. He opened the door and led me into a small, bare room. The vestry? I wasn't very clued up about the ins and outs of churches. He flipped an old-fashioned switch and a bare lightbulb hanging from the ceiling flickered on. He turned off the torch and slipped it into a pocket of his combats.

There were two camp chairs. On the flagstones between them was a thermos and two chipped green teacups. There was a small barred window, high up, and a plain wooden crucifix hanging on the whitewashed wall above an empty bookshelf. And that was it. It was more like a cell than a room – not exactly the cosy setting you'd imagine for a nice cup of tea with the local priest – and again I thought of how Martindale made me think of a monk.

We sat down and I stretched my legs out, rubbing my knees.

'Painful?' Martindale asked as he poured two cups from the thermos.

'Weather, you know. Bit of a chill and they seize up, like.'

The tea was milky with lots of sugar. Just the way Stevie liked it. I gulped it down, trying not to gag.

'So, what have you been thinking since our first meeting? Are your feelings about being here any clearer?'

I'd had plenty of time to think about what I was going to say, to come up with something that would convince Martindale that I was the kind of mindless zombie he was looking for, but putting things into words wasn't one of Stevie's strong points. If I sounded too convincing, I knew Martindale wouldn't be convinced at all. I decided to let Stevie have first go, and if it really was total garbage, I'd step in.

I drained my cup and put it down carefully on the floor. 'I walk a lot, you know,' I said. 'At night, mostly. Even when I'm knackered and all I want is to sleep, I get up, start walking – don't know where I'm going, you know. Nowhere. Just walking. Me feet are killing me sometimes, but I don't stop. Not until . . . I don't know.'

Martindale was nodding, looking at me with those laser-beam eyes.

'Thing is . . .' I screwed up my eyes, groping for the right words. 'The thing is, I walk and walk and walk – I've got all this . . . you know, I can keep going all night, I think I could walk forever sometimes. I don't mind the pain. I don't mind being hungry. It don't bother me.'

I lifted my head and our eyes briefly met before I looked away.

'But I ain't going anywhere, you know? I want to be going somewhere. I don't even care where it is. End of the fucking world, I don't care. Right off the edge. I just want to be going . . . somewhere.'

I slumped in the chair and closed my eyes with the effort of trying to squeeze out so many words in the right order.

I blinked, and I could see Martindale was still nodding.

'No one goes so far as he who knows not where he is going,' he said.

I looked at him blankly.

'Oliver Cromwell.' He smiled. 'Never mind. The point is, I think I understand what you're talking about, Stevie. You've got an energy, a tremendous energy in you. A fire. You may not understand where it comes from, but I do . . . I really do. It comes from God. It's the fire of the Holy Spirit that's burning in you, that makes you walk. And you might think all your life you've been going nowhere – you've just been trudging on and on through pain, through rejection, through misery, through violence, through loneliness – but all that trudging has actually brought you here.'

'But—'

He put his hand on my shoulder. 'Not that this is your final destination, Stevie. No, no. This is just a stop. A station along the way. But now you're on the right track, do you see? You can begin the real part of your journey from here.'

I closed my eyes and took a deep breath, clenching my fists. 'I don't understand. I don't understand anything. I don't know why I come here.'

'That's OK, Stevie. That's OK. I know this may sound strange, but that's how I know it was meant. That's how I know the Holy Spirit has been directing your steps. No one goes so far as he who knows not where he is going, remember? And you are going to go far, Stevie, I promise. Further than you have ever dreamed. You are going to do wonderful things for God.'

'I don't understand. What am I going to do? I can't do anything. I've never been able to do anything – except fuck everything up.'

'Trust me, Stevie. You can do so much more than you think. Remember, you have that special energy within you, the fire that comes straight from God. We just need to harness it, to direct it.'

'How?'

He leaned forward in the chair. 'Do you trust me, Stevie?'

I looked at him. I didn't have to think about it. 'Yeah. Yeah, I do.'

He sat back. 'Then everything will become clear. You just have to be patient, give it time. The Holy Spirit has brought you here. And God will take you the rest of the way. You don't have to think for yourself any more, Stevie. You don't have to worry if you're doing the right thing ever again. You're in God's hands now.'

I felt a warm wave washing over me, through me. I didn't have to worry about anything any more. I didn't have to be angry any more. All the shit that had been happening ever since I could remember, all the fighting, the crying, the beatings I'd taken, the ones I'd dished out, all the fury about what I'd never had and could never have, all the shit I'd taken from cunts who thought I had less right to exist than a dog: I could let it all go. Martindale would take it away. God would take it all away, and scatter it all into space.

My chest started heaving and I could feel hot tears trickling down my face. I tried to speak but it felt like something was stuck in my throat. My mouth wouldn't work, even though there were words trying to get out. Martindale was sitting looking at me with a smile at the corners of his mouth, waiting.

'Just tell me what you want me to do,' I said.

'First we have to cleanse you, Stevie. We have to empty you out.'

I nodded. That sounded good.

'We have to make a bonfire – a bonfire of the spirit. We're going to throw all the garbage from your life onto it, so it turns to ashes and blows away. Everything in your life up to this moment is going to burn, until there's nothing left. No more bad thoughts. No more bad memories. No more . . . Stevie Nichols.'

'And . . . then?' I managed to say.

Martindale folded his hands in his lap. He wasn't smiling any more.

'Then you'll be ready to do God's work.'

31

I stood under the shower, letting the scalding water wash away Stevie's rancid stink, while the last vestiges of his fucked-up personality finally drained from my mind. On the walk back, I'd had a struggle putting him back in his box. The plan had been to get Martindale to swallow the bait – and he had – but Stevie was the one who ended up getting hooked. As I'd shuffled away from the church, shoulders hunched, hood down, hands in my pockets, I'd tried to put a lid on his excitement, but it kept fizzing up to the surface, like a can of Coke I'd chugged down too quickly. Martindale's spiel about incinerating the old Stevie and his shitty life had really got to him. He couldn't bloody wait.

I dried myself with a towel and scooped Stevie's clothes up off the floor. One day I'd happily chuck them into the incinerator, too, just like Stevie, happy to be rid of them both, but not yet. I shoved the dirty clothes into a clear plastic bag and tied it off with a strip of duct tape before putting it into the washing basket. There was a clean pair of jeans and a white T-shirt on the toilet lid, and it was only after I'd put them on that I finally felt a hundred per cent myself.

Not that that meant I felt particularly great, but at least it was an improvement on Stevie. I couldn't fault him; he'd done a good job. But once Martindale really got to work on him, I knew I was going to have a hell of a job keeping him under control.

I wondered if Mrs Allenby was right and I was falling apart. Or did I still have what it takes, like Alex believed? I had a feeling that getting sucked into Martindale's twisted world was going to test me to breaking point. *Fine*, I thought. At least then we'd find out.

I felt a chill go through me. Once I'd submitted myself to Martindale's brainwashing, I wouldn't be able to call for backup. We wouldn't be able to risk using radio transmitters. I'd be totally alone.

I walked barefoot into the kitchen, looking for something to eat. I opened the fridge. A half-empty carton of soy milk and a packet of . . . tofu, whatever that was. It looked as if it might be handy for grouting tiles in the bathroom, but not much else. I was debating whether I could be arsed to go out and get some supplies or just make do with a cup of tea and some of that soy stuff when I felt my phone buzzing in my back pocket.

'Logan.'

'Hello. It's Lucy. Sorry, it's late – or early. I shouldn't be calling, but I felt bad I didn't call you back right away.'

I had to stop myself from grinning.

'No, it's fine, I wasn't asleep or anything. You got my message, then. Well, obviously. Sorry it was a bit garbled. I was sort of taken by surprise, if you know what I mean.'

'Oh God! The old greeting. I'm so sorry. That must have freaked you out.'

'No . . . it was stupid of me. I should have realized.'

'I've got to change it – I know I have. But I can't face it. Just saying "Hello, this is Lucy" seems like too much. I don't know why.'

'Yeah, I understand. You could always just get an automatic one – you know, not your voice.'

'Yes, I should do that. I will.'

I didn't know what to say next. I liked just knowing she was there, on the other end of the phone. It made me feel better. But this was supposed to be a conversation. If I didn't say something, she'd think I was nuts or just annoyed she'd called in the middle of the night. Luckily, she broke the silence before I could come up with something stupid.

'I know this sounds bonkers, but I was going to go out for something to eat. I haven't done any shopping since . . . since, you know. And I don't like going places where I might bump into someone I know, so that leaves going somewhere at three in the morning.'

'Do you know anywhere?'

'There's a place in Soho, on Greek Street, that's open all night.'

'How far are you?'

A hesitation. 'Not far. You?'

'I can be there in half an hour.'

'Great. I'll see you there, then.'

'OK.'

I ended the call and put my phone back in my pocket. I'd already done a lot of walking tonight. But that was with Stevie's knackered knees and fucked-up feet. *I* still had plenty of miles left in me. I put on socks and trainers and grabbed a trackie top, then stepped out into the cool night air.

The diner was surprisingly busy. Most of the customers sitting at the plain Formica tables were in their twenties or younger, nursing cups of coffee and looking like they were trying to come down off whatever drugs they were on. There was an old dear in a windcheater a couple of sizes too big for her, holding the plastic menu out stiffly in front of her without looking at it. I had the feeling she'd been sitting like that for a while and the teenage waitress lounging by the counter had learned to ignore her. No money, but nowhere else to go. Or nowhere she wanted to go.

I saw Lucy at a table against the wall at the back and walked over. She was wearing a raincoat buttoned up to the neck, and maybe because it was the middle of the night I couldn't stop myself wondering what she was wearing underneath.

I gave myself a mental slap. Maybe this wasn't such a good idea after all.

She passed over a menu as I sat down. 'Are you sure you're hungry?'

She had her hair in a tight ponytail, and it made her look as if she was showing her face properly for the first time. I noticed her eyes were green and her skin looked very pale under the fluorescent light. She was wearing just enough make-up to make it look as if she wasn't.

'I could eat a horse. I genuinely couldn't tell you the last time I ate.'

She smiled. 'Lucky I called, then.'

I smiled back. 'Yeah. Yeah, it was.'

'So what have you been doing that's so fascinating you forgot to eat?'

'I . . . I've just been walking around, mostly.'

I winced. That sounded fucking stupid. I should have figured out a proper cover story before I left the flat.

'Trouble sleeping?'

If only she knew.

'Yeah, something like that. What are you having?' I asked, keen to get off the subject of what I'd been doing with my time.

'A burger,' she said. 'And not the vegan one. With chips and an entire bucket of ketchup, if they have it.'

I grinned. 'Sounds good.'

I waved at the waitress and she practically sprinted over, obviously thrilled that someone was actually ordering food.

Lucy looked up at her. 'The burger. With chips. And any trimmings, if you have them.'

'Same,' I said.

The waitress scribbled something down and scurried off before we could change our minds. It clearly wasn't the sort of place where they asked you how you wanted your burger done, and that suited me fine. As far as I was concerned there was cooked and uncooked, and I trusted the chef to figure out which was the right one.

I slid the menu back across the table. 'So what have you been up to?'

I gave myself another mental slap. Harder this time. She'd just lost her entire family. She'd been about to throw herself off a bridge. *So what have you been up to? Oh, you know, this and that. Looking at a new colour scheme for the lounge. Pruning the wisteria. Running a nice, relaxing bath so I can slit my wrists.*

Luckily she didn't seem offended. 'Funeral arrangements, mostly. I can think of better ways of trying to take your mind off things, frankly.'

I nodded. 'I was lucky. I had a mate who did all that for me. I stayed blind drunk until the day of the funeral.'

I felt my guts twisting at the memory.

'Was it hard?' she asked, and I could tell she was afraid, afraid she wouldn't be able to go through with it.

'If you do it sober, yes. Nothing harder. Sorry.'

She reached out and touched my hand. 'No, I want the truth. I think that's why I find it easy to talk to you. You don't shy away, or get squeamish. You just give it to me straight.'

I didn't know what to say to that.

Our burgers arrived, practically flung down in front of us with a challenging look from the waitress, as if to say, 'Don't blame me – you ordered it.'

Lucy emptied the bottle of ketchup onto her chips as promised and we both grabbed our burgers and got stuck in. She looked as if she was properly letting go for the first time, dropping bits of food onto her plate and getting her fingers sticky with ketchup. Her burger disappeared in half a dozen bites and she grinned at me across the table, wiping her mouth with the back of her hand. I swallowed the last of mine and grinned back. You could only eat like that with someone else who'd lost everything, both knowing that being hungry and taking pleasure in satisfying that hunger wasn't a betrayal. It just meant, for better or worse, you were still alive. Still human. It wasn't something to be ashamed of. It was just the way it was.

She looked at me with a wicked glint in her eye. I knew what she was about to say.

'Sure, why not,' I said, waving the waitress over again. It wasn't as if the other customers were keeping her busy.

'Can I get you coffee or dessert?' she asked.

'Maybe later,' Lucy said, smiling. 'We'd like two more burgers, please.'

The waitress nodded. As she took our order to the kitchen, she glanced back over her shoulder as if she couldn't quite believe we were serious.

We took the second burgers more slowly. I couldn't help thinking it was like when you had sex with someone you'd fancied for a while. The first time was fast and furious, just pent-up lust being unleashed. Then the second time was gentler, more controlled. Better.

We ate in silence. Every now and then our eyes would meet and we'd quickly glance away.

I pushed my plate away and sat back. 'That was a good idea of yours.'

She picked up a slice of pickle, then halfway to her lips, put it down. 'God, I'm done.'

She smiled, sheepishly now, as if the same thoughts had been going through her head as mine. She started wiping her fingers carefully on her napkin. For the first time, there seemed to be an awkwardness between us.

'So,' she said finally. 'What do we do now?'

32

The atmosphere was different when I walked through the door and into the Clearwater Security office the next morning. Everyone was there, already assembled at the conference table, Ryan with his laptop open, Mrs Allenby with her notepad at the ready. Alan was sitting next to Alex, nervously wiping his glasses on a handkerchief and looking as if he wished he had a bit of kit to tinker with. Alex had her arms folded, her game face on.

All eyes turned to me.

'Well?' Mrs Allenby asked.

'I think he's our man,' I said simply.

She let out a long breath and nodded. As I sat down between Ryan and Alex, I could feel a surge of electricity around the table.

'You're sure?'

'Oh, yeah. He's serious, and I don't mean about doling out soup and all that. He's targeting vulnerable individuals for some sort of brainwashing. I did my best lost sheep act, and he practically swallowed me whole.'

Mrs Allenby looked at me. 'And you think you can handle it, being in the belly of the beast? You're comfortable submitting yourself to this "brainwashing"?'

Comfortable? Not the word I would have used, but I could see she was looking for chinks in my armour, any little sign that I would crack under pressure.

'I've done the training – interrogation resistance,' I said coolly.

'And?'

'Flying colours.'

She didn't look convinced. She maintained eye contact, daring me to look away. She would have made a decent interrogator herself, I thought.

'I don't know,' she said. 'I don't know if we can risk it. If he's as good as you're suggesting, he could unmask you, and then we've lost him. He'll just go to ground.'

'Won't happen,' I said firmly.

'I've seen Logan in situations like this,' Alex said. 'He knows what he's doing.'

Mrs Allenby gave her a withering look. '*Situations like this?* I'm not sure there are any training courses that can prepare you for the kind of intensive psychological assault that Martindale seems to have in mind.'

'Maybe not, but—'

'I'm sorry, Logan has done a first-class job of getting Martindale to expose himself. Now we're sure he's our man, the sensible thing would be to put the church under continuous surveillance and—'

I slammed my fist on the table, rattling the coffee cups. '*Bollocks!*'

For a moment no one said anything. Alan looked as if he wanted the ground to swallow him up.

'Look,' I said, in a calmer voice. 'With all due respect, right now we know absolutely fuck all. We don't know what the connection is with Weston. We don't even know for sure if Shlovsky's involved. We don't know what Martindale's planning, let alone how he's going to do it or what his homeless recruits have got to do with it. And like you say, the clock is ticking. We've got no idea how close to midnight we are. For all we know, it could all be about to kick off. We can't afford to fanny around keeping tabs on Martindale. If we're going to stop this thing, we need to be on the inside, now, and I can do that. I'm halfway there. If we back out now we'd be cutting off our noses to spite our faces. Isn't that the whole point of Blindeye? Martindale's opened the door. We have to take our chance while we can, otherwise it's going to slam in our faces. We won't get another one.'

I sat back with my arms folded. That was a long speech for me, and if they wanted an encore, they weren't going to get it.

Mrs Allenby tapped her pencil on the table, thinking it over. 'Mr Oldfield? Are we any closer to establishing the connection between Weston and Martindale?'

Ryan put his laptop to one side. 'I've been thinking about it. Let's assume Weston found Martindale and not the other way around. We're also assuming no prior connection; they weren't altar boys together, or anything like that. So that means Weston is searching and ends up finding Martindale. What's he looking for? He's Shlovsky's point man, so actually the first question is, why Weston and not Titov? Given their history – the fact that he's Shlovsky's personal bodyguard – you'd think Titov would be the most trusted, especially for something as sensitive as this. But no, for some reason he picks Weston. Why? Well, the obvious difference is he's British. It could be that using him is a way of disguising the Russian connection. That would make sense, if the crucial thing is to keep Moscow's fingerprints off it. But maybe there's more to it. Anyway, we've got Weston, and he's looking for someone who is willing and capable of executing a terror attack. Where's the obvious place to look?'

'Islamists,' Alex said. 'He just needs to connect with a radical preacher in a mosque that isn't under surveillance.'

Ryan nodded. 'Agreed. But he doesn't do that, or at least that's not where his search leads him. He ends up somewhere rather different.'

'St Saviour's,' Mrs Allenby said.

'Yes. Exactly.'

She pursed her lips. 'We seem to be going round in circles, Mr Oldfield.'

'Sorry,' Ryan said. 'But sometimes when you find yourself in a labyrinth, that's what you have to do, in my experience. At least at first.'

She didn't look convinced, but nodded for him to carry on.

'So I was trying to think like Weston, and of course I started off trawling the usual jihadi websites. Then – assuming he knows what he's doing – I dug a bit deeper, into the dark web, where, unfortunately, the real extremists advertise themselves.'

Alex looked bewildered. 'But we know he didn't find one of them.'

Ryan pulled at his goatee. 'Maybe he did.'

'You mean St Saviour's has a site on the dark web?'

'Well, not St Saviour's exactly. But I did come across something interesting. Something that could possibly tie in with Martindale. You remember he was studying the crusades? Quite an odd subject for a theology student.'

'Why do you say that?' Mrs Allenby asked.

'Well, most Christians would admit that the crusades were more about making money than saving souls. And sometimes worse things than that. It's hard to make the case that there was anything spiritual about them, when all's said and done.'

'But Martindale did?'

'I don't know. He never completed his thesis, so it isn't logged anywhere. I'm only guessing. But maybe he was taking the very unfashionable line that the crusades could be morally justified, despite all the greed and bloodshed. Perhaps he got into an argument with his tutors at All Souls about it and that's why he never finished his degree.'

'This is all very interesting, Mr Oldfield, but what's it got to do with the dark web?' Mrs Allenby asked, losing patience.

'The thing is, I came across a site called Tenth Crusade,'

Ryan said. 'There were nine crusades – nine major ones, anyway, if you don't count off-the-cuff raids and bits of freebooting that didn't have the blessing of the Church.'

'So what's the tenth one?' Alex asked. 'I mean, the crusades were all about taking Jerusalem back from the Turks or Saracens or whatever, weren't they?'

Ryan nodded. 'That was the justification, anyway.'

'So you reckon Martindale's recruiting an army of dossers to lay siege to Jerusalem? Not sure the IDF would take too kindly to that.'

Ryan smiled. 'A bit impractical, I agree. Although there was a Children's Crusade, which had about the same chance of success. But no, I don't think he's planning on marching on Jerusalem – at least, not the actual one.'

Alex tilted her head to one side. 'So . . . what?'

'There's another element to this Tenth Crusade website.' Ryan turned to me. 'Did Martindale mention anything about William Blake?'

'Who?'

'Come on, you must have sung "And did those feet in ancient times . . ."'

'Sorry, mate, not with you. Blake? No. He did quote someone. Don't remember. Began with a C.'

'And your point is?' Mrs Allenby asked.

'Well, Blake thought Jerusalem was an idea. That it needed to be "builded here . . ."'

'"In England's green and pleasant land",' Mrs Allenby finished.

'Exactly.'

Alex looked confused. 'So . . . if Jerusalem is here, then how is the Tenth Crusade all about taking it back? Back from who?'

'The Muslims, I assume,' Ryan said.

We all thought about that for a moment. I had to admit, it was starting to make sense.

Mrs Allenby tapped her pencil on the table for a few moments. 'But we don't know if this has got anything to do with Martindale. We could be making connections that don't exist. We can't afford to get this wrong.'

'No,' admitted Ryan. 'We don't know if Martindale and the Tenth Crusade are connected.'

'But there is one way we can find out,' I said.

Mrs Allenby sighed. She put her pen down and looked at the table for a moment. 'All right,' she said. 'But for God's sake be careful.'

33

I was sitting at the kitchen table with a cup of tea when Alan texted. I was making a to-do list in my head: things I needed to get sorted before I went back to St Saviour's. I had a hunch that the 'cleansing' process would start right away. Martindale had to have a place that was secure, where you could hide someone away for an extended period without anyone noticing – where, for all I knew, no one could hear you scream. Somewhere out in the sticks – an isolated farmhouse – would be perfect. Wherever it was, that's where I'd be going, but how long I'd be there was anyone's guess. Which was why I had to get my ducks in a row now. After all, there was always a chance that I wasn't coming back.

If Lucy called and I couldn't answer, I didn't want her thinking I'd got cold feet. I didn't want her tipping back into the abyss – not because of me. I'd have to tell her I was going away for a while – but where? So far I'd managed to skirt around the subject of what I did for a living, but I wouldn't be able to keep that up forever. I'd have to come up with a story that included a plausible reason for disappearing at short notice for an unspecified length of time with no means of communicating. I was still waiting for inspiration to strike.

I'd violated my probation and was going back to jail? Or volunteering for rehab? I owed money to a loan shark and the blokes with baseball bats were after me? None of these really fitted with what I'd already told her, though I'd told her so little it probably didn't matter. Or, if I was being honest with myself, was the real reason I didn't fancy any of these scenarios: what they would make Lucy think of me?

People do funny things when they're grieving. I knew that as well as anyone. Someone stops you from topping yourself and you can end up thinking they're an angel sent down from heaven especially for you, that it was meant – any kind of bollocks. So if you then find out they're actually a jailbird, or a junkie, or a gambler, that could jolt you back into reality and make you realize that your knight in shining armour was just a fantasy. It might be enough to make you think you were right the first time and decide to have another crack at suicide, this time with a bit of practical experience under your belt. Or it might just make you wonder what the hell you thought you were doing getting mixed up with such a lowlife.

You might just come to your senses.

And perhaps that was what I was really afraid of.

So, I had to find a way of telling Lucy I was going away for a while. I couldn't tell her where or why, she wouldn't be able to phone or text, and I didn't know when I'd be back. But not to worry, and whatever you do, don't decide you're probably better off not seeing me again anyway.

Yeah, that was going to work.

Which left me with two options: either I could tell her the truth, that I was a former MI5 surveillance officer now working for an unofficial and totally deniable covert organization that occasionally murdered people and frequently broke the law; that I was currently engaged in an operation involving submitting myself to a brainwashing programme that might well compromise my already fragile mental health, not to mention risking my physical safety, and that even if I came out of that in one piece, I had a strong suspicion that two other members of the team had been murdered by person or persons unknown and the rest of us might still be under threat.

Or I could come up with a clever cover story that explained my falling off the grid for a while without making her think there was anything dodgy going on. On paper, that was definitely the best option, but however hard I tried, so far I hadn't got any further than the first line, which went something like, 'Lucy, you might find this hard to believe, but . . .'

Which meant Alan's text was actually a welcome distraction.

Might have some news on that Interflora delivery. Call me.

I pressed his number.

'Alan, mate. What's up? Where are you?'

'Um . . . in the office.'

I looked at my watch. 'You on your own?'

'Yeah.'

'What the fuck are you doing?'

'Oh, you know, this and that. I like to keep things tidy, you know.'

It sounded a lot to me like Alan had lost his nerve, that he was scared to leave the office. I wondered how long he'd been camping there and felt a tinge of guilt: I'd been so wrapped up in my own problems, I hadn't really spared a thought for how he was handling things.

'You want to meet somewhere?'

A pause. 'Well, I don't know . . .'

'OK, mate, I'm coming to get you, and then we'll sort something out, all right?'

I could hear him wheezing down the phone, like he was having some sort of asthma attack.

'All right.'

Thirty minutes later I was walking past the Clearwater Security building, checking the vehicles parked on the double yellows and residents' bays on both sides of the street. No occupants, as far as I could see. Apart from the cars, the street was empty. I turned the corner and ducked into the doorway of a wine shop. Alan answered on the first ring.

'I'm on the street, mate. You OK to move?'

'You not coming up?'

'No, that makes me visible, yeah? I'm just going to be watching. What I want you to do is leave the building, run a pattern, and I'll see if I can spot anything that isn't kosher, OK?'

'How far behind me you going to be?'

Bloody hell, he was twitchy. 'Don't worry, close enough, mate. We'll go round the houses a couple of times and then it'll all be hunky-dory, no worries. Outside in four minutes, yeah?'

He said OK but he didn't sound happy. I walked briskly round the block and into the newsagent on the corner. Two minutes later I saw Alan walk past, swaddled in a dark rain-coat, while I pretended to scan the tabloid headlines. I waited another two, fiddling with my change, to see if anyone else went by. All clear. I walked out with a *Mirror* tucked under my arm and headed back towards the Clearwater building. Two blokes – twenties, beards, casual clothes – passed me. My antennae didn't twitch, but you never know. I increased my pace, crossed over and started walking back the other way, twenty yards behind them. It wasn't exactly out of the manual, and if there was a bigger team, my one-eighty would have been spotted for sure, but as long as it was just these two, I reckoned I should still be in the clear.

When they got to the end of the street they stopped and turned.

Shit.

I put my head down and kept going. They crossed the road over to my side and I had to slow down to let them pass. One of them gave me a hard look, and I stopped, breathing steadily, making sure my hands were loose, main-taining neutral eye contact and keeping the second bloke in my peripheral vision while I waited for them to make a move.

The way these things usually worked, it would probably be the quiet one, while the aggressive one kept your attention, but I was taking no chances.

'Cheers, mate.' The second one gave his mate a playful shove in the back and flashed me an apologetic smile as they went past and dived into the pub on the corner.

'No worries.' I let out a breath and walked past.

I quickly looked round to make sure I hadn't missed anything while this little sideshow was going on. An old geezer in a flat cap was crossing the road towards me and I pretended to look at my watch, waiting to see which way he went, but he definitely had the look of a man who desperately needed that first pint, and confirmed my guess by ducking into the pub too.

For a millisecond, I thought about following. We could have all got pissed together and they could have sorted out my love life. But I quickly shook that thought off and crossed over to the other corner instead, passing the newsagent and following in Alan's footsteps towards the next junction. There were two blokes in suits sitting in a dark Audi, which didn't smell right, but the location didn't make sense unless they were part of a bigger team with multiple vehicles, so I made a mental note of the registration and let them go. All my instincts told me we were in the clear, but I stuck to the rest of the plan anyway, and ten minutes later Alan and I were in the snug of The Butcher's Dog with a couple of pints of lager in front of us. He necked half of it before I'd even had a chance to sit down, looked at the half-empty glass for a second, then picked it up again and drained the rest. Pale and pasty had always been his style, but now his skin looked grey, his face puffy. I watched as a little bit of colour came back into his cheeks and he started to look slightly more human again. Amazing what a pint of lager could do, if you drank it quickly enough. There wasn't anything it could do for the smell of stale sweat and unwashed clothes, though.

'Better?'

He nodded, wiping his mouth with the back of his hand. 'Yeah.'

'How long you been holed up in there?'

He shook his head. 'Long enough.'

I poked him in the chest. 'You should have bloody said something, you twat.'

He flinched. 'Like what? I can't be doing with all this counter-surveillance lark. It's doing my head in. I like to be in my workshop, keeping out of harm's way, you know that.'

I took a swig of my pint. 'It'll all be over soon, one way or the other.'

'Great. That makes me feel so much better. Cheers, mate.'

I shrugged. I wasn't going to make him any false promises. 'Let me get you another, and then you can tell me what you've found.'

The bar was quiet, and it didn't take me long to get the barman's attention. I put the two fresh pints on the table and sat down again. Alan took a dainty sip, the effort of not downing it in one clearly visible on his face. 'Daisy, you said?'

'That's right.' I felt my chest tightening. 'Had any luck?'

He took another sip. 'What's this all about, then?'

I had to think quickly. 'It was just something that came up when Alex was having her little chat with Ekaterina Shlovsky. Just a remark that didn't quite make sense. A loose end, you know?'

'Why all the cloak and dagger, then?'

I took a long pull on my drink to buy myself some time. Good question. I realized that I'd been taking Alan a bit for granted. Socially awkward he might be, but he wasn't stupid. I was going to have to come up with something a bit better.

'You know me, Alan: I'm like a dog with a bone sometimes. If the Shlovskys have got any dark secrets, I want to know what they are. Just in case.'

He peered at me. 'In case of what?'

'In case this whole thing goes tits-up and we need some leverage. What if we've got the whole thing arse-backwards, and Shlovsky's not involved in any kind of terror plot after all? What if he finds out we've planted a listening device in his wife's dressing room? The Kremlin might be putting the squeeze on, but he's still one of HMRC's most valued customers. And we know the PM is wary of pissing him off. Someone might just decide to throw us to the wolves. In which case, it's not who you know, but what you know about who you know that counts, if you get my drift.'

Alan looked at me quizzically. I could tell he wasn't buying it.

'And you want to keep Mrs Allenby out of the loop because . . .?'

'She's part of the establishment, mate. If it comes to throwing us to the wolves, she wouldn't think twice. She doesn't want us wasting time on an insurance policy, does she?'

Alan looked down at his pint. 'OK,' he said. From the flat tone of his voice, I was guessing that meant, 'OK, so you're not going to tell me the truth.'

'So . . .?' I looked at him expectantly.

'The word "Daisy" did come up a few times in one conversation between Ekaterina Shlovsky and Anastasia. Lots of crying involved on both ends, so it would have been hard to make out what they were saying in English, let alone Russian, to be honest, but the context seemed to be something bad that happened – something they both feel terrible about. Anastasia was the first to mention it, and that started her mother off and then before you know it they're both wailing down the phone and it's hard to make head or tail of any of it – especially when I reckon Mrs S had been on the sauce.' He looked at me. 'Does any of that make sense?'

I thought about it for moment. 'What was the date of this conversation?'

'Er . . . September fifteenth, I think.'

'And that was the only time they talked about Daisy?'

'If you can call it talking, yep.'

'Did any other names come up in the same conversation?'

'One, yeah. Mikhail. Just the once – and that set Mrs S off on a proper crying jag. I thought she was going to do herself an injury. I almost called 999.'

'Funny,' I said.

'Mikhail's the brother, isn't he? A couple of years older.'

I nodded. 'If that's the Mikhail they're talking about.' But I was sure it was. And I was beginning to see what might have happened. It would help if I could talk to Daisy – see how she reacted if I mentioned the word 'Mikhail' in front of her. But I wasn't going to get a chance to do that. I'd have to go with my gut and do a bit more digging.

'You happy to carry on with this for a bit? It won't be for long, I promise.'

Alan made a face, as if to say, *That's what I think about your promises, mate*, but then he shrugged and said, 'Sure. I'm all for insurance policies. Pensions, too. So long as you're alive to cash them in,' he added grimly.

'I want you to focus on Mikhail, the brother.' My gut told me they wouldn't mention Daisy again. Not until the next anniversary, anyway. 'Anything that comes up in connection with him. Especially connected to that date.'

'And what do you think's going to come up? What do you reckon he's done, this lad?'

'I'm not sure yet, mate, not sure.'

But I was.

34

Maybe it was because I was thinking about Martindale and St Saviour's and I had religion on my mind – and also the fact that this was going to be my last meeting at Clearwater for a while – but as Alex poured the coffee and a plate of biscuits was pushed round the conference table, I couldn't help thinking of the Last Supper. Did that make me Jesus? Was I about to go out and get crucified? Would I die and rise again? That sounded pretty much like what Martindale had in mind for Stevie Nichols: get rid of the old Stevie and replace him with a blank canvas, someone who Martindale could mould into whatever shape he wanted.

The question was, would the old Matt Logan survive the process?

What about Judas, then? Was there someone sitting round the table planning to betray me? I looked at Mrs Allenby, calmly making notes in her little book. Was she putting a line through my name while I was watching? Had she done the same thing with Craig and Claire?

She turned to me, as if she could read my thoughts. 'You're sure about the tracker?'

'Hundred per cent.'

'Even though Mr Woodburn assures me he can provide one small enough to be woven into your clothing? It will be essentially undetectable, unless Martindale has some fairly sophisticated equipment, and it's hard to see how he could have acquired anything of that nature.'

I shook my head. 'Chances are he'll get rid of whatever I'm wearing.'

'But what if he doesn't?' she persisted.

What I wanted to tell her was that it didn't matter if the tracker was undetectable. I knew if we had the tools and someone with some basic surgical skills, we could even implant it, make it to all intents and purposes invisible. But Martindale would *know*. I could feel it in my bones. I had to go in clean.

And what good would it do anyway? They might know my location, but they wouldn't know if I was alive or dead. I could be a maggoty corpse and they'd be none the wiser. The point was, no one could help me once I was in Martindale's clutches. I was beginning to think the whole tracking device thing was just about making *them* feel better.

'Sorry, it's just a gut thing. It's got to feel right.'

She gave me a long look over the top of her glasses, trying to decide how stubborn I was going to be. 'If that's the way you want it,' she said finally. 'But it's against my advice. We will obviously keep eyes on the church as much as we are able, but with the resources we have . . .' She let the sentence trail off. We all knew there was no way we could monitor the comings and goings at St Saviour's 24/7, which meant there was really no point bothering at all. Alex would watch me in, but that was about it.

I looked round the table. Ryan and Alan avoided eye contact nervously, like they thought I was about to go off on a suicide mission. Mrs Allenby had her head in her notes. Maybe she was underlining 'against my advice' to cover her arse if there was ever an official inquiry. But there was nothing official about Blindeye, so what would be the point? Just force of habit, perhaps.

Alex was the only one who looked at me. I tried to read her expression. It was a mixture of concern and curiosity, like she knew I was hiding stuff from her. Which I was. And I felt bad about it. I looked away.

'There are two further items on the agenda,' Mrs Allenby said. 'Mr Woodburn?'

Alan sat up straighter in his chair. 'Yeah, the visual feed from the house – I was just looking through what we got before it conked out. Nothing really, just the usual vehicles coming and going for the most part, but anything we hadn't seen before, I put the registration number into the system just to see what came up. Anyway, there was a Jag which made an appearance at 2.45 a.m. on the twelfth. It got my attention just because of the odd time, you know. It went out of visual before we could clock any passengers, but I ran the plates and something a bit funny came up.'

'Like what?' Alex asked.

'Well, nothing,' Alan said.

'What's funny about that?'

'It was blocked. Access denied.'

Ryan got there first. 'Meaning it was an official government vehicle.'

Alex opened her eyes wide. 'Bloody hell.'

'Any way of identifying it?' I asked.

Alan looked at Ryan.

'There's a lot of them. Hundreds, maybe,' Ryan said. 'Hmm, might have to think about that one.'

'Do,' said Mrs Allenby. 'And lastly . . .' She reached down and pulled something out of a bag at her feet. Two slim manila files dropped to the table. 'I've been thinking about your concerns regarding Miss Maxwell and Mr McKinley. I may have been a trifle hasty in my initial response. I've now had an opportunity to consult with the Director General, and after considering the matter, he decided it was justified to . . . obtain these.'

Well, that's a turn-up for the books, I thought. *Maybe she isn't the Judas after all.*

She placed both hands on the files, as if she was reluctant to give them up. 'Needless to say, obtaining them was not without its risks. Possession of them is not without its risks, either. And there is a strict time limit to our access.' She pushed them over towards Ryan. 'So you need to work quickly, and ensure they do not leave this room.'

I could see Ryan was having a hard time not grinning like the Cheshire Cat. At last he had some data to crunch. He looked like a kid who'd just been given a big bag of sweets by an auntie who usually just handed out apples.

'Of course. I'll start going through them as soon as we're finished,' he said.

I'd been worried the rest of the Blindeye team would be twiddling their thumbs after I went underground at St Saviour's. Now it looked like they'd have their hands full. Alex would be keeping an eye on the church, Ryan would be analysing Claire's and Craig's files, and Alan would be trying to identify Viktor Shlovsky's mystery visitor – not to mention a bit of research on Mikhail Shlovsky on the side. There were plenty of questions we still needed answers to, but I couldn't think about them now. I had to focus on what I was about to do. I shifted in my chair, keen to get going.

'I'm not sure we're quite finished, Mr Logan,' Mrs Allenby said, sensing my impatience. 'We need to set a time limit for communication. If you haven't got a message to us after three days, I'm sending Miss Short in.'

'Too soon,' I said quickly.

'When then?' Mrs Allenby asked.

I put my hands down flat on the table. 'There's no . . . Look, we're going in blind here. I may not have any way of knowing what day it is. We've got to assume he'll be trying to disorient me. I might walk out of there in a couple of days or it could be a lot longer. Who knows? If we put an artificial time limit on it, we risk blowing the whole thing up. You're just going to have to trust me . . .'

'. . . and hope for the best,' Mrs Allenby added wryly.

'Something like that,' I said.

She didn't look happy. 'I'm afraid I'm not going to just sit here and wait indefinitely. That would be reckless. After six days, if we've heard nothing, I'm going to get you out.'

I opened my mouth then shut it again. I could tell from her expression she wasn't going to budge. Not having a contingency plan – even if that plan meant fucking everything up – clearly just went against the grain.

Six days, then. 'Fair enough.'

'Right,' Mrs Allenby said firmly. 'We all have things to do.'

I stood up and nodded to Ryan, who was already flicking through the files. 'Good luck with that.'

'Cheers, and you,' he said, looking up briefly.

I nodded at Alan and he nodded back.

Then I turned to Alex. 'A quick word?'

We walked over to the kitchen area.

'Don't worry about a thing,' she said breezily. 'I'm going to be your guardian angel.'

I smiled. 'Just keep your wings well hidden, yeah?'

'Always,' she said.

'And don't be too keen. The one thing we don't want to do is spook this guy. I'll find a way of getting a message to you. Just be patient, OK?'

She nodded. 'OK.'

'One more thing.' I paused, not really knowing what I was going to say. 'Look, I know I've been a bit . . . mysterious recently. I haven't been a very good friend. It's just . . . there's some shit going on.'

She folded her arms. 'Great. Thanks for the explanation. "Some shit going on." That clears that up, then.'

I sighed. 'You know what I mean.'

'No, actually, I don't,' she said. 'I mean, there's plenty of shit going on, and we seem to be in the middle of most of it, but that doesn't explain why you won't tell me what's going on in that thick head of yours.'

I started to say something but she put a finger to my lips.

'Don't. I know you well enough to know when you've got something to say, you'll say it. You saved my life once, so I'm not going to go off you, however much of a surly bastard you are.'

She took her finger away.

'Thanks,' I said. 'When this is over, I'll try and explain.'

She nodded, a sceptical half-smile playing at the corners of her mouth.

Fair enough, I thought. I wanted to tell her that I couldn't think of anyone better to have my back, but at that moment I felt a sharp tug on my sleeve. I looked round, surprised.

Who . . .?

Then I twigged. It was Stevie, bored with all this talk and wanting to get going. The sad bastard just couldn't wait for his makeover.

I turned away from Alex, muttering under my breath. 'Careful what you wish for, Stevie, mate, careful what you bloody wish for.'

35

We didn't order the burgers this time – not even one. We were just like all the other night owls scattered round the diner, nursing cups of coffee that were slowly going cold in front of us.

'Thanks for coming,' I said.

She reached for my hand. 'Don't be silly. You said you had something important to tell me.'

'Yeah. Look, this is difficult . . .'

She took her hand back, her eyes suddenly wide.

'No, no, it's not that,' I said quickly.

She closed her eyes and took a couple of long, deep breaths, nodding to herself.

'Please, Lucy,' I said, beginning to panic. Shit, I was doing this all wrong. I reached over slowly and touched the ends of her fingers with my own. She opened her eyes and stared at me.

'I thought you were about to say you didn't want to see me again.'

'No, no, no,' I said, shaking my head.

'I mean, I wouldn't blame you, obviously. It's not like I'm

much of a catch, am I? Not with all my . . . What's the word? *Baggage*. If you got cold feet after . . . last time – that would be perfectly understandable.'

'I didn't,' I said. 'The opposite, actually.'

She raised an eyebrow. 'What is the opposite of cold feet?'

'I don't know – hot something,' I said.

She nodded. 'Hot something. Well, that's good, I suppose.' She laughed, then wiped her eyes. 'Sorry. You gave me a bit of a shock, that's all.'

I pulled her hand towards mine. 'I didn't mean to.' I wanted to say something nice now, something reassuring, like *Let's spend the day together*, but I knew I couldn't. Instead, I was going to make her cry again.

'Why don't you start over,' she said, giving my hand a squeeze.

'OK.' I took a deep breath. There was no way of sugar-coating it. 'I'm going to have to go away for a while. I won't be able to call you or even send a message. And I can't tell you why.'

There, I'd said it. She looked at me for a long time, her expression blank.

'How long?'

'I don't know.'

'But . . . weeks? Months? Longer?'

'Weeks . . . probably.'

She seemed relieved. 'OK. Weeks.' She looked as if she was processing that, thinking about not being able to call me up at any time of the day or night, knowing I'd be there for her.

'If I haven't got in touch by the end of the month, then that probably means I'm . . .' I couldn't bring myself to say it.

'Not coming back at all?'

I looked down at our intertwined hands.

'Jesus! You're saying you might get killed! What the hell are you mixed up in?'

I shook my head. 'I can't tell you. I wish I could, but I can't. It wouldn't do any good. It wouldn't be safe.'

She looked shocked. 'You mean *I* wouldn't be safe?'

I nodded. 'Look, if you decide it's no good – this is no good, if you want to . . .'

She pulled her hands away and wrapped them round herself. 'Oh, shut up. Shut up.'

She hugged herself for a while, then reached into the pocket of her raincoat and pulled out a tissue. She dabbed her eyes then blew her nose.

'I'll wait. I can wait,' she said.

I felt the rock that had been squeezing my chest suddenly being lifted off.

'On one condition.' I looked at her. She held my gaze, a fierceness in her eyes. 'When you come back . . . *if* you come back, you have to tell me everything.'

So here it was. The thing I'd been avoiding for so long. It seemed I couldn't dodge it any longer. I'd known I was going to have to face up to it at some point – after all, what sort of a relationship could you have with someone if you couldn't tell them what you were doing when you weren't with them? – but I hadn't been expecting the moment to come so soon. Now it had, I felt sick, dizzy. But in one way it was a relief.

'OK,' I said.

'Promise?'

'I promise.'

She sniffed. 'Then I promise to stay strong until then. No jumping off bridges or . . . anything like that.'

'Good,' I said. I needed to hear her say it. I just wasn't sure I believed it. She read the uncertainty on my face.

'Really.'

We both knew there was nothing more to say. She got up and pushed her chair in. I started to get up but she put a hand on my arm. 'No, stay.' She walked to the door, gave me one last quick glance as she opened it, then walked out onto the street.

I sat for a moment, watching her walk past the window, head down. Then I pulled a tenner out of my wallet, put it down on the table under a saucer and followed.

On the street I wondered what I was doing. Was it just that I wasn't going to see her for a long time – for all I knew, never again – and couldn't let her go? Or was it something else, something I didn't want to admit to myself?

It was drizzly and cold, as well as late, but Soho was still busy. I dodged round a group of kids sharing a bottle of something, laughing and joking, stepping into the road just as Lucy turned the corner into Old Compton Street. She was walking quickly, so I started to jog. At the corner I could see her twenty yards ahead, just in front of a couple of blokes holding hands. I hung back, not wanting to get too close, waiting until there were a few more bodies between us, then carried on. She was walking purposefully, but keeping an eye on the handful of cars cruising slowly towards Charing Cross Road.

Then she stopped. I ducked into a shop doorway. A dark saloon pulled up and she opened one of the rear passenger doors and got in. I stayed in the shadows as the car drove past, but I could see clearly. There were two men in the front, clean-shaven, dark jackets. The driver was wearing a tie. In the back was a woman, middle-aged, blonde hair. Lucy sat next to her, staring straight ahead, her expression blank.

I stayed where I was for a long time, trying to process what I'd just seen. After all the emotions I'd gone through at the diner, I felt numb. Paralysed. Unable to think.

After a while a young bloke in a filthy windcheater and torn trackie bottoms stopped, a grubby hand held out. 'Sorry to bother you, mate,' he said in a raspy voice, 'but I'm trying to get some money for something to eat.' I pulled out my wallet and emptied it out into his outstretched hand. A tenner blew away in the breeze before he could close his fist over the rest of the notes. His mouth opened and he looked at me, lost for words.

I shifted myself past him out of the doorway and started putting one foot in front of the other mechanically, heading west towards Wardour Street.

36

An hour and a half later I was standing in the rain in front of St Saviour's, wet through, my bones aching. Despite the cold and the rain I felt as if I could have stood there forever. Pain, discomfort, hunger: I didn't feel any of it. I no longer cared what happened.

After a while – it could have been a minute or much longer – the door opened and a figure slipped out. He stood on the steps, trying to keep out of the worst of the rain, and looked around. It was Martindale, wearing the same dark combats and hoodie as before. As soon as he saw me, he raised a hand.

'Stevie. There you are.'

I looked at him without moving. I could have stayed where I was, just standing there like a statue, until he gave up and went back inside. Or I could have turned around and walked away. It didn't really matter. But instead I stepped forward, my sodden trainers squelching on the flagstones, and followed him inside.

He shut the door and drew across the heavy bolts. There was a hurricane lamp by the altar, and he went and picked it up. As its beam played across the inside of the church, I thought it looked even more ramshackle than before. There were buckets on the floor, presumably to catch the water leaking from the roof, and what looked like sodden hymn books were lying in random piles. There were splashes of white paint across the back of one of the pews – or maybe it was graffiti – and a filthy tarpaulin was draped over the font. It was hard to imagine Martindale actually conducting any services here. The whole place looked as if it was about to be demolished.

'This way.'

He opened the door into the little room where we'd had our talk and put the lamp on the floor. But instead of sitting down, he moved over to the bookshelf under the crucifix and started moving it to one side.

'Give us a hand, Stevie, would you?'

I got on the other end and shoved as he pulled. It was surprisingly heavy, even though there weren't any books on it, and it took a fair bit of grunting and heaving to shift it.

'That'll do.'

The bookshelf had been hiding a set of double doors, three or four feet high, set into the wall, the handles padlocked together with a heavy chain. Martindale pulled a bunch of keys from a pocket of his combats and sorted through them until he found the right one. He opened the padlock and freed the chain, then pulled the doors open. The light from the lamp was now shining into a narrow, low-ceilinged room.

'Watch your head,' he said, nudging me forward with his hand. I thought maybe he was going to shut the door behind me and leave me there, but instead he hunched forward and followed me through, closing the doors behind us. Bent over with my hands on my knees, I looked around. The room was empty, with bare, whitewashed walls and an old carpet covering most of the floor. Martindale started rolling the carpet up from one end, and without being asked, I knelt down and helped him push it against the far wall. A thick cloud of acrid dust made us both close our eyes. When I opened them, I was looking at a trapdoor set in the floor.

Martindale lifted up one of the doors by its handle, releasing a gust of cold, stale air, and then the other one. I peered down into the hole and saw the top of an old wooden ladder.

'This is where it can get a bit tricky,' Martindale said. 'I'm going to have to let you go first and you're going to have to feel your way a bit, I'm afraid. Just take it slowly and you'll be all right.'

He pointed the lamp down into the hole as I got on my knees, then put one leg down, feeling for the rungs. Once I'd got one foot securely in, I started lowering myself down, gripping the sides of the ladder tightly. It wobbled slightly under my weight.

'Don't worry, it's quite safe,' Martindale said.

I made my way down steadily, and as soon as I got my feet on the floor, Martindale followed, holding the lamp in one hand and feeling his way down the ladder with the other.

'Interesting history, St Saviour's,' he said once he'd reached the bottom, sweeping the beam of the lamp across the low rectangular space we were now standing in. One wall was brick, but the others looked as if they were made out of solid stone. One of them had a dark, worn-looking door set into it.

'Officially, the first St Saviour's was built in 1152 by King Stephen, not long before he died. Of course, there's nothing left of the original structure – at least not above ground. Lots of knocking bits down and rebuilding them over the years. But there had been chapels of some sort on this site for who knows how long even before Stephen. Hence all the chambers and tunnels down here. The last rector was a bit of a history buff – he discovered a couple of tombs nobody knew about – but I think I've outdone him. I suppose I should have told the diocese about all this –' he swept the torch through 360 degrees again – 'but what would be the point? They'd probably just shut it all up and throw away the key. Health and safety and all that nonsense. Or worse: turn it into a tourist attraction, like the Temple of Mithras.'

I wondered why he was banging on about all of this crap. Did he really think Stevie gave a rat's arse about King Stephen or the Temple of Doom or whatever it was? Then it hit me. It didn't really matter *what* he said: he was just distracting Stevie, keeping him calm, talking any old bollocks to keep him from having second thoughts about what he was getting himself into.

For the first time I started to notice the cold and a shiver went through me.

Martindale nudged me towards the door, then felt in his pocket and came up with a big brass key. The door was low and narrow and the dark wood was chipped and scarred. He turned the key in the lock and the door scraped against the floor as he pulled it open.

'I'll go first,' he said, holding the lamp out in front of him. We entered a narrow passage. I put my hand out and felt cold, damp stone. 'I'm pretty certain there's an underground river pretty close. When there's a lot of rain it can get a bit wet down here.'

He turned a corner and the light disappeared. I felt my way along until I saw him again, unlocking another door just like the first. He waited until I'd caught him up and pushed me through. 'Watch your head.'

The room was small, maybe ten foot by ten. The walls were dark brick and the floor looked like hard-packed earth. Heavy wooden beams made up the ceiling. In one corner was a three-legged stool. In the other were two metal buckets. One of them was full of water.

'This used to be an ossuary. When I discovered it, it was full of bones. Impossible to tell how old, but judging from the state of them, I'd say they went back to well before King Stephen's time.' Martindale shrugged off his backpack and unzipped it, pulling out a black bin bag and a grey blanket. 'Right. The first thing, Stevie, is to get rid of your old clothes. They're a symbol of your old life, the old Stevie, so that's where we'll begin. Then, one by one, we're going to strip away the other layers, the layers of the self, until you're spiritually naked as well as physically. Then you can be reborn.' He looked at me. 'It sounds easy, doesn't it? Like peeling an onion. But I'm afraid, like an onion, there will be a few tears. The old self, old habits, old memories; they won't give up without a fight. Have you ever gone cold turkey, Stevie?'

'Once,' I said.

He nodded. 'This will be worse.'

I thought maybe he was going to give me one last chance to pull out, but he just looked at me with a mixture of sadness and anticipation, the way you'd look at something you were never going to see again.

I started to peel off my clothes and Martindale scooped them into the bin bag. When I was finished he handed me the blanket. 'It can get a bit chilly down here. OK, I'm going to leave you for a while, so you can get used to your new surroundings. When I come back –' he smiled, and the lamplight glinted on his glasses – 'we'll begin.'

I watched him turn and walk through the door. When he closed it behind him, the darkness was total. I listened to the key scraping in the lock, then his footsteps along the passage, gradually fainter and fainter. I heard the creak of the other door, the sound of another key being turned, and then silence.

Darkness and silence. My new home. I wrapped the blanket round myself, then slowly felt my way around, touching the walls, the floor, the stool, the buckets – round and round until I had a mental picture in my head of where everything was. It wasn't much, but it might end up being the only thing I had to hold on to.

Reaching a corner, I sat down, wedging myself between the walls, feeling the icy touch of the old bricks on my shoulders through the thin blanket. I closed my eyes, then opened them. No difference. The same impenetrable dark. That would be the first stage of the disorientation process, blurring the distinction between inner and outer, between what you could see and what was just in your head, between what was imagined and what was real. I knew it would start to unsettle me before too long – opening my eyes and the world refusing to appear – but for the moment I was happy to give myself up to it. Real darkness is something we never really experience any more. It was like we were more afraid of it than even our caveman ancestors must have been. But at this moment, it felt like something I desperately needed.

It was when I started to see things that the problems would start.

37

The sound of Martindale opening the door came sooner than I had expected. Not that I had any real idea how much time had passed. But I'd thought he would let Stevie stew for a bit longer, let the darkness and the silence soften him up before he got to work on him. Maybe he thought Stevie was so weak-minded to begin with that it wouldn't take much to turn him to jelly. Or maybe he was just eager to get on with the job: there must be a clock ticking for him, too, after all.

Martindale put the lamp down on the floor, angling it so it shone behind him, making a dim halo on the wall. He sat down on the stool and shifted round to face me.

'I want you to recall a memory for me.'

His voice had changed. This wasn't the chatty priest any more, burbling on about ancient artefacts. He sounded cold, impersonal, all business. Was this the first glimpse of the real Paul Martindale? The other thing I noticed was that he hadn't called me Stevie. It was a small thing, but chilling in its way. Stevie Nichols was already history. I was sure he would never use his name again, confident that the man who walked out of this miserable cell would be a different person entirely. But why, if he wanted Stevie to forget who he was, was he asking him to remember?

'OK,' I said. 'What?'

'Let's go back to your childhood. What's the first thing you can remember?'

I closed my eyes. *Come on, Stevie*. He seemed reluctant, like he'd gone into his shell since arriving at the church. Self-defence mechanism maybe? When it came to the crunch, had he decided he really wanted to hang on to who he was and his miserable bloody life?

Slowly an image formed in my mind. A bright, sunny day. I had to squint when I looked up. I was, what, four? Five? I was wearing a pale-blue T-shirt with a brown stain on it that wouldn't come out, however many times it was washed. And the grey shorts I hated because they were always slipping down. They belonged to someone else, someone bigger, but they were all I had. The other kids were always taking the piss, trying to pull them down.

'Well? What do you remember?'

'I was little. Must have been at the orphanage. But we was outside, somewhere. There was grass. It was sunny.'

'That's clear in your head?'

'Yeah.'

'Then what happened?'

'There was a girl. There weren't usually girls. We wasn't supposed to mix with them, you know? Stupid – we was only little kids. Fucking nuns, what did they think we was going to do?' I lost my train of thought for a moment, thinking about the nuns and all the things they tried to stop you doing, which was pretty much anything that wasn't scrubbing floors or praying or going to sleep.

'Go on.'

'This girl. She had blonde frizzy hair. I'd never seen that before. I thought it was . . . I dunno. Anyway, she came over and smiled at me, so I looked round, thinking someone was behind me and was going to whack me – you know, she was just distracting me – but there wasn't anyone there. Then she pulled her hand out from behind her back and she had a paper bag in it. She held it out, like. "D'you wanna sweet?" she said. "My name's Rosie." I still didn't trust her, you know, so I just looked at her, all that corkscrewy hair waving about in the wind. She was smiling, but with her teeth together, which I thought was funny. "Go on, put your hand in," she said. So I did, like. I still thought there'd be a trick, like the bag was full of dog shit or something.'

'And was it?'

'No. There was sweets. They were round. Big. I pulled one out. "They're gobstoppers," she said. "You can have one." I remember I put it in my pocket and she laughed. I kept it in my pocket for days. Every now and then I'd put my hand in and feel it. It was sticky. I thought it must be getting smaller. Then one morning it was gone.'

For a moment I felt everything Stevie was feeling. No one had ever given me anything before. Only taken things away. I was sorry I'd never told her my name. I thought if I'd told her my name, one day I'd see her again and she'd remember, but because I hadn't she'd forget about me.

'And you remember all that?'

'Yeah.'

'Are you sure?'

'What d'you mean?'

'I just talked to her.'

'Who?'

'Rosie.' He jerked his head towards the ceiling. 'She's upstairs. We were just having a cup of tea.' He smiled. 'I do see what you mean about the hair. But the rest of her's changed quite a lot, I'm afraid.'

I sat up straighter, confused. 'What . . . I dunno what you—'

He wrinkled his nose. 'Not a pretty sight. Never mind. Anyway, she told me all about it.'

'What d'you mean? About what?' I could feel my heart rate rising fast.

'The gobstopper. You know it was poisoned? Rat poison, she said. She wanted you to eat it so she could watch you die. It would have been very painful.' He shook his head sadly. 'Nasty little bitch.'

I closed my eyes. I watched Rosie smile again. Now, with her teeth clenched, her expression somehow didn't look so friendly.

'You're lying!' I shouted as loud as I could, but my voice came out a feeble, strangled bark.

Martindale didn't move. 'You think about her, don't you?

Not all the time. Months might go by – years, even. And then when you're feeling down, one of your especially black moods, you think back to when she offered you a sweet. And you imagine bumping into her again – the grown-up Rosie – you imagine she's beautiful now, and she remembers you; she's never forgotten, and just like you, she's been thinking of you for all these years.'

I clenched my fists and shook my head violently from side to side like a dog trying to escape its leash.

Why is he saying this? Why can't he just shut up?

'Well, it's true: she has been thinking about you. Ever since you put the gobstopper in your pocket and walked away, she's been wondering if you ate it. She's been imagining the look on your face when the pain hit you, she's been imagining you frothing at the mouth, your eyes bulging, your black, swollen tongue sticking out. When she's feeling a bit down, she thinks about it and it cheers her up, im-agining you in unbearable pain, squirming like a worm on a hook, choking your life out.'

I suddenly felt a stab of pain in my guts. A wave of nausea swept through me and I toppled over, retching. In two violent spams, I emptied the contents of my stomach before my cheek hit the floor, then lay there, my face inches from the spreading pool, panting, overwhelmed with the sour stench of vomit now filling the room.

I opened my eyes. If Martindale was sickened by the smell, he didn't show it. If anything, his expression was one of satisfaction.

'I think that's enough for now. Funny how things aren't always quite the way we remember them, isn't it? I'll let you have a rest and a think, and then I'll be back.'

38

It was the cold that eventually woke me up. I tried to lift my face off the floor, but it seemed to be stuck to the slowly drying vomit. I pulled harder and managed to sit up. The blanket had fallen away and I pulled it round myself and just sat there, trying to hug some warmth into my bones. After a while, I tried standing, but my hamstrings instantly cramped up and I toppled back down, so I crawled instead, trying to access my mental map of the room to locate the buckets. My outstretched hand first found the stool and I instinctively pulled it back, as if Martindale might somehow still be there. I took a deep breath, the stinking air almost making me gag, and inched my way round to where I guessed the buckets would be. The water in the first bucket was ice-cold, but I didn't care. I scooped out a handful and splashed it over my face, wiping away the filth. I kept going until the smell was out of my nostrils and I could breathe normally, then lowered my face to the bucket and drank. I slowly levered myself up until I could stand, then started slowly pacing round my cell, trying to get my circulation going again. Once I was loose, I felt my way round to the opposite corner and sat down, wrapping the blanket around me as tightly as I could.

I closed my eyes. I couldn't feel Stevie anywhere. He just seemed to have disappeared. I let my mind wander and eventually I found him, curled up tightly into a ball, trying to make himself as small as he could, a tiny, tiny invisible speck floating in the vast, empty dark. I shook my head sadly. If he thought he could hide from Martindale as easily as that, he had another think coming. But he'd find that out soon enough. I let him drift on while I focused on what I needed to do.

The first thing was to give myself some basic mental tasks. How big is the cell? How many feet from side to side? What's the distance from floor to ceiling? Then, when I'd exhausted all the possibilities of mental calculation, I'd try some simple memory tests. First off, FA Cup winners, going back as far as I could. Then scores. Then scorers. Then back to the beginning and do the teams, starting with the keeper, then right back, left back . . .

I wasn't in school much when I was a kid, and didn't pay any attention when I was, so you could ask me kings and queens of England and I'd be stuck after Elizabeth II. But that didn't mean I wasn't any good at absorbing information; it just meant I could never be arsed if there didn't seem to be any point to it. Football would definitely keep me going for a good while, and then there was all the stuff I learned in the army, starting with every kind of weapon I'd ever handled, imagining field-stripping them in the dark . . . Anything would do, so long as it was just information, numbers, data.

No emotional content. That was the thing to avoid. The trick was going to be to let Martindale fuck with Stevie's memories until he went mad without letting the same thing happen to me. Focusing on the physical stuff would be a useful distraction: pain, cold, hunger – whatever. And then routine mental tasks: calculations, memory games. Anything neutral. Anything to keep Martindale away from the important stuff.

I got up and started carefully inching my way around the walls, planting each foot neatly after the other. Let's say each foot is ten inches long, just to make things a bit more interesting, then when it comes to the height of the walls, we'd do the width of a hand – say, four inches? I nodded to myself: sounds good.

I plodded on, round and round, totting it all up in my head and storing it away. I had no real sense of time, but it felt as if I must have been going for two hours at least – maybe three? – before my concentration started to waver. I felt my way over to the bucket and gulped down another scoop of water. I could have had more but I needed to ration myself: I'd used up at least half in cleaning myself up and I didn't know when Martindale would be back. I was getting hungry now, too, beginning to feel a bit woozy as my blood sugar hovered around zero. Soon I'd be running on empty, and that would bring its own problems. But for the moment I was OK, as long as I didn't get too dehydrated. Stevie chucking his guts up hadn't helped.

I decided to have a rest. I went back to my corner, almost

stubbing my toe on the legs of the stool, then remembering where it was just in time. I wedged myself between the walls, pulling the blanket over my knees. I felt the darkness and the silence closing over me as my mind went quiet. It was like going under when you were exhausted from treading water. I felt a hand grasping my ankle, pulling me down. For a second I let go, surrendering to the familiar touch. *No!* I shook myself alert and got my head above water again.

Come on, focus. What next? OK, got it: you're going on the tube from Uxbridge to Epping. Which lines? How many stops? Count them: Hillingdon, Ickenham, Ruislip, Eastcote – no – Ruislip Manor, then Eastcote, then . . . is it North Harrow or West Harrow? Or Harrow-on-the-Hill? Shit, go back to the beginning, see the map in your head. OK – Uxbridge, Hillingdon . . .

39

I heard the soft scrape of shoes on stone and suddenly became alert. Had I been asleep? My sense of time was totally gone. Martindale could have been away for an hour or a whole day. I stopped and listened. Nothing. Was it my imagination? Maybe it was just rats. There must be plenty down here, after all. What did Martindale say this room used to be: an ossuary? Full of bones, at any rate. They'd be hundreds of years old, though. Not much left to gnaw on. There could always be a new lot, of course, if things went wrong. I could end up propped up in the corner just like Daisy. Would anyone ever find me? Maybe not for another few hundred years. That would give the rats plenty of time to pick me clean.

Fuck. Stop that.

I heard the clunk of the lock and then the creak of the door opening. A gust of chilly air blew into the room as the light from Martindale's lamp swept round the walls. He stood for a moment, looking down at me, without speaking, then sat down on the stool, placing the lamp on the floor beside him. I shut my eyes, the sudden brightness making me dizzy.

'It's probably a bit bright for you, isn't it? You're getting used to the dark.' He reached into a pocket of his combats and pulled out a candle and a box of matches. 'This will be a bit less uncomfortable.' He struck a match and held it to the wick until it spluttered alight, then set the candle down carefully on the floor, before turning off the lamp. I opened my eyes. Martindale's face seemed to be floating in the gloom, just visible in the candlelight. Somewhere deep inside, I could feel Stevie trying to worm his way further into the dark.

'I hope you're feeling rested, because it's time for another little trip down memory lane.'

I nodded, slowly, but Martindale seemed to sense that Stevie wasn't entirely present. I couldn't see his eyes clearly but I knew he was looking at me, waiting patiently. Slowly, reluctantly, Stevie uncurled, like a kid playing sardines whose hiding place had just been discovered.

'OK,' Martindale said. 'You're probably feeling a little hungry. If you concentrate hard and do what I ask, maybe I'll bring you something.'

'OK, yeah,' I said, my voice barely a whisper.

'Your mother,' he said.

'I don't—'

'Yes, you do.' His voice was firm. 'You *do*. You've just chosen not to remember. I can't think why you'd do that – a boy deliberately forgetting his own mother? That's not very nice, is it?'

I felt a flutter of panic. Stevie was fully present now. 'But she – I don't know – got rid of me, when I was a baby. So I can't remember her, can I?'

Martindale sighed heavily. 'That's the story you've told yourself, but we both know it's not true. You've just tried to block her out. But that's going to stop, right now.'

My breathing quickened. 'OK.'

'Good. Let's start with your first summer holiday.'

Nothing. My mind was a blank.

'Come on – Bournemouth. You went to the beach. What was the weather like?'

I paused. Stevie had never been to Bournemouth. He didn't even know where it was. But it was no use him saying that. Martindale was like an irresistible force. Stevie was just too weak to resist. I closed my eyes and tried to think. At first there was nothing. Then suddenly I could picture it.

'It . . . rained,' I said.

'Yes! It poured down, didn't it! What did you do?'

'Made sandcastles on the beach, I suppose.'

'In the rain?'

A pause.

'Yeah.'

'What was your mother doing?'

It was miraculous, as if Martindale had conjured her out of thin air. There she was, the mother he'd never seen. He could have reached out and touched her. 'She . . . had an umbrella. She stood and watched. She was smoking a cigarette. She was . . . always smoking cigarettes.'

Martindale was nodding. 'Did it make her clothes smell? Could you smell it when she held you?'

I found myself grinning. 'Yeah. I liked it.'

'When you smell cigarette smoke, do you think of her?'

'Yeah. Always.'

'Was she pretty? She had dark hair, didn't she?'

'Yeah. And long. Really long. All the way down her back.'

Martindale didn't say anything for a while, letting the smell and the look and the feel of her fill Stevie's mind.

'She really loved you, didn't she? What was that? I can't hear you.'

I opened my mouth but no words came out. A dam-burst of emotions was filling me up and I felt myself starting to choke.

'She . . . she . . .'

'Come on, say it.'

I toppled over, retching, but my stomach was empty and nothing came out.

'Say it!'

'Yes! She loved me.'

'Good. Good. And how did she show that she loved you?'

I shook my head. 'No . . . please.'

'Come on, don't be shy!' He was leaning forward eagerly on his stool now. I thought of a fisherman watching his float bobbing, waiting for the moment to strike.

I was rocking from side to side now, moaning. I felt Stevie slipping away.

Martindale could sense it, too. 'You can smell the cigarettes in her hair,' he said, raising his voice. 'Your face is in her hair, that lovely long hair. You liked to put your face in it. You put your arms round her neck, didn't you? Holding on tight. And then she turned her face to you and looked at you, and she smiled, didn't she? And you smiled back, because you were so happy she was there, and you loved her so much, and then she . . .'

He stood up, a faceless, shadowy figure towering over me. I cringed back, like a dog waiting to be kicked.

'Say it!' he shouted.

Stevie was on the verge of blacking out. I took a huge breath, trying to fill my lungs . . .

'*She kissed me!*' I screamed, then sank back, like a puppet with all its strings suddenly cut, my head bumping against the wall.

Martindale stood for a moment, looking down at me, then sat back down on the stool. The candle had fallen over, and he picked it up carefully and stood it upright. He lit another match and the flame flickered back into life.

'Very good,' he said. 'I'm glad you can remember that. You're still remembering it, aren't you?'

I made a sound.

'I'll take that as a yes. A mother's love: we all need that, don't we? Without it we'd be . . . nothing. Nothing at all.'

I felt sick, knowing what was about to happen.

Time stretched out. Martindale didn't seem to be in any hurry to deliver the final blow. *Just fucking get on with it*, I thought.

'I said I'd get you some food, didn't I? What would you like?' He waited. 'That's all right, I'll just grab what I can find. Oh, before I go, just one thing you should know.'

He came and squatted down beside me. I couldn't see him properly, but I could feel his breath on my face.

'Your mother,' he said in a soft voice. 'She died soon after you were born. So I'm not sure who the woman on the beach was. Or the little boy for that matter. Strange, isn't it? Because you remember her so clearly.'

He waited to see if he'd get a response. But there was nothing. Then he turned and walked to the door.

40

It was the gnawing hunger pains that eventually brought me back to my senses. I was lying on my side, clutching the blanket, my face against the cold floor. Far off, very faintly, I could hear a child crying. It felt as if I'd been listening to it for a long time. Could there be a child down here, somewhere in another cell? I didn't understand. What would Martindale want with a child? Then I realized: it was Stevie. I listened. It was getting fainter. Soon it would stop. And then Stevie would be ready for the next stage, the next phase of the cleansing process. I could feel him already, beginning to loosen and fall apart, like an overdone chicken. I wondered what Martindale was going to do next, what bone he was going to pull.

I got onto my hands and knees and crawled towards the buckets. I wasn't thirsty, but I was desperate to put something in my mouth. Martindale had said something about bringing food. When had that been? I felt along the floor with my fingers. A bowl. A metal bowl. I put my finger inside. There was a smear of something; it felt like porridge, but thinner. Some kind of gruel. I scraped it up and shovelled it into my mouth. It was barely a mouthful and tasted of nothing, but I started salivating, just the same. I worked my fingers around the sides, trying to get every last scrap, desperately licking and sucking my fingers until there was nothing left.

So he had left food. Had I already eaten the rest of the bowl? Why didn't I remember? Or maybe the rats had been at it. Or had he left the bowl with just a spoonful of food in it just to fuck with me? More mind games. Maybe he'd calculated that it was just enough to keep me going, just enough to keep me alert and receptive without actually making me feel any less hungry. I put the bowl down and methodically searched the floor in case there was anything else, even sticking my fingers hopefully into the half-dried patch of vomit, but that seemed to be it. For a moment I had the thought that Stevie had eaten the rest of the bowl without telling me and felt a flash of anger.

I shook my head. *Steady, Logan.*

I drank a scoop of water, splashed another scoop onto my face, and went back to my corner, wrapping the blanket round my shoulders. *Stevie's close to breaking point*, I told myself. *You just have to hold your shit together until he cracks, and remember not to go crazy along with him.*

You can do that, right?

I nodded to myself. *Yeah. Piece of piss.*

OK, what next?

How about some exercise? Fifty circuits of the cell, maybe? Just to get the circulation going and keep everything from seizing up?

I wasn't sure I had the energy. I would need what little I

had left to try and stay alert, focused. Silly to waste it on doing press-ups.

Concentrating on the body, on physical sensations, was good, though. It was a way of keeping yourself grounded. I decided to do a full inventory, starting at the bottom with my feet and working my way upwards, focusing on what I could feel. I spread the blanket and laid myself out flat. An uncontrollable wave of shivering went through me.

OK, that's a good place to start. Cold, you're unbelievably fucking cold. Good. It's when you stop feeling cold you have to worry. OK, let's get back to the feet: apart from the cold, what can you feel? Those broken toes from two years ago: still aching a bit, or is that just imagination? And what about your dodgy Achilles? Still a bit sore?

I worked my way up, willing sensation into my muscles and tendons, trying to bring the map of my body to life, remembering old injuries – along with the stories that went with them – and tracing long-healed scars, until I could feel a faint buzzing going all the way through me from head to toe.

Right. Next.

Where had I got to with the cup finals? For a moment I was confused: had I already started or had I just been thinking about it? I had a feeling I'd got to 1974 but I couldn't be sure. *Never mind; let's start there, anyway.* I could always go back to the beginning.

Right. 1974. Liverpool and Newcastle. Three–nil Liverpool. Bill Shankly still in charge. Was it his last game? Can't remember

– come back to that. Scorers: Keegan, Heighway . . . Shit, who scored the third? Keegan, Heighway . . . Toshack? No. Let me think. Let's go through the team.

'Keegan.'

I looked up. Daisy was sitting on the stool.

I blinked and looked again.

'Still here,' she said with a giggle. 'Not pleased to see me? Anyway, it was Keegan. He scored two.' She shook her head. 'You call yourself a football fan?'

Her hair was very blonde, almost dazzling. I didn't remember it being frizzy. I also wondered how I was able to see her, since there was no light.

'It's my inner glow, in case you're wondering,' she said with another laugh.

I felt if I said anything, if I acknowledged her presence, it would only make her more real.

'You're welcome,' she said. 'Any time. A bottomless treasure trove of useless information, that's me.'

I couldn't help staring at her, even though I desperately wanted her not to be there. She seemed pleased.

'Don't you think I'm looking well?'

I opened my mouth, then quickly shut it again. She was looking lovely.

'Better than you, anyway. Aren't they feeding you down here? You look a bit pale, to be honest. It's not really meant for regular people down here. You should be dead, strictly speaking.' She looked at me curiously. 'You're not dead, are you?'

'No,' I whispered.

She laughed delightedly, clapping her hands. 'He speaks! Not dead, then. Very good. Being dead's no fun, I can tell you. Not at first, anyway. You get used to it after a while, though. Then it can have its moments, I suppose.' She looked around. 'Where's the other one?'

I concentrated on keeping my lips shut tight.

'Hiding. Silly boy.' She shook her head. 'I don't know, the pair of you.'

The longer this went on, the more real she seemed to be getting. I felt torn in half. There were so many things I wanted to ask her. Plus it was company. But I also desperately wanted her to go away. How could I make her go away? I was sure she'd go if Martindale came back, but I didn't want that. Anything was preferable to that.

'You feeling peckish?'

My stomach clenched.

'I've got a little something here, if you are. Don't show your friend, though, or he'll want one, too.'

She was holding something in her fist. Her fingers were very pale. Her fingernails were blood-red.

'Do you want to see?' Her eyes sparkled and she was grinning. 'If you don't say anything, that means yes!'

I bit my lip, tasting blood.

'*Ta da!*' She opened her fist, revealing what looked like a purple golf ball in her palm. 'Look at that! It's almost as big as I am!' she squealed.

She held it closer and I could see that it was a gobstopper.

'They're not so easy to get hold of these days, you know,' she said. 'Not great big ones like this. Well, do you want it?'

I couldn't help staring at it. It seemed to be slowly growing bigger as I watched, glistening in the glow of her bone-white fingers. At first it had looked purple, but now it seemed darker, almost black. I wondered what would happen if I put it in my mouth. It wasn't real, after all. The sugary, artificial taste of it was making my mouth water. Surely it couldn't do me any harm?

'Go on,' she said. She seemed to have got closer without moving. I licked my lips. I was trying to keep as still as possible, but my hand seemed to be moving of its own accord, slowly reaching out. 'Go on! That's it!' I looked up and saw she was grinning, her tiny pearl-white teeth clenched together.

I heard the sudden rattle of a key in the lock. Her head snapped round, and she snatched her hand back, closing her fingers over the gobstopper.

The door began to open and the light from Martindale's hurricane lamp swept round the room. As it touched her, she started to fade.

'Saved by the bell,' she said in an annoyed voice, before vanishing.

41

Martindale stood in the middle of the room with the lamp in his hand, looking at me curiously. I realized I still had my hand out. I pulled it back and hid it in the folds of the blanket, keeping my eyes on the floor while I shuffled back further into my corner. He shone the lamp over the buckets and the tin bowl. I saw the glint of a metal spoon in the far corner. 'We'd better empty that,' he said. I assumed he meant the bucket I was supposed to piss and shit in. 'And get you some more water. It looks like you were hungry.' He put the lamp down so it was pointed almost directly at me, moved the stool nearer and sat down.

Even with my eyes closed, the light was blinding. My head began to throb. I could tell he was looking at me, examining me carefully to see how much resistance was left, how much of Stevie remained to be disassembled.

My eye started to twitch. I realized my mouth was open, a thin strand of drool hanging down, but I couldn't seem to close it. My hands started clutching each other under the blanket.

That wasn't Daisy, I said to myself.

Then who was it? You saw her, didn't you? Stevie's fucked off. He's had enough of this lark. You're the only one left. So it must be you that's going mad.

I opened my eyes, afraid that I'd been speaking aloud. I was sure Martindale must have heard me, but his face showed no reaction. He was still looking at me dispassionately, like I was some sort of bug under a microscope. I couldn't help glancing over his shoulder, afraid Daisy would be there with her poisoned gobstopper, but there was no one else in the room.

That wasn't Daisy.

Who was it, then?

Nobody.

She wasn't real, then?

No.

Funny – she seemed to think you *were real. She must be seeing things. Maybe she's gone mad.*

Yes.

Not you, then?

No. NO!

I was sure I'd shouted, but there was still no reaction from Martindale. He was holding one of my eyes open with his thumb and forefinger, gazing into my pupil. Then he picked up one of my hands, held it for a moment, then let it go. It flopped back onto my lap, a dead thing. Satisfied, he pushed the stool back into the centre of the room and sat down again, looking at me thoughtfully. After a while he nodded to himself, apparently happy with what he saw.

'I think you might be ready for a little experiment,' he said. 'Just to see how far along we are.'

I knew what Martindale was trying to do. He was scrambling Stevie's memories so he couldn't tell what was real and what wasn't. And if you can't trust your memories, then you can't be sure you are who you think you are. Stevie Nichols would cease to exist. Stevie Nichols, who'd never existed in the first place. I felt as if I'd once had a plan, a very clever plan, but now I'd forgotten what it was.

'I want you to think back to – not so far back this time – let's say a couple of years. Just pick an ordinary day.'

Two years. Sarah and Joseph and me were a family then. An ordinary day.

No!

I wasn't going to let him do this. I *couldn't* let him do this. Not Sarah. Not Joseph. I needed Stevie. *Come on, you stupid bastard, where are you? You can't just fuck off out of it like this!*

A look of concern passed across Martindale's face. He could see how tense I was, my body going rigid, all my muscles clenched. I tried to relax. I couldn't let him see I was resisting.

Come on, Stevie – I need you now*!*

An image suddenly came into my head. I'm sitting in a narrow alley behind a shopping centre. My legs are in a filthy old sleeping bag, my knees curled up, just like I am now. I've got a bottle of brandy – a half bottle, but it's almost full – the real stuff. I take a swig and let the liquor slowly burn down my throat. The taste is so sweet. I don't think

I've ever tasted anything so good. I don't remember where it came from or how I got it, and I don't care. It's mine and I'm going to drink the lot.

Martindale could see from the way my eyelids were fluttering that I was remembering something. 'What can you see?' he asked.

'I've got some brandy,' I said. It was Stevie's voice, not mine. 'I'm just having a little drink, you know?'

Martindale nodded. 'That must be nice. All on your own.'

'Yeah. I'm in that alley behind the shops, you know?' In my head I took another swig.

'All right. I want you to do something for me now.'

I wiped my hand across my mouth. 'OK.'

'I want you to look at yourself. Imagine you're floating, just hovering right above yourself, looking down. Like a drone.'

I tried that. There was Stevie in his filthy coat, his sleeping bag wrapped round his knees like an old lady feeling the cold, clutching a bottle of amber liquid.

'Can you see yourself?'

I nodded. 'Yeah.'

'OK. Let's pull back a bit further. You're at the entrance to the alley now. You're standing, watching. What can you see?'

I narrowed my eyes. 'Bloke in the corner in a sleeping bag.'

'What's he doing?'

'Drinking. He's got a bottle. Brandy, it looks like.'

'Do you recognize him?'

'Yeah, it's Stevie.'

'Whose brandy is it?'

'I . . . what?'

'It's yours, isn't it? A whole bottle. All yours. And he took it. Look, he's drinking it now. The rate he's going, soon there won't be any left. How does that make you feel?'

'Thieving cunt,' I said, without thinking.

Martindale was nodding encouragingly. 'Yes! You don't like him, do you?'

'He's a cunt. Nobody likes him. He makes shit up all the time.'

'What are you going to do, then?'

'Get my fucking bottle back.'

I walked quickly down the alley, stepping over a pool of piss. Stevie was just raising the bottle to his mouth when I kicked him in the legs, hard. He squealed and dropped the bottle. It smashed on the concrete, the yellow liquid mixing with the filth to make a dark puddle.

'You stupid fucking bastard!' I shouted, kicking him again. He rolled up into a ball, his hands covering his face. I kicked him in the ribs as hard as I could and then again, until I heard something crack. He rolled back over, his hands clutching his side, moaning, and I thought, *Right, I'm going to fucking do you now*, and I took a couple of steps back, like I was about to take a penalty, and—

'Enough!'

My eyes snapped open. Martindale was leaning over me. 'We can leave him now.'

I was breathing hard. Despite the cold, I could feel sweat

gathering on my forehead and trickling down the back of my neck. 'OK.'

He stroked his stubble thoughtfully. 'That was good. Very good. I think you might almost be ready.'

I lay down, exhausted, my head resting on my hand.

After a while I opened my eyes. The room was pitch-black. Martindale had gone. I slowly crawled round the room, feeling the walls, the stool, the buckets. One of them was now empty, the other full with water again. I did another careful circuit, stopping every now and then to listen. I wanted to make sure he wasn't hiding in a corner, holding his breath.

Eventually I was satisfied: all clear.

I took a scoop of water and swilled it round my mouth before spitting it out. I did that twice more until the taste of the brandy was completely gone, then had a drink. There was no food. Unless Martindale had brought some and I'd forgotten. I couldn't tell if I was hungry or not.

But I felt better now. Calmer. I'd managed to keep Martindale from fucking with my memories. Stevie had come up trumps. I just needed to keep going. I'd try and do a few stretches, then go back to the cup finals routine.

Actually, maybe not. I didn't want Daisy coming back.

'Thank goodness for that. Stupid bloody game.'

I kept my eyes shut for as long as I could, my heart hammering, but I couldn't keep it up forever. I opened my eyes and there was Lucy, standing in front of the door in her raincoat, looking very tall. Her hair was wet and she was holding her phone to her ear.

'Terrible reception down here, you know.'

I felt helpless. There was nothing I could do to make her go away. I breathed in and out a few times. *Might as well just go with the flow*, I thought.

'Two minds with a single thought,' she said, putting her phone in her pocket with a frown. '"Go with the flow." That was what I had in mind, until you stepped in. Didn't he say there was a river down here? One of the lost rivers of London, I suppose. Like the Fleet. How romantic!'

I made myself look at her. 'There's something I want to ask you,' I said.

She cocked her head to one side. Water dripped from her hair and onto the floor. 'What?'

'Those people – when you got into the car, after we met at that diner – who were they?'

'What people? What are you talking about?'

'You know what I'm talking about. I saw you. There were three of them. Two men in the front and then a woman in the back.'

She took a step back. 'I got the tube home that night. You're imagining things. I think you've been in this place too long. If you think back, you'll remember, you saw me walk to the end of the road, then you followed me all the way to the station. You do remember that now, don't you?'

I closed my eyes. I could see her. She kept walking. There was no car. No one stopped. She kept going until she reached the end of the road.

'Stop it!' I shouted, clamping my hands over my eyes. 'Stop it!'

Silence. I kept my hands where they were. I listened, my eyes tight shut. Nothing. I waited for as long as I could, then opened them.

'Hello.'

It was Sarah. *Oh God, please no. Please not that.*

'It's OK, Logan. It's all right. This is really me.'

I breathed out. I wanted to believe her. God, how I wanted to believe her.

'Come on, you can look at me,' she said gently.

I looked up, into her eyes. She was smiling.

'It'll be all right. You're strong. And you've got me and Joseph. You can get through this.'

'I'm a bit fucked up, Sarah,' I said.

'Not where it counts,' she said. 'Where it counts you're all right.'

I reached out my hand. I so wanted to touch her.

She pulled away. 'You know we can't do that, Logan.'

I nodded. 'I know. It's just . . . I need something to hold on to. Something real.'

'Just think why you're doing this,' she said. 'That's real.'

'I don't know if that's enough,' I said. 'I'm scared.'

She looked at me sadly, then blew me a kiss. I felt a gentle waft of air against my cheek. And then she was gone.

42

I slept after that. I didn't have any bad dreams, and when I woke up I felt better. Still woozy and a bit hypo; my bones ached and my limbs felt weak – but my head felt OK. Well, maybe not OK exactly. But at least when I opened my eyes, I wasn't terrified of what I was going to see.

Now it was just a case of waiting for Martindale to make an appearance. All I had to do was keep my shit together until then. He seemed to think Stevie was ready for the next stage of the process. I was really hoping it would take place somewhere that didn't smell of shit and vomit, somewhere with central heating and running water, even. A place that didn't make you feel as if you'd been buried alive.

That was the thing at the back of my mind that was starting to nag at me. What if Stevie had actually failed the audition? What if Martindale wasn't coming back, but was just going to leave me here? I had most of a bucket of water. How long could I last after that ran out? Without some more calories, the cold would get me fairly soon as well. It was just a question of whether hypothermia or dehydration did for me first. Freezing to death would be preferable, I guessed. They say you actually start to feel quite warm towards the end. Dying of thirst I really didn't fancy. Those seemed to be the choices. Unless I decided to top myself before it got to that point. If I managed to get the handle off the bucket, maybe I could sharpen an end against the wall, then open a vein. Drowning wasn't an option, which was a relief; I'd never fancied that. I never understood why anyone would choose to go that way, when you could just swallow a few pills . . .

Shit. Better stop that train of thought before it gets started. My out-of-control thoughts were taking me places I really didn't want to go.

What to do? I didn't have the energy to crawl around the cell, let alone walk. The idea of doing sit-ups was a fucking joke. I didn't think I had the strength to even play memory games. There was nothing to do but just sit still and conserve what little energy I had. Try not to think too much. Try not to do anything. And just hope that if I had any more hallucinations, Sarah would come and help me out. That was a funny thought: if I started seeing things, my dead wife would put a stop to it. I had a good chuckle at that one.

Counting. I could always do that, to help keep things on an even keel. Start at zero and keep going for as long as I could and if I forgot where I'd got to, just start again from the beginning. *Out loud?* No, that felt like too much of an effort. Just in my head. *OK, here goes.*

I got to 212 before I got stuck. Something about that number just stopped me in my tracks. What the hell was it? I couldn't say the next number, even in my head. I started from zero again and the same thing happened. What the fuck? Then it hit me: it was a house number. The little house where we used to live before Sarah and Joseph were killed. 212 Garden Close. *Shit.* What could be more neutral than numbers? What could be safer? It seemed like memories were everywhere, just waiting to ambush you. *Never mind. You can deal with it. Get to 212 again, say a little prayer, and then move on. Easy.*

I'd lost count of how many times I'd had to start over, but I was somewhere in the nine hundred and somethings when I heard the sound of footsteps. *Good.* Martindale wasn't just going to leave me here, then. The door opened. A figure entered, dressed in a pale monk's robe, with the cowl pulled down over their face. Was it Martindale? For a moment I wondered if maybe he'd sent someone else to finish me off. He must have seen the look on my face because he pulled back the cowl to show himself.

'You're wondering why I'm not dressed as usual? I'm sorry – I didn't mean to alarm you. I'm dressed for a ceremony, a very solemn religious ceremony.'

I felt my eyelid fluttering. 'What . . .?'

'A funeral.'

I tried to swallow but my mouth was too dry. A funeral? He was holding the lamp in his left hand, but his right was hidden in the sleeve of his robe. Was he holding some sort of weapon? Not so long ago, I would have been able to disarm him easily, but now? I wasn't sure I'd be able to stand up if I tried.

He reached forward and I saw he was holding an energy bar in a bright-red wrapper.

'Here. Take it.'

I looked at it, and instantly felt a dribble of saliva running out of the corner of my mouth. But something stopped me from grabbing it. Could it be poisoned? That would definitely be the easiest way to do it. No fuss, no mess. I felt like a sailor marooned on a raft with no water, deciding whether to just dip his hand into the sea . . . It looked so good, and after all, what was the alternative: starving to death?

I took it and started fumbling with the wrapper.

'Let me help you.' He tore it open and shook the bar into my palm. I took a bite, trying to chew slowly so I didn't choke. My jaw ached with the unfamiliar effort, and the taste of sugar was so strong it almost made me gag, but eventually I managed to get it down. The rush of glucose into my bloodstream was instantaneous.

'Have some water.' He brought over the bucket and I put my face down to it and drank until I started to feel sick. 'Not too much,' he said, taking it away.

He put the bucket down, positioned the lamp so it cast a gentle glow across the wall behind him and sat down on the stool. I wiped a hand across my face and leaned back.

'You remember that down and out who stole your brandy?'

I nodded. 'Yeah.'

'What was his name?'

'Stevie.'

'Stevie. That's it. Can you picture him now? I think he's in the same place we left him.'

I closed my eyes. Stevie was curled up in his sleeping bag. He'd pulled it right up to cover his face, but it wasn't long enough, and while he slept, he'd straightened his legs and pulled it down, so now his head was resting on the ground. His mouth was open and his breath was coming in short little gasps. His face was smeared with dirt but you could still see his skin was very pale.

'What's he doing?' Martindale asked.

'Sleeping,' I said.

'Can you see him breathing?'

'Yeah.'

'All right. Now I want you to imagine his heart. It doesn't look right, does it?'

'No.'

'Can you describe it?'

'It looks funny.'

'How do you mean?'

'It's black. It's full of this black stuff. It's all sticky, like it's clogged up.'

'That must make it hard for it to keep beating. Is it still beating?'

'Yeah . . . just.'

'It's going to stop soon, though, isn't it?'

'Yeah.'

'Is it stopping now?' His voice was almost a whisper.

'Yeah, yeah it is.' I watched Stevie's shrunken, fucked-up heart twitch once, twice, then no more.

'Is he dead?'

'I think so, yeah.'

Martindale crossed himself. 'He's at peace now.'

I nodded. I felt a weird calm passing through me.

'We can't leave him, though, can we?' Martindale said.

'No.'

'Ashes to ashes. We must commit his body to the flames. Have you got that bottle and the lighter?'

'Yes.' I had. I was holding them in my hands. If I'd looked down I would have seen them.

'Do it, then.'

I shook the bottle over the sleeping bag, saving a last splash for his head, the spirit soaking into his hair. Then I flicked the lighter and held it to the end of the sleeping bag until it caught. Soon the whole thing was engulfed in flames. I watched Stevie's skin crinkle and blacken under his fiery halo. I stood back. Soon I heard his bones begin to crack. He seemed to jerk inside the sleeping bag, as if he'd briefly come alive again, but it was only the snap, crackle and pop of his body disintegrating in the intense heat, like dry twigs on a bonfire. The fire raged even more fiercely, and in a few minutes, there was nothing left but a heap of ashes dancing in the air as the breeze took them. Then the wind got stronger, swirling the ashes away, more and more, until there was nothing left but a long grey smear on the concrete.

'Gone?' Martindale breathed.

'Yeah,' I said.

No more Stevie. I felt a massive surge of relief. I'd passed the first part of the test.

Then I felt a quick stab of panic.

Who the fuck was I supposed to be now, then?

43

Martindale helped me up and led me gently out of the cell with the blanket round my shoulders. As we inched our way slowly through the passage together, leaving the sickly stench of burned flesh behind us, I could barely feel the floor under my feet, they were so numb. I stumbled a couple of times, but Martindale caught me before I fell and hauled me back upright. It felt strange, hanging on to him for dear life when all I wanted to do was smash his head against the wall.

Climbing up the ladder took forever. Each step seemed to take all the strength I had, even with Martindale pushing from behind. But eventually I managed to crawl out into the little room and then finally into the room with the bookcase. I glanced up at the crucifix and thought of Stevie. At least his suffering was over.

Martindale locked the doors and pushed the bookshelf back against the wall. I stood in the middle of the room, uncertain of what to do next.

'Let's get you cleaned up,' he said. 'Then you can have something to eat.'

He steered me through the door and back into the interior of the church. The only light was from his lamp, and that was beginning to dim. *So it's night*, I thought. It was almost as if no time had passed at all, and everything that had happened in that terrible cell was just a bad dream. He shone the beam towards a short flight of steps with a door at the bottom.

'There's a shower. It's a bit cramped, but there's hot water. And a toothbrush. Just give me that –' he took the blanket – 'and there'll be some fresh clothes for you when you're finished.'

I grunted, not yet trusting myself to speak, and walked down the steps. Now that I didn't have Stevie to fall back on, I was afraid that at any moment he'd take a look at me and see I was a fake.

The shower room was bare concrete, and the water was only lukewarm and barely more than a trickle, but I didn't care. I stood under it for as long as I dared, soaping myself from head to foot, scraping my flesh with my nails, then starting all over again. When the little bar of soap was almost worn away to nothing, I turned the water off and picked up the toothbrush, using the last of the soap as toothpaste. There was a tatty old hand towel on a rail, and I used that to dry myself as best I could.

Martindale was holding out something white when I opened the door. At first I thought it was a dressing gown, but then I realized it was a robe – a monk's robe like the one he was wearing.

He saw my hesitation. 'Take it. It symbolizes purity. A new beginning.'

I slipped it over my head and tied the cord round my waist, then followed him into the vestry. There were two chairs, lit by the bare bulb hanging from the ceiling. We sat down, facing each other.

'How are you feeling? I mean, physically.'

'OK,' I said.

'And in your mind?'

I shook my head, as if there were no words.

That seemed to be the right response. 'Good. Now, do you know who you are?'

'No.' I tried to make it sound as if I wasn't bothered.

'Can you remember anything about your life before you came here?'

'No.' Same flat tone.

'Do you know your name – what people call you?'

'No.'

'Shall we give you a new name?'

I shrugged. 'If you like.'

'We'll call you Peter. Like the disciple. In the Bible. I don't suppose you've done much Bible reading?'

'No.'

'But you can read?'

I felt as if I was stepping onto thin ice. 'Yes. I think so. I don't know.'

'Well, we'll find out. Not that it matters. The Holy Spirit will speak to you directly now, through me. Do you believe that the Holy Spirit can speak through me? That when I tell you something, it comes from God – that it's God's word?'

'Yes.'

'And you will obey God's commands without thought, without question?'

'Yes.'

'Because if you don't – if you disobey God's commands, any of God's commands – then you will cease to exist. *Instantly*. Like the flame of a candle being snuffed out. Because He has made you for one reason and one reason only: to do His will.'

I nodded. For a moment I did believe it.

'But if you obey him – if you do His will faithfully – then He will love you as a son. Your brothers and sisters will be angels, and they will be your family forever.'

He stood up and put his hands on my shoulders. I swear I could feel a glow flowing through his fingertips and into my body. I thought he was going to say something, some sort of blessing, but after a minute I realized he wasn't. He was waiting for *me* to say something.

I took a deep breath. 'What does He want me to do?'

44

Alex had her arms crossed and was shaking her head. 'He said to wait – until he can get a message out.'

'We can't wait forever,' Mrs Allenby said evenly. She took a sip of her coffee.

'You said six days.'

'Six days is too long.'

'But—'

'I know what I said,' Mrs Allenby cut in tersely, putting her cup down carefully on the table. 'But that was never going to be realistic. We should have gone in after seventy-two hours. That's quite long enough. I only waited until now because . . . well, I thought I'd give him another twelve hours because he was so adamant. Now I'm beginning to worry that could have been a fatal mistake.'

'It could be a fatal mistake if we go in now and Martindale gets spooked,' Alex said.

Mrs Allenby took her glasses off and put them carefully into a small green leather case, then snapped it shut. 'I am relying on you *not* to spook him.'

'You won't give him one more—'

'No!' Mrs Allenby's voice wasn't loud, but Ryan and Alan found themselves sitting back in their seats as if she'd just delivered a full-on hairdryer. 'Time is running out and I will not waste any more of it.'

She locked eyes with Alex. Alex stared back, an expression of defiance on her face, then looked away. 'Fine.' She got up, pulled her motorcycle jacket from the back of the chair and walked to the door.

'Thank you, my dear,' Mrs Allenby said without looking up.

Now that she knew she had no choice, Alex found herself racing to get to the church, as if all the anxiety she'd been keeping a lid on had been released by Mrs Allenby's order. Maybe it was too long. Alex had wanted to do it Logan's way, but perhaps trusting his instincts had been a mistake – just misplaced loyalty. He had been acting strangely for a while, she had to admit. Maybe his judgement was shot.

Still, it made sense to wait until there was a service; otherwise she'd have to come up with an excuse for sneaking around, and she didn't want to go there quite yet. First she just wanted to take a look – see the lie of the land – before deciding how to play things. She'd parked a couple of streets away, and now she was standing in the shadows between a white van and a skip overflowing with builder's rubble and broken furniture, with a good view of the front of the church. At first she thought she must have got the time wrong, or Martindale had stopped celebrating mass at all. She hadn't seen a soul go anywhere near the church. With nothing else to look at, she'd found herself birdwatching. A flock of pigeons wheeled one way, then the other, over the church, making her think they'd been alarmed by a predator, but if there was a hawk about, she couldn't see it. Then, with five minutes to go, an old lady with tight white curls and a bent back appeared, opened the big wooden door and slipped inside, followed by a bloke in his twenties with a wispy beard and the unmistakeable look of a junkie, and soon half a dozen more went in, of various ages and types, but all looking equally battered by life. She slipped out from behind the van. After a hurried trip to her local Oxfam shop, she'd worried she'd maybe overdone the shabbiness. She hadn't even washed the clothes before she put them on. But now it looked as if she was going to blend in just fine.

Inside, the church looked as if it was either in the middle of a major renovation or about to be demolished. There were ladders and buckets against one wall, and a section of the roof looked as if it had been hastily covered over with plastic sheeting. The pews looked relatively new, but at least one row seemed to be missing, and the row at the back had a sheet draped over it at one end. She took a seat on the aisle, in the second pew, which gave her a decent view of the rest of the congregation, shuffling and coughing their way into their places. She looked towards the altar. There didn't seem to be a pulpit, and there was no sign of Martindale. She knelt down, rested her elbows on the back of the next pew and put her hands together. She heard the soft muttering of prayer in a language she didn't know from somewhere in front of her.

With her eyes closed, she still felt the figure go past her down the aisle. When she looked up he was resting his hands on the altar. Medium height, slim build, thinning blond hair and steel-rimmed glasses, he had the look of a priest, even if he wasn't wearing any of the regulation vestments, just dark trousers and a black shirt, the collar undone.

'In the name of the Father, the Son and the Holy Ghost, amen.' His voice was deeper than she thought it would be, carrying easily through the cavernous space. Muttered amens came from the hunched figures scattered around her. 'Let us first give thanks for His bounty . . .'

She'd been expecting something a bit more . . . radical. Martindale might not quite dress the part, but he sounded like every other priest she'd ever heard, just droning on in this fuddy-duddy way, like he was reading an autocue. *His bounty?* As far as she could see, Martindale's congregation had all been right at the back of the queue when the bounty was being handed out. So what the hell were they supposed to be giving thanks for? *Thanks for precisely nothing, mate.* It was this sort of nonsense that had made her an atheist as soon as she'd understood what the word meant. She realized she'd folded her arms crossly, and quickly put her hands together in prayer again. She also realized Martindale was probably too smart to wear his heart on his sleeve. The old dear with the crooked back probably looked back fondly to the days when the mass was said in Latin: she might forgive

Martindale his shabby clothes, but if he started preaching revolution, she'd no doubt be straight off to the bishop to complain. Which might explain why the revolution hadn't happened yet.

As Martindale droned on, Alex checked out the rest of the congregation. There were eight of them – nine including herself – spread out as if they were trying to put as much distance between each other as they could. It didn't seem very Christian: love thy neighbour, and all that. It made her think of perverts watching dirty movies, all pretending they weren't really there. She couldn't get a good look at the one on the last pew, nearest the door, without making it obvious what she was doing, but she could see the rest reasonably clearly without turning her head: three women, two old, one baby mother probably still in her teens; and five men, none of them in the best of health, judging by the wheezing and coughing, and at least a couple of them living on the streets, if the sour smell wafting through the church was anything to go by.

No Logan.

She risked a look at the guy to her left, pretending to have a crick in her neck: comb-over; pale, puffy face. Nope.

Which left Plan B: wait until the church was empty and Martindale had fucked off, and then break in and have a little look around. Not ideal.

She watched Martindale at the altar. 'The peace of the Lord be with you always,' he intoned solemnly.

'And with your spirit,' came the muttered response.

'Let us offer each other the sign of peace,' Martindale said.

Along the pews, the ragged congregation shifted reluctantly towards each other. Two old biddies in the front shook hands with each other then put their hands back in their laps, eyes fixed rigidly to the front. *So much for brotherly love*, Alex thought.

She felt a gentle tap on her shoulder. It was Logan, holding out his hand. Where the hell had he sprung from?

'Fancy seeing you here. Didn't think you were the religious type,' he said as she grasped his hand.

'Bloody hell, Logan, I thought you were—'

'Shh, don't talk now.' He took his hand away and she felt a crumpled piece of paper in her palm. She quickly pocketed it as Logan shuffled back to the end of the pew.

The van was parked under an old railway bridge half a mile from the church. A ragged queue of homeless people – most of them men – lined up patiently, waiting to be given a styrofoam cup of soup and a sandwich wrapped in cling film. Alex sat against the wall opposite, feeling the cold through her thin skirt as she watched Logan doling out the free food. There was someone else in the van with him, because she occasionally saw him turn his head and smile, but she couldn't see them properly. She hoped if it was Martindale, he wouldn't see her and recognize her from the service.

After a while she allowed herself to slide down the wall and gently topple over, like she was pissed or just passing out from exhaustion. Out of the corner of her eye she could see Logan pointing towards her and saying something to the other person in the van. A minute later he'd left the van and was crouching over her with a cup of soup steaming in his hand. He touched her shoulder with his other hand.

'Are you all right?'

'Never better,' she whispered, giving him a little grin from her prone position. 'Is that chicken, by any chance?'

'Tomato, I'm afraid. It's all we do. Anything else upsets the vegans.'

'There's homeless vegans?'

'There's homeless everything,' he said. 'Look, we don't have much time. Let me sit you up and you have some of this soup while I talk. OK?'

Alex nodded, slowly pushing herself back up against the wall. 'You've lost weight,' she said, taking the cup. 'And I'm not sure the shaved look is really you.'

'Yeah, never mind that. Listen, Ryan was right. Since I passed the audition, I've had nothing but the bloody crusades, morning, noon and night. It's like doing fucking history GCSE.'

'How would you know?'

'Shut up. Anyway, he definitely thinks we're all living in Jerusalem East Seventeen, and it's time we took it back, and then Christ will turn up waving a big sword made of fire or something and we'll all live happily ever after.'

Alex took a sip of the soup, then made a face. 'Tomato, you said?'

'Or mushroom. Same difference.'

'And what does "taking it back" mean, exactly?'

'That's what I don't know yet. But he's a fanatic. He's capable of anything. Whatever it is he's planning, it's going to be big.'

'And what's your role in all this?'

'We're going to be the points of God's spear, that's what he calls it.'

'We?'

'There's four of us, I think. All simple-minded fucks-ups just like me, who've had their brains scooped out and replaced by this crazy religious stuff.'

Alex sat up straighter. 'And you're all right?'

'So far. He's a sick bastard, though. I think he enjoys fucking with people's minds. He's good at it, too. He would have made a top interrogator – seems to just have a knack for figuring out your weak spots and then sticking the knife in.'

She saw Logan shudder.

'So what do we do now?'

'I can't leave the church, except when I'm helping the homeless, like now – which really means recruiting for Martindale.'

'Identifying psychologically vulnerable people?'

'Basically.'

'Jesus.'

'I don't think Jesus knows too much about it, to be honest. Look, I've got to go. He's got eyes in the back of his fucking head, this one.'

'You're scared of him?'

'Too fucking right I am.'

'So how will we stay in contact?'

'There's bins down the side of the church. It's my job to take out the slops. Look under the grey bin. Careful of the rats, though.'

Alex nodded, handing back the cup. 'Talking of slops. Quickly, before you go. I need to tell you what Ryan found in the files.'

45

As John drove the van back to the lock-up round the corner form the church, I thought about what Alex had told me. Ryan had been through Craig's and Claire's files forwards, backwards and sideways and found precisely nothing – or at least nothing that suggested why they should have become targets. I already knew the basics: Craig had grown up on a council estate in Glasgow, and then got a scholarship to Edinburgh University to study history – which is where he got the tap on the shoulder and was recruited as an intelligence officer, before moving to the A4 surveillance team. Claire, I remembered, had a military background as an avionics technician and had applied for a job as a mobile surveillance officer on the MI5 website. Nothing out of the ordinary in any of that, and according to Alex, Ryan hadn't found anything else that raised a red flag.

Except for one thing. For two months, between the beginning of February and the end of March 2016, they'd both taken a sabbatical. Nothing particularly unusual in that: recent experiences had made MI5 wary of burnout; better to give your officers a decent chance to clear their heads and recharge their batteries every once in a while – especially if they were on the front line of the war against home-grown terrorists – than keep pushing them until one day the lights just went out, with potentially hundreds of lives on the line. Claire and Craig had both done their time. They were both due a break.

But at precisely the same time? What were the chances of that?

Certainly neither of them had ever mentioned it. But then why would you? If you'd taken time out because you were worried you were losing your edge – or your bottle – it wasn't exactly something you were going to share with your new colleagues over a cup of tea in the canteen. And if you'd spent the time away from work redecorating the spare bedroom or putting your record collection in alphabetical order, that wasn't going to make for scintillating conversation either.

So it could be nothing. Or . . . what? How could taking time off work at the same time explain why, three years later, they both got killed? Unless what they were doing was so secret that it didn't even appear in their files. For fuck's sake, they were already keeping tabs on potential terror plots, treading that fine line between giving the bastards enough rope to hang themselves and letting them slip out of their clutches – what could be more sensitive than that?

John pulled the van up in front of the church and sat there for a moment without speaking. At first, I'd found these little moments when someone seemed to have pressed his 'pause' button a bit unsettling, thinking he was about to have some sort of turn. But I'd learned it just meant he was working up the courage to open his mouth. Not that what he eventually said was ever really worth the wait. Either Martindale had done a particularly thorough job of scrambling his brains or there hadn't been much there to scramble in the first place. I waited patiently, wishing I had a cigarette, which was odd, because I'd never been a smoker. Stevie's legacy, I supposed. The silly bastard hadn't entirely gone, then.

'You go back inside. I'll sort out the van.' John glanced over at me, then went back to staring through the windscreen.

'You sure?' *Shit.* Don't ask him a question or we could be here all night. 'All right,' I added quickly, opening the door and jumping out.

The church was dark when I slipped inside. No sign of Martindale. I thought about having a bit of a snoop around before bedding down in the little storeroom by the vestry that was now my home, but something stopped me.

'Peter.'

I turned towards the sound of his voice. He was sitting in one of the pews, the back of his head barely distinguishable from the surrounding dark.

'Come and sit with me.'

I walked over and sat down next to him.

'How did things go tonight?'

'Good,' I said in a toneless voice.

I heard him breathe in and out slowly, as if he was deciding something.

'I think it's time to share God's plan with you. Do you think you're ready?'

I tried to sound calm, even though my pulse was racing. 'Yes.'

'We are going to start a war, in this green and pleasant land. A war between Christ and his enemies. A war in which there can only be one winner, and the defeated will be utterly destroyed. We will wash the streets of Jerusalem with their blood, wash them clean so they are fit for the feet of Our Lord to tread.'

He was still looking straight ahead at the blacked-out windows and the darkened altar. I wondered what he was seeing.

'And God has chosen you to strike the first blow.'

This was it. This was what we'd been waiting for.

I concentrated on keeping my hands still, trying not to show any signs of the adrenaline pumping through my body, waiting for him to say more.

Come on!

'And I heard a great voice coming out of the temple, saying to the seven angels, go your ways and pour out the phials of the wrath of God upon the face of the earth.'

I nodded, as if I understood, but biblical mumbo-jumbo wasn't what I needed at that moment. What did he want me to fucking *do*?

'The phials of the wrath of God,' he repeated. 'Would you believe that they are here, right now, in this very church, beneath our feet?'

He didn't move his head, but I could tell he was smiling. 'The technical term is ZX4. It's a kind of nerve agent. Like Novichok. Have you heard of that?'

Had I? I tossed a coin in my head. Tails. 'Yeah. Bastard Russians.'

He chuckled. 'Yes!'

I knew I should just keep quiet, like the empty vessel I was now. I just followed orders: there was no reason for me to be curious about anything. But I had to ask.

'This ZX-whatever stuff – is that Russian, too?'

This time he turned towards me as he shook his head. 'Oh, no. ZX4 is British, made here in a dark Satanic mill called Porton Down. It's our country's dirtiest secret – our very own biological superweapon.'

What? My mind was spinning. I'd never heard of ZX4, but I knew we didn't have any biological weapons – not since we signed the Biological Weapons Convention treaty back in the Seventies.

I grunted, as if it might as well have come from Tesco for all I cared, praying he wouldn't be able to resist telling me more.

'We should have destroyed it, of course. And officially, we did. But somehow a few ounces got kept back. For a rainy day, perhaps – or for when God saw fit to use it.'

Was all that really possible? And if it was, how the bloody hell did Martindale get his hands on the stuff?

'A miracle,' I said solemnly, rocking gently backwards and forwards on the pew.

'In a way,' Martindale said. 'Happily there are people in the establishment, people in the army, in the intelligence services – in the government, even – who still believe that this is a Christian country and are willing to help us reclaim it from those who want to turn it into a caliphate.'

Willing to help . . .

Was he saying he'd been given the ZX4 by someone on our side? Someone with access to a secret stock of the stuff at Porton Down? *With the idea of using it on our own people?* I was trying to think how high up that would have to go.

Right to the top.

46

Ryan pushed the files across the table. Mrs Allenby looked down at them but didn't pick them up.

'You're sure there's nothing else there that could help us?' she asked.

'Nothing that I can find,' Ryan said with a frown. 'I've cross-referenced everything – every date, every place, even just keywords.'

'And they never worked together?' Alex asked.

Ryan shook his head. 'They were never assigned to the same op. They went on a training course together. That's all.'

Mrs Allenby looked thoughtful. 'What course?'

Ryan looked down at the notes he'd scribbled on a legal pad. 'It was a technical thing. Learning how to use some new audio kit. I'm surprised you weren't on it, Alan.'

'When did you say it was?' Alan asked.

'Um, let me see – September 2015.'

'Oh yes. I remember. I was supposed to be tech support on that, but something came up – some problems with the radios on one of the teams, and by the time it was sorted, it was more or less finished.'

'Do we know who else was on it?' Mrs Allenby asked.

Ryan flipped through his notes. 'It was quite small, if I remember. Here we go: Frank Hemmings, Dana Till, Geoff Winter – all A4 people.'

'Any of those names ring a bell?' Mrs Allenby asked, looking around the table.

Alex shrugged. 'What sort of bell? I knew Geoff Winter a little bit. He seemed all right.'

Mrs Allenby sighed, then looked pointedly at Ryan. 'Well, I'm not about to dig out all of their files to see if there's any correlation with Mr McKinley and Miss Maxwell, if that's what you're thinking. This was risky enough,' she added, pulling the two manila files towards her, as if she couldn't wait to put them back where they belonged.

'There was someone else on the course, now that I remember,' Alan said, pushing his glasses more firmly onto the bridge of his nose. 'At least, he was on the original list of attendees. John Tenniel.'

Ryan looked bemused. 'You're sure? His name definitely wasn't in the file.'

Alan nodded. 'DCI Tenniel. That's why I remembered. I thought, what's a detective chief inspector doing on an MI5 training course?'

'Where was he from?' Mrs Allenby asked.

'National Crime Agency, if I remember. Yeah, that was it.'

'Not unheard of,' Mrs Allenby said, tapping her pen

thoughtfully on the table. 'Especially if he was involved in a major operation with a strong surveillance element. Let's have a look at him, shall we?'

Ryan had already started scrolling through Tenniel's record. 'OK, a bit of an old-fashioned thief-taker. He seems to have taken down one or two big names who the Serious Organized Crime Agency had been trying to nail for years. Commendations up the wazoo, then fast-tracked promotion until he gets the plum job at the NCA. Very impressive.'

'But what's he got to do with Craig and Claire?' Alex asked. 'I mean, so they're on the same course. They have a coffee and a chat, and then he goes back to the day job. So what?'

Mrs Allenby continued tapping her pen, then stopped abruptly. 'Let's scroll forward a few months – to March, or perhaps April of the following year. What's Tenniel doing then?'

Ryan tapped away at the keyboard for a minute. 'OK, nothing, nothing . . . Oh, wait, here we go, April sixteenth 2016.'

He turned his laptop around. On the screen was a grainy black-and-white shot of an industrial-looking building. A man was being led out of the front door by two policemen towards a waiting van, his hands cuffed in front of him. Armed police in Kevlar vests could be seen waiting in the wings. The man was thick-set, late fifties, early sixties, with short dark hair, prominent eyebrows and a couple of days of stubble. His jaw was set, a look of cold fury in his dark eyes.

'Terry Mason,' Alex said, nodding to herself. 'I remember

now. The last of the old-style East End gangsters – at least that's how the tabloids liked to portray him. Didn't he hook up with some Albanian people-smugglers?'

'That's right,' Ryan said. 'He repurposed a whole fleet of trucks he owned. Made millions – basically he was a slave trader. God knows how many people's lives he ruined.' He shook his head. 'Evil bastard.'

'And vicious, too,' Alex said. 'He had a run-in with some Turkish drug gang before that. He was taking a piece of the action so they could operate on his territory and then they decided they didn't need to pay up any more.'

'So he burned their restaurant down, after jamming the doors so no one could get out,' Ryan said.

'Like you say, evil bastard,' Alex said. 'But what's Terry Mason got to do with anything?'

Mrs Allenby sat back in her seat, looking at Ryan. 'Did it say in the files how Mr McKinley and Miss Short did on the course evaluation?'

'Er . . . yes. Top marks, both of them.'

She smiled. 'Then I have an idea what may have happened.'

'Well, I'm glad someone does,' Alex said, looking at her quizzically.

'Let's just look at it logically,' Mrs Allenby said. 'One piece at a time. Detective Chief Inspector Tenniel has a reputation for getting his clutches on criminals who have so far proved rather slippery. However, for most of his career he's been a big fish in a small pond. Now he's facing a rather stiffer challenge: Terry Mason. The Met have had Mason in their sights for years but have never been able to pull the trigger. Unless Mason makes an uncharacteristic slip, how is Tenniel going to succeed where everyone else has failed?'

'He's looking for something new – a game-changer,' Ryan said, beginning to understand where Mrs Allenby was going.

'Yes,' she said. 'He gets himself on an MI5 surveillance technology course and likes what he sees. If I could utilize some of this new kit, he thinks, that might just give me the edge I need. Of course, when it comes to surveillance, the police and MI5 operate under different rules, but maybe he's found a way round that. Anyway, he gets chatting to a couple of A4 people on the course – the people he thinks are the most capable. Perhaps he thought they had other qualities, too, that made them suitable for what he had in mind. Perhaps he told them – in the strictest confidence – about the undercover operation to take Mason down. Perhaps he also told them about some of the more despicable things Mason had done – perhaps things that never made it to court. At any event, a few months later, these two A4 operatives both go on extended leave at the same time, and within a few days of their returning to duty, Terry Mason is arrested. Sometime after that he's convicted on multiple counts of fraud, extortion, kidnapping and murder. The judge opts for the heaviest sentence possible, ensuring Mason remains in prison for the rest of his life.'

'That certainly all makes sense,' Ryan said.

'OK,' Alex said. 'I'll buy into all of that. But it doesn't tell us if Claire and Craig were murdered, and if so, by who.'

'If they were involved in the NCA operation, then somebody took a good deal of trouble to cover it up,' Mrs Allenby said.

'But why?' Alex insisted.

'That I don't know,' Mrs Allenby admitted. 'And whatever the reason, I can't imagine whoever did so would then think them enough of a threat to have them murdered.'

'What if it's revenge?' Alan said.

'What do you mean?' Mrs Allenby asked.

'Terry Mason's associates, gang members.'

She shook her head. 'The ones that didn't go down with him, who slipped through the net – you'd expect them to keep a low profile, to try not to attract attention. Would it be in their interests to start murdering people?'

'Family, then.'

Mrs Allenby looked thoughtful. 'There was a son, I remember. And the wife, of course.'

'Stephanie,' Ryan said, looking at his screen. 'She looks like a piece of work.'

'They tried to get both of them on conspiracy charges, I think, but there wasn't enough evidence.'

'Or the evidence was never admissible in court,' Alex said.

'Which rather supports our theory,' Mrs Allenby said.

Alex pulled on a strand of hair and started twisting it. 'So let's say it's the son or the mother, or the two of them together. They're out to get whoever put Mason behind bars. How would they know about Craig and Claire's involvement?'

'That *is* a mystery,' Mrs Allenby admitted with a frown.

'How many people would have known?' Ryan asked.

Mrs Allenby looked at him. 'On the police side, probably only Tenniel. There would be no reason to tell the rest of his team the identities of their new colleagues. And then on our side, someone must have signed off on their temporary assignment, of course.'

'Should we take a look at Tenniel, then?' Alex asked.

'In an ideal world,' Mrs Allenby said. 'But in case you're forgetting, at this precise moment, we have a terror attack to stop.'

47

I didn't have a shred of doubt that Martindale was deadly serious. Now that I'd learned a little bit about the crusades, I realized that the idea of killing hundreds, if not thousands of people in the most brutal and bloody way possible just because they believed in a different God used to be considered quite normal. So maybe if you spent years immersed in that bloody history, it became normal for you too. Perhaps that had been Martindale's own kind of brainwashing experience. So the question wasn't whether he was willing to expose untold numbers of innocent people to a deadly nerve agent, but whether he actually had the means to do it. The more I thought about it, the more I reckoned his story of an establishment plot to get rid of the country's Muslim population with some leftover stocks of a banned biological weapon was a load of bollocks. Not that there weren't probably plenty of high court judges and retired colonels who'd like nothing better than to turn the clock back so far it told the time in Latin, but would they really be able to get their hands on a load of ZX4? If the government really did hold back some stock of the stuff, would anyone really be foolish enough to hand it over to someone like Martindale, a religious maniac with at least a couple of screws fairly obviously loose?

There was only one way to find out. Martindale had said the phials were literally under our feet. So they were somewhere in the maze of tunnels where my brain had just spent a few days in the tumble dryer. If I was honest, I fancied going back down there about as much as I did jumping into an open grave, but the more I thought about it, the more I knew it was what I had to do.

Martindale was in and out of the church at all sorts of odd hours, so I never knew when he was going to pop up. Plus I still had a feeling I couldn't shake that he could see inside my head when he wanted. I knew if I wasn't careful, I was going to turn into one of those sad fucks who line their hats with tinfoil to block the CIA's mind-control beams. But then, you don't know what mind control is until some bastard has had a go doing it to you. You couldn't blame people for taking precautions. The point was, I wasn't going to take a chance that Martindale might turn up just as I was jemmying open the door behind the bookshelf. I needed to know I had a decent window.

Tonight, though, I knew he'd gone out with John in the van. They'd do the soup kitchen thing, then trawl around known homeless spots for another couple of hours ministering to the poor and fucked-up. I didn't know where the other two were, but if they did make an appearance, I reckoned I could convince them whatever it looked like I was doing, it was God's will. They'd be so full of the fear of the Almighty, I was pretty sure it wouldn't be hard to scare the poor bastards.

That left me with two problems: how to unlock the padlocks and how to see what the fuck I was doing. Martindale took his big bunch of keys with him wherever he went, but I reckoned I could pick the locks if I could find something the right shape. It was a long shot, but two of the old dears who came to Martindale's services always had their hair up and I reckoned they must be full of pins. It took me a while, but after crawling around on my hands and knees between the pews for an hour until my knees were rubbed raw, I eventually found one. Martindale never left the hurricane lamp in the church – too much of a fire risk with all these brainless zombies around, maybe – but that was less of a problem. There was a box of matches for lighting votive candles which I'd pocketed earlier. Luckily, there were enough in the box that he hopefully wouldn't notice a few missing.

As soon as I found the hairpin, I pushed the bookshelf aside and went to work. The padlocks were a bit rusty, and a couple of times I thought the hairpin was going to snap, but I kept at it, and after a couple of minutes I was in the little room with the trap door. Opening that was easy enough, but looking down into the black hole below, I felt a wave of dread that made me feel physically sick. I felt like someone who'd just pulled themselves out of a swimming pool full of sharks standing on the top board.

C'mon. Pull yourself together. Nothing but rats down there. And a few old bones.

And maybe a stash of one of the world's deadliest toxins.

I took a deep breath and put one leg down the hole until I could feel one of the rungs of the ladder under my foot. I wasn't going to try holding a match in one hand while I felt my way down, so the darkness was total. As if to compensate, my sense of smell instantly went into overdrive. Smoke, vomit, piss and week-old shit seemed to suddenly blossom in the stale air, but that must have been my imagination.

When my feet were finally on firm ground, I lit a match. The bad smells vanished as the walls of the chamber came to brief life in front of my eyes. I reckoned if the stuff was down here, it would be well hidden, somewhere deeper, so I didn't bother looking around. I just needed to see where the doors to the passage were. The match went out and I walked carefully in the dark until I could touch the doors with my outstretched hand. I then lit another match and went to work on the lock.

Once I was in the passage, again I just went by feel. I took it slowly, keeping one hand pressed to the cold stone of the wall on my left, until I came to the door. The one that opened onto my cell. It was firmly padlocked, but something told me he wouldn't have hidden anything there, so there was no point looking inside. Or was I just too much of a coward to go in?

I tried to clear my mind so I could think straight.

I *was* scared. The idea of being buried alive in that room

still gave me nightmares. I knew as soon as I walked in, I'd be terrified of the door clanging shut behind me and the sound of the key securing the padlock. I couldn't do it.

OK. But there's no point coming all the way down here and not taking a look. If I lit a couple of matches, I'd be able to see enough without having to step through the door.

Deal?

Deal.

I slipped the hairpin into the lock and started twisting. My hand was shaking so much it almost slipped out of my fingers. The lock looked old enough; I just had to hope it wasn't so old it was buggered up with rust. I pulled the hairpin out, took a breath and tried again. Better. The lock snapped open with a click. I pulled the door open. Inside was nothing but blackness. I fumbled three matches out of the box and struck them, holding the flame out at arm's length. I didn't know what I'd been expecting, but when I saw the room was empty, my knees went weak with relief. No ghosts. No phantoms. Not even the stool or the buckets. And the smell had gone. Martindale must have cleaned up. I took a step forward, my hand still holding firmly on to the edge of the door so it couldn't swing shut behind me, and took one long last look around the walls before the matches sputtered out. Unless he'd buried them, the containers of ZX4, or whatever it was, weren't here.

So did that mean they didn't exist? Martindale had talked about the chambers and passages under the church as if they were a regular warren; perhaps there were more tunnels, more chambers I couldn't see. Maybe the trapdoor in the little room next to the vestry wasn't the only entrance to the maze. I realized it would take a proper team, with decent lights and digging tools, to really scope the place out. Maybe something that could detect traces of biological weapons, too. That thought made me shudder. The truth was, unless I struck lucky, there was no way of knowing what was stashed down here without bringing a fully kitted-out biohazard crew in, and I didn't think even Mrs Allenby could conjure one of those out of thin air.

I stepped back and closed the door, snapping the padlock closed, then started feeling my way back along the passage. After a couple of paces I stopped in my tracks. Both times Martindale had led me through, we'd felt our way along the same wall, the one now on my right. With the hurricane lamp in his right hand, that had made sense coming in, but on the way out I now remembered he'd transferred the lamp to his left hand, leaving his right free to feel along the wall. Why? Why didn't he want to touch the other wall? Or was it that he didn't want *me* to?

I shifted to my left and started inching my way along, brushing the fingers of my left hand up and down the wall in a sweeping motion. I remembered counting the steps on the way in, in a vain attempt to make some sort of plan of the tunnels in my head. Ten steps: that meant the turn was just ahead and the passage would bend round to my right. But as I felt down, my fingers touched empty air. I knelt down and started feeling with both hands. There was a gap in the wall a couple of feet wide, starting about eighteen inches off the floor. I lit a match and peered in. It clearly extended for several yards, but the match flame couldn't illuminate any further than that.

Only one thing for it, then. I put my head in and then my shoulders, then shuffled forward on my elbows until I could hoist my legs in after me. It was a tight squeeze but by rolling from side to side, I was able to push myself along. I stopped. What about getting back out again if I came to a dead end? I tried going backwards, pushing back with my elbows on the slippery stone. Not so easy. A lot slower. But doable. Then another thought hit me. What if the tunnel suddenly narrowed and I got stuck?

Shit. I felt my pulse quicken. This was worse than being shut up in that bloody torture chamber. In the inky blackness I had no way of telling how far the tunnel went in or what was waiting for me at the end. For all I knew I was about to go sliding head first into a medieval cesspit.

I took a moment to get my breathing under control. I had to decide. Chicken out and never know what was down here? Or push on and take my chances? In the end I decided to keep going; I'd taken enough chances just coming down here. I might as well keep pushing my luck until it ran out.

That was when I heard the voices.

48

Alan was sitting at his work station trying to knead the kinks out of his neck when his phone beeped. He looked at the message.

'Jesus H fucking Christ.'

Mrs Allenby had just taken her coat from the stand by the door. 'What is it?'

Alex and Ryan were in the kitchen area, waiting for the kettle to boil. They walked across to look over Alan's shoulder.

'That Jag – you know, with the dodgy number plate? I've just found out who it belongs to. Well, not who it belongs to, exactly, but—'

'What are you talking about?' Mrs Allenby said, putting her coat down on the back of a chair.

'It's the PM's. There are two. That's one of them.'

Mrs Allenby swivelled the chair around and sat down. 'Are you sure?'

Alan nodded.

'So it might not have been her in the car?'

'Those vehicles are only used to ferry the PM around. If

one of them is driving somewhere at three in the morning, then she's in the back.'

Ryan was shaking his head in disbelief. 'Bloody hell.'

'I was just making coffee, but I think I might need something stronger now,' Alex said.

'I think we all might,' agreed Mrs Allenby, her hand on her cheek. 'And there's no question it's . . .?'

'No,' Alan said. 'I've looked at the footage maybe a dozen times. There's no mistake.'

'So the PM was visiting Viktor Shlovsky in the middle of the night,' Alex said, almost laughing. 'I'm still trying to get my head round it.'

'Well, at least that explains why she didn't want Shlovsky put under surveillance,' Mrs Allenby said wryly.

'But surely she can't be part of . . .' Alex's voice trailed off, as if she couldn't bring herself to actually say it.

'Hold on a minute,' Ryan said. 'Alan, have you got the log for that night?'

Alan reached for a thick A4 notepad. 'Yep.'

'Is there anything else, apart from the mystery Jag?'

Alan turned the pages. 'Yeah, Shlovsky leaves at about ten thirty.'

'With the full security detachment?'

'Um, yeah, it looks like Titov was driving and Weston was riding shotgun.'

'And when did they get back?'

Alan licked his finger and ran it down the page. 'That's

funny. I haven't got anything down here. I remember the feed was playing up a bit, so maybe we just missed them.'

'Or maybe they didn't come back, not until much later.'

'But if the PM wasn't meeting with Shlovsky, what was she doing there?' Mrs Allenby asked.

'Maybe she turned up unexpectedly. Maybe it was an emergency, and she couldn't let Shlovsky know she was coming,' Alex suggested.

Mrs Allenby looked horrified as the possibilities went through her head. 'An emergency? What kind of emergency would bring the Prime Minister of Great Britain running to meet with a corrupt Russian oligarch in the middle of the night?'

'If that was the case, if she found he wasn't at home, then she'd just turn round and go straight home, wouldn't you think?' said Ryan. 'No reason to hang around – in fact, the less time she's there, the better.'

'But the Jag didn't leave for another hour,' Alan said, looking at his notes.

'So maybe she didn't turn up on the off-chance at all,' Alex said. 'Maybe she knew Shlovsky wouldn't be there. She came to see someone else.'

49

There were two of them, speaking in low voices, but all the tunnels and chambers under the church must have had an effect like some sort of whispering gallery: it sounded as if they were only a few feet away.

I pushed myself on a couple of yards, trying to keep the scraping sounds to a minimum: if I could hear them, then they could hear me. I stopped. The voices were louder now, so I was definitely getting nearer. But I still couldn't hear what they were saying.

I moved forward carefully. After about ten yards I saw a flicker of light ahead of me and instinctively ducked, almost smacking my nose on the cold stone of the tunnel floor. I looked up slowly and the light was gone. Inching forward again, I reached a right-angled turn. That's where the light was coming from.

Crammed into the tunnel like a hot dog sausage in a bun, I was completely vulnerable. If anyone saw me, I'd be totally at their mercy. But I wasn't going to turn back now. On the other hand, I didn't want to draw attention to myself if I could help it, so I slowed down to a snail's pace as I wriggled forward until I was able to turn my head and look round the corner. Light danced across a wall but that was all I could see. The tunnel came to an abrupt end after three or four feet. I was guessing it came out near the top of some sort of room, and that's where the voices were coming from. I could hear them quite distinctly now, but if I was going to see them, I was going to have to squeeze my torso into the right angle, leaving my legs behind in the main passage. Worth the risk? I didn't have room to toss a coin, so I decided to go for it.

After a laborious few minutes of slow-motion crawling I was lying on my side, my legs jack-knifed behind me, with a partial view of another brick-lined cell. Two men were standing near the wall, looking down at something by their feet, but the only way I could get a glimpse of it was by sticking my head over the lip of the tunnel and I wasn't about to do that.

'This is the last one?' It was Martindale.

'Yes. That's all of it. All there is.' The second man spoke quickly, his voice clipped. It had a penetrating, parade-ground feel. He was wearing a blazer and a checked shirt, with what looked like a regimental tie.

Douglas Weston.

'We're very grateful,' Martindale said.

Weston gave a sharp nod. 'Don't let us down. The future of this country is in your hands now.'

'Please give your . . . associates our thanks,' Martindale said. 'We've been planning this a long time. But everything's in place now. And with God's help, nothing can go wrong.'

So that was it. It all suddenly made sense. That was why it was Weston and not Titov who had made contact with Martindale: Weston was a British Army officer from his upper-class accent to his spit-shined shoes. The perfect embodiment of the Establishment, with friends in high places who all shared Martindale's vision of a purified Christian nation. Or, at least, that's what Martindale had been led to believe.

So what was the stuff Weston had just handed over? If it was true that we'd held back some of our stock of ZX4 when we'd signed the BWC treaty, that would be about as top secret as it gets. If word got out, that would be enough to bring down the government and probably half the army top brass along with it. There's no way a middle-ranking ex-army officer in the pay of a Russian billionaire would get a sniff of it.

So what was it? Something a bit less deadly but easier to get your hands on? Like anthrax, maybe? But then why tell Martindale it was ZX4?

Maybe if I listened a bit longer, I thought, I'd get another piece of the jigsaw. Then another thought struck me: I didn't know how Martindale and Weston had accessed the room they were now in, but presumably when they were finished down there, Martindale would be coming back to the church. I needed to be safely tucked up in my little broom cupboard when he did.

I slowly pushed myself off the wall and started to shuffle backwards towards the main tunnel.

That was when I saw the rat.

He must have been creeping along ahead of me in the passageway and I'd been slowly boxing him in. When he ran out of road he had no choice but to hunker down and stay as still as he could. Which is why I hadn't noticed him. But starting to move again had obviously spooked him. He was now silhouetted against the wall of the chamber, twitching like crazy, obviously trying to decide whether to stick or twist.

Just stay where you are, you silly fucker, I thought, *and everything'll be fine*. I dragged myself back another foot or so.

See? I'm going away. Give me another five minutes and I'll be out of your hair.

I could see his beady little eyes fixed on mine as I inched further away. I was almost at the point of being able to pull my torso round the corner when he darted forward in a mad dash to squeeze past me, then changed his mind and scrambled back towards the end of the tunnel, stopping just short of the lip. The scraping sound of his feet against the stone seemed ridiculously loud. I stopped dead, holding my breath.

Down below, Martindale and Weston stopped dead, too.

'Did you hear that?' Weston asked. 'Could anyone else be down here?'

'No, it's all totally secure. Only I have access.' Martindale's tone was soothing. For the first time, I almost felt myself warming to him.

'Then what was that noise?'

'We do get rats down here,' Martindale said. 'Big ones, sometimes.'

Weston grunted non-committally. 'I haven't seen any.'

Martindale didn't say anything. I could almost feel Weston staring up at the hole in the wall.

'Do you have a ladder or anything?'

'There's one leading down from the vestry to another section of the tunnels. I suppose we could go and get it.'

There was a pause. Weston was thinking about it. 'What about those crates? A couple of them should do it, if they'll take my weight. I just want to have a peek up there.'

'Sure. If you like.' I heard steps on the dirt floor as Martindale went to get them.

Fuck. What to do now? I couldn't move, but if I stayed where I was, in less than a minute I'd be looking Weston in the eye.

The rat was still frozen to the spot. I decided there was only one thing for it. But I'd have to be quick. I slowly pushed my shoulders forward, then whipped out a hand and grabbed him. He went mental, squealing and biting like a demon, but I held on tight, then pulled my arm back as far as I could and flung him towards the hole. He flew away from me, then seemed to stop, and I thought I'd blown it, before he suddenly dropped out of sight. There was a soft thump as he hit the floor, then I heard him skittering away.

There was an intake of breath from down below. Then a quick laugh. 'Ha! You were right, it was a rat.'

'Do you still want to take a look up there?'

'No, no need. But no harm in double-checking everything's secure upstairs, if you don't mind.'

'Of course,' Martindale said.

I closed my eyes and took a series of deep, slow breaths. I could feel my hand beginning to throb where the little fucker had bitten me. I just had to hope he hadn't given me the plague or some other fucking disease that had been festering down here since old King Stephen's time. Leprosy, say. I started to feel nauseous. I could feel the prickle of sweat on my forehead. *Calm down, you stupid fucker. You can't get ill that quick. Just take a breather and get your head straight.*

But I couldn't afford to take a breather. I needed to retrace my steps, locking everything behind me, before Martindale got back to the front of the church.

50

I pushed the bookshelf back as quietly as I could, hoping I'd managed to get it more or less in the right place. I remembered the crucifix was above it and a couple of inches to the left of dead centre, but it was too dark to really see and I wasn't about to turn the light on to check. I crept out of the vestry and down the steps to my little cubbyhole. An old sleeping bag was laid out on the floor, just fitting into the cramped space. A tattered paperback Bible lay on the floor beside it, along with an empty china cup. I slipped into the sleeping bag without taking off my clothes and listened.

Nothing. Just the wind flapping the plastic sheeting over the holes in the roof.

The sudden bark of a fox along the side of the church made me tense. Had I forgotten something? I went through a mental checklist: all the doors firmly closed, all the padlocks snapped shut. So why did I have this nagging feeling something wasn't right?

The matches. Shit. I felt in the pocket of my jeans and there they were. I needed to put them back with the candles by the altar. Or was that taking a stupid risk? I'd been lucky to make it back and get myself safely tucked in before Martindale reappeared. What were the chances he'd turn up now just when I was creeping around suspiciously? I could return the matches later, couldn't I? I remembered his habit of sometimes lighting a candle instead of using the lamp when he needed a bit of quality time with the Almighty in the wee hours. Nope: I couldn't take the risk. I had to get them back.

I got up and started feeling my way towards the altar in the dark. The flagstones were cold under my bare feet. The fox barked again, a high-pitched yelp that sounded like a cat being tortured. *Get on with it*, he seemed to be saying. I stubbed my toe painfully on the altar, but at least it meant I was in the right place. I reached out my hand and felt the edge of the tray full of candles with my fingers, then carefully placed the box of matches in its usual place. I resisted the urge to hurry back to my bed. The last thing I wanted to do was to knock over a can of paint or a bucket of rainwater now.

Still no sign of Martindale. Safely in my sleeping bag again, I finally relaxed, expecting the creak of the big door opening at any moment, knowing I'd covered my tracks. I waited five minutes. Then another five. I stopped relaxing.

I didn't know how Martindale and Weston had got into the room under the church. I had a fairly clear mental map of the bits of the labyrinth I'd been in, but I had trouble matching it to the layout of the church above ground. The second entrance could be anywhere – maybe not even in the church itself. But if Martindale was hurrying back to make sure the church was locked up tight, surely it wouldn't have taken him this long?

The thought occurred to me that Martindale was already in the church when I got to the vestry. He'd checked and found I'd gone AWOL and was waiting somewhere, biding his time until I returned. Would he have called Weston for backup? Were they both here? I listened, but all I could hear was my own breathing.

I was thinking about improvising some sort of weapon when I heard the scrape of the key in the church door. The door creaked open, then shut, followed by the heavy bolts clunking into place. There was no light. After a few seconds I heard his boots on the smooth stone, getting fainter as he went deeper into the church, towards the altar. Then a soft thump, as if he'd just dropped to his knees, followed by some indistinct mumbling. Was he giving thanks for the last canister of ZX4? Or double-checking with the Holy Spirit that it was OK to unleash it on the streets of London? Knowing Martindale, he wouldn't be having any doubts about what he was doing at this stage of the game. He was probably just asking the Almighty to make sure his zombie helpers didn't suddenly come to their senses.

I waited for as long as I could, fighting the urge to sleep. Either the adrenaline rush of my little adventure in the tunnel had seriously drained me or I had gone down with something nasty from that rat bite, but I was finding it hard to keep my eyes open. Or maybe it was some evolutionary thing: when it's dark and quiet, go to sleep. If you start crashing around in the middle of the night, the chances are something that can see and hear better than you is going to have you for breakfast.

Either way, it meant that when Martindale put his hand on my shoulder to shake me awake, I didn't have to pretend. For a moment I genuinely didn't know where I was.

'Peter,' he said. 'It's time we talked.'

I followed him into the church then stood in the aisle while he went and lit some candles. He was dressed in a dark monk's robe, the cowl down over his face. He blew the match out and pointed to the pews.

'Sit.'

I thought he was going to join me on the pew, but he remained standing. His face was in darkness, but I knew he was looking at me, those X-ray eyes trying to penetrate my skull. After a while he made a satisfied noise, as if he'd just made his mind up about something or the Holy Spirit had just given him the go-ahead.

'It's time for me to tell you the plan. God is pleased with your work and He has told me your spirit is now ready. Do you feel ready?'

My heart was pumping. I didn't feel tired any more.

'Yes.'

'Good. Then listen. The wrath of God has been prepared. The phials of the wrath of God are in our hands. The time has come to empty them out on the heads of Satan's followers.'

'When?' I asked.

'Soon. Very soon. First, I'm going to show you the phial – make sure you understand how it works, what you have to do. Then I'll tell you where you are going to release it.'

He reached into his robe and pulled out a steel canister, placing it carefully on the pew beside me. It was about nine inches tall, like a small thermos flask with a bulbous black top. On the side was a keypad with four digits.

'To open it, you must enter a code. A number. You must remember this number. Can you do that?'

I hesitated for a second. 'Yes.'

'It is a secret from God, so I cannot write it down. You must learn it. I will tell it to you now, and then tomorrow I will see if you have remembered.'

I nodded.

'Two one two seven.'

'Two one two seven,' I repeated. 'Two one two seven . . .' I carried on muttering the numbers under my breath.

He nodded under the cowl. 'Good.'

'And what do I do then?' I asked.

'The seal will be broken. You can lift the lid. Then you'll see a nozzle, like a spray – an aerosol. Just press the button – keep pressing, keep your finger on it – until it's empty.'

'Like you do with an air freshener?'

'Yes.' I couldn't see whether he was smiling, but he seemed to like that. 'An air freshener. Just imagine you're spraying a room, a room full of terrible smells – death and decay and corruption – and you're making it clean and new and sweet-smelling again, a place fit for Our Lord.'

I nodded, grinning. 'Yeah. I can do that.'

He reached into his robe again and came out with a crumpled sheet of paper. 'And this is where you must do it.'

I looked at it, resisting the temptation to snatch it out of his hand. I needed to seem eager, but not too eager. This was one piece of the jigsaw. But there were four us, four of his little brain-dead helpers, therefore four targets. I had to know the location of all of them. There was no way I could ask, and no reason for him to tell me. I was going to have to figure it out – or someone was – before we could stop it. One thing I was sure of, though: the attacks would be simultaneous.

He pushed the piece of paper towards me. 'Take it. Like the number, memorize the name and where it is. I've drawn a map so you can find your way from here. Then tomorrow, give it back and I'll burn it.'

He isn't completely mad, then, I thought. He'd send us out to do the killing and then wash his hands of the whole thing. Four homeless nobodies would sacrifice themselves to start a religious war and he'd just sit back and watch, knowing the evidence of what he'd done would be destroyed the moment we sucked in the first breath of ZX4.

The second part of his plan suddenly became clear in my mind. Analysis would show exactly what type of nerve agent had been used and where it had come from. The people who opened the canisters might be expendable, but behind them would be some real VIPs. Their names might never be revealed, but the fingerprints of Britain's ruling elite would be there for all to see. Would that be enough to set off the powder keg Martindale was praying for? Civil wars had been started for less, I reckoned. Retaliation, counter-retaliation: a lot of people would be dead before the cycle was over, that was for certain. And the country would be torn apart. No putting the lid back on after that. Anybody who still believed in loving thy neighbour could fuck off to Sweden.

I unfolded the piece of paper and looked at Martindale's map. The lines were thickly drawn and the names written in big capital letters, like he'd made it for a child. There was even a little drawing of the target, so I'd recognize it even if I didn't know the name. But I did. The irony of the whole thing hit me right between the eyes. Oh yes, I knew the Hanbury Place Mosque, all right. Back in the day, I'd spent many a happy hour pretending to be a homeless beggar squatting on the pavement opposite while secretly taking note of everyone who went in and came out, as we tried to keep track of a suspected terrorist cell.

Now I was a homeless person all over again.

But this time my job was a bit different.

This time I was going to watch the mosque filling up with the faithful and then go inside and kill every last one of them.

51

Alex didn't really mind poking around in rubbish bins; it was the dressing up she didn't like. But even she had to admit, if you didn't want to stand out like a sore thumb, you needed to look the part. Anyone up to their elbows in garbage who didn't already stink of the stuff was obviously Old Bill, or at best some kind of gutter journalist. Either way, you were going to attract attention, and that was something Alex couldn't afford to do. So as she entered the alleyway alongside the church, she wasn't sure if the smell of stale sweat and rotting food was coming from her or the row of bins at the end.

The grey one, Logan had said. In the uncertain glow of the one working street light they all looked grey. When she got close enough to see properly, she realized that was because they were.

Brilliant. When all this was over she'd definitely have a word. For now, she had no choice but to look under all of them. Which meant more time and more risk.

The other problem was that they were all full and weighed a ton. It looked like people had been chucking old bricks and bits of broken furniture on top of whatever other crap was in there, compacting it down to the consistency of concrete.

She put her hands on the rim and heaved. The bin lifted a couple of inches off the ground, but there was no way she could bend down and look underneath without it coming crashing down. She tried poking the toe of her boot under and wiggling it around, hoping that might turn up something, but nothing doing. It was hopeless. The other two bins looked even more crammed with shit. If she was going to get a proper look at what was underneath, she'd have to push the bins over, and that would sound like a bomb going off. She'd probably have dead people coming out of their graves to see what the commotion was all about, never mind the neighbours. No way was she going to risk that.

She took a step back, trying to figure out what to do before she became an object of suspicion just by being here this long. She gasped as something brushed her ankle. A lean-looking fox with dark ears was sniffing at the bins.

'Bloody hell, don't mind me,' she said, laughing.

The fox took no notice. It sniffed at each bin in turn. Whatever it was looking for didn't seem to be there. Alex folded her arms and watched, just happy for the moment to be in the presence of a wild animal, even if it was one that lived on takeaways in styrofoam boxes. The fox went back to the first bin, then put its snout to the ground, snuffling around at the bottom.

'I've tried that,' Alex said. 'It's harder than it looks.'

The fox carried on undeterred, then started scraping with

one of its paws. Alex leaned down to look. The fox seemed to have got hold of a piece of paper, tugging it out from under the bin with its teeth.

'Let me have a look at that,' she said, stepping forward. The fox looked over its shoulder, as if seeing Alex for the first time, and bolted.

Alex reached up and tipped the bin back, then scraped the rest of the paper out with the sole of her boot. She let the bin come to rest as gently as she could, picked the piece of paper up and carefully unfolded it. It was covered in writing but she quickly realized that wasn't going to help her. It was a page torn out of a hymn book. She held it up to the light. There were faint marks, as if someone had used a thumbnail to make impressions on the paper. At a certain angle, it almost looked like writing. This had to be it.

And if it wasn't? If it wasn't, she really didn't know what she was going to do.

Three and a half hours later, dressed in the same long, ragged skirt and stained puffer jacket, her hair in matted clumps hanging over her dirt-streaked face, Alex sat hunched against the wall of a derelict warehouse by the river. For the past twenty minutes she'd been walking round in circles, muttering loudly to herself: snatches of poetry she'd learned at school, imaginary shopping lists, the plots of TV soaps she'd watched – anything that came into her head – to reinforce the impression that she was someone probably best avoided. In the eyes of her fellow down and outs who were beginning to gather in a loose group in the centre of the empty space, a stronger deterrent was the fact that she didn't have a bottle or a smoke or anything else that might be worth trying to get off her. How long before someone decided to mess with her just for the sake of it was another matter. If Logan didn't turn up soon, she might have to move further down the riverbank to somewhere more secluded, even if it meant he might miss her altogether.

She'd just decided to give it another five minutes when she saw the van pull up. Thank fuck for that. A couple of the more together members of the group got up and sauntered over towards the van. She resisted the urge to go with them. Logan had to come to her, and in his own time. At least now everyone had something else to focus on apart from the crazy woman with the wild hair.

She watched as Logan and another man doled out soup and sandwiches from the van, then Logan walked into the warehouse and squatted down by the little group sitting or lying on the floor. She heard wheezing laughter, a few choice swear words, then Logan patted one old guy on the shoulder and moved off. He caught sight of her and changed direction.

'Before you say anything, I don't want any of your terrible soup,' Alex said.

'Your loss,' he said, shrugging.

'So what's happening?'

He laughed, as if she'd said something funny, and she grinned back, adding a cackle of her own.

'It's in the church. I've seen one of them, and the rest of it is—'

'Slow down – what are you talking about?' she said, still smiling and nodding.

Logan breathed in. 'He's got hold of a nerve agent. ZX4. From Weston. It's British –' he saw her expression change – 'don't ask. I don't know how much, but there are four of us, so four targets. Mine's a mosque, Hanbury Place, so we have to assume the other three are mosques as well. He's keeping it under the church – it's a bloody maze down there.'

Alex thought furiously. 'How will they get the stuff inside? Security's tight these days.'

'They won't have to. It'll be crowded enough outside.'

'Where are they?'

'Don't know. He keeps us all isolated most of the time, so he has control.' Logan looked over his shoulder. 'He's coming. I don't want him to start talking to you. He's a clever fucker and he'll suss you if you make a mistake.'

'Thanks for the vote of confidence.'

'You're welcome. Just get this back to the team, and when I know when it's kicking off I'll let you know. Figure out a plan.'

'You don't have one?'

He touched her shoulder. 'OK, you take care now,' he said in a loud voice. 'Try and find somewhere safe to sleep, yeah?'

She got to her feet and started walking towards the other end of the warehouse, away from Martindale, resisting the temptation to break into a jog.

52

'Bloody hell,' Ryan said. 'Four locations packed with people. We don't know what the delivery system is, but that's hundreds dead for sure. The ZX series is nasty stuff.'

'More to the point, it shouldn't exist,' Mrs Allenby said.

'So how the hell did Weston get his hands on it?' Alex asked.

Mrs Allenby thought for a moment. 'It seems to me there are two possibilities. Either somehow the stocks of ZX4 were not destroyed when the treaty was signed . . . possible, I suppose, but I would like to think that could not have happened. And I very much hope no one would have then handed it over to someone like Weston. That simply doesn't bear thinking about.'

'So what's the second possibility? That this isn't the real stuff at all?' Ryan asked.

'Then why say it is?' Alex objected. 'Martindale wouldn't care what it was as long as it did the job.'

'No, I'm guessing that Martindale really is in possession of ZX4,' Mrs Allenby said.

Alex looked confused. 'I don't get it. So . . .?'

'This is not common knowledge – in fact, I'm sure it's still classified – but I seem to remember there was a report back in the late Seventies – never confirmed, one source who we subsequently lost, but we took it seriously enough at the time – that the Russians had a programme to manufacture copies of British and American biological weapons.'

'Why would they do that?' Alex asked. 'Didn't they have enough of their own?'

'Oh, yes,' Mrs Allenby said. 'More than enough, I would say. But every batch of nerve agent is unique. If you have a good enough sample, it can be traced back to the factory that made it. The Salisbury attack, for instance: there was absolutely no doubt that it was Novichok. At first, you might think they'd been careless. But I don't think so. The Russians might have denied responsibility officially, but in reality they wanted any other defectors or double agents to know exactly who was responsible. They were saying: look, this is what we'll do if you betray us.'

'You've lost me,' Alex said. 'What's this got to do with ZX4?'

'If there was an attack on four British mosques and the nerve agent responsible was found to be ZX4, who do you think the finger would point to?'

There was silence round the table as the implications of that sunk in.

'So you think the Russians have been making their own ZX4 so they can use it in a false flag operation?'

Mrs Allenby nodded. 'That would certainly explain where Weston got it from.'

Alex sat forward. 'Remember that car that turned up, when we were first monitoring the house? Disappears into the garage then comes straight out again? Maybe that was a delivery.'

'And I don't think it was just pizza,' Ryan agreed. 'If it's true the Russians have been making their own knock-off ZX4, and Weston has handed it over to Martindale, then we need to call in the heavy mob – get the stuff out of the church before it can be used,' Ryan said.

Mrs Allenby looked at him. 'I don't think it's quite that simple. How would we convince them our information was reliable? And the stuff may not even be in the church any more. More to the point, think of the implications if a quantity of ZX4 is found in a church, ready to be used in a series of terror attacks. If Martindale spills the beans, the result could be almost as devastating to this country as if the attacks had actually taken place.'

'So it's down to us, then,' Alex said.

Mrs Allenby nodded. 'I'm afraid so.'

'And right now we only know the location of one of the targets.'

'So we'd better get our thinking caps on, hadn't we?' Mrs Allenby said.

53

Martindale had been behaving oddly all morning. Normally he'd arrive at the church around seven, then come and find me in my little cubbyhole, where I'd make sure I already had my head in the Bible he'd given me. We'd say some prayers together and he'd choose a passage – usually Matthew or Mark – and get me to read it aloud to him until I got to a word or a phrase that set him off for some reason and then he'd start talking in that low, soothing way he had, about Jesus or Jerusalem or whatever and I'd let it just flow over me, lulling me into a waking sleep. When he finished, I'd always feel nice and relaxed but somehow slower, like he'd given me some sort of tranquillizer. Was it actually a kind of hypnosis? Was that how he maintained control? All I knew was it took me a while to shake myself loose and start thinking clearly again.

Today had been different. I had no way of telling the time, but I knew Martindale was late. When he finally arrived, he was agitated, antsy, smiling and talking to himself. Our Bible-reading session was shorter than usual and this time he just let me read, as if for once he wanted me sharp and alert, not nodding off into dreamland. He told me to wait in the vestry, locking the door after him, while he ministered to the various people who turned up at the church door, but then after a while I heard the church door slamming shut and the key turning in the lock. That was something he never did during the day: the church was open to all comers. So what was he up to? After about half an hour he came back, blessed the little gaggle of regulars who'd been waiting outside, then shooed them out and locked up again. I could hear him mumbling some prayers inside the church and then he came and unlocked the vestry door.

I looked up from my Bible reading. He was dressed in his white monk's cowl. He just stood there, looking at me, and for a moment I was convinced he knew who I really was. Then he smiled.

'Do you remember the number?'

'Two one two seven,' I said without hesitation.

He nodded. 'And you have the map?'

I pulled it out of the front pocket of my jeans. He held out his hand and I let him take it. In his other hand he was holding a box of matches. He struck one and touched the paper to the flame, watching until it burned down to his fingers, then dropped the blackened fragments to the floor.

'It's time,' he said.

My stomach lurched, and the feeling of vague unease I'd had since waking up in the dark solidified into panic. What the bloody hell day was it?

Then I realized how badly I'd fucked up. I'd thought it

would happen in a few days; Alex and the team had time to figure out a plan. But my sense of time was skewed. Martindale had messed with my mind so I couldn't keep track of the days.

Today was Friday. Of course it bloody was.

And that meant Friday prayers.

Martindale's edginess, all his mysterious comings and goings: he'd been getting the others ready, a modern-day Guy Fawkes putting a match to his four fuses and his four barrels of gunpowder.

Did that mean they were already on the way to their targets? Friday prayers were at noon. That would be when he'd want the ZX4 to be released. So what was the time now? However long it would take me to walk to my target, the Hanbury Place Mosque – that was how much time we had.

I stood up, desperate now for him to send me on my way. He reached into his robe and pulled out a small backpack. I took it from him and he laid both hands on my shoulders.

'You will be with God very soon now, Peter. How does that make you feel?'

'Happy,' I said, trying to sound excited at the prospect of unleashing an agonizing death on hundreds of innocent people before receiving the congratulations of their creator.

'Then go with my blessing. Remember, have no fear. Stay calm. God will be with you at every moment. Walk steadily and you will be at your destination at the right time. When you are among them, open the phial.'

'Yes,' I said. I bowed my head. 'Thank you.'

I felt his hands leaving my shoulders. He went and stood by the door as I slung the backpack over my shoulders.

As I passed him he made the sign of the cross.

Outside, a light drizzle was starting to fall. I walked along the path, putting one foot mechanically in front of the other, resisting the temptation to break into a sprint until I'd turned the corner into the alley with the bins.

I saw a hunched figure coming towards me. *Shit.* I couldn't remember his name but I knew the shambling walk and the long, faded green coat. It was one of the down and outs from the warehouse by the river, and I knew if I raced past him as if my feet were on fire, he'd be sure to tell Martindale.

I stopped and made myself smile. 'How are you, brother?'

He smiled back, showing a few rotten stumps. 'He can't reach it, see? Not enough rope. I told him.'

I nodded. 'I must go now, brother.' I touched him lightly on the shoulder and walked on down the alley.

'Get some rope,' he called after me.

I raised a hand without looking back. I counted to twenty, then turned. He was gone.

Thank fuck. I raced to the end of the alley, my trainers slipping on the wet paving stones. To my left, through a wire fence, was a patch of waste ground overrun with weeds. I pushed through a gap in the fence and picked my way through the broken glass and empty laughing gas canisters until I reached a partially demolished wall on the other side. I carefully pulled out half a dozen bricks until I could see the top of a plastic supermarket bag, half buried in the earth. *Thank fuck*. I'd squirrelled it away the night before I let Stevie loose, and that was in the dark. I dug out a couple of scoops of earth with my hand to loosen it, then pulled it out. I started trying to unpick the knot at the top, but my fingers didn't seem to be working properly and in the end I just ripped the bag open. A phone and a backup charger tumbled out, along with a pair of earbuds. I attached the cable and waited for the phone to power up. When the screen lit up I entered the passcode, then went to contacts, scrolled through and hit Alex's number.

'Yes?'

'Alex, it's me.'

'Logan? Where the hell—'

'Just shut up and listen. It's happening now. Friday prayers. There are three more targets. We need to intercept the carriers before they get there.'

'Give me the names.'

'I don't have the fucking names.'

'Jesus. All right. Let me call you back.'

54

It was all happening just like O'Dwyer said it would. First the text, then the meet on the bridge, which he knew would be just to check he hadn't brought company, then the real meet which would be somewhere open, where everything would be on the table. Hansen was early – dawn just starting to silhouette the high-rises – which was deliberate, so they could have a good look at him, see he wasn't texting every five minutes, and – again – check he hadn't come mob-handed. He sat with his hands on the wheel, his lanky frame relaxed, looking straight ahead with no expression, the way you did when you'd been pulled over and the plods were searching the car. They could take all day, as far as he was concerned. He allowed himself a wry smile. Better safe than sorry.

When the Lexus nosed its way slowly into the car park, then stopped, its headlights aimed straight at him, he didn't move or take his hands off the wheel. This was the moment they'd take him, if that's what they were planning to do, while he was temporarily blinded by the headlights. There would be another car, hidden in the alley behind the car park, and they'd come storming out of there, one with a hammer to the driver's side window to get his attention, and then a second man would take the other window out – along with his head and most of his shoulders – with a shotgun. That's how he'd have done it, anyway.

Strangely, the thought of it didn't make him anxious. What was going to happen was going to happen. If it didn't go the way he'd planned, well, there was nothing he could do about it now. He blinked as the headlight beams swung away, and the car made a slow circle until it came to a halt, with the driver's side window alongside his own. He waited until the driver had powered their window down, then followed suit.

It was her. That was good. If it had been the boy, or just a couple of the goons, that would have complicated things. Or maybe just made them more simple. He would have been fucked.

'Mr Hansen,' she said, nodding.

He nodded back. It was best not to show he knew who she was, but a quick glance had confirmed her identity.

Stephanie Mason. Dressed in a too-tight tweed jacket and a floral silk scarf, with her horn-rimmed glasses and her hair in a neat perm, she looked like the headmistress of a posh girls' school – or a judge, maybe, one of those annoying old birds who insisted on giving you a half-hour lecture on the evils of crime before they delivered the pathetic wrist slap your brief had negotiated.

But Stephanie Mason was neither of those things. Before her old man had been put away, for all Hansen knew she'd spent her time making jam and pruning the roses. But not now. Now she was quickly building a reputation for ruthlessness – not to say vindictiveness – that made Terry look like a soft touch. Hansen wondered if she'd been the brains behind Terry's operation all along, and he'd just been the front man, only playing the part of the big-time East End villain. Well, she was certainly the boss now. Denny was still a kid, or behaved like one. He wasn't going to step into his dad's shoes any time soon. In fact, the rumour was he preferred high heels anyway.

'Do you know why I wanted to see you?' she asked.

'I can guess,' Hansen said.

'Your boss.'

'Associate,' Hansen said, feigning offence. 'Partner, maybe.'

'That's not quite the truth, though, is it?' she said. 'Who gives the orders?'

Hansen stayed silent.

'I think it's time you got a promotion, don't you? And Mr O'Dwyer got a corresponding . . . demotion.'

He turned to look at her, as if this was all a big surprise.

She held out a manila envelope. 'Twenty thousand. Half now, half on completion.'

He pretended to think about it, then nodded and took the envelope. He knew he'd never see the rest, but ten grand was ten grand.

'And if it's a nice clean job, I'm sure we'll be speaking again soon. With Mr O'Dwyer gone, you could find yourself a busy man.'

He powered the window up and turned on the ignition. This was the tricky bit, trying to make sure he left the car park first. He pulled away, aiming for the exit. In his rear-view mirror, the Lexus still hadn't moved. She might think he was being a little rude, but that didn't matter now.

As soon as he was out of the car park, he pulled over. He looked back. The Lexus was just starting to move. He picked up his phone from the seat beside him and flicked to the app. He pressed the icon and a keypad appeared. Glancing back at the Lexus again, he tapped in the three-digit code. She'd stopped, no doubt wondering what the hell he was doing. For a moment their eyes locked.

Then the windows disintegrated and one of the doors blew open as the Lexus was rocked by a huge fireball, followed by a deafening boom. Hansen watched the flames raging inside the car until he was satisfied there could be no survivors, then put the car in gear just as the first bits of debris started to rain down.

55

'Where is he?' Mrs Allenby asked.

'I don't know,' Alex said. 'Near the church, I think. He's just been given the green light by Martindale. The Hanbury Place Mosque. Friday prayers.'

'Of course,' said Mrs Allenby, shaking her head. She turned to Ryan. 'Can you show us on a map?'

'Already doing it,' Ryan muttered. He hit a few more keys then turned his laptop so they could all see it. 'OK, here's the mosque.' He drew a line with his finger. 'And here's St Saviour's. We don't know where the other carriers started from, but it must be relatively near the church.' He drew another line, a circle this time, with St Saviour's in the centre and touching the mosque at the bottom. 'So they're probably somewhere in this zone.'

'Fuck. There must be a dozen mosques in that area,' Alex said.

Ryan tapped the keys. 'Not a bad guess. Fifteen.'

Alex put her head in her hands. 'Jesus.'

They all looked at the circle on the map, hoping something – anything – would jump out at them.

Ryan pointed at the line from St Saviour's to the Hanbury Place Mosque. 'Don't you think that's odd?'

Mrs Allenby squinted at the map. 'What do you mean?'

'It's due south.'

Mrs Allenby looked at him. 'So what?'

'Well, it could be coincidence. He could have chosen that target for any number of reasons, I suppose, I mean—'

'Come on, spit it out, man.'

'What if it's a cross?'

Ryan started drawing more lines on the map. 'Look. You see? If you draw a line north–south through St Saviour's, and another east–west, you get a cross. It makes perfect sense if Martindale really wants to make a statement. The other targets should then be north, west and east of the church. And –' he drew another, slightly smaller circle within the first so they formed a doughnut shape – 'within this area here.'

'Right,' Mrs Allenby said. 'How many potential targets does that give us?'

They waited while Ryan tapped in the new parameters. 'To the east, there's one on Truman Street. To the north, there's . . . It looks like there's two possible – no, wait, this one's been shut down. OK, so just one, on Buxton Grove.'

Mrs Allenby turned to Alex. 'While we're still looking, get on to Logan – tell him about Truman Street. And does anyone know where the hell Mr Woodburn has got to?'

56

Five minutes had gone by. Five minutes of pacing up and down like a lunatic, checking my phone hadn't gone dead, taking my earbuds out and putting them back in.

'Logan, it's Alex.'

'Thank Christ. What's going on?'

'We reckon we've identified two of the other targets. Ryan's working on the last one. There's no way to be sure, but we think he's chosen the locations so they—'

'I don't give a fuck why he's chosen them – just fucking tell me.'

'Truman Street. Due east of the church.'

'I know where it is.'

'How long will it take you to get there?'

'I'll find out, won't I,' I said, taking off at a brisk jog. I could feel the canister as I ran. 'What about the others?'

'I'm getting on the bike now. I'll take the one north of the church. Any idea what I'm looking for?'

'They have backpacks. That's all I can tell you. But with a bit of luck they'll stand out. They won't be wearing shalwar kameez. Right, I'm going.'

'One more thing. The fourth one will be to the west of the church. I'll send the exact location when I have it, but just so you know.'

'OK. Good luck.'

'Yeah . . . you too.'

I was panting now. I wasn't even going full-out, but my time in the cell under the church had taken its toll. My lungs were burning, and I was starting to see stars.

I slowed down a little, until I could see straight again, and tried to take deep, slow breaths.

Fuck it, Logan, don't fall apart now.

I opened the map on my phone and tapped in the location. A maze of backstreets and footpaths winding through the low-rise estates lit up. I memorized the route and put the phone back in my pocket. If the carrier was maintaining normal walking pace like Martindale said, I might have a chance.

But I'd need to fucking run, not fanny about worrying whether or not I was going to black out. I thought about a quick prayer, just on the off-chance, then decided against it. After all Martindale's bullshit, I wasn't a hundred per cent sure whose side the man upstairs was on.

I put my foot down, pumping my arms to try and develop some sort of rhythm. *Jesus, you'd think I'm trying to run up Snowdon.* I ran down the middle of the street, then dodged back onto the pavement when a truck turned the corner and started barrelling towards me. Why didn't I put a fucking watch in the bag along with the phone so I could see how much time I had left? But, then again, what did it matter?

All I could do was try and find the guy as quickly as I could and hope to God Alex and the rest of them could do the same at the other locations.

At the end of the street I turned left past a boarded-up community centre and almost collided with a young mum pushing a buggy laden with shopping bags. I couldn't see a baby, but I mumbled 'sorry' anyway as I went past and heard a shrill 'fucking arsehole' in my wake. I was looking for a right turn, but after fifty yards the road started curving left instead and I slowed down, leaning forward, hands on knees, my chest heaving. I tried to picture the map in my head. Where was the fucking turn?

Fuck fuck fuck.

Suddenly it all became clear. My head was so fucked up I'd gone left instead of right, and now I was going north, not east. I turned round, squinting back up the road while I tried to fill my lungs.

And that was when I saw him. It was John, dressed in dark-blue trackie bottoms and a grey hoodie, his long legs swinging awkwardly, like a puppet's. He looked in my direction as he crossed the street. I looked away, then looked back. He was gone. Had he recognized me?

I sprinted after him. We were out of the estates onto a busier street lined with stalls selling old clothes, and at first I couldn't pick him out. Then I saw his big head bobbing as he dodged between two women coming out of a sari shop.

He was running.

57

The fat man was twitchy, no doubt about it. O'Dwyer had caught him looking curiously at people on the platform as they walked passed the bench, the way you would at someone you thought you'd recognized but you were trying to remember if you actually knew them or if they were just off the telly. He remembered once bumping into a bloke in the park and giving him a big smile and hello before he realized he was the twat who used to sit outside the tube with a mangy dog and a begging bowl. Or maybe the fat man was starting to lose his marbles and was worried he wouldn't recognize people he really did know.

Or, then again, maybe he thought someone had been following him for the last hour and was planning to push him under a train.

Which, of course, was the truth.

O'Dwyer thought about bailing, just calling it quits and going home. He didn't know why the fat man thought he was being followed – he wasn't being that slapdash, was he? – but even if he was just being paranoid, acting all nervous would make O'Dwyer's job a good deal harder.

He knew the smart thing was to leave it for another day. But then, there wouldn't be another day, would there? The whole point of doing it now was so it looked like he'd done all three jobs before Stephanie Mason got taken out. If someone in the family knew he'd baulked at the third one, it might look like he'd figured out that he was playing with fire – to put it mildly – and decided the least worst option was to remove his employer. Once she was gone, there'd be no point in offing the silly fat bastard.

He looked at his phone again. No fucking service, so he couldn't tell if Hansen had texted. Every instinct told him to finish the job, as if he was a loyal employee of the Mason family. Sometimes you had to abort – of course you did. But not just because the old git had got the collywobbles, surely?

He risked another glance down the platform. It was filling up, the next southbound train due in two minutes. The fat man would be getting on it. It was all shaping up nicely.

Fuck it. In for a penny. He pushed off the wall and started easing his way slowly through the crowd. Along the platform the fat man was getting up, his eyes darting around. Even at this distance, he could see his forehead was shiny with sweat. The fat man pushed a strand of hair away from his eyes and settled his glasses more firmly on his nose.

One minute.

The fat man stood behind the yellow line. He was obviously staking his claim to a spot where the doors would open and he could scuttle into a seat, if there was one. He wasn't going to risk not getting on the train, even if it was packed. O'Dwyer carefully manoeuvred past a gaggle of teenage girls loitering dangerously close to the tracks, thinking it might be quite helpful if one of them did face-plant onto the third rail, until he was just feet away from the fat man, then slipped in directly behind him. If the fat man turned now, he'd see him. He heard the screech of the oncoming train. The fat man looked longingly towards the tunnel, as if his salvation might be coming from that direc-tion. As the train emerged, O'Dwyer took a step forward and shoved the fat man hard in the back. He toppled forward, his arms flung out sideways as if he might be able to fly, then disappeared over the edge just as the train roared over him. O'Dwyer turned smartly away and was halfway to the exit before he heard the first screams.

58

Alex slowed to a crawl as she rounded the corner of Buxton Grove. She could see the mosque a hundred metres to her left, the copper dome shining through the drizzle, small groups of young men, most in shalwar kameez, already beginning to congregate outside. Her first instinct was to stay on the bike, to keep as mobile as possible, but if she spotted the carrier, she needed to be able to take him out then and there. She squeezed into a space between two cars, turned off the engine and took off her helmet – wondering if it was better to bring it with her to use as a makeshift weapon before deciding it was more important to stay light on her feet. She stashed it in her pannier.

She looked at her watch. Twenty minutes.

The mosque was at a junction where two streets funnelled into one. That meant there were three approaches. If he was coming from the direction of St Saviour's, which one would he use?

Shit. For all she knew he'd got there ahead of time and was now doubling back. No point even trying to figure it out. Just get out there into the crowd and start looking for a white guy with a backpack and a zombie look in his eye. She walked out into the road so she could see people clearly on both sides of the street. A cabbie coming up behind hooted and she skipped back onto the pavement, giving him the finger.

She spotted someone: short blond hair, backpack. She crossed over, skipped past a group of old men in shalwar kameez and put her hand on his shoulder. A woman, early twenties with pierced lips and eyebrows, spun round, shrugging Alex off.

'Fuck do you think you're doing?'

OK, this wasn't any good. She needed to get nearer to the mosque, then watch people coming to her.

'Sorry. Thought you were someone else.'

She stepped out into the road again and began to sprint, knowing she was making herself conspicuous. A bike swerved to avoid her as a group of boys caught sight of her and started calling and laughing. *Fuck it. No choice now.*

She stopped twenty metres short of the end of the road. There was quite a crowd now in front of the mosque, men chatting and arguing as they waited to go in. With her blonde hair and leathers, she knew she couldn't get any nearer without sparking a riot. She hung back, trying to figure out what to do next.

Something made her turn. On the other side of the road a man was standing, just like her, looking towards the mosque and wondering what to do next. His head was shaved and he looked pale, with dark circles under his eyes. His Adam's apple bobbed as he swallowed hard. The only problem was, he didn't have a backpack.

Then she saw it, discarded at his feet, her eyes drawn by his odd trainers – one red, one blue – while he cradled what looked like a thermos to his chest with both hands.

She took two steps back to remove herself from his peripheral vision, then crossed over and ducked into a boarded-up shop doorway a few yards behind him. His perfect stillness, while pedestrians flowed around him, made her think of Moses parting the Red Sea. But why had he frozen? Had he lost his nerve? Or was he trying to decide how much closer he dared to go?

Then she saw the subtle movement in his arms and shoulders and realized he must be opening the canister. Ten quick strides later he'd be in the midst of the worshippers.

There was no time to think. She stepped forward, hooked her arm through his and yanked him back. He teetered sideways and she pulled him further towards the alcove. She heard a loud yelp, more like a dog than a human being, as he swung his elbow back sharply, breaking her grip and hitting her in the mouth. Then he turned with a look of pure, animal fury and punched her in the face, breaking her nose. Alex stumbled, stunned by the pain, and felt him turn away. She reached out blindly, catching his sleeve, and pulled as hard as she could. He turned back towards her, holding the canister in one hand and swinging wildly with the other. She ducked down and to her left, his fist grazing her forehead, then brought her right knee up between his legs. He grunted, his teeth bared in a snarl of pain, and as his head came down instinctively, she pivoted to her right and brought her left knee up into his jaw with everything she had. The crack of breaking bone was like a pistol shot.

The canister clattered to the ground as he toppled forward. She scooped it up, stomped his head hard with her heel a couple of times, then turned and ran.

59

John had that funny way of walking, like a puppet being jerked around, and he'd probably never done any serious running in his life, but he was strong. Stronger than me, at any rate. Whenever his brainwashing had been, he'd had time to recover, to rebuild some of that lost muscle mass. He might not get any points for technique, but I knew if I didn't catch him within a hundred yards, I was fucked. My feet already felt as if they were only loosely attached to my body, but they still managed to send jolting shockwaves of pain up my legs and into my lower back. I gritted my teeth, knowing as soon as I stopped, I was going to throw up.

He glanced back as I hurled myself forward and we locked eyes for a moment. Was there something I could say that would make him pause? Could I convince him the Holy Spirit had decided to abort the mission at the last moment? Was there some biblical phrase that would stop him in his tracks? If there was, it didn't matter: he put his head down and the moment was gone.

He hit an old dear clutching heavy bags of shopping, sending her careering into a shop window, but it didn't seem to slow him down. A moment later, I hurdled her prostrate body, a bag of oranges tumbling into the gutter, but I wasn't getting any closer; in fact, he was starting to pull away, his gawky running action proving surprisingly effective.

I stopped, grabbing a lamp post for support, telling myself it was just for a moment. I just needed to get some air into my lungs, then I'd really give it everything. I held on tighter, waiting for a wave of dizziness to pass.

I spat a mouthful of bile onto the pavement and looked up. Thirty yards ahead, John had stopped, frozen in his tracks in the middle of the road like a cartoon character who'd just stepped off a cliff, before a black van suddenly slammed into him, sending him flying. There was a shout and the screaming of tyres as his body thudded onto the tarmac like a sack of cement. I pushed off from the lamp post and stumbled forward.

Crouching over his body, I ran my hands over him, pretending to feel for broken bones. Where was the fucking backpack? His eyes were glazing over, blood streaming from his mouth and ears, a strangled wheezing sound coming through his mashed-up teeth. I glanced round. The backpack was poking out from under a car. I made a grab for it as the van driver staggered over, his face white. He was holding his phone to his ear and his mouth was open, but no words were coming out. A man in a suit ran out of a shop doorway and started listening to John's chest. As more people started crowding round, I slipped away, unzipping the backpack and quickly transferring the contents to my own. I pulled my phone out. Fifteen minutes until Friday prayers. I wondered how Alex was getting on. Well, either she'd get her man or she wouldn't. No point double-teaming when there was one more target left. West of the church, she'd said. I started to run.

'What do you mean, there are no mosques? There must be.'

I was walking now. There was no point trying to run, even though there were only minutes left on the clock. I just couldn't do it. It was probably already too late, but I stumbled on anyway, not knowing what else to do. Alex's voice sounded muffled, like she had a bad cold and was breathing through her mouth.

'Ryan's got a list of every mosque in the fucking country. There just isn't one anywhere near where it should be.'

'Then maybe the cross thing is all bollocks,' I said.

'If that's true, then it could be anyfuckingwhere. And we've got five minutes.'

I looked around desperately, hoping to see someone hurrying down the road in a shalwar kameez, or just a sign in Arabic – anything. But the rain had got harder and the streets were emptying. There was no one. I scanned the rooftops, trying to see the glint of a dome – anything that stood out from the faceless two-storey terraces that made up this godforsaken part of London.

I stopped and leaned against the wall. I desperately wanted to sit down and close my eyes, but I knew if I did that I'd never get up again. I didn't bother looking at my phone to see the time. We were already too late.

That bastard Martindale. I imagined the smile on his face as he gave thanks for the news. Hundreds dead. The hospitals crammed with hundreds more desperate, dying people in terrible pain. Panic in the streets. Mothers, sisters, daughters weeping. Angry young men already plotting their revenge. Even if only one of the mosques had been hit, it would be enough. It was like 9/11: put enough planes in the sky, and at least one of them was bound to reach its target.

As if echoing my thoughts, I heard the cry of a child. I looked round. A woman in a full burka was hurrying four small boys across the street. She spoke sharply to one of them as she pushed him forward, provoking another yelp of protest. I watched as they made their way along the street through the rain then disappeared down a narrow side street. I pushed myself upright. Where were they going?

I watched for another minute. Another small boy hurried down the alley wearing shalwar kameez. Then two more.

Should I follow? Or keep looking for this damned mosque? Friday prayers would be beginning now. There would be nothing I could do except witness the devastation.

I waited for a bus to go past, then crossed the road. When I turned into the alley I started to hear voices. At the end, I could see figures scurrying past and quickened my pace to a pathetic, limping shuffle. The alley narrowed, then opened out into a housing estate. To my left, hemmed in by blocks of flats, was a squat prefab building. Women and children, with a handful of old men, were hurrying inside. A madrassa? An Islamic community centre? I didn't know exactly what it was, but I had a feeling I'd found what I'd been looking for.

I looked around. Standing in the shadow of the nearest block of flats, his back to the wall, was a young man. I'd never seen him before, but I instantly knew who he was. His head was shaved like mine and he was staring straight ahead with the look of someone who knew he was only a short step away from heaven. Maybe he was just filling his lungs with London's stinking air one more time, to remember all the shit he was leaving behind. The backpack at his feet was a giveaway too. As I watched, he reached down, unzipped it and pulled out the canister, then walked towards the building full of children.

I took a couple of steps towards him. He turned and looked at me, his fingers on the keypad. I stopped dead.

'It's over, brother,' I said, trying to sound friendly but a bit intimidating at the same time. 'Father Paul called it off. The Spirit of God spoke to him. He sent me to tell you. The time wasn't right. He wants us to bring the phials back to the church so they'll be safe.'

I watched his eyes flickering. He was trying to decide if I was for real or a phantom, a demon sent by hell to trick him. I saw his knuckles go white as his grip tightened on the canister. His fingers trembled over the keypad.

Then he smiled and I knew he'd decided. He looked at the keypad, his brow furrowing in concentration. Four numbers.

I threw myself forward, knowing it would be too late. I was about to be ZX4's first victim.

His smile grew wider, then I saw a shadow dart out, there

was a dull thump, and his head jerked forward. He stumbled, then fell to his knees, his head turned sideways at an odd angle. Through his pale lips, a long stream of blood splashed onto the grass.

Behind him, Alex stood there, breathing hard, her face swollen and bloody, her motorcycle helmet still held out in front of her like a baseball bat.

60

The door of St Saviour's was closed. I watched for five minutes from across the street, but nobody went in or out. The rain seemed to have kept the worshippers away. Or maybe something had told them today was not a good day to go to church.

I pushed the door open and slipped inside. The only light came from a flickering row of candles near the altar. The place seemed to be empty. Maybe he'd done a runner when he realized all his plans had come to nothing.

Then I saw him: head down, praying in the first row of pews. I closed the door and pulled the bolts across.

He turned at the noise. 'Peter? Is that you?' He stood, watching me carefully as I came towards him.

'My name's not Peter,' I said.

He narrowed his eyes. 'What happened?'

'What happened?' I smiled. 'I guess you could say I saw the light.'

For the first time I saw a flicker of uncertainty on his face. 'What about the others?'

'John's dead, or as good as. The others too, I reckon.'

'And what about the . . .?'

'The phials? God's wrath? They're in a safe place. I just came back to make sure there aren't any more.'

His face went slack as the last hope went out of him. I'd been pretty sure there were only four canisters; now I was certain.

'It's over,' I said.

He tensed, and for a moment I thought he was going to run, or go for a weapon. Then he let out a long breath and his shoulders relaxed. Perhaps he saw the look on my face and realized there was no point.

'Who are you?'

'I'm Stevie Nichols,' I said. 'You killed me, remember? But now I've come back to life.' I grinned. 'Like Jesus.'

He licked his lips. I could almost see his mind working, looking for a way out. 'What do you want, Stevie?'

'What do I want? I'd like my memories back. I'd like to be who I was – you know, when I was just an ordinary fuck-up. Before you killed me.'

He nodded. 'I can do that,' he said, taking a step towards me.

'Shut up, you murderous cunt,' I said, stopping him in his tracks.

He looked at me. Those X-ray eyes. 'You're not Stevie, are you?' he said slowly.

'It doesn't matter who I am,' I said. 'All that matters is that you're finished. The Tenth Crusade, brainwashing poor sad bastards to wage a holy fucking war while you sit here praying – all that's finished.'

He was silent for a moment. 'So what are you going to do? Have you come to arrest me?'

'I'm not a policeman,' I said.

'Then what?'

'I haven't decided yet – I mean, about your punishment. I think you need some time to reflect – have a nice long chat with God. Then we'll see. The Holy Spirit might speak to me, you never know.'

I took him by the arm and, again, for a moment I thought he was going to resist, but he must have felt the fierce strength that was suddenly coursing through me and went slack.

I pushed him towards the vestry. Once inside I pointed to the bookcase. He looked confused, then panicky, as he suddenly realized where we were going. I shoved him forward and together we moved the bookshelf aside.

'Where's the lamp?'

'Over there.' He pointed to the corner, his hand shaking.

I picked up the lamp and turned it on. 'The padlocks?'

He fumbled inside his robe and came out with the bunch of keys.

'Let's go.'

Nothing more was said as we made our way down the ladder into the bowels of the church, then along the dank passage to the cell where Stevie Nichols had died. I opened the door and pushed him in. In the beam of the lamp, I could see that it was still empty. *I should have at least brought down a bucket of water*, I thought. *Oh well, too late now.*

'What now?' he said. For the first time there was genuine fear in his voice.

'I'm going to leave you. The dark's a bit scary at first. And the cold. But you get used to it.'

He reached a hand out, as if he was going to tug at my sleeve, but I stepped back, out of reach.

'When are you going to come back?' His tone was pleading.

'Soon,' I said. 'When you've had time to think about things.'

'And then?'

'Like I said, then we'll see.'

I took one last look at him, his mouth open, lips trembling, eyes wide with terror, then walked out, slamming the door behind me.

As I went through the passage, I heard a sudden scurrying. I stopped for a moment and smiled.

Back in the vestry, I snapped the last padlock shut and heaved the bookcase back into place, then turned off the lamp and put it back in the corner. I shut the door behind me and groped my way to the altar. There was one candle left, sputtering feebly in the cold air. I blew it out, picked up the matches and lit three more, then stood back. No: one more. I lit a final candle.

'That's for you, Stevie.'

Opening the church door, I could see the rain was coming down even harder. The sky was so dark it almost seemed like night. I slipped out, closing the door behind me.

As I breathed in the damp air, I could feel the strength

beginning to leave me. I needed to get a move on, while I still could. I walked down the alley, past the bins, shivering as the rain soaked into my shirt.

When I got to the street behind the church, the gutters were already surging with water, the potholes in the road overflowing. I found a drain and knelt down on the kerb.

One by one, I slipped the keys off the keyring and dropped them through the grate.

61

It was a strange sight. Five glasses of champagne, along with an empty bottle, and beside them on the table, looking like some sort of weird cocktail shakers, four brushed-steel canisters containing one of the deadliest nerve agents ever made.

Mrs Allenby handed round the glasses, then picked one up for herself. 'Cheers,' she said, raising it towards me.

I took a sip, not quite sure what the alcohol was going to do to me. After a shower and a change of clothes that Alex had somehow found for me, I was feeling halfway normal again, but with everything my body had been through in the last few days, I wasn't taking any chances. I looked at Alex, with her fat lip and bandaged nose, and raised my glass.

'Cheers.'

'And you're certain this is all there is?' Mrs Allenby asked. 'He didn't have any more hidden in the church?'

'No, this is it,' I said.

'And there was no sign of Martindale?'

'I think he scarpered as soon as he realized the attacks hadn't happened. He must have thought John and the others had been arrested and would tell the police everything.'

'Where do you think he'll go?'

'He knows he can't run forever. I think he'll just crawl into a hole somewhere and top himself. I don't reckon we'll be seeing him again any time soon.'

Mrs Allenby nodded. 'Probably for the best.'

We all sipped our champagne in silence for a few moments, unable to take our eyes off the canisters.

'I'm sorry I missed all the action,' Alan said eventually.

'Don't worry, mate,' Ryan said, putting an arm round his shoulders. 'There was nothing much we could do at this end, anyway, when it came down to it.' He raised his glass to me and Alex. 'It was these two that got the job done.'

'Indeed,' said Mrs Allenby. 'If I had medals to hand out, you two would definitely be in line for very splendid ones. But this was a team effort. We wouldn't have been in a position to stop Martindale in the first place if it hadn't been for everybody's hard work.'

'Do they know who the bloke under the train was yet?' Alan asked.

'They just released it, yeah,' Ryan said. 'John Jennings, I think the name was.'

'Jesus.' Alan just managed to put his glass down before he dropped it.

Mrs Allenby put her own glass down. 'Mr Woodburn? What is it?'

'If it's the same bloke, John Jennings was the techie who took my place on that course, along with Claire and Craig.' He sat down, his face pale. 'That could have been me.'

We all let that sink in. 'So if it is the same John Jennings, and he was also seconded to Tenniel's squad surveilling Terry Mason . . .' I let the thought hang in the air.

'Then it looks like Mason's widow, or whoever it was, has now taken all three of them out,' Alex said.

'Yes, but how would she know?' Alan said. 'How would she know the identities of three MI5 surveillance operatives who were drafted into an undercover NCA team looking at her husband? You don't find out information like that on the gang widows grapevine.'

'Someone must have told her – someone on the inside,' Alex said.

Mrs Allenby looked thoughtful. 'Well, this is for another day, but perhaps we do need to take a closer look at John Tenniel. Not to mention Mrs Mason.'

'I'm afraid that won't be easy,' Ryan said.

'What do you mean?'

'Someone put a bomb under her car. At least, that's what it looks like. There's no official confirmation of the device yet, but she definitely isn't going to be available for interview.'

Mrs Allenby put a hand to her throat. 'Quite an eventful morning.'

I smiled wryly. 'You could say that.'

Alex nodded towards the canisters. 'What are we going to do with this lot? We can't just say we found it under a bush and hand it over to Porton Down. They'd stick us in a cell and throw away the key.'

'There would certainly be rather a lot of awkward questions

to answer,' Mrs Allenby agreed. 'For the moment we'll keep it here, in the safe.'

'There's a safe?' Alex said.

'Didn't I mention that?' Mrs Allenby said innocently. 'Clearwater is a security company, so I thought it stood to reason we ought to have one. I believe it's top of the range.'

'And then?' I asked.

'I'll have to talk to the Director General. Hopefully he'll be able to come up with a solution.'

'What about Shlovsky?' Alex asked. 'Do we let him just get on with his life as if nothing's happened?'

'We put a stop to an absolutely horrendous terror attack. We saved countless lives, and quite probably prevented an outbreak of bloody civil unrest. I think we are going to have to be satisfied with that.'

'No justice for Shlovsky, then? Is that because he's still protected by the PM?' Alex said with real bitterness. 'And to think I almost voted for her.'

'I might have something on that front,' Ryan said.

Mrs Allenby turned to him. 'Why didn't you tell me?'

'We had other things on our minds, I suppose,' he said apologetically. 'Anyway, once we knew the PM didn't turn up at Wyvern Lodge to see Viktor Shlovsky, I thought I'd have a look at his wife to see if there were any connections there.'

'And were there?'

'Possibly. The PM had a year abroad as part of her university degree course. In Geneva.'

'And I'll bet Ekaterina Shlovsky was there, too,' I said.

'Well, she wasn't Ekaterina Shlovsky then, of course, but she was studying art history. The two could certainly have met, maybe become friends.'

'There's a story there, I'll bet,' Alex said.

'Got to be,' I agreed. 'If the PM is willing to risk her career—'

'Not to mention the security of the fucking country,' Alex chipped in.

'I'll bet you anything Ekaterina Shlovsky has something on her,' I said. 'Either that or she did the PM a hell of a favour back in the day.'

'I'm free, if you were thinking of sending anyone to Geneva,' Alex said brightly, turning to Mrs Allenby.

'Again, for another day,' Mrs Allenby said. 'We'll need to think very carefully before we do anything precipitate. We'll be walking into a minefield. Anyway, I must go. All Clearwater Security employees should take a well-deserved break.' She nodded at me. 'You in particular, Mr Logan.' She turned back to the canisters. 'Now, we just need to put these things somewhere they can't do any harm.'

Ryan and Alex helped her scoop them up.

I followed Alan to the kitchen area. He opened a cupboard and pulled out a bottle. 'Twelve-year-old Macallan,' he said. 'I don't know about you, but I need a proper drink.'

He filled a couple of glasses. 'Slainte.'

'Happy holidays,' I said.

'Look, I'm sorry I wasn't here when it was all going down.

I know what Ryan said, but I should have been here. I guess I lost my nerve a bit.'

'Forget about it,' I said. 'Nothing you could have done. I'm just glad it wasn't you under that train.'

He nodded, then took another gulp. 'Anyway, I don't know if this is all too late, but I found out a bit about what you wanted.'

'Mikhail? The brother?'

'Yeah, seems he's a bit of a black sheep. Almost got chucked out of the posh boarding school they sent him to when he was fifteen. Complaints from a couple of girls in the village. Daddy coughed up for a new library and it all went away, but it looked like Mikhail didn't exactly mend his ways after that. A couple of police cautions – impossible to say if any money changed hands, but he seemed to have a knack of wriggling out of difficult situations.'

'Sexual assault?'

'Yeah, that seems to have been his thing. But nothing ever stuck.'

'And now he's safely tucked away in New York.' None of that surprised me. In fact, I would have put money on it. But there was still another piece of the puzzle I needed. I knew I couldn't push him, though. Either it was there, or it wasn't.

'You asked about Daisy, too, didn't you?' Alan said. 'To see if the name ever came up in relation to Mikhail.'

I took a sip of the Scotch, trying not to seem too eager. 'And did it?'

'Afraid not. Anastasia, the sister, was at another school only a few miles away. Seems there was always shenanigans with boys from Mikhail's place going over the wall, midnight trysts, that sort of thing. There was a bit of a scandal when her best friend disappeared. She'd been staying with them at Wyvern Lodge, then one day – poof – gone without trace.'

'What was her name?'

'Duscha. Duscha Zinchenko.' He looked at me. 'Does all that help at all?'

I finished the last of the whisky. 'Yeah. Yeah, it does. Thanks, mate.' I gave his shoulder a squeeze. 'Right, I'm off back to the flat to get some kip.'

'Well deserved,' he said.

'What about you?'

'Yeah, go back home, I suppose. I'm going to take the bus.'

Mrs Allenby had gone. Ryan was just clearing his desk, putting his laptop into a backpack.

'Look, when we've all got our heads back in place, we need to meet up for a drink – the whole team,' he said.

I looked at him.

'Well, maybe not Mrs Allenby. Not that there's anything . . .'

'Yeah, good idea. Now that we know there isn't anybody trying to kill us.'

'Exactly. I tell you, I can't remember the last time I had a proper night's sleep.'

'I'll bet. Right, text us, yeah?'

'Definitely.'

I put my hand on his arm. 'One thing. You can't remember what Weston's regiment was, can you? Before he went into MI?'

He grabbed his coat off the rack. 'Let me think . . . Oh yes, Twelfth Armoured Infantry Brigade. Any reason you need to know?'

I shook my head. 'Just curiosity.'

He nodded dubiously as he closed the door behind him.

'Pub?' Alex asked, putting her biker jacket on. 'Or hospital?'

'You can talk,' I said.

She shrugged. 'I was thinking of getting a nose job anyway. This way was cheaper.'

'And no waiting list,' I said.

'Exactly.'

'Look, Alex, I'd like to talk. It'll be a fucking boring evening for you and you probably won't get a word in edgeways, but if you can face it, that would be good.'

She gave me a kiss on the cheek. 'Of course. I'll bring a book if I get bored. I know: *Crime and Punishment.*'

I gave her a blank look.

'It's Russian. Very famous. Never mind. Give me a call when you're ready.'

'Thanks. Will do.'

'Don't forget to turn the alarms on.' She gave me a wave over her shoulder and left.

I stood for a moment, swaying a little, and I had to put my hands down on the table to steady myself. The booze had definitely been a mistake. Still, it wasn't every day you stopped a mass killing, was it? And there was still plenty of time to go back to the flat, sleep it off and then get ready. I felt I could sleep for a million years.

But if I wasn't going to have bad dreams, there was still one more thing I had to do.

62

This time I didn't bother covering my tracks. In fact, I wanted to leave as clear a trail as possible. I left the metal plate swinging down from one bolt, so anyone shining a torch up from below could see the open window where I'd got in, and heaved myself over the sill.

With my feet planted on the bare floorboards, I stopped and listened. All I could hear was the swooshing of branches in the wind and the slow drip of water from my rain jacket onto the floor. As I took the familiar route along the corridor and up the stairs, the house felt somehow emptier than before. But maybe that was just my imagination.

I opened the door and shone my torch into the room in a slow arc. Nothing had changed since the last time I'd been there. Daisy was still hunched in her corner, her head lolling to one side, her legs splayed, like an abandoned rag doll.

'Hello, Daisy,' I said.

I let the beam of the torch move slowly over her, the light glinting where the bare bone showed through the parchment skin. If she was pleased to see me, she didn't show it.

I went to the window and opened the shutter wide, then

shone the torch out into the dark so the light caught the water dripping from the trees. Would he see it? I couldn't be sure, but something told me he would occasionally look over, perhaps before he went to bed, just to make sure all was as it should be. I waved the torch around some more, wondering if I should have brought some music, blasting some heavy drum and bass out into the night. That would definitely have got his attention. But it might have got some of the neighbours out of their beds, too, and I didn't want that. Plus, Daisy didn't seem to be in a party mood.

What if he didn't come? How long could I keep this up? I hadn't really thought past this one night.

The video camera was still there, aimed at the front of Shlovsky's place. It didn't really matter now, but I took a break from the lightshow and put it in my daysack. I went back to waving the torch around, wishing I'd planned things better. Then, twenty minutes later, just as my arm was starting to cramp up, I heard it. Someone entering the house, the same way I had. The only difference was, they were trying to make as little noise as possible.

'He's coming,' I said to Daisy. 'But don't worry. Everything's going to be fine.'

I turned the torch off and waited.

I had to admit, he was good. After the initial soft thump of his feet as he jumped down from the window, I'd heard nothing, not even the creak of a floorboard. It was only when the door started slowly opening that I knew he was there. I waited behind the door as he moved cautiously into the room. I could see the beam of his torch playing across the floor and over the walls. Then it stopped. He was looking at Daisy.

That was my moment.

He was standing side-on to me and I caught him just as he turned with a right-hand punch to the kidney, followed by a ridge-hand to the throat with my left. As he instinctively tried to shift out of range, I slipped behind him and caught him in a chokehold, my forearm slammed against his throat like an iron bar. Instead of pulling against me, he let his weight fall back, trying to push me off balance, feeling behind him with his hands for anything he could grab or twist, but I planted my feet firmly, gritting my teeth as I kept the pressure on. Soon I could feel his body going slack, his hands falling limply to his sides, but I wasn't going to fall for that one, and made my grip even tighter. Then his head fell forward with a kind of choking grunt, and I knew he was out.

I lowered him gently to the ground and fished a pistol out of a shoulder rig under his jacket. It was a Browning 9 mm. I smiled. *Old school.* I didn't think he'd have anything else, but I frisked him thoroughly just to be sure. Satisfied he was clean, I kicked the Browning aside and dragged him over to the opposite corner to Daisy, propping him up against the wall. I took a pair of plastic handcuffs out of my jacket pocket, along with a roll of duct tape, secured his hands with the cuffs, then started winding the tape round his ankles. When he was all done, I stood back and took a proper look.

He was wearing jeans and trainers with an old tracksuit top: just the kind of gear you'd throw on if you had to get up quickly in the early hours. But there was something about him, even lying slumped unconscious in the corner, that smelled of the parade ground. Maybe the jeans were just a bit too clean, the side parting a bit too neat. Somehow, you couldn't help feeling this was a man who was most comfortable in uniform.

I looked over at Daisy. There was no sign the kerfuffle had disturbed her.

I picked up the torch and turned back to Weston. His chest was heaving, and his eyes began to flicker. I gave him a kick in the side, to speed things along, and he grunted, opening his eyes. I sensed him quickly assessing the situation.

'Who the hell are you?' he barked.

I frowned. 'People keep asking me that.'

He grunted again, testing the restraints on his hands. I saw his eyes flick towards the Browning, then over to me. He'd clearly been expecting to find a couple of kids messing about, or some knackered old junkie, not a man with duct tape and PlastiCuffs in his pocket.

'OK, what are you doing here, then? I'm sure you're aware this is private property.'

I had to say I was impressed. Here he was, disarmed and trussed up like a turkey, and still he was the one asking the questions. I reckoned he would have done well under interrogation.

'No one seems to be living here,' I said pleasantly.

He nodded. 'So you were hoping to squat here, were you? Filling the place with your shit.'

I stepped forward and gave him another kick in the kidney. 'Language, please. There's ladies present.'

He looked at me. The kick didn't seem to bother him, but he was now clearly wondering if I was mad. That would make me more dangerous.

'Anyway, so what if I am?' I said. 'You don't look rich enough to be the owner – even of a dump like this.'

'My employer is the owner, as it happens,' he said, as if he'd scored a point.

So that was it. Another piece of the jigsaw fell into place. Shlovsky had bought the house to make sure no one ever found what was hidden inside. And why not? It was probably only a few million, and buying a house on The Bishops Avenue and leaving it to rot was nothing out of the ordinary.

'Of course: Mr Shlovsky.'

I saw his eyes narrow. That had clearly rattled him. 'How do you . . .?'

'And you're Major Weston, formerly of Her Majesty's armed forces, but now a dogsbody for any scumbag who offers you enough money,' I continued.

'If you know that, then you know how much trouble you're in,' he said.

I looked down at him. 'From where I'm sitting, I'd say you were the one in trouble.'

He thought for a moment. 'What is it you want?'

I smiled. 'That's better. I just want to ask you a few questions. You see, something happened with the Shlovskys, and I'm not quite sure of all the details. I need you to fill in the gaps for me.'

'What sort of thing?' His tone was somewhere between compliant and combative. He was probably beginning to think this was some sort of kidnap plot.

'Well, let's start with Anastasia. And Mikhail. Mikhail's a nasty piece of work, I think. I reckon you've had to clean up one or two of his messes, somewhere along the line. Isn't that right?'

Weston didn't say anything.

'All right. Let's try another name. How about Duscha Zinchenko?'

I saw a slight tremor at the corner of his mouth.

'Doesn't ring any bells? Well, I'm going to tell you what I think happened to Duscha, and if I get any of it wrong, you can tell me – OK? Right. Duscha and Anastasia are best pals from school. In fact, they're such good mates that Duscha's always staying over. Maybe her family's still in Russia, or she has problems at home, I don't know. Anyway, Duscha's a lovely girl: slim as a wisp, long blonde hair, cheekbones to die for – that real Russian look, you know? So it's no surprise Mikhail takes a fancy to her. Or maybe he already knew her from school. Doesn't matter. The point is, one night things get out of hand. And where Mikhail's concerned, you know what that means. Did he rape her?'

I looked at Weston.

'Feel free to chip in at any point. No? OK, I'll carry on.

I think he did – or tried to – and she resisted. She's a spirited girl. She might be small, but she's strong, determined. I'll bet she fought like a vixen. He probably wasn't used to that. It made him angry. So he hit her. Duscha's not the sort of girl to let a thing like that go. So now we have a problem. If Mikhail's going to stay out of prison, someone needs to shut Duscha up. Permanently. Someone needs to finish her off. She needs a good hard whack, here.' I touched the side of my head.

I paused, trying to read his expression.

'So, another mess, another clean-up. But money and lawyers aren't going to be able to fix this one. We need to get rid of poor Duscha – put her somewhere nobody will find her. But somewhere close, where we can keep an eye. What about that empty old house across the road? Perfect. And just to make sure, Shlovsky buys it. Anastasia and her mother are distraught, of course. But do they want to see their beloved Mikhail go to jail? You know what happens to rapists in jail, even rich ones. Maybe especially rich ones. No point in two lives being ruined, is there? So they just cry quietly and let it go. How am I doing so far?'

'Do you want money?'

'Money? No. I just want you to tell me one thing.'

'What?'

'What did they call her? Did she have a nickname?'

'What has that got to—'

'Just tell me.'

'All right. Yes, I suppose. It was her initials for some

reason. Duscha Zinchenko. Dee Zee. Like the Americans would say it.'

I nodded. Of course. Dee Zee.

Daisy.

I shone the torch over at her so Weston could see the hole in her skull. To his credit, he didn't flinch.

'I've got a question for you,' he said.

I opened my arms. 'Fire away.'

'How did you know? How did you know all this?'

I jerked my head towards the corner. 'Daisy told me some of it.'

He nodded slowly, keeping eye contact. Now he really did know I was mad. 'But what about me? How did you know it was me?'

I put my hand in my pocket and pulled out something small and shiny, then flicked it towards him. He looked down at the cufflink as it landed between his legs.

'I expect you've been looking for that. It must have come off when you were dragging Daisy over here. Death or Glory. The Seventeenth Lancers – the Charge of the Light Brigade and all that. Of course, there hasn't been much call for a regiment of lancers for a while, so now they're part of the Twelfth Armoured Infantry Brigade. But it's still nice to remember the history, isn't it? Even if it did end up tripping you up.'

For the first time, he smiled. 'Well, well. Funny how things happen.'

'Yeah, ain't it just,' I said.

'What are you going to do?'

He probably had a faint hope I was going to turn him over to the police. Maybe he thought, with his connections, he could work something out.

'That's rather up to Daisy,' I said. I looked over. 'Daisy?'

I waited.

'Are you sure?'

I turned back to Weston.

Then I reached down and picked up the gun.

EPILOGUE

I'd forgotten how peaceful a golf course could be at night. The rain had stopped, the wind had blown away the clouds, and the light of a three-quarter moon meant I could see the dips and hollows of the fairway all the way to the green. Weird to think that in a few hours, the sun would be out and groups of old codgers would be trundling along with their cigars stuck between their teeth as if God was in his heaven and all was right with the world.

But it was this world – the night world where dark things happened – that felt like the real one. And this world, I knew, was where I belonged. It was only because of the terrible things that were done in the night world that the sun would come up tomorrow morning and the birds would start singing again, and the old codgers could have their game.

I looked over to my left, where three little bunkers were clustered together on the edge of the rough. A fox was running round in circles, dodging first one way then the other as it chased its tail. I'd never seen a fox do that. Fleas, I thought; they must be driving the poor bastard crazy.

Then I looked again and there was the shadowy figure of

a boy. He was running forward with his arms open, trying to catch the fox, while the fox kept darting out of reach, then spinning back to start the game again.

'Silly boy. He thinks it's a dog.'

Sarah was sitting on the ground beside me, the cool breeze blowing in her hair.

'I never got him a dog, did I? I know he wanted one,' I said.

'There wasn't time,' she said soothingly.

'There wasn't time for much,' I said.

'There was enough,' she said. 'Enough for the important things.'

She looked down at my hands. I felt the hot, sticky blood dripping onto the grass. 'I don't know how to wash this off,' I said.

'You can't,' she said, and her voice sounded sad.

Acknowledgements

I would like to thank Luigi, Bill, Alex and Wayne for all their hard work and patience. You understand how I work and you're always so supportive. Your experience within this industry is always comforting. In short, you are utterly brilliant.

My thanks and appreciation go out to my former department at Thames House for their patience and guidance. I will never break my oath to you.

I would also like to thank Riaz and Tiksha. Your love, support and friendship have always come without compromise. We love you all and look forward to our adventures together!

AVAILABLE NOW

The explosive true story of life in MI5 from
the number one bestselling author of *Soldier Spy*,
Tom Marcus. Turn the page to read an extract now . . .

PROLOGUE

It's the screams you hear first. There are men and women everywhere, from all walks of life, running, hiding, some frozen into petrified stillness. This isn't a normal scene in London, but it's one that is fast becoming anticipated.

Zero Six.

More carnage, as I see glimpses of bodies, the walking wounded and those who have already lost the fight. One or two people are recording what they can on their phones, handsets shaking uncontrollably. There's a flash of the three targets, wearing what look like very crude suicide vests, stalking more prey. The armed police close in, running fearlessly towards the fight.

Zero Six.

Right now, I know that MI5 officers will be reacting to a protocol designed to put every conceivable asset on the ground within minutes. Surveillance teams already on the ground will be redeployed. Those who had just finished and were at home with their families, or somewhere desperately trying to switch off, will be in their cars and with the teams immediately. The intelligence officers would be briefing the teams live on the radios, no time to bring them in. The operators in the teams, not just surveillance but the technical attack teams, the office geeks within Thames House, our cousins in Vauxhall Cross and the wobbly heads in Cheltenham, would be working together with one goal in mind: to stop the killers.

Zero Six, roger, en route.

The first shots ring out, and I know from the controlled manner this is almost certainly the police firearms officers. Over the past few years, due to the huge spike in the scale of terrorist activity and their capability, the Counter Terrorism Unit is now without question the best trained police force in the world. Tonight, just south of London Bridge, they are proving it, as the echoes of gunfire continue to bounce around the buildings, a brutal counterpoint to the screams.

My lungs spasm, gasping for air, as I realize I am frozen with my phone to my ear, waiting for an update from my team leader or the operations officer back at base.

'Breaking news here on Sky, as what's being described as a terrorist attack in the heart of London . . .'

Lowering my phone, I look at the blank black screen. No call. No messages. No longer frozen, I take a step back, soaking in my surroundings. *Fuck.* The TV is on, this is on the news. I'm not on the ground. I'm no longer in MI5. I'm not hearing my radio. It was an auditory hallucination. I've relapsed. *Get out, get out NOW!*

It's late at night and everyone in the house is asleep. I grab the door keys and leave, my legs instantly propelling me into a run I didn't know I needed. Moving faster and faster, I cover the couple of miles to a large wood.

I'm brought up short after vaulting a dry-stone wall that acts as a land boundary to a farm. It's dark around here – the immediate area is almost pitch-black thanks to the looming treeline.

As my heart and lungs struggle to replace the oxygen my muscles have burned through, I find myself sitting on this low wall looking towards a break in the trees through which I can see a valley and hills in the distance.

Zero Six.

FUCK OFF, THAT'S NOT ME ANY MORE!

I'm not M15 any more but I always will be. I'm no longer part of my team, but I can always hear them. I'm no longer hunting the most dangerous terrorists in the world, but every day I'm watching and waiting for them.

Even moving back along this dark, muddy track I'm trying to pick out a route in the shadows that will take me home a completely different way. Some call it paranoia; even the doctors I've dealt with in the past would classify my day-to-day behaviour as paranoid. PTSD or not, the curse engrained into me also keeps me alive.

Spotting a different route to take, I cut across an open field, dark silhouettes of cows moving slowly in the distance. I'm walking rather than running, giving myself time to face the demons I had convinced myself were gone. My mind is calmer by the time I creep back into the house. Resisting the urge to turn the news on, I strip out of my wet clothes and sit on the sofa thinking about the team. They'll be on the ground right now, helping to hunt down anyone associated with the London Bridge targets, anyone who could be waiting for the right time to launch their own attack.

I can imagine the speed at which the intelligence officers on the desk would be shifting through terabytes of live data, creating a triage of threats from thousands of targets.

I can almost hear the radio transmissions, the team leader calling in assets, continuous updates from Thames House, bikers blasting past every operator, all task-focused and doing everything humanly possible to prevent more attacks like this. Unfortunately, you can't stop every single one, it's impossible. And we will get hit again. It might be next week, might be next year, but it will happen. The thing to remember is that our intelligence and military is the best fighting force in the world. Like any world champion, some attacks will find a way through our defences, but we can take the blows and keep fighting. Our guard never drops. Together with my team, I helped stop hundreds of attacks over the years. They continue to do so today.

I wrote about some of my experiences as an MI5 officer in *Soldier Spy*. On the one hand, remembering the past showed me that having PTSD wasn't my fault. I wasn't a victim, just someone who got caught out in the open at all the wrong times. Revisiting my career for *I Spy* has allowed me to describe some of the operations I couldn't include in the first book and go deeper into the challenges that defined me, and the lessons learned along the way.

The memories of my team are so vivid, they stay with me. To this day I want to be back with them and instantly hate myself for it, because going back would take me away from my family. What I can do is remember them in my writing, and pay tribute to the bravery of the men and women of MI5.